begin *again*

begin *again*

a novel

JENSEN PARKER

Strangers Book Four

Made for More Publishing, LLC

BEGIN AGAIN

Cover Design: Jensen Parker

Alpha'd: Ashley Vaccaro, Samathan Ivy, and Miriam Al-Qhowdhaib

Editing: Sophie B. Murphy, Eloquent Inkblot LLC.

ISBN (e-book) : 979-8-9879868-9-9

ISBN (printed) : 979-8-9879868-8-2

Published by Made for More Publishing, LLC.

https://www.jensenparker.com

For the ones who have loved and lost, the ones who have had their hearts broken, and the ones who have lost it a time or two...Give yourself the grace you've given others and keep going.

Author's Note

Begin Again is the fourth book in the Strangers Series and can be read as a standalone. All books in the series are interconnected standalone stories, however, I suggest reading them in <u>order</u>. This book (more than the others) will rely on knowledge of the previous characters and books due to the nature of the story but was written so it can be enjoyed on its own. Be forewarned, there are spoilers for the other books...

This book contains scenes with discussions of mature subject matter, including amnesia, grief, anxiety, terminal illness, on-page sexual content, drinking, on-page violence, and explicit language, and is intended for mature audiences.

-Jensen

Strangers Series
Main Cast of Characters

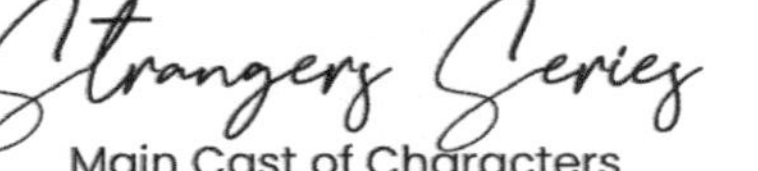

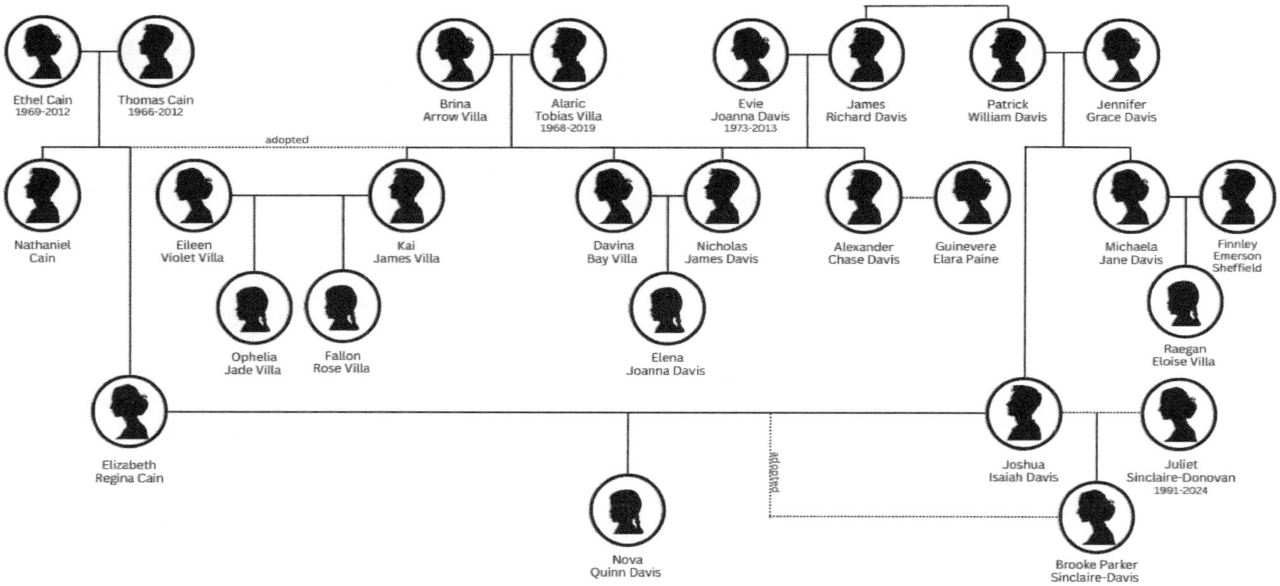

Characters are products of Jensen Parker's imagination or used fictitiously.

Ordinary - Alex Warren
Dancing Under Red Skies - Dermot Kennedy
Breathe - Fleurie & Tommee Profitt
Begin Again - The Summer Set
Comeback - Jonas Brothers
Restless Man - Radio Company
The Stranger - Ingrid Andress
my tears ricochet - Taylor Swift
All These Years - Camila Cabello
Begin Again - Colbie Caillat
Dancing With Your Ghost - Sasha Alex Sloan
Still in Love with You - Deeps
Bruised and Blooded - Seether
Easy on Me - No Resolve
Religiously - Bailey Zimmerman
This Love (Taylor's Version) - Taylor Swift
Begin Again - Didirri
Heaven Without You - Alex Warren
Give Me A Sign - Breaking Benjamin
How Do I Do This - Kelsea Ballerini
Sounds of Someday - Radio Company
Nervous - Nick Jonas
right where you left me (bonus track)
                                            - Taylor Swift
Watching over Me - Radio Company
Love Me Back - Max McNown
Strangers - Lewis Capaldi
If I Fall - Nick Jonas
Troubled Waters - Alex Warren
I Can Do Anything - Alexandra Kay
Hold On - Chord Overstreet
Let Me Go (feat. Chad Kroeger)
                                            - Avril Lavigne

Crossroads - I Prevail
Shameless - Camila Cabello
The Alchemy - Taylor Swift
Rome - Dermot Kennedy
Paper Planes - Alexander Jean
Half a Man - Dean Lewis
Find You - Nick Jonas
Brand New Day - Forty Foot Echo
Mountain With A View - Kelsea Ballerini
Life After You - Daughtry
Beautiful Things - Benson Boone
No I'm not in love - Tate McRae

Apple Music

Spotify

Stay - Miley Cyrus
Back to the Start - The Summer Set
Last Kiss (Taylor's Version) - Taylor Swift
Speechless - Dan + Shay
When I'm Gone - 3 Doors Down
Wish You The Best - Lewis Capaldi
I Dare You - Rascal Flatts & Jonas Brothers
Angels Like You - Miley Cyrus
Awaken - Breaking Benjamin
When You're Gone - Avril Lavigne
Nostalgia - Tate McRae
hummingbird - Carly Pearce

<u>CHARACTER CATCH UP</u>

I write my books as interconnected standalone stories, but you will see characters from the other books involved in this book's events.

If this is the first time we're meeting, WELCOME! Here's a little guide to get you caught up...

Nick Davis and **Nina Villa** have their own book, *Until Now,* which is the first book of the Strangers series. It's a fake dating, forced proximity, one-bed romance. As you will see in all of the books, they are what brings all of these characters together, so they will be involved (a lot!). *Begin Again* takes place almost ten years after the events of *Until Now.*

Michaela Davis and **Finn Sheffield** have their own book, ***Strictly Business,*** the second book of the Strangers series. It is an enemies-to-lovers, brother's best friend romance. Michaela is Josh's little sister and Finn is his best friend.

Elizabeth Cain-Davis and **Josh Davis** have their own book, ***Terms & Conditions,*** the third book of the Strangers series. It is a marriage of convenience (arranged marriage), marriage in trouble, second chance romance. Elizabeth is the adopted daughter of the Villa family and, therefore, is sometimes referred to as the third Villa child or sister to Nina and Kai. Josh is Michaela's older brother and Nick's cousin.

Alex Davis is Nick's little brother and Josh's cousin. He is engaged to **Guinevere (Lara) Daniels.**

Kai Villa is Nina's older brother, married to **Eileen Villa.**

Brooke (Brie) Sinclaire-Davis is Josh's daughter from a spring break fling in college. Elizabeth adopted Brie after her mother passed away.

Sheriff Beau Turner is the Sheriff of Spruce County, where Haven is located.

Sheriff Rhett Wilson is the Sheriff of Puck County.

Sergeant James Warren leads the State's investigation into a missing person in the book.

That's all I'm going to say about the characters for now! If you want to see the full connection between everyone, please check out the family tree provided a few pages ahead of this.

Happy reading.

One Year Ago

AN OVERWHELMING BLAST OF antiseptic fills my lungs when I suck in a breath for what feels like the first time in a year. Antiseptic, bleach, and the slightest tang of metal. I can almost taste it on my tongue. Speaking of my tongue, it feels like sandpaper against the roof of my mouth, and my throat feels like a thousand nails have been scraped across the raw flesh. The word is shrouded in darkness because my eyes won't open. No matter how hard I try, the muscles refuse to cooperate with my direction. Loud whooshes in my eardrums give way to a variety of sounds…

A door closes in the distance.

A few loud dings echo through the air.

Muffled voices speak behind a wall, but I can't make out what they're saying.

Finally, I force my eyelids open, blinking one, two, three times until finally the weights fall off, and they peel back to reveal a blinding light.

I try to shield my eyes, but my left arm feels like a ton of bricks, and it stays in place at my side. My right is easier and it moves freely. I rub my eyes until they adjust to reveal a… hospital room.

I'm in a hospital.

Why am I in a hospital?

I have to get out of here. I have to—

"Oh!" A shrill voice sends a jolt through my head, and the dull pain sitting in my left temple cracks my skull in two. The voice belongs to an older woman—a nurse—dressed in blue scrubs with yellow ducks on them. Her blonde hair is pulled into a tight bun on top of her head, and her eyes are hidden behind thick, round glasses. She stands in the doorway with a wide smile. "You're awake! Good. I'll get the doctor. He'll be so glad to hear this."

Maybe he can tell me why I'm here. Where is here anyway?

The nurse returns with a gray plastic pitcher and a white cup filled to the brim with ice chips.

"I was startin' to think you'd never wake up," she says, pouring water into the cup, opening the bendy straw, and stabbing it through the ice. She holds it up to my mouth. "Drink, sweetie, it'll help your throat. You've been out a few days. Guarantee your throat's as raw as sandpaper."

Her name tag dangles from a daisy clip off the pocket of her scrubs—*Janet,* it reads. She radiates the same energy you'd expect your grandma to have. She has crow's feet in the corners of her eyes and a smile that drags down around the sides of her lips. As she holds the cup to my mouth, I can see a jagged line on the outside of her thumb extending through her wrist to her arm.

"T-thank y-you," I rasp out, barely able to hear myself.

"Take it easy, darlin.' Don't want to strain yourself."

"Good morning, sunshine!"

My stomach twists in knots when an older man walks into the room. He's dressed professionally, with a white lab coat over his clothes, *Doctor Sanders, M.D.* embroidered above the left breast pocket. His stark white hair is perfectly styled with a small swoop over his forehead, a white mustache rests atop his upper lip, and I swear his striking blue eyes pierce through my soul. He reminds me of Dick Van Dyke in *Diagnosis: Murder.*

"Glad to see you're still with us. How are we feeling?" Doctor Sanders swoops down with his stethoscope, placing the cool metal against my chest. He moves it around my chest and then my back, and instinctively I take a few deep breaths. "You sound great," he says, straightening himself and wrapping the listening device around the back of his neck.

I take another sip of water, and the liquid soothes the rawness of my throat. "W-what happened?"

"Well." Doctor Sanders sighs and pulls the stool up next to the bed. He crosses one foot over his knee and leans back against the thin air. "I was kind of hoping you could tell me."

"What do you mean?"

"Ol' Bill Wyatt, his boy, and Mr. Blackwood found you wandering out in the woods 'bout two days ago. You were in pretty bad shape, son. Two bruised ribs, a sprained ankle, and a pretty bad hit to the ol' noggin. Looked like you'd been out there a while; you were severely dehydrated and chilled to the bone. Honestly, don't know how you were still up and movin' when they found you."

"I don't—I don't remember anything."

Doctor Sanders shares a look with Janet. I don't like that look. He looks back at me, asking, "You remember your name?"

"It's…It's…"

Oh, come on. I know my own fucking name.

How could I forget my name?

It's…it's right on the tip of my tongue! Ready to roll off the edge so I can tell him who the fuck I am and go the fuck home. *Home.* Where is home? And where am I right now? What happened to me? Why can't I remember *anything?*

My fists ball at my sides, grasping the cream, knit blanket covering my legs between my fingers. "It's…"

"Take it easy, son," Doctor Sanders says. "It's alright. We'll get this whole thing straightened out."

This time, he doesn't hide the concern etched in his features—his brow creases and his lips pull into a thin line, his eyes expressing a new level of pity—when he looks at the nurse. "Just give me a few minutes. I'm gonna make a few calls."

Before the door closes behind them, I hear them talking in hushed tones, trying to figure out what they're going to do. I can't decipher what they're saying, but I know it's not looking good for me. Having an amnesiac loony toon show up in their town is probably the last thing on their list of wants.

A black hole forms in my stomach, slowly sucking me inside of it. How could I forget who I am? What the hell happened to me and why was I wandering in the woods? Was I alone? Of course, I was alone. Sanders would've said if they found someone with me here in…I still don't know where the hell I am.

He said I was wandering in the woods…Well, that really narrows it down. There are a million different areas in the continental United States with woods. I am in the United States, right?

After what feels like hours have gone by, the door clicks open again. This time, Doctor Sanders is followed by two other men. One of them is an older man dressed in blue jeans and a button-up with a cowboy hat on his head. The other is a police officer. He's a tall, aging, dark-skinned man with thinning gray hair. His white button-up looks freshly pressed, with two patches on either arm and a thin black tie clipped to the middle of his shirt by a gold tie clip. The patch on his right sleeve reads *Bezer Police Department*. I notice a whiteboard behind his head: *Bezer General*. Janet's name badge says the same thing, and so does Doctor Sanders'.

Bezer.

Where the fuck is Bezer?

"What's your name, son?" the officer asks, and steps forward.

"I already told the doc, I don't know."

"Just give it another go for me."

I sigh. "It's…" A million names go through my mind, but not a single one hits home. I rub my eyes, trying to connect the dots, searching for anything that will tell me who I am, but I get nothing.

"Alright, take it easy," the officer says, patting my shoulder. "I'm Chief Sloan. I'm the officer who responded when Bill and Joe found you the other day. Do you remember any of this?"

I shake my head.

"I thought you said it wasn't that bad." Chief Sloan hisses over me toward the doctor.

"I said we couldn't be sure until he woke up," Sanders defends himself. "There's no way to tell what the body will do to protect itself. He's obviously been through something, that much was apparent from his injuries."

Chief Sloan sighs, rubbing the crease of his brow before he meets my eyes again.

"Where am I?" I ask.

Finally, the other man in the cowboy hat steps forward, clearing his throat. "Bezer. Bezer, Colorado."

Colorado? What the hell am I doing in Colorado?

The four of them look down at me, then at each other, a hint of pity etched in each of their features. They don't know what to do with me. They don't know who I am or what I'm doing here, but neither do I. They said I've been here for two days, but how long was I out in the wilderness before that? Isn't there anyone looking for me? Don't I have a family trying to find me? Or maybe I'm just a drifter, alone in the world with nothing to call my own, with no one to care if I find my way

home or not.
     "Welcome to the City of Refuge, son."

Part One

Him

one

NOW

THUNDER ROLLS THROUGH THE *sky, reminding me to pick up the pace because I have limited time before the heavens unleash their fury. I thought walking home from the gym would be a good way to cool down after a quick game of basketball with some of the guys, but the air is thick and sticky—and only getting worse. I'm sweatier than I was on the court, but there's no use trying to get a ride now. I'm only two blocks from home. Rounding the corner, my pace slows when I see a figure on the sidewalk not too far away. Not a figure…a person. A woman.*

She paces back and forth but never takes the final step forward that will lead her down the path to my apartment building. What is she doing? Another roar of thunder echoes above and I can feel the light mist of the impending rainstorm.

Please wait two more minutes so I can—

Holy shit.

My feet ground themselves in the cement. My heart swells, finally recognizing the woman in my path. What is she doing here? She's not supposed to be here.

Fuck, she looks good. The dark denim hugs her body in all

the right places, showing off the curve of her legs up to her ass, hidden just beneath her black overcoat. Her hair falls down her back in waves, almost reaching her hips.

She stops pacing long enough to pull out her phone and type something, her thumb hovering over the screen as another roll of thunder shudders above us. She sighs, stuffing the phone in her pocket without hitting send. "Fuck."

"Vulgar language for such a pretty mouth."

The woman turns on her heel, eyes wide, but the hesitation in her posture is long gone when she sprints to me. The basketball falls from my grasp, and I pull her into my arms, wasting no time pressing my mouth to hers. A soft moan resonates deep in my throat. It's been too damn long since I've had her in my arms or felt her lips against mine.

"I missed that."

She hums in agreement, and—

I jolt from my bed as another thunderous boom echoes, followed by a burning white streak of lightning. There aren't even five seconds before the next boom of thunder. I reach for the clock on my nightstand, where bright red numbers glare out at 3:02 a.m. A hand scrubs down my face, and I push myself out of bed. I have to be up in two hours anyway, and I know I won't be going back to sleep anytime soon. Not that I get much sleep as it is, but I would have liked to get a little more tonight. This is the furthest I've gotten in that same dream—the one I've had for months…Fucking storm had to go and ruin it.

Turning the faucet on when I walk into the bathroom, I wait for the water to warm before I let it run over my fingers. The temperature peaks and I fill my hands to rinse my face. The water washes away the last bit of sleep left in my eyes, but it can't erase the last eleven months.

How in the hell has it been eleven months?

Almost an entire fucking year since I arrived in Bezer,

Colorado. Since I woke up in a hospital room without a name or any recollection of who I am…Was…Am?

Or where I came from. And I'm not closer to finding out the truth today than I was three hundred and fifty-three days ago.

Letting the water swirl down the drain, I grip the edge of the sink and meet my reflection. I don't recognize the person staring back at me. It's like meeting the gaze of a stranger on the street, except I don't get to walk away from this stranger. I'm forever trapped in the same space as him.

The Blackwoods have been extremely supportive over the last year, more than I ever expected them to be. Joseph Blackwood is one of the men who found me wandering the forest in early April last year. He had been kind enough to give me a place to stay when I had nowhere to go and no money. While the idea of moving into the home of a stranger seemed like it should be a little concerning, it was better than spending an indeterminate amount of time in the hospital.

Besides, imagine being in his shoes. It couldn't have been any easier letting me walk through the door than it was for me to walk through it. Lately, I've wondered how long he'll continue to extend the same generosity. How long is too long? I'm not paying to live here, but I work on the ranch and around the house to earn my keep, doing the things Joseph can't anymore or his daughter—Charlie—doesn't want to. This past month, I've considered getting a job in town to supplement a little bit, maybe offering to give Joseph a little each month, but I'm not sure there's enough time in a day. I'm up by five o'clock every morning and work well past sundown, sometimes late into the night when I have trouble sleeping.

The room Joseph set me up in on the day Chief Sloan dropped me off wasn't much, but for now…it's home. It's small but charming, with original wood floors from when the house was built in the late 1800s, and I've always been curious about the stories they could tell. The stories the house could tell. The lives these walls have watched, the secrets they keep as they stand by keeping my own.

The wood-burning fireplace across from the foot of the bed was a blessing this past winter, better than even the modern-day heater Joseph had me install in the barn before it got too cold. I've spent many sleepless nights in the muted pink armchair near the fireplace, going through the hospital file labeled "John Doe" or with the sketchbook and pencil I picked up from the store in town.

The file is thin. There are only a few pages of notes from Doctor Sanders at Bezer General, with minimal information, and a copy of the police report Chief Sloan slipped me (even if he wasn't supposed to). Each time I go through the scribbled words I hope something new will catch my eye. I hope something will stick out and remind me of anything from my past life…But it never does.

Flipping open the file on the desk, I glance over the notes I had taken on the facts:

1. Found wandering the woods on the morning of April 10, 2028, by Bill Wyatt, his son, and Joseph Blackwood on their way to a hunting post. Out there for at least a day, possibly two, based on the level of dehydration. Almost hypothermic.

2. No identification.

3. Blow to the head, seemingly blunt force trauma. Deep laceration on left side of face. Sprained ankle. Bruised ribs. Amnesia.

4. Getting memory back has been a slow process. Small memories here and there, nothing concrete.

5. No one has come looking.

Next to the file is a blue spiral-bound notebook with every memory or dream I've had since I arrived in Bezer. They don't often vary, but I like to keep track of them in case something new happens to make an appearance. Turning the pages until I reach the next blank space, I write out the dream I've just woken up from, adding the color of her eyes (something I've never noticed before) and how she didn't hesitate to run straight into my arms. I've dreamed of this woman countless times. She is in almost every dream or memory I've had. I have a feeling she's the answer to everything…I just have to find her first.

A crash from downstairs shoots a jolt of adrenaline through my veins. What the hell was that?

Careful to avoid the spots on the old stairs I know will creak, I make my way down to the lower level of the house and immediately notice the light on in the kitchen. Craning my neck around the last few stairs, I expect to see Joseph's door open, but it's still sealed shut. He probably put his damn earplugs in…and when he does, he doesn't hear a damn thing. He'd sleep through the apocalypse if he went to bed with those things in.

When I take the final steps to the kitchen, my awareness falls. Joseph's daughter, Charlie, rummages through the cabinets, muttering to herself.

"Looking for something?"

The sound of my voice practically sends her shooting through the roof. She spins on her heel with wide eyes and loses her balance, falling onto the counter before crumbling to the ground. She giggles the whole way down.

"Are you drunk?" I ask, bending down to her level.

"No." She giggles and her head shakes back and forth against the white cabinet. "Y-you'reeeeeee drunk."

"Oh yeah, you're drunk." I sigh. "What are you doing down here?"

"I need a snack!"

I take in her appearance—black pleather jeans, a one-shouldered black top, black heeled booties, and large silver hoop earrings. It looks like she just walked in the door. I caught a glimpse of her jumping in her truck while making my rounds in the barn after dinner. That had to have been around seven. Did she just get back? The stove clock reads 3:34 a.m.

"Did you just get home?"

"Yeah, so?" Charlie quips. "You're not my dad."

"No, but you're gonna wake him up if you're not quiet."

Charlie huffs, folding her arms. "You're bossy. I don't like you."

I roll my eyes, putting one arm under her legs and the other around her back to lift her off the ground.

"Put me down, Xavier! I'm not a child."

When I was still at the hospital, we all agreed on the name Xavier. I can't remember how we decided on it, but at the time, anything was better than being the nameless freak. "Then stop acting like it," I say.

Charlie tries to push me away as I walk toward the stairs, but her attempts have no effect on me. "I can w-walk, Xavier. Let me walk!"

"Okay, just be quiet!" I hiss, looking her straight in the eye. I glance down the hall at Joseph's door. Just because he *can* sleep through anything, doesn't mean he *will*. The last thing I need is him coming out at three in the morning to find me carrying his drunk daughter up the stairs. "If I put you down, will you be quiet?" She starts to open her mouth, but I stop her. "Ah! Say something else and I'm carrying your drunk ass upstairs. Got it?"

Charlie huffs, mumbling something that sounds like "you're mean," but does as she's told.

I slowly set her back on her feet, but her ankles wobble in the booted heels. She clutches at me, trying to steady herself, and it sends us both tumbling a few paces. When I look up to check on her, we're mere centimeters apart, so close I can smell the vodka and citrus on her breath as I look directly into her green eyes. She sucks in her bottom lip, gaze dropping down to mine and back.

"Zay," she whispers, starting to close the gap between us.

Oh no. I cannot let this happen, especially not in this state. Clearing my throat, I take a step back. "Let's go, Charlie."

Her arms fall to her sides as she stands there like a scolded child. Her eyes narrow, staring at the ground, piecing together what just happened. When she straightens her back, she seems a little less wobbly on her feet, as if the whole thing sobered her up a bit.

That theory goes out the window when she takes her first step, her ankle giving way beneath her. She almost crashes into the banister, but I catch her before she does.

"I can do it!" Charlie swats at my hand.

"Not unless you want to tumble down the stairs in those damn shoes," I say, rolling my eyes and picking her up again.

I leave the door of her bedroom open when I walk in and set her on the edge of her bed. This is supposed to be a quick trip in and out, there is no need to hang around, but Charlie has other plans. She flops back onto the bed and lifts one of her boots. "Help me."

"Charlie."

"Please," she whines.

I sigh but step back into the room, kneeling in front of her to remove the shoes. Unzipping the boots, I tug them off her feet and place them neatly at the foot of the bed for her to put away when she wakes up. "Okay, Char, time for bed. Let's go."

"Are you gonna read me a bedtime story?" She giggles, lifting up on her forearms to stare down the bed at me.

"No." I pull myself up from the floor.

"You're no fun, *Xavier*," she huffs. "Or whatever your name is."

I glance over my shoulder to see she has flopped back on

the bed with her arms crossed over her chest. Her auburn hair has started to fall out of the updo she had it in, splayed out beneath her head as she glares up at the ceiling.

God, she's so dramatic.

I roll my eyes, looking through the dresser for something a little less…tight for her to sleep in, trying to ignore the slight sting in my chest. I shouldn't let her words affect me so much, I know that, but they sting. I thought we had gotten past the attitude but guess not.

"Middle and bottom drawer," she calls from her place, her words more sober than they have been all night. She continues to stare at the ceiling when I place a pair of sweats and an oversized T-shirt on the bed next to her.

"Goodnight, Charlie," I say and leave without waiting for a response.

Things with Charlie are complicated. They have been from the moment I stepped foot on Blackwood Ranch. The welcoming committee wasn't exactly…welcoming at first. I can't blame her. She didn't know me any better than I knew myself. Every day I wake up, I wake up a new person. But as I've settled into life on the ranch, Charlie and I have found common ground, albeit still shaky at times, and settled into something, too…Even if I'm not exactly sure what that means.

I open my bedroom door to get ready for work, I can't help but think about how we've ended up here…

two

One Year Ago
April 2028

MY HEAD SNAPS FORWARD from its resting place against the cool window, pulling me instantly from sleep, and I have to look around to catch my bearings. To remember where I am. The police SUV climbs up the dirt road of a mountain with nothing but thick trees and brush on either side. To my left is Chief Daniel Sloan, dressed in a starched white button-up with a navy blue tie secured by a gold tie clip, all underneath a black jacket with a sleeve patch that reads *Bezer Police Department*. There's a white cowboy hat on the bench between us.

Taking a deep breath, I rub my hand over my shaved head and settle back into my seat. I hadn't been asleep long, but I wonder if I had been able to get a few more minutes if I would have been able to dream of something and it would trigger another memory or a name or anything…

"You okay over there?" Chief Sloan asks.

"Y-yeah," I say. "Good to go."

"You sure you want to do this?"

"Do I have another option?"

It's been three days since I woke up in Bezer General

Hospital. Doctor Sanders said there isn't anything we can do… It's up to me to remember. And so far, there have been no signs of that happening soon.

Yesterday afternoon, there was a discussion between Doctor Sanders, Chief Sloan, and Mr. Blackwood about what to do with me. The doctor was adamant there must be some way to identify me—fingerprints? DNA? Anything?

"We ran his prints," Chief Sloan had said, standing in the hospital room. "I took 'em when he came in, but nothing showed up in our database."

"What's that mean?" Mr. Blackwood asked. Joseph Blackwood was one of the men who had found me on the outskirts of town two days prior. He was a gruff man with a head full of white hair and a white beard. His broad stance oozed confidence, a kind of confidence only certain individuals had. I was surprised when he walked in with Sloan that morning, unsure what insight he could offer into the situation, but at that point, I was open to just about anything.

"Just means he's never been arrested. And I'm sorry to say, but until we figure out who he is, or someone comes looking for him…we can't let him leave."

"Well, what are we supposed to do with him?" Doctor Sanders asked, his fingers rubbing the white mustache resting on his upper lip. His striking blue eyes narrowed on Sloane.

"Well, we can put his photo up," Sloan said. "I've alerted the sheriff, gave him a copy of the photo too, but he hasn't had any reports come in." His words trailed off, shoulders raised in a shrug. He didn't say the thing we were all thinking: If I had been in Bezer at least four days at that point, and no one had filed a missing person report yet, what were the odds of them doing it at all? Chief Sloan shrugged, hands gripping his waistband. "There isn't much else I can do until he remembers something."

The pounding in my head grew with each word as I listened

to them continue to go back and forth. The light became too bright, and the sounds of the machines pierced my eardrums. The only thing I could hear was the loud whoosh of blood as it coursed through my veins, making the throbbing between my eyes worse.

A cold hand ushered me to lie back, and I could faintly hear Doctor Sanders on the other side of the thunderous pounding. "Okay, that's enough for today."

A moment later, the nurse walked in with a Tylenol and an ice pack, taking over for the doctor and helping me settle back onto the bed.

"Look." Chief Sloan sighed. "I wish there was more I could do, but this is how we have to proceed when dealing with a John Doe."

John Doe.

John? Hmm, no.

Johnny? Nope.

"You have no identity, no money, and nowhere to go. So, for the foreseeable future, you'll be right here until we figure out what to do with you."

"Actually," Joseph said, combing the ends of his beard. "I have an idea."

"Joe," Sloan warned.

"I need some help around the ranch." Joseph turned from Sloan to me. "You any good with your hands?"

"I guess so," I said.

"I need some help getting things fixed up and help with some ranch work. In exchange, I'm happy to put you up in a room at our bed and breakfast."

"Re-establishing a routine can be helpful to jog the ol' noggin," Doctor Sanders said when Sloan tried to counter Joseph's offer.

"It's up to you, son," Sloan said, and all three men looked at me. "You can stay here, or you can take Joe up on his offer."

And that's how I ended up in Chief Sloan's police cruiser, heading up the mountain to Blackwood Ranch. If my only choices were sitting in a hospital room or working around a ranch, I'd take the latter.

The ranch sits a few miles up a dirt road off a dead-end street perpendicular to Main Street. Bezer is a small, off-the-grid type town in the Rocky Mountains. The whole place looks like it's stuck in the 1950s, with Main Street thriving as the central part of the community. It's an odd sight. I may not remember my name, but I'm pretty sure small towns like this don't exist anymore.

The thick brush on either side of the road loosens until it's completely gone, opening to a wide clearing. The rolling hills and mountains in the background look more like a painting than real life. Black iron letters spell out *Blackwood Ranch* above the open gate the dirt road runs through, and a homestead becomes visible. A white farmhouse with a barn about a hundred yards north and an old red tractor that looks like it hasn't run in a long time is parked outside. Not too far from the tractor is a dusty blue pickup truck with a white stripe down the sides that also looks like it hasn't run in quite some time.

Sloan lets his foot off the gas, coming through another patch of trees and creeping toward the house until he comes to a complete stop. My stomach drops when he maneuvers the stick shift to park. I have no idea what I'm walking into, or what to expect from Mr. Blackwood, but Chief Sloan and Doctor Sanders seem to think he's a good enough guy. He appears well-respected, but what if he's secretly a serial killer?

What? It could happen.

Joseph stands on the front porch of the farmhouse. It's bigger than it looked from the gate, towering over me as I step out of the car. I shade my eyes from the spring sun and a cool wind whips around the door. Goosebumps rise across my skin beneath the coat Sloan had given me before we left the hospital. His wife had taken the liberty to gather some clothes for me. She'd picked out some of his old clothes that didn't fit him anymore and even went to the store to get whatever she couldn't find at home. It wasn't much, but it was a start. The house is secluded and surrounded by acres upon acres of untouched land, with no sign of anyone for miles. The only sounds are from the birds in the sky and a horse's whinny from the direction of the barn.

"Thanks for bringing him up, Danny," Joseph calls to Chief Sloan. He's wearing the same thing he wore both times he visited the hospital—Wrangler blue jeans, a plaid button-up, brown boots, and a brown cowboy hat.

"You got it, Joe." Sloan waves to him. "You sure about this? We can figure something out if—"

"Oh, no, it's no trouble. I can use the help. The ol' ticker ain't what it used to be, y'know? And I had to let my guys go. It's just been me and Charlie, so an extra pair of hands is gonna help a lot."

The hinge of the screen door creaks as an auburn-haired girl steps out of the house. The hinge grinds away at something deep inside me and I make a mental note to grease it as soon as possible. She looks around at the three of us before turning to Joe. "Who is that?"

"Charlie this…What did we say again?"

"Xavier," I answer.

"Right, right. Charlie, this is Xavier. He's gonna be staying with us for a bit," Joseph explains, and Charlie's eyes narrow toward me. "He's gonna help out around the ranch while—"

"Dad, we can't afford—"

"It's no trouble. We already worked out the details."

"What's that supposed to mean?" Charlie's glare turns on her father.

"Don't worry about it, Char," Joseph says, wrapping his

arm around her shoulders. "He's just here until he can get the ol' noggin working again. It's no trouble, is it, Xavier?"

"No trouble at all," I say with a brief smile.

"He's happy to have a roof over his head." Chief Sloan chuckles and a heavy hand clamps down on my shoulder, urging me forward. "Well, I best be getting back to the station," the chief says, rubbing his hands together when the wind blows again. "Gotta finish up a few things, and Doris'll have my head if I'm late for dinner again."

"Thanks again, Danny," Joe says. "Tell Doris I said hey!"

Sloan waves over his shoulder and hops into the cruiser, starting the trek back down the mountain.

I watch the taillights for a moment longer, gripping the handles of the drawstring and plastic bags in my hands a little tighter. The contents of the drawstring bag from the hospital are all I have left of my past—a pair of gym shorts and one tennis shoe. The hospital had to cut me out of the shirt I had been wearing, it was torn and covered in blood, from a head wound and countless scratches and scrapes across my body. No one knew where my other shoe was. I wasn't wearing it when they found me.

"Well, c'mon, boy, let me show you to your room," Joseph calls from the porch behind me.

Taking a deep breath, I finally turn on my heel and follow him inside the house, passing by Charlie, who glares at me the whole way in.

Joseph leads me upstairs and down the hall to a bedroom, next to the communal bathroom. The room is decorated to match the farmhouse aesthetic. A blue patchwork quilt covers the queen-sized mattress with a matching blue rug on the floor, a carved wood dresser against the exterior wall, and a desk in the corner to the left of the bed. All that's missing is some rooster décor.

"This'll be alright?" Joseph asks.

"It'll be perfect." I set my bags on the bed, but don't let go of the handles. "Anything is better than another night in that hospital bed."

Joseph laughs and pats me on the back. "You can say that again. I couldn't wait to get out of there when I had heart surgery a couple years ago. Well, make yourself at home, Xavier. Dinner is at six, make sure you wash up."

"Yes, sir."

"Enough of the 'sirs.' You can call me Joe."

I nod, smiling toward the older man, and wait until I hear his retreating footsteps completely disappear before I let out the breath I've been holding. With another look around the room, it all starts to sink in…This is home for the next however many days…weeks…months…

Until someone figures out who I am or the Blackwoods get tired of me.

It's homey, but it's not *home*.

"Just because my dad is okay with you being here, doesn't mean I am." Charlie stands in the doorway, arms crossed tightly over her chest. No longer blinded by the sun I get a proper look at her. She's pretty, with auburn hair falling below her shoulders and a slender figure. She doesn't wear much makeup, if any, and is dressed in blue jeans and a plaid flannel tucked into her waist—like her father. But something about her feels out of place, like she's playing the role of the rancher's daughter, not that she is one. Her eyes narrow, looking me up and down, and she says, "I don't know what kind of 'deal' you have worked out with him—"

"That's not any of your business, is it?"

Charlie scoffs. "There's something about you…I don't like this."

"Well, if you know something that can help me get out of here quicker, by all means…I'd love to know."

"My dad thinks everyone can be trusted, but I don't, and I

sure as hell don't trust you."

I roll my eyes. This tough girl routine is going to get real old, real fast if I'm stuck here for a while. "There's nothing here that I want, Charlotte."

That's the formal name for Charlie, right?

"It's Charlie," she quips. "And what was your name again?" A devilish grin spreads across her lips as she kicks off the wall and disappears down the hall.

three

April 2028

WALKING INTO THE BARN the next morning, I had no idea what to expect. Joseph said it needed work, but he forgot to mention how much.

Last night, Joseph wasted no time listing off the biggest things that troubled the ranch, but as I got ready for bed, I thought the old barn was the best place to start. Having the barn as a workplace in case the weather decided to unleash one final cold spell seemed like a good idea. It is April, after all, and being up this far up in the mountains, there is always a possibility for snow.

How do I know that? I thought as I changed into my pajamas. Was it common knowledge? The kind of thing everyone knew? No, it couldn't be. The thought seemed like it would be more common to someone used to this area. Was this a clue? Was I from around here?

My first night at the ranch had been uneventful, thankfully. Charlie had been absent when I came down at six o'clock on the dot for dinner, and I would never tell Joseph, but I was grateful. The thought of dealing with her across the table made my head hurt.

Joseph spent most of the meal recounting the story of Blackwood Ranch. It was a rundown farmhouse built in the 1800s set for demolition after it sat abandoned for so long, but his parents bought it instead because his mother always had a soft spot for the old place. They hated to see something with so much history torn down. She had always dreamed of opening a bed and breakfast in their small town, a place where visitors could come to enjoy the simple life that Bezer had to offer. A place of refuge away from the hustle and bustle of the rest of the ever-changing world. His parents opened the Blackwood Ranch B&B when Joseph was five years old and ran it until he took over when his mother passed twenty years ago. He loved that Charlie had been able to grow up in the same place he had. Charlie's mother had died when Charlie was six years old, so it had been the two of them and whatever guests for a long while now.

The once steady stream of guests they used to see every year had dwindled to maybe one or two a year recently. Joseph knew the decline was partially due to a lack of an online presence, but that's not what Bezer was about. If he had gone this long without the internet, he'd be fine…He could've asked Charlie for help, but he said she had been so busy in San Diego the last few years, that he didn't want to bother her.

I found myself growing more curious about what the future held as I listened to Joseph's story. What would happen if they continued down the same road, refusing to enter the modern age? If you wanted to be noticed, you had to have an online presence, and if you didn't it was considered "sus."

"Had to let some of my best hands go." Joseph sighed from the head of the eight-top wooden table in the dining room. "That's why I could use your help around here. In recent years, my health hasn't been the best. I've had to cut back on the manual side of things. And Charlie, God bless her, she tries but can only do so much."

I had no qualms about helping out, I was grateful to have a real bed to sleep in and food that wasn't being pushed out of a hospital kitchen.

When I went to bed last night, my muscles instantly relaxed against the mattress, which was surprisingly plush—far better than the one I had been sleeping on at the hospital. But even so, I struggled to fall asleep, and when I finally did, it felt like two seconds later my alarm was blaring in my ear. And that's how I ended up walking into the barn at five o'clock this morning to get a better idea of what needed to be done.

Charlie's SUV was back underneath the carport when I stepped out the front door this morning. *Goody.* That meant I would have to deal with her at some point and with whatever attitude she decided to throw my way. The thought gave me a headache. Look, I get it, she didn't like the idea of a strange man walking into the house, but what's the difference between me and one of their typical bed and breakfast guests? Minus the lack of an identity...

When I gave the barn a good look-over this morning, it became obvious it was a good thing I decided to start there. The roof had been patched before the winter, but it still needed to be completely repaired. A handful of pieces of siding needed to be replaced—some were broken and others were missing completely. One of the doors that enclosed the indoor riding arena needed to be put back on the track. Two stalls needed the floors repaired, and one gate needed to be put back on the hinge. And finally, one of the main barn doors needed to be replaced due to a chunk missing from the bottom and wood rot. That didn't even include the room that looked like a makeshift tack room in total disarray, seemingly left unfinished by the prior ranch hands.

I have already pulled the main entry door off the hinge to get a better look at the damage, and it was obvious the whole thing needed to be replaced. Repairing it would be more work than building a new one, meaning I will have to replace the other one so they match—nonetheless, it seems like the easier option. As I stared at the door, I wondered if I knew *how* to do something like that. The knowledge of deciding to build two new doors versus repairing the one came naturally from somewhere within the depths of my mind. That meant I must know *something* about construction...Right?

I'm disappointed when I reach for the coffee tumbler I found in the cabinet this morning and find it practically empty. With a heavy sigh, I take my jacket from the hook on the wall and shrug it back over my shoulders, heading toward the house to get a refill and change clothes. The temperatures haven't warmed up from earlier this morning, but I won't need as many layers as I anticipated. Even though the barn needs more work than I hoped, it maintains a good amount of warmth within its walls. Once I get into the thick of things, I doubt I'll want this many layers on.

Walking into the house, I barely step over the threshold before I hear voices down the hall from the kitchen. And I immediately recognize them as Charlie and Joseph, the former expressing her latest grievance to the latter. I use my free hand to quietly close the door behind me, trying to conceal my arrival a little longer—and if you're wondering, yes, I greased the hell out of that damn hinge before I did anything else this morning.

"How can you be so naive?" Charlie huffs.

"Charlie—"

"No! Those people have been after this place for years. *Years*, Dad! Just last week they left a message on the answering machine trying to set up a meeting with you. Now all of the sudden this guy shows up with amnesia."

"Charlie, he really does have—"

"That's bullshit!" A slam echoes down the hall, presumably

one of the cabinet doors, as she tries to get her point across.

Does she ever let the man finish a damn sentence?

"You have such a wild imagination. Honey, this is nothing more than a coincidence."

"I don't believe in coincidences," Charlie says. "Dad, I'm serious. Why aren't you more concerned about this?"

"*If*, and that's a big if, Xavier is who you think he is...we'll handle it when the time comes. But I don't think you need to worry about this. Besides, even if he is some big architect or whatever you think he is, won't it be nice to have someone who knows how to work with their hands?"

I stare down at my hands, flexing them—opening and closing them a few times, trying to will the knowledge they hold from within—before I take a deep breath and walk down the hallway.

My arrival is met with an exaggerated groan from Charlie, but Joseph smiles brightly. "G'morning, Xavier! You were out there bright and early this morning."

"Yes, s—Joe." I catch myself before the word *sir* comes out, offering a tight smile. "Yeah, I, uh...I don't get much sleep right now."

"That's okay, I'm sure it'll get easier as you start to...get back into the swing of things."

Remember.

As you start to remember, is what Joseph meant to say.

"Anyways," he continues. "Can we get you anything? More coffee?"

"Please." I sigh. "It was a bit chilly this morning."

"Charlie here was just sayin' we're supposed to get snow this weekend."

"That's what I was afraid of." I roll my shoulders, straightening the length of my spine, and crack my neck. "I started the barn this morning so there would be a space to work in case it happened."

Joseph chuckles. "You talk like you're from around here."

His statement lingers in the air, the three of us staring at one another, waiting for my response. Charlie, who has been invested in the crossword puzzle pulled from her father's newspaper, lifts her gaze to the conversation.

"I, uh…I don't think I am," I stammer out. "I just…Well, I don't know. I thought—"

"Don't hurt yourself, son." Joseph lifts both hands, dropping his copy of the *Bezer Times* on the table. "I just meant that most people who know that sort of thing are usually familiar with the mountains." He offers me a smile before he turns to his daughter. "Charlie, why don't you make a fresh pot so Xavier has something to keep him warm out there?"

She looks up from her crossword again with a glare. "He knows where it is."

"Actually—"

Her glare turns on me when I try to refute her argument. I don't know where it is, the coffee had already been brewed when I got up this morning. The pot was one of the only modern things Joseph had around here. It was one of those programmable coffee pots you can set to brew at a certain time.

"C'mon, Char, make your ol' dad a pot, will ya?" Joseph pushes.

Charlie stares at her father for a moment longer before she sighs, rolling her eyes. The chair's feet scrape against the wood floor as she pushes back from the table, not bothering to push it back in. She begins grabbing items to make the fresh pot from various cabinets and I step up beside her, looking over her shoulder as she prepares the ingredients.

Charlie's movements pause briefly, and she glances at me from the corner of her eye. "What are you doing?"

"Well, I figured I'd better watch…You said I knew where everything was, so I'm making sure you do it right."

The wooden coffee spoon clatters from her hands onto the counter and she spins on her heel to give her dad the most *are you fucking kidding me* look I've ever seen. Joseph laughs, shaking his head as he returns to the newspaper in his hands.

"You seem to have this under control," I say, and I'm surprised she doesn't get whiplash from how quickly she turns back around. I watch her frustration grow at the smirk on my lips. "Am I good to run upstairs real quick or do you need me to make sure you got it?"

"You're an ass."

I shrug and walk backward until I'm out of the kitchen. I can hear her slam the cabinet with a frustrated growl as I climb the stairs to change.

After tightening the nut and bolt that bolsters the final board of the door, I use the drill to add a final screw in each joist. I run my hand over the board, noting where it still feels a little coarse to the touch, and wipe the dust off on my jeans. While the main boards of each door are in place, I still have to add the diagonal pieces that will add extra support to the joists on each one. Grabbing one of the boards meant for that exact purpose, I place it on the makeshift table saw comprised of a larger piece of plywood and two sawhorses.

Footsteps walk up the gravel leading from the house to the barn, but they're not heavy enough to be Joseph, which means it's the only other person here. When I came downstairs earlier, she was nowhere to be seen, but my tumbler had been filled and resealed, ready and waiting on the counter.

My suspicions are confirmed when I look over my shoulder. She's dressed now, no longer in her sweats and loose-fitting sweater from earlier, with a windbreaker over her shoulders and her auburn hair pulled into a ponytail on top of her head, stuck through a fleece headband that covers her ears. It's gotten colder in the last few hours, especially now that the sun has started to set. I had hoped to finish the door and siding today, but the door has taken a little longer than anticipated. However, it felt like the most important thing to finish. I couldn't leave the barn wide open with two horses inside.

Charlie stops about five feet from me, arms crossed over her chest.

"Something you need?" I ask when she doesn't say anything, continuing to stand there.

"Dad said to tell you dinner is ready." Her lips pull into a firm line. "I yelled, but I guess you didn't hear me."

Did she really? I don't remember hearing anything and it's not like there's much noise out here that would drown her out. Then again…I do have the radio playing.

"You didn't need to trek out here to tell me that," I say.

"I don't need another lecture from my dad, so yeah, I kind of did."

I laugh and motion to the board that I was about to cut before she showed up. "I need to finish these doors and then I'll head in."

Charlie nods and turns to go back inside. As I'm about to push the saw blade through the red-marked line on the board, I realize she's still standing there. I glance over my shoulder again to find her staring straight at me. More specifically, at my arms. Unlike Charlie, I had shed my layers—even after changing earlier—because I was burning up from the constant motion.

"Need something else?" I ask.

Charlie rips her gaze from my arms as if my words break her trance and she shakes her head vigorously.

"It'll go faster if I have some help. Hold this up for me?"

"Big strong man can't hold up his wood?"

I roll my eyes but motion for her to come closer before finishing the cuts to make the diagonal boards. Charlie's steps are hesitant, still maintaining distance between us.

"Hold this here." I show her where to place her hands on the board so that it rests at an angle between the two joists on the front of the door.

She's standing so close now that I can feel the cold clinging to her jacket against my bare arm. Her gaze is on me instead of the task at hand, and when I turn to tell her to focus, the words get lost when I look into her eyes. From this distance, I notice the specks of gold hidden within her forest-green orbs. They're pretty—really pretty.

Not as pretty as hers.

As whose? Where did that come from?

Charlie clears her throat expectantly, ripping her gaze from mine. "Dinner is getting cold."

"Right...Sorry." I shake my head, clearing all thoughts of the last minute, and return to the task.

Drilling the board into place should have been easier with her help, but it did the opposite, making it more difficult. I continuously maneuver around her, finding the right angle to drill, putting us in some awkward positions.

When the final screw is in place, I take a step back and examine our work. It will do for now. I'll need to secure the board to the joists and then do the other door, but it will be easier without her help.

"Charlie?" I hear Joseph call in the distance without any issues, making me think she didn't even try to yell for me like she said. "Xavier? You guys coming?"

"On our way, Dad!" Charlie yells back, turning back to me. "We better go. He made chili and he *hates* waiting for his chili."

"Go ahead." I nod toward the house. "I need to finish these and then I'll be right in."

Her gaze narrows, and she looks like she is about to argue with me, but she doesn't. She turns on her heel to begin the walk back to the house, but she stops...again. Now a few steps away, she turns back around and stuffs her hands in her pockets, not coming any closer. "You *really* don't remember anything?"

I laugh. "I really don't remember anything."

"How is that possible? I mean, how do you just wake up with no recollection of who you are?"

"One of the world's greatest mysteries, I suppose."

Charlie huffs and I can tell she wants to ask me more, but she swallows whatever question sits on the tip of her tongue.

When she's finally gone my shoulders fall with a deep sigh. I wish I had the answers she's looking for, the ones I'm looking for, but unfortunately...I don't. I would love to remember something (anything) because that would mean I get to go home. I'm grateful to Joseph for giving me a warm bed, food, and something to keep my head and hands busy—to keep my mind off the situation—but there's a yearning deep in my soul for the life waiting on the other side of that smoke wall clouding my mind.

four

August 2028

FOUR MONTHS. ONE HUNDRED and twenty-three days. That's how many mornings I've woken up at Blackwood Ranch. How do I know? I've kept a running tally in the notebook on the desk in my room. The top margin of the very first page is covered in little tally marks for every day I've been here. Every day I haven't remembered who I am. Every day no one has come looking for me.

Sometimes when I drive into town, I stop by the police station and check in with Chief Sloan to see if there are any updates, but it's the same answer every time: "Sorry, kid. Nothin's coming in yet." Which he usually follows up with, "I'm sure somethin'll turn up eventually."

Well, eventually hasn't happened yet and I'm starting to lose hope that it ever will. I wonder if my few "memories"—if you can even call them that—are memories at all. Or maybe they are, but from a life I no longer have the privilege of knowing. Maybe an ex-girlfriend? A brother I no longer speak to? Or maybe they're dreams my mind has created to give me a sense of false hope for something that doesn't exist at all.

The sun beats down on the open riding arena a few hundred yards from the house, not far from the barn. The back left corner of the large, fenced circle is shaded by a patch of trees that extend out from the wilderness like a vein, where Joseph and Melody Jones watch Charlie give Melody's daughter a riding lesson. It's something Charlie started about two months ago at her father's request, but she only offers lessons to a few select students. She didn't seem happy when Joseph brought up the idea, but it wasn't my place to ask questions. I thought it seemed like an odd request, Charlie barely spent time in or near the barn unless she was mucking stalls—an observation I'd never made until she was forced to spend time in the barn with her students.

Joseph leans against the steel pipe fence, one boot up on the bottom rung, as he squints against the bright August sun. Melody sits at the picnic table, dressed in clothes that make her look like she took a wrong turn and ended up at a farm instead of brunch at the country club. I'm surprised she even sits on the picnic table, not afraid that she might get something on the expensive-looking pants.

As I get closer, I hear mumbled instructions from Charlie who stands in the middle of the arena. She holds a long rope allowing her to maintain some control while she gives the girl a chance to do it herself as the horse prances in a circle.

"Oh, hello, Xavier!" Joseph says, turning toward me. "Mel, you met Xavier yet?"

"Yes, we met last time." Melody smiles, her smile ghostly white against the stain on her lips. "Nice to see you again, Xavier."

"Mrs. Jones," I say with a nod. "Jenny's looking good out there."

"Isn't she?" A look of pride crosses her features when she glances back at her daughter. "Charlie's lessons have been doing wonders!"

Joseph shakes his head. "I tried to tell her she needed to do this a while ago, but that girl is stubborn as a damn mule."

"Well, I'm glad you finally convinced her, Joe. Did I tell you Jenny wants to get into barrel racing like Charlie?"

"Charlie used to race?" I ask. The girl who will barely even go near one of the horses used to barrel race? That doesn't seem likely.

"She was one of the best!"

"My wife was good, but Charlie was great," Joe says, a nostalgic smile crossing his lips. "She used to be a big name on the circuit."

"Used to?" I glance over at Charlie, who is oblivious to the conversation about her past. I wonder if that *used to* is part of why she seems so unhappy sometimes. I catch the last seconds of a look shared between Melody and Joseph before the former sighs and focuses on Jenny, who has started a series of jumps on the other side of the arena.

"You've probably noticed Charlie doesn't have much to do with the horses," Joseph says, catching my attention. "She was thrown from her horse, Arthur, a few years ago in the middle of an event. Arthur got spooked, no one knows why, but the whole thing was a circus." He kicks something invisible in the dirt beneath the fence before straightening his back and looking at me. "When Charlie came to, she didn't want anything to do with the sport again."

"Well." Melody scoffs. "Can you blame the poor girl? That must've been scary. One minute you're on the back of your horse doin' something as easy as breathin' and the next you're waking up on the ground, lucky not to be paralyzed."

Well, shit.

I didn't think about it that way.

"And that's why she ended up goin' to college. How could I fight her on it when something like that happened? Before the accident, she had applied to school but decided to go professional instead."

"San Diego?" I ask, remembering a coffee mug in the kitchen and Joseph's history lesson from my first night here.

"Yep." Joseph sighs. "Packed up and moved to the West Coast until a few months before you got here, Xavier."

Jenny guides the horse over the final hurdle before trotting to Charlie with a proud smile.

"I've never seen her ride either of the horses in the barn," I say.

"She doesn't ride anymore. Hasn't since the accident. Before these lessons, I was lucky she even mucked the stalls."

A smile, a genuine smile, splits Charlie's face when she watches Jenny perform the circuit one more time before the girl breaks into a chorus of "Look at me, Mom!" and takes a lap around the arena. I catch Charlie's eye when Jenny trots by and the right side of my mouth tugs up briefly. She reciprocates it. Charlie's disdain for me has dampened in the last few weeks. I don't know what brought her sudden change of heart, but I'm not complaining. Even though we've been more cordial toward one another, there is an underlying tension I don't quite understand. It might have something to do with whatever she *thinks* I'm doing here. Something to do with that conversation I overheard on my first day here. She said there were people after this place. Why, though? It isn't like Bezer is the next hot spot for development…At least it doesn't seem like it.

Or maybe it's something to do with how I catch her staring at me when she thinks I'm not looking. She has gotten a little bolder in her flirtations, but each time I shoot them down. I don't know who I am. How can I even think about offering myself to someone? The thought of jumping into something with her seems insane. I'm not ready for that.

"She seems pretty okay with them now. You think she'll ever ride again?" I ask.

"One can hope," Joseph says. "But I doubt it. Her horse died not long after she ran off to San Diego. They were best friends. I'm not sure she'd have it in her to go out there without him."

"Poor thing was probably heartbroken," Melody says, meeting us at the fence.

Joseph nods. "She won't say it, but it tore Charlie up, too. She wouldn't want to face that again."

"That black one in the barn isn't hers?" I ask.

"Shadow?" Joseph asks, sharing a confused glance with Melody before they look at me. "No. No, Shadow is a rescue that no one else wanted. Stubborn-ass horse. Mean as a snake, too. I leave him alone, let him do what he wants, and he doesn't bother me none. It's better than what he was dealing with before."

"He doesn't seem too bad."

"What do you mean?"

"Well, he lets me pet him whenever I'm in the barn. Never gives me any issues mucking the stall or anything." With each word, their eyes grow to be about the size of dinner plates. I'm starting to think I'm the first person Shadow has ever warmed up to.

"He let you pet him?" Joseph can barely get the words out as Charlie joins us underneath the shade. He scoffs, looking at her. "You'll never believe what Xavier just told me."

"You finally remembered who you are and you're leaving?" Charlie's face glows with fake excitement and I roll my eyes.

"He was able to pet Shadow," Joseph says. Charlie's face falls. "You should put Xavier in the ring with him. See what happens."

"Can you even ride?" Charlie hisses.

Is she really asking me that? I don't know if I can ride a horse. I don't even know if I've ever been around a horse before, but neither one on this ranch has kicked me yet, and they don't seem to mind when I'm around them. That has to be a good sign. Right? I shrug. "Only one way to find out, I guess."

"This is a bad idea, Dad. That could've been a fluke, we don't know—"

"I pet him every day."

Joseph offers his daughter an *I told you so* look and she shakes her head. Pinching the bridge of her nose, she sighs. "I don't like this. We don't even know if he can ride. What if he falls and it makes whatever he has going on worse?"

"Or what if he falls and it makes him remember?" Joseph says with a straight face, but I know he's only saying it to get a rise out of his daughter. And it works, her eyes blazing with fury. "I'm only kidding, Char. Let's give it a shot, and if it still seems like a bad idea, you can end lessons dead stop."

Charlie glares at me. "Fine, but if anything, and I mean *anything*, goes wrong…That's it."

I'm not sure what makes me go along with Joseph's request—horseback riding lessons aren't a requirement of my role at the ranch—but I do it anyway. Maybe it's my curiosity about Shadow, maybe it's my curiosity about Charlie, or maybe it's both. Whatever the reason, I raise my right hand to my forehead in a mock salute, and say, "You're the boss."

Her gaze narrows even further before she closes her eyes, hearing the hoofs of the horse Jenny rides come closer. Taking a breath, she re-centers herself and turns on her heel to finish the lesson.

I wait until she's gone to turn back to Joseph. "So, the real reason I came out here, Joseph, is to let you know I fixed that leak under the sink. Gonna need to replace some of that cabinet beneath it, bit of wood rot under there from the moisture."

"You have enough wood in the barn?" Joseph asks, not taking his eyes off Charlie.

"Should, but I'll be able to tell once I get more into it."

"Don't get in too deep, it's not that much trouble."

That's a weird thing to say. I shrug. "I don't mind. Helps me take my mind off things."

"Any luck in the memory department?" Joseph finally looks over at me, and his question earns Melody's attention, too.

"I get a little here and there, but nothing…big." I glance out over the rolling acres of the ranch. "Nothing that tells me anything."

"Don't worry, dear," Melody says. "You'll get there soon enough, I'm sure. Don't stress yourself too much or you could make it worse."

"You're right, Mrs. Jones…Well, I'm gonna go finish up that sink. Make sure there's enough wood."

A week after Joseph suggests putting me in the arena with Shadow, Charlie asks me if I *really* want to give it a try. The thought of getting on the back of a horse is a bit nerve-racking, but it can't be that hard, right? After dinner, she knocks on my door and tells me to meet her in the barn in the morning. We'll get in a lesson before the August heat rolls in and before the afternoon sun stands overhead. The weather has taken a turn for the worse in the last few days, and by noon the heat will reach close to one-hundred degrees. It's beautiful but hot, and I'll have to check on the fence at the farthest part of the ranch where Joseph says it looks like there's some damage from a summer storm a few nights ago.

The next morning, Charlie walks into the barn as I finish cleaning Lady's stall—the same horse Jenny had been riding during her lesson last week—and she doesn't look happy. I'm not surprised. I'm used to her morning moods but today seems worse than normal. Charlotte Blackwood is the furthest thing from a morning person, requiring *at least* one cup of coffee before anyone talks to her. And from the looks of it, I don't think she's even close to finishing that first cup, or maybe today is a two-cup kind of day.

"Mornin', Char," I call over my shoulder, but she only grunts. Charlie sits on the plywood box across the hall from the stall, her legs pulled up to her chest, sipping from the travel mug on the top of her jean-clad thighs. "What cup is that?"

"One."

"Talk to me when you're done with it."

"Shut up." Charlie rolls her eyes, but her face falls when I step outside the stall. Her eyes travel up the length of my body as I lean against the rake and when she meets my raised brow, she quickly looks away, knowing she's been caught. She clears her throat. "Hurry up. I want to get this over with."

I try to hide my smirk, shaking my head and putting away the muck rake. "Anything I can do to get things moving for this lesson?"

Charlie points toward the tack room I cleaned up about a month ago. When I first walked in, I didn't think it would be that bad—maybe a day or two to get it organized—but it had taken me almost a week to get it in good working order. Finishing the remodel that had been started but never finished was next on my list after mending the fence. That damn fence has become a nuisance. Something is always going wrong with it. It's an old fence—I don't think it's been replaced since it was first installed however many years ago—but Joseph refuses to let me do any replacements unless it's absolutely necessary. It's getting to the point where slapping on a Band-Aid on and calling it good won't work anymore.

"Get your tack ready," she says after a sip of coffee. When I look at her like she has three heads, she rolls her eyes for the millionth time. "Saddle. Bridle. Pads."

I repeat the words as I walk through the tack room, using only the knowledge and limited experience of seeing horses on television to find what look to be the right items.

Her instructions continue with brushing Shadow before putting together the saddle. The whole time, Charlie watches from her place on the box with an unreadable expression, almost a mix of amazement, confusion, and irritation.

Next comes the tack, and from her throne, she gives me the order in which it should go: pads, saddle, buckle the girth ("What is a girth?" "The belt," she says rolling her eyes), fit the bridle ("No, you put the mouthpiece in first."), and adjust where needed.

"What the fuck?" Charlie says under her breath when I lead Shadow out of the barn by the reins. Her gaze is still slightly narrowed in confusion when she follows us into the outdoor arena. "Do you want me to take the reins while you mount?"

"What do you think?" I ask Shadow, earning a huff in response.

When I look at Charlie for interpretation, she only shrugs. "Let's try it. See what happens."

Shadow stamps his front feet, but to my surprise, he allows Charlie to take hold of the leather guides.

She doesn't even try to hide the shock written on her face when I hoist myself on his back, swinging my leg over and landing in the saddle like I've been doing it my entire life. Shadow doesn't seem phased by the added weight on his back, standing ready and waiting for instruction.

"You look surprised," I say.

"I am." Charlie laughs, tucking a piece of hair behind her ear. "This is…incredible. This is the first time he's ever allowed anything like this. I can't believe it." Her hand raises like she's going to pet the bridge of Shadow's nose, but the horse takes a step back, forcing me to grab hold of the horn. "Still not a fan of me, got it. Here, you take the reins."

We spend the next two hours going 'round and 'round the arena, even taking a few jumps (because Shadow didn't feel like listening to Charlie's instruction *not* to go over there), before Joseph parks his truck under the carport and joins us.

"You seem pretty comfortable up there," Joseph says, leaning over the fence. "You sure you've never ridden before?"

"I went with what I've seen in the movies," I say, earning an eye roll from Charlie.

"A little unorthodox, but I like it."

"Don't encourage him, Dad."

"So, is it safe to say I was right?" I hear Joseph ask when Shadow and I approach the two of them.

Charlie sighs, pushing herself off the fence. "Yes, you were right."

"Wait, wait, can you say that again? I need to get it on tape. Xavier, hurry, get somethin' to record it with!"

five

September 2028

"WHAT IF WE TRY something different today?" I follow Charlie out to the barn. She had to work this morning, which pushed our riding time back to the evening before dinner. Not that I minded. I don't need Charlie here anymore, but she likes to be, so I indulge her. Shadow and I have gone out alone a few times now that I know what's needed. Sometimes, I prefer taking him across the property instead of the truck. It's more relaxing, Shadow can stretch his legs and I can breathe without someone looking over my shoulder.

"Like what?"

"You go for a ride."

"What kind of ride are we talking?" Charlie asks with a raised brow and a confident smirk.

Not the kind she's thinking about.

"How about we start with Lady," I say, trying to change the subject back to the matter at hand, but I can feel the flames of embarrassment rising in my cheeks.

"Wait, you want to give me a lesson?"

"Do you *need* a lesson in riding?"

Charlie's eyes light up. I swear the question wasn't meant to sound as dirty as it did, but there's no taking it back now.

Clearing my throat, I say, "I hear you used to be pretty good...At racing, I mean."

Charlie scoffs. "A long, long time ago. I don't—" She takes a deep breath. "That's not me anymore."

"Why'd you stop?"

The conversation takes a more serious turn than it had moments ago. "If you know I used to ride, you know why I stopped."

"I don't see what's stopping you." I shrug. "Everybody falls sometimes. Just a matter of getting back up."

"What are you? An inspirational quote desk calendar?" Charlie laughs. She grasps the muscle of my bicep through the checkered flannel, giving my arm a playful shove.

While my "pep talk" may sound like one of those inspirational quotes you see on a poster inside a classroom or on a breakroom wall, it doesn't make it any less true.

"C'mon, I already cleared it with Lady. She's down if you are."

"You already cleared it with—" Charlie looks between me and the chestnut-colored horse, who pokes her head through the stall opening.

"I'll be right here with you," I say, taking one of her hands and gently placing it on Lady's nose. With small strokes, I feel the tension in Charlie's hand begin to lessen and she willfully pets the horse herself. My hand falls to her side, watching as her walls begin to crumble, and I can't fight back the smile. "C'mon, Char, you got this."

Charlie looks over her shoulder at me, and even though there is still a small amount of hesitation in her eyes, she nods. Looking back at Lady, she says, "No funny business."

Lady huffs in response before throwing her head up and down.

"Tack up," I say. "Let me see how a pro does it."

It doesn't take her long to prep Lady for their ride, less than it took me the first time I got on a horse, but who's counting? When she's finished, Charlie guides Lady out of the barn. We still have a few months left of nice weather before we'll have to move lessons inside, but I don't think a little cold weather will bother Shadow.

Charlie stands beside Lady, her hand resting on the horse's shoulder, but she doesn't move to hoist herself up. Her eyes flutter closed and Lady doesn't move a muscle, almost like she knows that Charlie needs this moment to prepare herself.

Honestly, if she decided to turn and run, I'd let her. She accepted the invitation, and that was honestly more than I expected. If she walked away right now, that would be fine. At least she tried. It's a step in the right direction.

Taking a deep breath, Charlie tips Lady's nose toward her but still doesn't make the jump. I'm about to tell her we can try again tomorrow, but with another breath, she lifts her left foot into the stirrup, makes a quick hop, grabs the cantle, and glides her right leg over Lady's back in one fluid motion. She makes the whole process look as easy as breathing—for someone like her, it must be second nature. Charlie adjusts herself in the saddle, her body tense at first, but with every passing second, she relaxes further.

"How's that feel?" I ask, patting the back of her thigh.

"It feels...good." Charlie smiles.

"I don't want to push you too far. If you want to be done—"

"No." She cuts me off. "No. I'm good." She leans down and pets Lady's neck before giving Lady's sides a gentle squeeze with her calves. At the silent command, the horse begins to move forward. It doesn't take long before they're trotting and then cantering and then they break into a full-on gallop.

"Well, I'll be damned," I hear over my shoulder. Joseph walks up the hill from the house with a proud smile. "How'd you do it?"

"I asked," I say with a simple shrug.

The better question is *why* I did it, but that answer is much more complicated. Charlie and I aren't exactly…friends, but after seeing how she is with the horses, I think she missed this part of her life. And if anyone could understand feeling like a piece of you is missing, it's me. Joseph had been kind enough to open his home to me and give me a chance at a (somewhat) normal life when I didn't know what normal meant. Helping Charlie get back to what she loved feels like a small step on the road to repay him for that generosity.

Joseph offers a quiet "huh," rubbing the scruff on his cheeks. He looks between me and his daughter before shaking his head with a small laugh. "Whatever you're doing, Xavier, keep it up."

Charlie and Lady come to a stop in front of us, the biggest smile yet plastered on Charlie's lips.

"You look good up there, kid," Joseph says, matching her smile. "How's it feel?"

"Good. Really good." She reaches down to pet Lady again.

"Well, I came to tell you dinner is done, but I don't want to rush this." Joseph motions between the three of us, a smirk tugging on his lips.

"Five more minutes?" Charlie asks, and her father doesn't even fight it. He waves us off and turns on his heel to head for the house. When I begin to do the same, Charlie calls out to me. "Can you stay with me?"

"I think you got the hang of it."

"Please?" Her pleading green eyes grasp my heartstrings, and I find it incredibly hard to say no. She doesn't need me here, but she *wants* me here, and for some reason that feels like reason enough to stick around.

$$six$$

October 2028

WHEN I WOKE UP this morning, there was a pit in my stomach and a wave of anxiety in the air that wasn't there when I went to bed last night. Like I'm missing something. Of course, I'm missing something. I've been missing my fucking memory for six fucking months, almost seven now. That thought put me in a sour mood from the moment I opened my eyes. Looking in the mirror, I decided to go into town and talk to Sloan. There had to be *something* else we could do besides sit around and wait, because that method wasn't working.

Bezer is covered in Halloween decorations in preparation for tomorrow. I didn't realize they were so into this time of year, but then again, I haven't come into town in almost two weeks. I've been busy at the ranch prepping for the winter. They're saying it's going to be a doozy this year, but they say that every year, don't they?

The parking lot of the police station is empty, except for the one SUV that I know belongs to Sloan. Bezer has not kept up with modern times and normally that's probably fine—it works for them—but when I'm trying to find my way *out* and back into the real world...their lack of modernity is deeply concerning. I still have yet to find a computer that's up to date around here. The station is similar to the rest of town: stuck in the past. It's a small two-room brick building with a single holding cell and two desks that face each other. And the Bezer Police Department isn't much of a department at all. It consists of two officers—Chief of Police Daniel Sloan and Officer Jack Burnes—and one volunteer who fills in when needed, Emma Pearce. I'm not sure Emma has any authority to arrest people or do anything, but in a town like Bezer, there isn't much need for it anyway.

"Slow day?" I ask, knocking on the open door that reads *Chief Sloan.*

The older man looks up from the newspaper on his desk. "You have no idea."

"Shouldn't you be prepping for Halloween or something?"

Sloan laughs, folding the newspaper before he leans back in his chair. "I don't know where you're from, but around here—"

"Me either." I roll my eyes, sitting in the chair across from him.

That really makes him laugh. "Well, around here, we aren't exactly a rowdy bunch. Unless you end up at the rodeo. Then things tend to get a little riled up."

"Noted."

"What can I do for you, Xavier?" Sloan folds his hands over his stomach.

"Just checking to see if you've heard anything."

Sloan matches my sigh. He lifts his glasses to rest on his head, rubbing his eyes.

"I know. I know you'd tell me if you had, but Sloan...you have to understand where I'm coming from."

"I get it." He replaces the wired rims on his nose. "I do. I want nothin' more than to help you get the hell out of here, but when nothing is coming in, there's nothing I can do. My hands are tied in this situation."

"The sheriff hasn't heard anything? I thought you said he put me up on the missing person boards."

"He did."

"You're sure?"

Sloan looks at me strangely, but I think it's a reasonable request. "Of course. Why wouldn't he?"

"It's been *six* months, Danny."

Out of everyone in this town, I feel the most comfortable with Danny Sloan. He is the first real person who didn't look at me like I was crazy or have that pitiful look in their eye. You know the one. It's the look you give a kicked dog before you reach your hand out, trying to comfort it. Danny and his wife are the only two people in town who have never looked at me like that—including Joseph and Charlie. And over the past four months, I've gotten closer to the Sloans after Danny came out to the ranch one day to invite me to dinner. His wife Doris wanted to make sure I was eating more than stew and chili because everyone knew that was about all Joseph made nowadays. Since then, dinner with the Sloans has become a thing every few weeks.

"I know." Sloan sighs, sitting forward. "And I can't imagine being in your shoes. Truly, Xavier, I wish there was something more I could do."

"Can you doublecheck with the sheriff? Make sure they put it out there. Ask them to repost it, maybe? If it's been a while, maybe a refresh will help."

Sloan scratches the gray stubble on his face before his shoulders fall and he nods. "I'll see what I can do."

"Thank you, Danny."

He offers one single nod but doesn't move an inch. There's something different about him, almost like he can't wait for me to leave as he sits behind his desk with his hands folded neatly and a straight smile. It reminds me of the same one he wears when trying to be serious, but even that smile has more pull to it.

"We still on for dinner next week?" I ask, testing the waters.

"Of course. Doris said she's gonna make something new…I told her not to do one of her experiments on us, but she seems to think we'll love it."

"So, pizza?"

"Probably." Sloan laughs and the tension melts away from his features, easing my anxiety. "We'll have to try it regardless. You know that."

I cringe. "Don't worry, I remember the chicken and sweet potato enchilada bake-thing she made."

Despite how bad it tasted, we powered through, determined not to hurt her feelings after she worked so hard on the dish. Doris wasn't so forgiving, though. She choked down three bites before she dropped her fork and pushed the plate away, saying she couldn't take another. She grabbed her purse and walked out the door, returning not long after with two large pizzas.

"Please don't remind me about that one." He laughs and when the dust settles, he heaves a deep sigh. "Look, Xavier, if I hear anything else, I'll let you know."

"Thanks, Danny."

seven

December 2028

WHEN I WAKE UP on Christmas morning, I don't open my eyes immediately, offering the same small prayer I had last night before falling asleep. I recite my one Christmas wish this year for anyone listening, hoping it will come true if I say it enough times. Squeezing my eyes tightly, I open them and blink rapidly to adjust to the dark room around me, disappointment settling in almost immediately. My wish didn't come true. I'm still in the same room I fell asleep last night. I had hoped and prayed and wished (and prayed some more) that when I opened my eyes, I would be back home in the comfort of my bed with whoever was out there waiting for me, and this would have all been a bad dream. I'm not so lucky...

And it leaves me wondering: If the "magic" of Christmas can't cure this, is there anything that can?

Pulling myself out of bed, I'm not filled with the Christmas spirit and don't feel like joining in whatever traditions the Blackwoods have. So, I get dressed and head straight for the barn, planning to spend the entire day working to keep my mind off things.

My plan works until well past sundown when the clock on the wall reads six o'clock in the evening and Charlie strolls into the barn.

"Dad said to tell you to get your ass inside," she says, still bundled up to ward off the weather outside.

"Thanks, but no thanks. I'm not really in the mood to celebrate Christmas right now, Charlie." I continue cleaning out Lady's stall for the second time today. I've been doing anything to keep myself busy and avoid being roped into their celebration.

"That's exactly why you should." Charlie stands there a moment longer, waiting for me to respond, but this time I ignore her. "I made red velvet cake. I remembered you said you liked it." She huffs when I still ignore her. "C'mon, Zay, you need to eat something. Come inside and get something in your stomach. Then you can come out here and brood some more."

Charlie smiles when my gaze finally snaps to her. When I step out of the stall, I say, "I am not brooding."

"That's exactly what you're doing. And I respect it, I love a good brooding session as much as the next person, but you can't avoid the basic human necessities to keep doing it."

There's a reason Joseph sent her out there instead of coming out himself. If I said no enough times, Joseph would leave me be, but he knows Charlie won't leave until I agree to come inside. She's just that damn stubborn. And if I don't agree here in the next few minutes, she will come over, rip this rake from my hands, and drag me inside whether I want to go or not.

"Fine, Charlie." I sigh, glancing back into the stall. "Let me finish this stall and then I'll be in." But she doesn't move an inch. She crosses her arms over her chest, which puffs out her already puffy coat even further, making her look like the Stay Puft Marshmallow Man.

"What's so funny?" Charlie asks when I laugh.

"You look ridiculous." I grab the bucket filled with bedding and spread it across the floor, half expecting her to ask me *why* she looks ridiculous, but the question never comes. Instead, she stands with her arms still crossed, and I can hear the impatient tapping of her boot against the concrete floor.

It takes less than five minutes to finish the stall and move Lady back into it, offering the horse an apple, before I turn back to Charlie, who cocks her brow. "Are you ready now?"

I nod, grabbing my brown Carhartt from the coat hook and slipping my arms through it.

"You look like the Stay Puft Marshmallow Man," I say when we walk outside, stuffing my hands into my coat pockets. Charlie's brows knit together, confused by what I just said. "You asked what was so funny earlier. That's what I was laughing at. When you crossed your arms, it made you look like that oversized marshmallow man from *Ghostbusters*."

"I do not!"

"Your coat is white, and it's big and puffy. That is exactly who you look like."

Charlie's next step is closer to me, using her shoulder to shove into me, the motion sending me stumbling a few steps to my right. My foot catches on something protruding from the snow and I lose my balance. I tumble into the fresh, powdery snow that had fallen while I was brooding in the barn, laughing the whole time.

"Xavier!" Charlie runs after me. "Are you okay?"

"I'm fine," I say, still laughing.

"You almost gave me a heart attack." She extends her hand out to help me up.

"You? You're the one who pushed me." I sit up and reach for her hand, but instead of standing, I pull her down into the snow with me and she screams, making contact with the cold substance. "Now we're even," I say, looking down at her.

"You jerk!" Charlie throws snow at me, but I turn in time to avoid it hitting my face.

"Don't start something unless you're prepared to finish it, Charlotte." I gather a mound of snow in my hands, compacting it into a ball. Opening my hands, I show her the snowball, my brow lifted in question. But Charlie already has one ready. She tosses it at me, and before I know it, we're in the midst of a snow fight, neither one of us making it quite to the snow*ball* part before throwing it at the other.

"Okay, okay, I surrender!" Charlie laughs, lifting her hands in the air.

When I drop the snow in my hands, she smashes a final ball in my face before scrambling to her feet. I do the same, grabbing her ankle, and somewhere in the mix of it all, the world spins before she lands on top of me. Her hands brace on either side of my head and our breaths mingle between us in heavy pants. I watch her throat swell with a hard swallow, her green eyes dipping to my lips before meeting my stare again. I don't realize what's happening until her lips are on mine. The first kiss is soft and hesitant, and I'm too stunned to react. Sure, there has been...something between us, but I wasn't expecting this.

Her kiss becomes more confident when I don't reject or push her away. She nips at my bottom lip and traces her tongue along the seam of my lips. When I comply, opening my mouth to her, she dominates. Her tongue tangles with mine and this feels like a first. I can't remember a woman being so dominating before, but that's not saying much, since I can't remember anything.

"Charlie!" Joseph's voice rings out through the air, breaking the trance.

Her lips are swollen from the kiss when we part, and I push a few strands of hair that blow in the wind behind her ear. Charlie starts to lean in again, but I turn my face so her lips land on my cheek. A look of hurt crosses her features.

Joseph calls again, and I'm surprised he can't see us. When I lean forward, I realize we're out of view behind the small peninsula of trees that branch out on the right side of the barn.

Charlie sits up and her hips move against mine in a fluid motion. It elicits a strangled moan from me. Without warning, she grinds her hips against mine again, and fuck…the friction is magical, but I can't let this continue. We need to go before Joseph comes looking and finds us like this. My hands land on her hips, stopping her movements. "We need to go before he comes looking for you." She tries to move her hips again, but I hold her steady. "Charlie, you've got to stop."

"C'mon, Zay," she whines, her breath hot against the shell of my ear when she leans back down. "I can return what I got you if you want to unwrap *me* instead."

That might be the corniest thing I've ever heard, or maybe it's because Charlie said it. I bite back the laugh threatening to spill from my lips, and she straightens her back.

"Are you laughing?" she hisses.

"I'm sorry, that was just…That was so corny."

Charlie huffs, bracing her palms on my chest to push herself off the ground. She doesn't offer her hand this time, instead marching down the hill toward the house without a second glance.

Despite being soaked to the bone, I lay there a moment longer, staring up at the expansive sky. A multitude of stars twinkle above me, but one in particular shines brighter than the others. There's a tug on my heart with each wink from high above, a feeling deep within that there is more out there. It makes me wonder if someone is looking up at the same sky, hoping we'll be together again someday. I wonder if I'm their Christmas wish, the same way they were mine.

eight

February 2029

THE PAST TWO AND a half months have gone about as well as you'd expect after the incident on Christmas, and it was like hitting the factory reset button with Charlie. When I walked into the house after our kiss, I went straight upstairs to change out of my wet clothes before joining the Blackwoods in the living room. Charlie wasted no time practically throwing her gift at me. The thin rectangle was wrapped in green stripes with a large red bow. Untying the ribbon, I slid my finger underneath the single piece of tape that held the paper together and unwrapped it to reveal a black box. Inside the box was a black leather wallet.

"Thank you, Char," I said, but she refused to look at me, gaze locked on the tree in the corner. I looked at Joseph, who shrugged. He wasn't going to ask questions. He was used to her mood swings and figured it was best to let it go. And because I didn't feel like explaining to the man who had taken a risk by welcoming me into his home *why* his daughter was upset, I let it go, too.

Charlie has kept her distance since that night, until today.

She skips down the stairs, making a spectacle of her entrance to breakfast and reminding her father loudly that she has a date tonight. From my place at the coffee maker, I shake my head and take a long sip after filling my mug. This is the most she has spoken around me and it's pretty obvious what she is trying to do. Apparently, I'm not the only one to think so.

"That was weird, right?" Joseph asks when Charlie traipses upstairs to continue her prep for her special evening—eight hours early.

"That was weird," I agree, sitting at the table to finish my breakfast.

"You have any plans tonight?" He turns the page of his newspaper without looking up, and I laugh. That was a silly question. Of course, I didn't have plans. "Nice guy like you should have plans."

"It's Valentine's Day. You take a girl out tonight and she's gonna think you're ready for marriage."

"Ain't that the truth," Joseph mumbles, finally looking up from the paper. He folds it in half and leaves it on the table. "Well, should I plan a special dinner for the two of us then?"

I shrug. "Sounds good to me." Finishing the last of my eggs and coffee, I wash my dishes and leave them to dry on the rack. "I'm heading into town. You need anything?"

"Nope, you have a great day, *sweetie*! And make sure to tell Danny I said hey." Joseph waves as I walk out of the kitchen. I wave my cheeks, playing along with his antics, only to turn and practically run into Charlie. Her gaze and lips pull into a thin line, glaring between us.

"Oh, I'm sorry, did we disturb your mental preparation for your *special* night?" I ask, placing a hand over my heart in fake sentiment. The question earns a chuckle from Joseph behind me, but a searing glance from Charlie, who pushes by me to enter the kitchen. She walks straight to the coffee maker, pours a cup, and leaves. I vaguely hear something like "assholes" under her breath when she passes by, but don't call her out.

It's well past eleven o'clock when I walk back inside, sweat dripping down my temples from a workout in the barn. The indoor riding arena has become my personal indoor track, giving me a place to run and work through my thoughts when it's too cold (or dark) to do it outside. Before I find the first step, the phone rings in the kitchen.

What the hell?

The scene is perfect for a scary movie—a quiet, dimly lit farmhouse in the middle of nowhere, everyone in bed except the lone main character who has just returned from the barn, and the phone rings in the dark kitchen. When I answer, will there be a killer on the other end?

"Hello?" I answer, half expecting a strange voice on the other end. Instead, it's the sound of a crowded bar.

"Is this the Blackwood residence?"

"Depends. Who's asking?"

"I'm sorry to call, but we have Charlie here and there's no way she can drive."

Worry floods my veins. "Is she okay?"

"Oh yeah, she's fine, just had a few too many."

That worry turns into irritation. Are you kidding me? I thought she was on a date. Why isn't that asshole bringing her home?

"Where is she?" I ask.

"Layne's."

"I'll be there in twenty," I say, slamming the phone back on the receiver. Layne's is a local dive bar off Main Street. From what I understand, it's the place to be. That's not saying much when it's one of only two bars in town and happens to be the one that attracts the younger crowd.

It takes me twenty-two minutes to pull into the bar's parking lot and I immediately spot Charlie posted up against the wall by the door *without* a coat on. What the fuck is she doing? It's two degrees outside!

I jump out and walk over to where Charlie stands, her eyes glassy as she stares off in the distance. She practically jumps out of her skin when I touch her shoulder. Her skin feels like a solid block of ice under my fingertips, the mesh long-sleeve turtleneck doing nothing to fight off the cold. Her hazy stare meets mine before she scoffs, rolling her eyes. "What the fuck do you want?"

"We're going home, Charlie. Let's go." I try to place my jacket over her exposed shoulders, but she shrugs out of my touch. "Charlie, please don't fight me on this. I don't feel like explaining to your dad that you froze to death outside a bar."

"And why should I? You don't care!" She takes a large step away from me, tripping over her feet when she stumbles off the sidewalk but catching herself on one of the cars nearby. "See, I don't need *your* help."

"Charlie, for the love of God, please don't do this right now. Let me take you home."

"No! I don't want you anywhere near me. You asshole. You...You...You..." I wait for her to finish the thought, but she can't find the words. Instead, she groans and stomps toward my waiting truck, stumbling every few steps. Before I can turn to follow, the door to the bar opens and a guy dressed in all black peeks his head out.

He curses under his breath when he doesn't see Charlie on the wall anymore. His eyes scan the lot before landing on me. "Hey! Have you seen a girl with reddish-brown hair? About yay-high. Wearing this black see-through-looking thing. Bit of a 'tude." When he finishes describing the drunk woman I've been trying to wrangle, I point behind me to where she's struggling to pull herself up into the passenger seat. "Oh, thank God. You're the one I talked to on the phone?" He breathes a sigh of relief. "Thanks for coming to get her. Poor thing got stood up."

Shit. That explains a lot.

"Thanks for calling," I say, turning on my heel and jogging to the truck where she still struggles to get in. Planting my hands on her hips, I lift her easily into the seat. When I buckle her seatbelt, I try not to think about how close our faces are and how the sweet smell of her perfume fills my senses with each inhale. Clearing my throat, I lock the door and close it before I walk around to the driver's seat.

We drive for ten minutes in silence before I hear a quiet sniffle from her side of the cab. When I glance over Charlie, she tries to hide that she's wiping her eyes, but the smeared makeup gives it away. "Wanna talk about it?"

I can feel her gaze shift in my direction, but she doesn't say anything. I turn to look at her, meeting her eyes for a brief second, before returning my gaze to the road. "I'm sorry, Charlie."

"No, you're not." Her eyes move to look straight ahead.

"I am. I know you were excited about tonight. I'm sorry that it ended like this." My hand grips the steering wheel, pissed off at the fucker who did this. Sure, we haven't been getting along—had we ever truly gotten along?—but that doesn't mean she deserves to be stood up. "You deserve better than this, Charlie."

She scoffs. "That's rich coming from you."

"Charlie, look...What happened on Christmas—"

"Don't," she whispers, looking down at her hands folded on her lap. When I try to continue, she repeats herself, louder this time. "I don't want to hear that you're sorry, Zay! I don't...I don't care. You've made it clear how you feel about me, and I've accepted that."

"Charlie, I don't know *how* I feel about you! I don't even know who I am! How am I supposed to offer myself to you when I don't even know my fucking name?" I look between her and the road so many times, I almost make myself dizzy. "I don't know if someone is out there looking for me or if I'm alone in this world. I don't know anything. And it's not fair to you or me to even think about getting involved with you."

My knuckles tighten around the steering wheel. I wish she'd get it through her thick head that the problem isn't her. It's me. It's all me.

Silence envelopes us for the rest of the car ride through town and up the mountain to Blackwood Ranch. When the gate is illuminated in the headlights, Charlie lets her head fall back against the headrest and sighs.

A few minutes later, I park under the carport on the side of the farmhouse but don't get out of the cab. Charlie doesn't, either, instead turning her head to look at me, and there's a deep sadness in her eyes. "I'm sorry, Xavier. For being such a bitch to you."

"You're not a bitch. You're just...stubborn." That's one way to put it.

Charlie laughs, biting down on her lip. "Thanks for coming to get me."

I reach over and squeeze her thigh. "Anytime, Char."

She places her hand on top of mine, and the air becomes heavier than it was a moment ago. Charlie swallows before she moves my fingers up her thigh to the hemline of the black pleather skirt.

"Charlie," I warn.

"Please," she begs.

I shake my head, pulling my hand from under hers. "Not

like this, Charlie."

"I want this, Xavier! I want you."

"Not like this. I'm not...I'm not ready for something like this and neither are you." Maybe I'll be able to give her what she wants one day but today is not that day. "Now, let's go get you to bed."

Charlie sighs but doesn't fight me anymore. I make my way to join her on the other side, where she tries to step down from the cab but struggles in her heels. I wrap my arm around her waist, hoisting her from the seat and setting her feet firmly on the ground.

"You okay?" I ask, and she gives me a small smile in return. It doesn't quite reach her eyes, but it's enough for now. "You'll be okay, Charlie. I promise." I nod, attempting to continue to convince her of the sentiment.

"Thank you, Zay." She looks down at her feet. "Can we not tell my dad about this?"

"Might be a little hard to keep it a secret when you're home but your truck isn't."

"Oh, right," she says, tucking her hair behind her ear.

"C'mon, let's get you to bed," I say, wrapping my arm around her waist and guiding her toward the house.

The whole way inside, Charlie maintains a comfortable distance between us.

"Can you manage getting into bed without falling and hurting yourself?" I ask.

"I think so." She smiles up at me before pressing a chaste kiss to my cheek. "Thanks, Zay." Without looking back, she enters her room and closes the door.

Less than a minute later, I'm back in my bedroom. I throw myself onto the bed, not caring that I still desperately need a shower. When my head hits the pillow, I can barely keep my eyes open, and the thoughts of Charlie are quickly replaced by the woman I've dreamed of almost every night since arriving in Bezer.

Her face is still trapped in the fog plaguing my mind, but I know there's something important about her. I think she's the key to figuring out who I am. This woman is one of the reasons I can't give Charlie what she wants…I can't offer myself to Charlie when I feel like I've already done so with this other woman.

There's an ache in my chest when I think about her. A longing for something missing, and I know it's her. But how do I explain that to Charlie? I can't. She'd never understand. Hell, I don't understand. And now I'm starting to wonder if I ever will.

nine

Now

A CRASH FROM DOWNSTAIRS brings an abrupt end to scribbling down the dream I just woke up from. It's the same one I've had countless times since arriving in Bezer, but this time when I found the same woman outside the apartment building, she ran to me and kissed me. I'm careful to avoid the creaking spots of the old stairs in the farmhouse as I walk downstairs to investigate, but my defenses fail when I see *who* is behind the disturbance.

Charlie rummages through the cabinets in the kitchen, muttering to herself about needing a snack, and something about Cooper.

"Looking for something?" I ask, and the sound of my voice sends her tumbling to the ground in those godforsaken heels. The same pair she wore the last time I had to pick her up from the bar on Valentine's Day.

The next thirty minutes are a mixture of trying to get her upstairs to her room without waking up her dad and keeping as much distance between us as possible. She tends to get a little handsy when she's drunk, especially the last few times.

This will make three times I've come downstairs to find her stumbling around, and I can only hope we're not going to make a habit out of it.

"Middle and bottom drawer," Charlie calls from the bed when I attempt to find her pajamas. She stares at the ceiling the whole time, even when I drop a pair of sweats and an oversized T-shirt on the bed.

"Goodnight Charlie," I say and leave without waiting for a response.

"Get any warmer out there?" Joseph asks from the stove when I walk into the kitchen the afternoon after Charlie's late-night kitchen escapade. He stirs something in a pot, probably his "famous" stew, the perfect meal to fight the nip that lingers in the cold air outside. Tomorrow is the first of April. It should be warming up soon, but the forecast has been calling for cold weather through the next week.

"Still pretty chilly," I say, lifting my ball cap and running my fingers over my scalp. My hair is longer than it has been for most of the last year. I've been thinking about letting it grow again. Who knows, maybe a change in appearance will help trigger something.

"Sure hope it breaks for the festival next weekend." As my time here ticks by, Joseph has been telling me more and more about life in Bezer, including the Blossom Festival, one of Bezer's proudest traditions. A yearly event on the first Saturday of April, the Blossom Festival celebrates the new year and the blossoming of new life that comes with the end of winter. The day is filled with live bands, a rodeo, a carnival, and local vendors. This year is the first time Charlie will be in the rodeo in over a decade. "I'd hate for you to miss it."

I can only nod in response because I don't know what to say. While I appreciate everything Joseph has done for me the past year, every day I wake up hoping it will be my last one here— hoping I'll finally remember something, or that someone will rescue me. The festival is supposed to be a celebration, but I'm not in the mood to celebrate much of anything that coincides with the one-year mark of my arrival in town. Thinking about still being here at the end of the week, let alone tomorrow or the day after, is enough to throw me into the thick of the depression I've been fighting my way out of for months. Every day is a challenge, some worse than others, but I remind myself there are worse places to be. At least I'm alive with a roof over my head, food on the table, and a warm bed to sleep in...

"Might be a good distraction for you," Joseph adds when I still don't say anything.

I hum in response, filling my coffee tumbler from the fresh pot that has finished brewing. When I turn, ready to face the cold again, I'm face-to-face with Charlie in the doorway. She's dressed in a different set of pajamas than the ones I pulled out for her at three-thirty this morning.

"Well, good mornin', sunshine! 'Bout time you got up," Joseph calls over his shoulder, a slight chuckle in his tone.

"Can you not be so loud?" Charlie grimaces.

"What's wrong, darlin'?"

"I have a massive headache, and I feel nauseous."

"You sick?"

I don't move from my place against the counter, I'm too interested to see where this will go. Charlie is her father's pride and joy, and I've realized that he tends to turn a blind eye to his daughter's antics—especially when it comes to partying. I raise a brow when she looks at me. What is she going to say? Time is ticking, and she better come up with something soon.

"No, I, uh...I just stayed up too late," she stutters.

Finally, Joseph slams the wooden spoon down and turns to look at her. "Charlotte Grace Blackwood, were you hangin' around that Hayes boy again?"

Let me correct what I said earlier...He turns a blind eye to her antics, except when it comes to her hanging out with her ex-boyfriend. According to conversations I've overheard between Joseph and his friend, Bill Wyatt, Cooper Hayes is bad news, alongside his friend, Dakota. They're the town's local bad boys. Whenever there's trouble, you'd usually find them at the center of it. But for some reason, nothing ever stuck, and they always walked free.

Charlie has been adamant she isn't interested in her high school sweetheart anymore, but it seems like they've been running into each other more than normal since he and Dakota made their big return to town two weeks ago. I haven't seen them, but town has been buzzing with the news ever since.

"Cooper?" Charlie scoffs. "Yeah, right."

Joseph's face says he doesn't believe her.

"I wasn't! I mean, yeah, he was there, but—"

I scoff, cutting her off.

"Something you wanna say, *Xavier?*" she hisses.

"Nope," I say, taking a sip of coffee. "Nothing at all."

"Your face says otherwise."

"That's enough, Charlie." Her father sighs. "Go get cleaned up and take a Tylenol. I need you to do the stalls."

Charlie glares at me. "You're not done? It's like...two o'clock!"

"And I needed him to do some other stuff this morning. So, you're on stall duty."

"I can manage the stalls, Joe," I say. "I was gonna work on the tractor some more, but I can do that later. I'm sure Charlie would much rather stay inside and nurse her...headache." I take another sip of coffee, catching her glare over the rim of my mug.

Joseph looks between us, before shaking his head. "Obviously, I'm missing somethin' here, and you know what? I don't want to know. You two can figure it out yourselves."

"Don't worry about it, *Princess*," I say to Charlie, walking out of the kitchen. "I can handle it today, but you owe me." I wink at her from the door and leave, but within seconds I hear her frustrated groan before she stomps up the stairs and slams her bedroom door.

I hum along to the rock song playing on the boombox on the ledge above the tack room entrance. The stalls aren't too bad, all things considered. I've been taking my time, enjoying the solitude working in the barn offers. The barn has become somewhat of my safe space at the ranch. A place I can disappear for a while without any interruptions, working on different projects. Since my arrival, I've found that working with my hands is one of my favorite ways to work through whatever thoughts are swirling in my mind.

As I finish spreading a fresh layer of bedding on the stall floor, I turn to the stall next door, where Shadow waits impatiently. I tried putting him in the pasture for fresh air, but he refused. I swear if he were a human, he'd be standing there with a raised brow, critiquing everything I'm doing, complaining about it taking so long...but I love that damn horse. "C'mon, Shadow, you're all clean, bud."

The black horse huffs in response.

"I know, I know. I won't take so long next time," I say, rubbing the bridge of his nose before taking hold of the halter and guiding him into his stall.

I learned that Shadow came to the ranch not long before I

did. We were like kindred spirits, both lost and trying to find our place in the world. Loners with no other place to go, and Bezer had offered us refuge. It seemed fitting that we ended up here considering that's what the town calls itself—the City of Refuge. Sloan had asked Joseph to take the horse in after he'd been found at an abandoned farm with evidence of abuse and mistreatment for who knows how long.

"I still can't believe you're the one who could break that damn horse."

Over my shoulder, Charlie stands at the entrance of the barn. Locking the stall door, I grab one of the apples I had swiped for Shadow and pass it to him, ignoring her.

Charlie sighs. "I'm sorry for earlier." She walks farther inside, digging her hands into her coat pockets. "I shouldn't have been such a bitch when you could've easily outed me to my dad."

"I didn't have to do anything; you did that yourself." I rub the bridge of Shadow's nose before turning to look at her. "I thought you were over Cooper."

"We were just talking." Charlie shrugs.

I lean my elbow against the stall door, lips pulling into a line. "And drinking."

"How is that any of your business, huh?"

"When you come home in the middle of the night drunk off your ass, waking everyone in the house up—me included—it becomes my business."

Okay, maybe she didn't wake me up, per se, but if I hadn't been awake because of the storm...she would have done so.

"Besides, what kind of jackass feeds someone drinks and doesn't make sure they get home okay? You shouldn't have been driving in that state."

"You're ridiculous, you know that?"

"How's that?" I ask, handing Shadow another apple.

Charlie takes a few steps closer but maintains a good

distance between us. "You say you don't want anything to do with me, but you get jealous when I hang out with my ex."

"Your ex who is notorious for causing trouble around town." I shake my head, turning away from her to put the muck tools away. This conversation is going nowhere and is going to end in an argument. One that I don't care to have. "Be careful, Charlie. I'd hate to see you end up on the wrong side of things."

"That what happened to you?"

Her words stop me.

"How else would you end up in this situation, right?" The only sound is the shrug of her shoulders in her windbreaker. Biting down on her lip, she rolls her eyes and steps back. "Whatever. You want to continue to pine after something that hasn't come looking for you in almost a year instead of seeing what's right in front of you, be my guest."

ten

"GETTIN' ANYWHERE WITH THIS old thing?" Joseph's muffled words catch my attention before I hear his hand knock on the edge of the truck's body.

Before the dead of winter set in, I asked Joseph if I could work on the old Ford. He told me it had been sitting outside the barn for at least ten years, so he wasn't sure much could be done with it, but I was welcome to try. Since then, it has been my pet project to pass the time. Something that I could call my own, instead of picking up other things to do around the ranch. It has been a few months since I got my hands dirty under the hood. The heavy snow that fell this past winter made it nearly impossible to work on it because I couldn't get it inside the barn. But now with the temperatures rising and snow melting…I could finally get back to it. And it feels great.

"We're getting somewhere, but not quite there yet," I say, crawling from under the truck. "Need something?"

"Actually, yes." Joseph wrings his hands before he folds them, leaning over the bed. He waits until I'm fully on my feet to continue. "I know you and Charlie have had your…

differences the past year."

That's one way to put it. After our little spat in the barn yesterday, she's been doing her best to ignore me.

"But tomorrow is her birthday and…Well, she's supposed to go out tonight with her friends, and it seems like any time she goes out lately, Cooper shows up. But if you were there—"

"Joe." I sigh and pull one of the work towels through the open cab window to wipe my hands. "You know I'd do anything for you, but—"

"I know that you two aren't exactly friends, but I think if you gave one another a chance, you'd actually see you could be! You're not as different as you might think."

I rub the crease between my brows. I'm starting to get the feeling no matter what I say, I'm not getting out of this. Not if I want a (somewhat) peaceful night. If he tries to tell Charlie she can't go out with her friends because of his fear that Cooper will show up…it'll be World War III in the Blackwood household. And if she goes out without a chaperone, she will most likely wake me up at three in the morning again.

"Just think about it, hmm? She's supposed to leave in a bit to meet them."

"Fine. But I'm not going to be happy about it."

I know I'm going to regret this. This is a bad idea, but how can I say no to Joseph? This man took me in when I had nowhere else to go, no questions asked—okay, maybe a few questions asked, but not really—and he hasn't asked much of me outside my normal workload. I owe him this much…

"You have no idea how much I appreciate this, Xavier!"

I grunt in response, turning my back to him to put my tools away. At least I have one thing going for me…I'm not the person who has to tell Charlie that I'll be her babysitter tonight. Joseph can do that.

"I cannot believe my dad is making you come tonight." Charlie huffs with her arms crossed tightly over her chest. That's at least the third time she has said it since we left the ranch. I'm sure she'll say it at least one more time before we get to Layne's Dive Bar. "I'm a grown woman. I don't need someone to *babysit* me."

My eyes remain on the road ahead, ignoring her. I haven't responded the other times she has said it, and this time isn't any different. Because that's what she wants…She's baiting me, hoping I'll say something to add fuel to her fire, and I will not fall for it.

"I'm not a child."

I roll my eyes and mumble, "Sure are acting like one."

"What was that?"

Great. Good job, Xavier. You weren't supposed to say anything. Now look what you've done.

"Nothing." I toss a sweet smile over my shoulder, pulling into the parking lot.

Charlie barely lets me pull the truck to a complete stop before she jumps out, making a beeline for the front door.

"You owe me, Joe," I whisper, rubbing my face, and climb out of the truck. This is going to be a long night, the kind of night that is bound to have consequences. What those consequences would look like…I'm not sure, but I know they can't be good.

The heavy metal door sticks when I try to open it, requiring a good tug to free it. No one had gone in behind Charlie, and while the door might be a little sticky sometimes, I can almost guarantee this extra-strength hold is intentional. When I finally get inside, I spot her auburn waves leaning halfway over the bar, pointing to something on the wall before batting her eyelashes at the bartender.

Oh, for the love of God.

Is this what I have to deal with all night?

The bartender offers a wink before he starts mixing her drink, keeping his attention solely on her. Charlie swings her hips from side to side against the edge of the bar before throwing her head back in laughter. She's really laying it on thick.

Before I even step up to the bar, I catch the eye of the bartender. He turns on a dime, focusing on whatever drink she just ordered.

Charlie glances over her shoulder to see who so rudely interrupted their conversation and rolls her eyes, climbing off the bar. "What's it going to take to make you go away?"

"Sorry, Char. You're stuck with me."

"Can you at least try not to be a buzzkill?" She groans, swiping the drink off the bar. The bartender set it down and walked away without a second glance. I barely registered him to begin with. "I know my dad sent you to—"

"Your dad only sent me to make sure you don't do anything stupid." I shrug, stepping up to the bar. "You wanna get wasted? Be my guest. Just don't do anything *stupid.*"

Charlie steps into me, looking up from underneath her long lashes. She gingerly places the straw against her tongue and sucks. "What constitutes stupid?"

My lips pull into a firm line, staring down at her.

"I'm kidding!" She doubles over in laughter. "C'mon, since I can't get rid of you, I guess I should introduce you to my friends." Charlie drags me toward the farthest corner of the bar, where a few people have already taken up residence near the billiards tables.

"And who is this?" A blonde girl purrs, and it's hard to miss the glare Charlie sends her way. "Is this the—"

"My dad made me bring him," Charlie cuts her off. "He promised not to get in the way tonight. Right, Zay?"

"It'll be like I'm not even here," I say.

"That's a bit hard to imagine when you're right there," a

different blonde says.

I'm going to call them Blonde #1 and Blonde #2. That seems easier than trying to remember their names. I'll never see these people again, so why do I care?

"Is that such a bad thing?" I ask Blonde #2, earning a glare from Charlie. It's a threat, telling me to be nice to her friends. "Whatever, I'm going to get a beer."

I thought birthdays were supposed to be fun. This is anything but fun...Tonight has been dragging. Every time I glance at the clock behind the bar, it's only been another five minutes. How long am I supposed to sit here? I might combust if I have to sit here for another two or three hours. I can think of a million other things I'd rather do, but I remind myself that I'm doing this for Joseph. And, I guess, for Charlie, too. It is her thirtieth birthday, after all.

So far, there have been no signs of Cooper.

Thank God. If it stays that way, I can report to Joseph that nothing happened, and he won't ask me to tag along with Charlie and her friends next time.

"This is so exhilarating, ain't it?" the guy I nicknamed "Cowboy" says, sidling up next to me at the high-top table. I think Charlie said his real name is Jackson, and he's dating Blonde #4. "You're Xavier, right? The guy who doesn't know who he is."

I nod.

"I'm Jackson." He sticks his hand out toward me. So, I was right...His name is Jackson. At least I know my short-term memory still works. "I belong to Katy, the one sitting across from Charlie over there."

Jackson points to the high top a few tables down where Charlie sits with five other girls, all blonde except one. Why does she have so many blonde friends?

"Nice to meet you," I say, shaking his hand.

"I didn't know you and Charlie were a thing."

My brow cocks. "We're not."

Why would he say that?

"Oh." Jackson hesitates, looking between me and the girls' table. "I guess I thought you were because you're here tonight. I mean…You've been living up at the ranch and Charlie has told Katy all about—"

"Jackson!" A shrill scream comes from the other side of the room. We both turn to see Katy flagging down her boyfriend with wide eyes. She and Charlie practically sprint to our table. "Honey, it's our turn to play darts. Come on!"

"But I was—"

"Now!" Katy heaves Jackson off the barstool and back across the room to the darts area.

"Should we play some pool?" Charlie asks, cutting me off when I try to ask her what in the hell just happened. She gnaws on the corner of her mouth, glancing toward the darts game where Katy has already begun to scold Jackson for almost spilling the beans. "One of the tables finally opened up."

A smirk tugs on my lips. She knows that she's been caught. Jackson was one second from spilling the beans earlier, and with how squeamish the thought seemed to make her, I wanted to push the subject further. "Lead the way."

Charlie swims her way through the crowd that has started to gather inside Layne's, and I stay one step behind. She sets up the rack when we reach the billiards table.

"How 'bout we make things interesting," I say, downing the rest of my beer.

"How so?" she asks without looking up from her task.

"For every ball I pocket, *you* have to tell me a secret."

"I don't have any secrets."

"No?" My brow raises. "Then it won't matter if I win."

"And what do I get if I pocket a ball?" Charlie asks, looking up at me, bent over the side of the table. If I were any other man, I'd probably enjoy the view. Hell, who am I kidding? Seeing her bent over the edge with her perky ass in the air is a sight, but I can't let it distract me from the task at hand.

"I'll remove a piece of clothing."

That stops her dead in her tracks, fumbling with the rack in her hands.

"We...I...Xavier, we're in a public bar!"

"And?"

Charlie glances around the room, leaning in to speak a little softer. "I'm really good at pool. You'll be naked in front of the whole town!"

She's right. I'm not wearing much, but I'm not worried. At least, I don't think I am. I hope I know what I'm doing.

"Sure about that?" I ask with a lot more confidence than I feel on the inside.

"You seem very confident for someone who can't even remember his own name."

Damn, that stings a bit. That is her favorite thing to use against me. Whenever I get a little too comfortable, she has to remind me that I'm still the town freak who can't remember a damn thing about himself.

Grabbing two pool sticks, I hand one over to her. "Are you in or not?"

Charlie's gaze narrows, but I see the fire ignite in them. She's intrigued and wants to know what game I'm playing. When she reaches out to take the stick, she lets her fingers ghost over mine before wrapping her hand around the shaft and sauntering to the other side of the table. "Your break or mine?"

"You go ahead. I'll give you a head start."

Charlie rolls her eyes but lines herself up at the opposite end of the table, bending over the edge again, and I push down any thoughts that might distract me from the game. Her tongue pokes out the side of her mouth as she sends the stick straight into the center of the white ball, breaking the rack and sending one ball into a pocket. It's a stripe.

She looks up from the table with a raised brow. She doesn't think I'm serious about the stipulations. I prove her wrong by shrugging the leather jacket off my shoulders and hanging it on the back of a nearby chair.

Charlie lands another ball in a corner pocket, and I remove my long-sleeve Henley, leaving me in a white T-shirt. I watch her throat swell as she swallows before dropping her gaze to the green felt.

She lines up to make another shot, but it's a scratch, landing the cue ball in a side pocket. She tries not to react, but the corners of her mouth fall for half a second before she fixes her face. She's disappointed.

With a smirk, I pull the cue ball from the pocket, setting it at the end of the table. Finding the easiest ball to pocket, I line up the shot and sink it. "You wanna tell me that secret now or later?"

By now, a small crowd has gathered to watch the show, including Katy and Jackson.

"My first kiss was in the back of this bar," Charlie grumbles.

"Classy." I smirk, lining up another shot and sinking it again.

The process repeats until there are only two balls left. Each secret she has shared so far reveals a little more about her, but none tell me what I really want to know.

"With this next one, I get to ask you a question and you have to tell me the truth. Deal?"

"Better hope you make it, then."

I smirk, sinking the ball into the corner pocket without

looking. That earns the biggest eye roll of the evening. "Why were you so scared for Jackson to talk to me earlier?"

"I wasn't."

"You and Katy about lost your minds seeing us talking." My weight shifts onto the pool stick as I lean down toward her. "Scared he might say something he's not supposed to?"

Charlie doesn't back down. Instead, she stands up taller.

"Ticktock, Char."

"That's *none* of your business," she hisses.

Out of the corner of my eye, I notice Katy silently reprimanding her boyfriend with a stern look. He wasn't supposed to be talking with me earlier. He knows something, and whatever it is (it's not too hard to figure out), they worry he'll let it slip. But that's a secret Charlie won't let go easily; it will take more than a wager on a billiards game to make that happen.

I shrug, taking a step back from her. "Rules of the game, Charlie."

Charlie's mouth opens and closes twice as she tries to think of the answer to give me. And before she offers it up, there's a loud commotion behind us.

"Where's the birthday girl?" a voice booms and the crowd parts like the Red Sea, where a monster of a man stands. He's at least six foot one, maybe taller with a mesomorph physique. Broad shoulders give way to thick biceps that strain underneath the black T-shirt. Blonde hair has been cropped close to his scalp. His overall image exudes dominance and power, but the kind of power that gets you into trouble. I glance at Charlie, but she's too busy staring at the newcomer, and she looks pissed.

"There you are!" He wraps Charlie in a tight hug, sweeping her off her feet and swinging her to-and-fro, even when she tries to push him away. "I've been looking all over for ya, baby."

"Get off, Coop!" Charlie scolds.

Shit. I sigh. I thought we were going to get lucky and go a whole night without him showing up.

"Aw, come on, babe. Don't be like that," Cooper pleads, but she pushes him away still. He doesn't take the hint, wrapping his arm around her shoulders and pulling her deeper into his embrace.

When they turn toward me, it feels like the world slows down...I'm almost certain my heart stopped for a moment. I don't know how it's possible, but I'm pretty damn sure it did.

I know him, and not because I know his name or have heard the stories about him. There's something about him that feels...familiar.

"What are you doing here?" Cooper hisses when we finally make eye contact. His reaction is all the confirmation I need. There is history here, but how is that possible? I've never seen this man before now.

Charlie finally breaks free from his hold, taking two big steps away from him and closer to me. "Zay, this Cooper...my *ex*-boyfriend."

"Oh, don't be like that, Char." His attention returns to her, almost like he's already forgotten I'm even here. "I've missed you!"

"That's how you ended up in bed with Missy?"

"You were gone!" Cooper defends himself, earning an eye roll from the green-eyed beauty. "How many times do I have to apologize for—"

"Save it for one of your fuck buddies, Coop. I don't care! We are never getting back together."

Cooper tries to say more, but this time I step in. "I think it's time you leave."

"You movin' in on my girl, city boy?"

"Nobody is moving in on me, Cooper Hayes." Charlie huffs, planting her hands on his chest to push him out of the billiards area. "And the only person *moving* better be you. Moving on out of here."

Cooper doesn't budge. His feet remain planted in the same spot, her shoves barely even registering to him.

Charlie groans in frustration. "Cooper, get out now!"

He finally relents when she practically punches his chest. Turning away from me to look at Charlie, he says, "Why don't you come with me, babe? We can talk. That's all I want."

"I'd rather bury myself six feet under."

That was dramatic.

"I can make that happen." Cooper smirks and Charlie deadpans. "I'm only kiddin', baby!" He kisses her forehead and allows her to push him through the crowd. I watch them swim through the sea of people until they disappear out the front door.

I know I should follow, but the weight that has settled in my stomach after seeing him tells me otherwise. Despite what Cooper said, I'm sure he *can* and has buried someone "six feet under."

After about five minutes, the door swings open again, and Charlie walks back inside...alone. She looks even more annoyed than she did when she walked out.

"Everything okay, birthday girl?" Katy asks when Charlie rejoins us.

"Can we go?" Charlie asks me, ignoring her friend.

"You sure?" I ask. "We can stick around for another—"

"No, I want to go home." Charlie doesn't wait for any more conversation, ripping her jacket and purse off the back of the chair and walking straight out the front door.

"Well, looks like we're leaving. Have a good night, everyone," I say, offering an apologetic smile for the way she ditched her friends.

Leaving the bar, I find her propped up against the side of the truck. Her hands stuffed deep in her coat pockets, Charlie stares down at her shoe that toes through the gravel beneath her feet.

"Let's go, troublemaker," I say, opening the passenger door for her. Unexpectedly, she doesn't say anything in return, only climbs into the seat without a word.

That's odd.

"I can't believe you dated that guy," I add after I've settled into my seat.

Charlie scoffs. "Coop wasn't always that way. He used to be pretty sweet when you got to know him."

"Sure."

"It was high school," she says with a shrug. "Live and learn, I guess."

"Hmmm."

"Don't *hmmm* me." She points one of her fingers at me from across the front seat.

"I didn't say anything!" I laugh and lift my hands in surrender.

"You didn't have to. It was written all over your face." Charlie sighs, one of those full-body sighs you feel deep within as it rolls through you. She keeps her gaze locked on her hands as her fingers twist around each other. "Please don't tell my dad about this. I don't want him thinking I'm running around with Cooper again. He already does, or you wouldn't be here. But I don't need him knowing that Coop showed up tonight. He'll never let me leave the house."

"Hate to break it to you, Charlie," I say, peering over my shoulder out the back window to pull out of the parking spot. "You're a thirty-year-old woman. You can do what you want."

"MORNING, MR. SULLIVAN," I say with a wave as I walk into Sullivan's Hardware two days after Charlie's birthday fiasco. I don't have to look at the old man to know he only offers a simple nod in return, which is more than he used to give me.

Sullivan's Hardware is the main source of materials for a variety of things in Bezer, from construction materials to general household needs to DIY project supplies to farm necessities. You could walk in and find just about anything you were looking for. The first time I came in, Mr. Sullivan stood behind the counter, inputting the price of each item into the register (by hand), and was about to give me the total when Charlie appeared from the back. I was surprised to see her. What was she doing there?

"Mr. Sullivan, he's with us," Charlie said, setting the load in her arms on the counter. That's when I noticed the apron tied around her waist and realized she worked at the hardware store. "This is Xavier. He's helping Dad up at the ranch."

Mr. Sullivan's gaze narrowed on me before he rolled his eyes and walked away from the counter. He grumbled to himself the whole way back to his chair a few feet away.

"You're good, Xavier. Anything you get here goes on the tab," Charlie said, pushing the bag of smaller items forward. "Don't mind him, he's just an ol' grump. It's part of his charm. Ain't that right, Mr. Sullivan?" Her question earned a grumble and huff from behind the newspaper in his hands.

But she was right. I have come to appreciate his grumpy charm.

Howard Sullivan is a quiet, reserved man who always has his nose in the newspaper—but not one of the mainstream ones. No, he refused to carry those papers filled with "unreliable bullshit," as he put it when I asked him for a copy once. I hoped if I could get my hands on one, I could find something that would point me in the right direction, but Mr. Sullivan shot that idea down before it ever got off the ground. A few more stops around town proved everyone in Bezer felt the same way Mr. Sullivan did about the news. Not to mention, asking someone around here about a computer that isn't from the '00s might be a sin.

I stroll through the aisles, picking up a new pair of pliers and an oil filter for the truck before going out back to grab some barbed wire for the fence that needs to be repaired...again. This is the third time I've had to fix the same section of fence. Either I have no idea what I'm doing (a strong possibility) or someone doesn't want it there. I think some sections need to be completely replaced and the fence will be fine, but Joseph refuses to let me do so. Says it's not worth the hassle.

I'm surprised I haven't seen Charlie yet. She usually makes her way out of the back by now when I come into the store. Then again, maybe she's not working, but she wasn't at home this morning when I left. Joseph didn't seem too worried about it, so she must not be anywhere Cooper could get to her.

When he asked about our night out, I left the part about Cooper out of it. I wasn't lying. Joseph didn't ask, so I didn't tell. I simply left it at:

Things were fine. (Things were fine until Cooper showed up.)

Charlie had fun. (Charlie did have fun until Cooper showed up.)

Her friends were nice. (And her friends were nice, even Jackson who almost spilled whatever secrets Charlie has been keeping.)

Mr. Sullivan glances over the counter, taking a quick inventory of the items I've collected, before grumbling to himself and sitting back in his chair.

"See you later, Mr. Sullivan," I call over my shoulder and walk out the door, but this time he shoves his nose further into the paper. "See you 'round, Xavier," I say, mimicking his nonexistent answer to my goodbye.

Loading up the truck takes less than two minutes and returning the cart to Sullivan's takes one more minute, but I should've been paying more attention to my surroundings in those three minutes. One man walks around the back of the truck, and another walks toward me on the sidewalk. This one I recognize instantly: Cooper Hayes. He stops, toeing the sidewalk edge and blocking me in the space between my truck and the one next to me.

"You're supposed to be dead," the other man says, gnawing on a toothpick between his teeth. I can only assume this is his partner in crime, Dakota Johnson. Black ink creeps up his right arm disappearing underneath the sleeve of his gray T-shirt—intricate markings of some sort. His eyes, black and ominous, are hidden in the shade of the baseball cap on top of long black hair pulled into a bun at the base of his neck, matching the color of his full beard. He's at least the same height as Cooper, maybe an inch or two shorter.

"Am I?" I look between them. I have nothing to defend myself with other than the keys in my hand. Everything else, including the gun Joseph gave me for *emergencies,* is inside the truck. Some good it'll do me there. "Guess it didn't stick."

Cooper steps closer, sticking his finger into my chest and staring down at me. "We don't like smartasses." He towers over me by at least four inches, probably more. Despite the adrenaline beginning to pump through my veins and the little voice in my head screaming *danger,* I don't back down.

"What a relief." I scoff. "Neither do I."

"We don't like games either!" Cooper practically yells in my face. "We should take you out back and finish what we started back at Achor."

Achor? What's that?

"What's stopping you?" I glance back at the other man and see him in the same spot, his hands draped over the edge of the truck bed, still gnawing on the sliver of wood between his teeth. "You boys don't seem like the kind to care what the town has to say about you."

Cooper starts to take a final step into me, but Dakota clears his throat. "Coop."

Out of the corner of my eye, an SUV rolls to a stop behind my truck on the main drag. The window rolls down and I don't have to look to know who is in the driver's seat. "Mornin', boys," Chief Danny Sloan calls through the window. "What seems to be the trouble?"

"No problem, Sloan." Dakota offers him a smile over his shoulder. "Just sayin' hello to an old friend, that's all."

Sloan looks at me with a cocked brow. "You know these boys?"

"News to me," I say, earning a laugh from the chief.

The door to Sullivan's swings open with the ring of the bell, catching our attention. An older man I've never seen before walks out and cases the scene. His lanky frame and handlebar mustache underneath the white cowboy hat remind you of what a rugged cowboy in these parts should look like.

"Everything okay out here?" his baritone voice rings out.

"Your boys are harassing our newest local, Red," Sloan yells to the older man. *Red*...that's the name I've heard Joseph and Bill Wyatt mention when talking about Cooper and Dakota before.

"Cooper Hayes!" Charlie comes barreling out of the hardware store not even a second later. "I told you to stop comin' around here! How many times do I have to tell you before you get it through your thick skull? I am not going on a date with you. And if you don't stop bothering Xavier, I'm gonna tell Daddy. I bet he'd love to know you're still bothering our guests."

Dakota rolls his eyes and steps away from my truck, shuffling around the back of the one parked next to me. Cooper isn't as easy to give up. He stands his ground, fists clenched at his sides.

"C'mon, boys," Red says with a deep chuckle. He tips his hat toward Sloan. "We don't need any trouble 'round here. Let's go." Red offers me a tight smile and a curt nod, and something in those steely blue eyes sends a shiver down my spine.

"This isn't over *Xavier*," Cooper says as Red plants a hand on his shoulder, directing him away. Dakota is already ahead of them on the sidewalk. It would seem this fight is over...for now. I don't think this will be the last time I see them. And now, thanks to Charlie, they know where I'm staying. The thought of them showing up at the ranch settles a heavy weight in my stomach.

"Xavier," Sloan calls, interrupting my thoughts. "Do yourself a favor and stay away from those boys, huh? Nothing but trouble. You too, Charlie!"

"Yeah, yeah, Danny," Charlie says, waving him off.

"Wouldn't want your daddy knowin' 'bout this, would ya?"

Charlie's head whips back around to him. "You wouldn't."

"Only if you promise not to get involved with him again."

"I swear on my mother's grave, I am *not* getting involved with the likes of Cooper Hayes again." Charlie's eyes meet mine for a brief second, her tongue poking out to wet her lips when she looks away. "He's following me, Danny. Just ask Xavier."

"Well, maybe you *should* tell your daddy, then. He's 'bout the only one Coop listens to besides ol' Red." Sloan puts the SUV into gear and begins to slowly roll forward. "Just stay away from 'em, yeah?"

twelve

A FRUSTRATED GROAN ECHOES down the hall of the barn where I finish the newly installed indoor wash stall. The old one suffered from age and a poorly designed plumbing system that did nothing but cause issues and random leaks. The amount of secret mold hiding behind the paneling wasn't surprising when I saw what was happening behind those soft boards. Drilling in the final screw to hold up the mounted plastic shower caddy, I chuckle, hearing another groan of frustration come from the indoor riding arena.

"Sounds like things aren't going so well in there," I yell down to Shadow, who's poking his head out of his stall. He huffs in response before retreating inside.

My curiosity gets the best of me, and I decide to see how things are going. Surely, it can't be *that* bad.

Reaching the arena, I lean against the doorframe and watch as Charlie and Lady kick up dirt, hauling ass around three barrels in the shape of a clover. Charlie rounds the center barrel and pushes Lady forward to the opposite end of the arena. Even when they reach their destination, Lady doesn't slow down until after a few more gallops.

"Sixteen-point-seven seconds!" Charlie's friend Katy yells from the other end with a stopwatch in her hands. She and Jackson have been here almost every night since we went to the bar almost a week ago. While Katy helps Charlie in her riding endeavors, Jackson usually putzes around. Sometimes he finds me and offers to help with whatever I'm working on. It's been nice having the extra hands, especially while working on the shower.

Charlie tosses her head back in frustration, covering her face.

"It's a good number!" Katy all but yells, frustrated herself. This is how it's been every night: Charlie disappointed in her time, while Katy tries to encourage her but ends up annoyed with her best friend's need to be perfect.

"That's slow, Katy. That's on the high end of a typical time!"

"You're just getting back into it, Char. You can't be too hard on yourself," Jackson says.

"You need to get out of your head," I call down the arena, and all heads turn toward me.

"Stay out of this, would you?" Charlie rolls her eyes, but the twitch in the corner of her mouth says the opposite.

"Seems like you need a little motivation." I walk farther inside and approach Lady, rubbing the bridge of her nose along the white mark.

"And what did you have in mind?"

I shrug, looking up at her from under my lashes with a smirk. From the corner of my eye, I can see Katy looking between us, then at Jackson, and then back at us. Her mouth spreads into a wide smile.

"You're insufferable. Go back to work," Charlie says, attempting to swat me away from Lady.

Katy cups her mouth to make sure we hear her loud and clear when she says, "Would y'all like us to leave you alone or—"

"What are you talking about?" Charlie whips her head around to glare at Katy.

"Oh, nothing!" Her smirk says it all.

"I have an idea!" Jackson practically jumps out of his seat.

Oh no, I have a bad feeling about this. Katy must have the same feeling by the way she covers her face.

"If you beat sixteen seconds, Xavier has to take you on a date!"

"Jacks!" Katy hisses.

"What?" He shrugs. "It's not like everyone doesn't see it."

I swallow the lump in my throat, ignoring Charlie when she glances down at me, keeping my gaze locked on the dirt floor beneath my feet. "I'm, uh...I'm gonna go check on the shower."

"Fuck." I sigh when a piece of barbed wire slices through the glove covering my hand. The end of the large spike nicks my hand, drawing blood to the surface immediately. That wouldn't happen normally, but these gloves are worn to hell. I've meant to get new ones every time I go into town but keep forgetting. Today has not been my day...First, it was waking up to find we were out of coffee, then a flat tire on the truck gave me a late start, and now...this. "What else could go wrong?"

I probably shouldn't say that so loud. Who knows what is out here waiting for the opportunity to fuck with the rest of my day.

Ripping the glove from my left hand, I toss it through the open truck window before I open the door and dig through the glove compartment for something to cover my hand.

The wound isn't too deep, but it'll keep bleeding if I don't do something. I need to get through at least one section before I go back to the house and properly dress it. I hope Charlie and Joseph have already left for town.

Tomorrow is the Blossom Festival, and they're supposed to be in town to help finish setting up. I know I should join them, but I declined the offer when they invited me. I need some space. I need to clear my head after the last few days. Working on the fence offers me that.

When I left Charlie and her friends in the barn last night, I intended to spend the rest of my night in my room, leaving almost zero chance of running into her again. But it wasn't enough. I needed to get out of the house. I needed breathing room. That's how I ended up at the small diner at the edge of town, properly named End of the Line Diner. Joseph has recently started giving me a small stipend for my work around the ranch, which felt wrong at first, like I was taking advantage of him when he was already letting me stay here for free. But it's nice to go out and buy things for myself and feel a bit more independent.

As I walked into the diner, the waitress, Helen, waved to me from behind the counter and motioned to the corner booth. It was my normal spot on nights like that. Nights when being behind the safety of my bedroom door wasn't enough. Nights when I couldn't sleep no matter how hard I tried. Nights when my mind went in endless circles trying to make sense of everything. Helen passed a coffee and breakfast platter in front of me before scurrying back over to the counter to talk to the other patrons.

It has been practically a year since I woke up in the hospital and up until now, I'd held out hope (even if only a small amount) someone, anyone, was out there looking for me. Someone moving heaven and earth to find me and bring me home. But the longer I'm stuck in Bezer, the more I lose faith in the idea. Maybe no one cared I was gone. Maybe I didn't have any friends or family to care. If someone *was* coming, they would've been here by now…Right?

Was I supposed to stay in Bezer the rest of my life? I'd have to. I'd have no other choice. I didn't know where I'd go. How was I supposed to live when I didn't know who I was? Should I move on and make a new life? But what if I woke up one day and miraculously remembered everything? Who is the girl that plagues me? And why can I see her but not remember her? Is she the answer to all of this?

The more questions that ran through my mind, the tighter my chest became as I sat there.

"You okay, darlin'?" Helen asked. It was the same thing she always started with. When I came in, Helen would leave me alone for the most part, almost everyone did around here, but she always made sure my cup was full for however long I was there.

"Y-yeah, thanks, Helen."

"Wanna talk about it?"

That was a first.

"No," I said, shaking my head. "Nothing to talk about."

"Now, I know that's not true. I get the feeling you have quite the story, but"—she glanced at the door when another customer walked in—"maybe another time."

Normally, my trips to the diner helped me relax and get out of my head, but it did the opposite last night. Too many things swirling around inside with no idea what to do. This back and forth with Charlie had been going on for a long time, and the longer I'm in Bezer, the more obvious it's becoming there might be something between us. The thought terrifies me. How am I supposed to jump into something when I don't know what could be out there waiting for me? There has always been a little voice in the back of my mind and a tug on my heart telling me not to jump in with both feet. But maybe it's time to test the waters…

The sound of an engine catches my attention, and I see Charlie's truck making its way through the field. She parks a few yards away and keeps a small distance between us after climbing out of the cab.

"Something I can help you with?"

"I'm sorry." The words look like they pain her to even say.

"For?"

"What Jackson said last night."

"Look, Charlie—"

She cuts me off, taking another step closer with a hand raised. "No, I get it. I know I haven't been the most…agreeable since you got here, but…" She chews on her bottom lip, scraping the toe of her boot across the dirt. "I haven't been fair to you, Xavier. And I know I can't expect you to…feel the same way. You don't even know who you are. Expecting anything from you isn't fair. I'm sorry."

"You're right," I say, folding my arms over my chest.

Her eyes are immediately drawn to the blood on the ripped piece of cloth I used to cover my left hand. Without warning, she closes the space between us, taking my hand in both of hers to examine the wound. "What happened?" Her touch is soft and delicate around the slice.

"It's a small cut. I'm fine." I remove my left hand from her grasp, using my right one to lift her chin and meet my gaze. "Charlie, you're right. It's not fair, but it's not fair for me to lead you on, either."

"You haven't." She places a hand on my chest when I try to argue. "Truly, Xavier…This is on me."

Hearing her take the full blame for what has transpired between us makes me feel like shit. This is not all on her. While I've done a pretty good job maintaining distance between us, especially when I can feel her closing the gap, I've slipped from time to time, too. And let's not forget the billiards game on her birthday...

"Let's do it," I say without thinking. God knows if I think about it, I'll back out. Charlie looks up at me skeptically. Closing my good hand around hers on my chest, I say, "Let's go on a...date."

"You don't seem too sure."

"No, yeah...Let's do it. The festival is tomorrow. Why not then?"

Charlie chews on the idea for a moment, longer than I expected her to, but a smile finally crosses her lips. "Okay, if you're sure."

I'm not.

I'm not sure about this, but it feels like the right thing to do when she is standing here chastising herself for something that isn't entirely her fault. I don't trust myself to respond verbally; instead, I lift the corners of my mouth with a small nod.

The confirmation gives her a little extra pep in her step when she takes two steps back. "Okay, well..." She glances back down at my injured hand. "Are you sure you're okay? I'm supposed to leave, but—"

"I'm fine, Charlie. I'm about to head back and get something to cover it up. I'll be fine. It's not that bad, see?" I flex my left hand and try not to wince at the twinge when my skin tugs against the edges of the slice.

"Okay, if you're sure...Dad and I are meeting Katy in town to help set up and—" Charlie trips over air on the way back to her truck. She's nervous. The only other time I've seen her nervous was before she got on Lady for the first time, but these are different kinds of nerves. My brow raises, watching as she continues to walk backward, rambling on about God knows what because I stopped listening.

When she's finally gone, I take a deep breath and scrub my good hand down my face. This is a bad idea, or maybe it's my nerves kicking in. Either way, it's not like one date means we're walking down the aisle. It doesn't mean we have to kiss. We're only spending time together and getting to know each other better. Nothing more. Nothing less.

thirteen

EVERYONE IN TOWN MUST be at this festival. There's barely enough room to breathe, let alone walk in any general direction. There's been a constant tightness in my throat, a constriction around my heart, from the moment we walked up Main Street and saw the crowd. This whole thing is overwhelming, to say the least. I blindly follow Charlie, her hand gripping mine to keep from getting lost in the crowd, and I can't help but notice how her hand feels in mine. It's soft—almost too soft— for someone who does more manual labor than the average woman. Her fingers grip mine a little too tight, making up for the gaps between our linked appendages because of how skinny hers are. Every so often, she tosses a smile my way, and I do my best to reciprocate it, hoping she can't tell I'm not present at the moment.

I could barely sleep last night, that's saying something considering I don't get much sleep as it is, and it wasn't only due to the nerves about my impending day with Charlie.

When I returned from working on the fence, I expected to find Joseph's truck parked beside the house, but it was still missing. I sent a silent prayer of thanks up to the heavens. That meant he and Charlie were still in town and I had some uninterrupted time to decompress. The thought of running to the diner for dinner crossed my mind because having to cook sounded terrible after working in the field all day, but first, I needed a shower. About halfway through my shower, I decided I definitely wouldn't be cooking, especially when the slice across my palm began to throb. I had almost forgotten about it until I had to peel the wrap from my skin, where it was sticking to the wound. Okay, maybe it was a little worse than I initially thought, but I didn't think it needed stitches. It was going to hurt like a bitch for a few days, but I'd survive.

Helen's face lit up when I walked into the diner, but her eyes immediately dropped to the white bandage wrapped tightly around the middle of my hand. "What happened to you?"

"Fence got the best of me." I yawned, taking the coffee mug she set on the end of the table.

"Yeah, those fences can be real dicks. Don't worry, darlin', I'm sure you'll get 'im next time." Helen's raspy laugh echoed through the almost empty diner as she sauntered away to throw my order on a ticket.

Business at the diner was slow and Helen took the opportunity to sit with me while I ate. While I had come looking for peace and quiet, I appreciated her company. She talked at a fast pace. Sometimes it was hard to keep up with her. She filled me in on some of the latest gossip going around town—I was glad to know I was no longer the town's only source of entertainment—and told me a little more about herself. She had worked at the diner for the better part of thirty years, something to keep her busy after her kids left the nest. Sometimes working here felt like raising kids, but she enjoyed it, nonetheless. I enjoyed the company and getting to know her. It would be nice to have another person in town I could lean on who wasn't Danny Sloan or Joseph. While Helen might carry a look of pity in her eyes whenever I first walk in the door, she doesn't treat me like a Chinadoll.

As I dug through my pocket for the wallet Charlie had gotten me for Christmas, Chief Sloan walked in with Jack Burnes behind him, dressed in uniform. Before they sidled up to the counter, Sloan noticed me. He whispered something to his counterpart before sliding into the opposite side of my booth.

"Somethin' I can get you Sloan?" Helen asked, returning for my tab.

"Just a coffee for now, and I'll take it up there." Sloan pointed up at the counter where Jack glanced through the menu. As if he needed to look.

"Long night ahead?"

"Little bit. Thanks, Helen."

His answer seemed odd. Bezer rarely saw crime, which is why the town could afford such a small force. For Sloan to have to work a late night made me think something was going on. Shit, was it the festival? My stomach dropped thinking about Joseph and Charlie being there to set up.

Before I could ask what happened, Sloan cleared his throat and said, "I don't want you to get your hopes up."

Despite what he said, my hopes skyrocketed. "Did you find something?"

"I said *don't* get your hopes up." Sloan laughed. "But maybe. The sheriff called, and—"

"What did he say?"

"—I think he might have something. Now, Xavier, I don't want you to get too excited, okay? This could be nothing."

"But what if it's something?"

"We'll cross that bridge if we get there."

The hope I had been feeling moments earlier deflated a little. It had to. Sloan was right. Whatever news the Sheriff had could be nothing.

"I gotta head out to Fox Grove shortly and talk with him. You'll be at the festival tomorrow?" Sloan asked, and I nodded. "I'll let you know if I find anything."

Even though I tried to maintain a level head about what Sloan had said, I still questioned, *What if it turns into something?* It could be the answer to everything. It could mean getting to go *home.* The thought of being one step closer to knowing who I am made me feel like I was floating, only to be brought crashing down when I parked in front of the white farmhouse after dinner. I was supposed to go on a "date" with Charlie the next morning. How could I when I knew I might be leaving soon? It felt wrong to think about canceling when I knew how excited Charlie was, but my hesitation only grew thinking about it.

"Xavier?" Charlie's voice pulls me from my thoughts of the night before. And when I look down to meet her green eyes, a thought runs through my head. *She's not her.*

Who the hell is *her?*

"You okay? You spaced out there for a minute."

More like most of the day.

I nod and say, "Y-yeah, I'm fine. Just a little tired, I guess. Didn't sleep much last night."

"Me either." She smiles, squeezing my hand, but she doesn't realize neither of us got much sleep for entirely different reasons.

Our day together has been fine. I can't complain too much, it's been nice getting to know Charlie away from the ranch. Seeing her let loose with her friends and laugh is something she doesn't do often. She's too worried about her father and handling the day-to-day work on the ranch. Even though it's been nice to see this side of her, I can't decide what's holding me back from allowing myself to enjoy it. Was it because of what Sloan said last night or because I'm just not interested in her? Either way, I'm not falling for this girl the same way she seems to be for me. And knowing that makes me feel even worse because I'm still not as invested in this as Charlie.

Down on the other side of the festival, the cover band returns to the stage, and after a quick thank you for the warm welcome, they start playing another song. The noise has been a great buffer most of the day, but the song they start with sends my mind spiraling...

I walk through the front door and straight to the kitchen as the same country song plays over the radio speakers. A woman stands at the sink, washing dishes as she hums along to the tune, and the sight of her makes my heart swell. Wrapping my arms around her waist, I press my lips against the warm, tanned skin of her neck. Her head falls back against my shoulder, granting me further access to the column of her throat, and a hum of approval comes from her. With a final kiss, I take her right hand and tug it to my chest, pulling her close to dance with her. I sing along to the song, and she laughs when I twirl her out from my chest before pulling her back in. As the final chorus plays, she wraps her hand around the nape of my neck, her fingers playing with the hair there, and she leans her head against my chest.

I kiss her temple as the song ends, but we still sway together in the middle of the kitchen.

"I miss you," I whisper against her skin.

"You have no idea." The woman brings our swaying to a halt and leans back to—

"Earth to Xavier!" Charlie shouts.

I shake my head, pinching the bridge of my nose between my eyes. *What the fuck was that?* Opening my eyes again, I'm met with expectant green ones. "I'm...I'm sorry, Charlie. I got...distracted for a second."

"You've been distracted all day," she huffs.

"I know." I reach for her hand when she tries to walk away. "Charlie, wait, I'm sorry. Really, I am. It's been a weird day."

She wants to be mad, and I can't say I blame her, but the annoyance begins to fall from her features.

With a slight huff, she readjusts her hand to hold my good one, and I do my best not to reject it. I don't need to start a war right now. Swinging our hands slightly, she says, "I have to get to Lady soon, but I'm dying for a coffee."

"Let's get you one," I say with a small smile, motioning for her to lead the way.

Charlie gets annoyed when I pay for her coffee, saying something along the lines of she "can pay for her own damn coffee," but I refuse to let her. I'm a gentleman and this is technically a date. She has thirty minutes before she needs to be down at the event tent where the rodeo is set to take place, but she doesn't want to be too early, so we find a table on the outskirts of the food area.

"How do you like it so far?" Charlie asks, taking a sip of coffee.

"The festival?"

What she means is: how do I like her so far? She disguises the question by talking about the festival instead.

"It's…fun. I get the appeal. Company isn't too bad, either."

"You're just saying that." Charlie rolls her eyes.

"No, I'm not." Okay, maybe a little, but I won't tell her. I promised her today, so I need to make good on my promise… even if I haven't been doing a good job of it thus far. "Charlie, I'm sorry I've been so distracted. I promise not to let it happen the rest of the day."

"Everything okay?"

"Everything is—"

"Xavier!" Chief Sloan shouts when he and Doris break through the crowd. "There you are. I was starting to think I wasn't going to see you." Sloan whispers something to his wife as they approach the table, and she nods. "Charlie, you mind if I steal him for a minute?"

"Be my guest, Danny. Not like we're on a date or anything," Charlie says, lifting her brows briefly before smiling at him.

"Don't worry, I'll keep you company," Doris says, sitting beside her.

"You're better company, anyway."

"Don't you know it?"

I hear them giggle as I follow Sloan through a small crowd of people and behind the food vendors, giving us a quieter and more private place to talk, away from the prying eyes and listening ears of everyone in the damn city.

"What did the sheriff say?" I ask, earning a sigh from Sloan. "I don't like the sound of that."

"Xavier, I'm sorry, but there wasn't anything. It was for someone completely different."

A swell of emotions floods my entire being, but I bite down on my bottom lip, trying to hold them back. Tears burn the corner of my eyes, but I fight like hell to keep them inside, to keep it all inside.

"I'm so sorry. I was...I really thought this was it, but I guess it just wasn't your time yet."

I can't bring myself to look him in the eye. I'm scared if I do, I'll finally break. And I have to hold it together until I get back to the house. I can't allow myself to break when I just promised Charlie I'd be on my A-game the rest of the night. She's counting on me. But as I stare up into the abyss above us, I wonder if this is some kind of punishment for something I've done in the past. Am I doomed to walk the earth day in and day out without a single idea of who I am or where I come from? A single tear slips down my cheek when I ask, "Do you think anyone even cares that I'm gone?"

"Trust me, kid. There are people out there looking for you."

My gaze falls back to Chief Sloan. Something in his voice strikes a chord in my mind. Why did he say it like *that*?

"I mean, I have no doubt in my mind about it," he says,

almost like he's trying to cover his tracks. "How could they not be?" Sloan clears his throat and pats me on the back. "Don't give up yet, okay?"

I rub the emotion from my eyes, taking a deep breath to try and eliminate the rest of it still clawing its way to the forefront of my mind. "What's the use? It's been over a year. If there was someone looking, they probably think I'm dead at this point."

"Don't say that. Please don't give up, Xavier. We'll keep fighting. We will figure this out." Sloan grips my shoulder. "It's going to happen. Might take some more time, but it's gonna happen. For tonight, enjoy the festival. Who knows, this might be the only time you get to do so." He smiles before pushing me forward and leading me back toward the girls.

Before the Sloans leave, Doris reminds me about dinner next week. She'll be making pot roast—my favorite of her homecooked meals—and I wouldn't miss it. They wish Charlie good luck before disappearing into the crowd. And when they're gone, I close my eyes and take one final breath. I have to hold my shit together for a little while longer. I can't let Charlie know something is—

"Is everything okay?" Charlie asks.

"Hmm? Oh yeah, everything is fine."

"Do you want to leave? I get it if you—"

"No." I cut her off. "No, I think this is just what I need to take my mind off things." I stick my hand out toward her. Charlie looks down at it, surprised, but takes it anyway, lacing her bony fingers through mine. "Besides, I can't miss watching you race."

fourteen

ABOUT A MONTH AFTER Charlie started riding again, she walked into the kitchen, sat at the breakfast table, looked her dad in the eye, and said she wanted to race again. More specifically, she wanted to race at the upcoming Blossom Festival, and that's how I learned all about the town's annual tradition of welcoming spring. Joseph seemed like the only person who wasn't surprised by her admission, saying the sport runs in her blood and she would have gotten back there eventually.

Despite practicing almost every night since I know Charlie isn't happy with her time. She hasn't been able to beat her record of 14.9 seconds. And while it's not the overall fastest record in the sport, it was Charlie's personal best, and she wanted to beat it.

Tonight.

She wanted to beat it tonight.

"She only needs to beat fifteen," Katy says from her spot between me and Jackson in the stands. When news spread about Charlie making her return to the circuit, the whole town buzzed with excitement—it had been almost a decade since her last race—and it felt like *everyone* was crammed inside the tiny arena to watch.

Joseph sits on my left with folded hands hanging between his knees. He's been unusually quiet since he joined us, and something tells me it has to do with the two men I saw him talking to earlier. They looked comfortable in their conversation on the outskirts of the festival, but there was a subtle tension in Joseph's smile, one I've only seen whenever he talks about the stresses of running the ranch. I turned to ask Charlie if she knew who the men were, but she was too deep in a conversation with Katy to notice anything unusual.

"You know who you're talking about, right?" Jackson asks, shoving a few pieces of popcorn in his mouth. Katy gives him a straight face, and Jackson shrugs, tossing another piece into his mouth. Katy is right though. Every other rider had already gone and the fastest time so far was 15.3 seconds. Charlie has to beat that number to win tonight, even if it isn't beating her personal best.

I didn't understand the concept of barrel racing until Charlie explained it to me when we set up the barrels the first time she practiced. Barrel racing is a rodeo event where the rider and horse go around three barrels placed in a triangular pattern. They race around each one, creating a cloverleaf pattern, before crossing the finish line. Whoever does it the fastest…wins! Seemed like an odd thing to get into, not exactly something you casually stumble upon. Joseph explained his wife had been into barrel racing; she did it more for fun, while Charlie did it for the competition.

I see Charlie direct Lady into the corral as two men finish setting up for the final race and the air becomes thick with anticipation. Charlie changed into a black button-up tucked neatly into her blue jeans, and a white cowboy hat now sits on her head. She wears it for good luck—at least that's what she said earlier. The hat belonged to her mother, and Charlie hadn't worn it since her accident, but this seemed like the perfect time to dust it off.

If I were in that corral right now, I'd look a lot more nervous than her. Charlie looks calmer than she has all day leading up to this very moment, and I wonder if the nerves have finally settled or if she's good at hiding them when she's in the zone. She strokes Lady's neck, saying something to the horse before righting herself in the saddle.

Before I know it, the gun goes off and Charlie bolts out of the corral. She directs Lady to the right, going around the first barrel in a tight circle, missing it within a quarter of an inch. How in the hell did she not touch that thing? She moves on to the second barrel, then the third before racing to the finish line. It all happened so fast, if you blink, you'd miss it.

Katy jumps up from her seat, a death grip on Jackson's hand, and her eyes glaze over with fresh tears as Charlie pushes Lady to cross the line. They don't stop until they reach the end of the straightaway. I don't have to look at the clock to know the outcome, because Katy screams and jumps in place. The rest of the crowd erupts within a second behind her.

Charlie catches her breath, stroking Lady's side, before a smile splits her face in half. I meet her eye when they do a victory lap, and she tips her hat toward me. Jackson pats me on the back with a smirk as Charlie tugs on the reins to finally maneuver Lady out of the arena. I watch her the entire way until she disappears, and only then do I catch a glimpse of the clock. It's stopped at 15.0 seconds.

While she may not have beaten her personal best, Charlie

won the competition, and it was one hell of a comeback. I'm damn sure proud of her. I just hope she's proud of herself. Who else can say they returned and won the competition after an eight-year hiatus?

Charlie has been surrounded from the moment she dismounted Lady, and when Katy and Jackson began to fight their way through the crowd, I took the opportunity to slip away from all the excitement. The Blossom Festival is set up on the outskirts of downtown Bezer, with a spectacular view of the surrounding mountains. If I can get far enough out of the crowd, I can probably find a quiet place to get some fresh air and take a moment to breathe. I swim through the sea of people until I finally reach the edge of the festival and step down from the pavement into the grass. The moon hangs high above the towering mountain's peak, illuminating the ground below and showcasing the open field I walk through.

Grasping the wood fence at the edge of the clearing, I take a long, deep breath, and all the emotions from earlier come rushing back. I knew better than to get my hopes up. I knew better than to assume Sloan's meeting with the sheriff meant I'd be closer to the truth. All that does is lead to disappointment. But I couldn't help myself. It's hard not to get excited at the prospect of it all. Nausea rises in my throat, and I struggle to force it back down.

How could this happen to me?

The problem is, I don't even know who I am. What if something like this was normal for someone like me? What if no one was looking for me because no one was surprised I went missing? That doesn't make sense...What about the woman who shows up in those memories? Surely, she'd be looking for me. Wouldn't she? Or was that someone that I only used to know?

What if I truly was all alone in the world?

Tears prick my eyes when I look up to the night sky, full of stars that twinkle and shine brightly. "Am I supposed to give up? Is that what this means?" I ask, hoping for an answer from anyone or anything that's listening. "Because that's what it feels like."

It just wasn't your time yet, Sloan said earlier, and all I can think is if not now, then when? It's been a year. How long am I supposed to wait for something that may never come? *There are people out there looking for you.* That was the other thing Sloan said. And the way he said it made it seem like...like he knew something. Was there more to the story about his meeting with the sheriff than he let on?

"You gotta give me something," I whisper, hanging my head. "Something that tells me what I'm supposed to do."

A voice rings out.

I look over my shoulder toward the direction it came from, I don't see anyone, but I know I heard it...Or maybe I'm imagining things.

Great, another thing to add to the list of things wrong with me.

"Not exactly what I was hoping for," I say to the brightest star above me.

"Xavier!" a woman's voice calls from the crowd.

"Oh, you've got to be kidding me," I whisper, and she calls again. "Fine. *Fine.*" I groan, rubbing my face and rolling my shoulders to compose myself before I head back into the festival. They're not wrong when you say to be careful what you wish for, this isn't exactly the sign I was hoping for, but it's the only one I've got.

Slipping through the crowd still in the arena, I find Charlie in the same place I left her. Weird. If she's here...then who called me? It was probably Katy. I don't see her face in the crowd, Charlie probably sent her looking for me. When Charlie turns around, my heart stops at the sight of the large bouquet of lilies wrapped in brown paper in her hands and...

The annoyance rolls off me in waves as I march across the room toward the door, but something catches my eye before I reach my destination. An oversized bouquet of roses and lilies sits in the center of a round table.

Odd...I didn't order those.

"What is that?" I ask, strolling over to the table. I hear her voice from behind me ask what I'm talking about, but I don't turn around, too busy digging through the flowers for a card.

And when I find it, my thumb swipes across the words written on it: Thanks for an unforgettable night. Can't wait for the next one. x

I swear I can feel the color physically drain from my face and the anxiety inject itself into my veins. My heart aches reading the words over and over again. What the fuck is this?

"What the fuck?" I finally get the words out. I turn to confront her, who in the hell is sending her flowers with a note like this?

A hand on my shoulder sends me jumping back and my chest heaves with two shallow breaths. Joseph lifts his hand and takes a step back. "Whoa, you okay, son?"

"Huh?" When I meet his gaze, I exhale, a little calmer than a second ago. Looking around, I'm reminded of where I am, and it's not where I was being confronted with the possibility of...whatever the hell that was. "Oh, yeah. Sorry, I was—"

"You remember something?" He cocks his brow.

"I don't...I don't know. Maybe?" I rub the crease between my brows. "It's probably nothing."

Charlie skips up to us, practically shoving the flowers into my nose. "Aren't they pretty? Daddy got them for me!"

"Yeah," I say with a half-smile. "They're great." But all these flowers do is remind me of the words on the card.

Thanks for an unforgettable night. Can't wait for the next one. x

Was that why no one had come looking for me? Was the

woman I'd been dreaming of having an affair? Was she the reason I had been out at…What was it Cooper said? Achor? When Cooper first mentioned the name, I had no idea what he was talking about, but after some conversations with Sloan, I've determined Achor is a mountain a few hours from here.

Was this woman the reason I was at Achor the day I went missing?

Was this the sign I had asked for?

"Where did you run off to? I was looking for you when I—"

"I needed some air," I say. "Got pretty crowded in here, y'know?"

Charlie nods, adjusting the bouquet before she gives it to her father, along with her hat. "Can you take these home?"

"You staying?" Joseph asks, and Charlie nods. "Xavier, you hanging around with her?"

Part of me wants to say no, I'm going back to the ranch, too, but I did promise Charlie we'd have a better date than we had been. So, I guess, I'm stuck here. "Yes, sir."

"You'll make sure she doesn't get into trouble, right?"

"Of course."

"If you're asking if he'll make sure I don't run off with Coop, then you have no worries, Dad," Charlie interjects.

"I didn't say that," Joseph says with a shrug.

"You didn't have to." Charlie rolls her eyes and her dad kisses her on the forehead, waving goodbye to Katy and Jackson when they reappear. When he's gone, Charlie beams up at me. "We have a date to finish."

fifteen

JACKSON STRUGGLES TO KEEP up with Katy when she drags him to the dance floor. The four of us have spent the last hour wandering through the festival, or what's left. Most everyone left after the rodeo, and while there are still a good number of people here, it's significantly less than earlier. It makes it easier to enjoy the festivities without fighting to get around like a school of fish swimming upstream. Charlie's hand brushes against mine before she intertwines our fingers. The movement draws my attention to our hands and then back up to meet her eyes. "Do you want to join them?"

"I don't…dance."

"Oh, c'mon. You don't know unless you try!" She tries to pull me toward the dance floor, but I maintain my stance.

"Charlie—"

"Just one, that's all I ask," she pleads, looking up at me from underneath her lashes. "And if you hate it, we never have to do it again."

The idea still sounds terrible, but slowly, she pries my feet from their place as she lures me onto the makeshift dance floor in front of the stage. A new song starts, and we find our place in the crowd near Katy and Jackson. Charlie steps up to me, draping her arms around my neck and interlocking her fingers to rest them there. Her nails ghost across my skin, sending a shiver down my spine. Instinctively, my hands land on her waist, and her brow raises, curious.

We sway left to right, as most people do in the crowd, keeping it simple and easy. Being this close to her makes every one of my nerves stand at attention. I can't decide if it's a good kind of attention or one that makes me want to go home and put at least a few walls between us.

"See? Not so bad," she says as my gaze sweeps over the crowd.

I offer her a tight smile when I look back down at her. The longer we're in this position, the more the feel of her body against mine doesn't feel…right. Is that the word? No. Foreign? She feels foreign to me like we're two pieces of a puzzle being forced together because we don't match.

"Thanks, by the way."

"For what?" I ask.

"Helping me start riding again." Charlie shrugs, chewing on her bottom lip. "I was so nervous after what happened with my accident, I was sure I'd never do it again. And then here you come and—"

"You're welcome."

"No, really, Zay. Thank you. Your help was a big part of why I could go out there tonight. If it hadn't been for you—"

"Well, it wasn't me out there. That was all you."

Charlie scoffs. "I didn't even make my personal best."

"You still won. You'll get there. Don't be so hard on yourself, Charlie."

"What did Danny want earlier, by the way? I wanted to ask, but you seemed pretty shaken up." Charlie looks up at me with big eyes, probably hoping I'll share some of my secrets with her.

"It was nothing." I lift my shoulders in a small shrug.

"Didn't seem like nothing," she says, but I don't answer. It's none of her business what Sloan and I talked about earlier. Charlie almost stops moving, but I don't let her. "You're really not going to tell me?"

"There's nothing to tell." It's not a complete lie. There is nothing to tell. We are no closer to finding the truth than before.

"Well look who it is," a voice says from behind us. There's a hint of danger woven delicately through the words, and my blood runs cold. The world around us stops. I should've known this would happen, I'm a little surprised it didn't happen sooner.

Charlie's entire being goes rigid before she turns around to face him. "What are you doing here, Coop?"

"I should've known you'd be with this city boy." Cooper scoffs. He licks his lips, looking me up and down—a predator stalking its prey—probably salivating at the thought of finally getting his hands on me. "I don't get it, Char. What's your deal with him?" Cooper takes Charlie by the hand, trying to pull her forward.

"Stop it, Coop!" Charlie promptly removes her hand from his and takes two large steps back. "You need to leave. Nobody wants you here."

Cooper rolls his eyes, adjusting his backward baseball cap. "It's a party for the whole town! Am I not allowed to join?"

"I'd rather you didn't."

Katy and Jackson break through the crowd and join the showdown, but Jackson keeps his arm in front of Katy so she can't step forward. His block doesn't stop her from throwing out an insult to Charlie's ex-boyfriend. "Why don't you go back to the hole you crawled out of, Coop?"

"Aw, Katy, don't be like that. I know you missed me, too."

Cooper touches where his heart should be, offering the blonde what I think is meant to be a sincere smile, but it looks pretty antagonizing if you ask me.

"In your dreams, Hayes. C'mon, Char, let's go." Katy grabs Charlie's arm and gives Jackson and me a look that tells us to follow. Cooper steps in front of her, blocking our path to leave, and the discussion is starting to gain the attention of onlookers in the crowd.

Great, this is great.

"What are you doing with *him?*" Cooper hisses at Charlie, motioning toward me.

Charlie crosses her arms. "Not that it's any of your business, but we were just dancing."

"No one dances with my girl," Cooper says, taking a step toward her, and I do the same. His eyes meet mine before a smile spreads on his lips and his tongue swipes across his teeth. Shit, this is about to get ugly.

"I am not *your* girl, Coop." Charlie stabs a finger into his chest. "Get a fucking life."

Cooper grabs Charlie's arm when she tries to push past him, but I take hold of her at the same time and pull her to stand behind me. "Dude, you need to back off," I say.

"And what are you gonna do about it?" Cooper laughs, and I feel like I'm talking to one of those high school bullies who's finally being stood up to. God, is that what this is? I can't be the first person who has stood up to this asshole.

"She wants to be left alone. I don't know how many times she needs to tell you." I watch his fists clench and unclench at his sides before he rolls his neck. Shit, I am not in the mood for a fight, but it looks like I'm about to get one. "Maybe you were dropped one too many times as a baby, but when a girl tells you to leave them alone, that means leave them alone."

"Oh, looks who's playing hero *again*," Dakota says, stepping through the crowd and catching my attention. Did he say again?

"You don't want to get in the middle of this, city boy," Cooper adds.

Why does he keep calling me that?

"Back off. There's no reason to start something when everyone is here to have a good time," I say.

"I don't know." Cooper shrugs, glancing toward his counterpart. "What do you think, Koda? I think this place could use a pick-me-up."

"Cooper, no," Charlie pleads.

"Oh, definitely," Dakota says. A sick smile tugs his lips upward. He and Cooper start to move closer, but their encroachment isn't enough for me to back down.

What you might call stupid…I call innate stubbornness.

"Xavier, no. Do not let them bait you into this," Charlie says, clutching my arm. She uses her other arm to try and push Cooper away. "Cooper, stop it!"

"You sure you wanna do this, city boy?" Cooper asks, stepping into me, his chest pressed up against mine. His breath is rotten enough to make me want to take a step back, but if I back down now, I don't think it will end well for me. Not that it's going to end well anyway. "I promise you, she ain't worth it."

I don't know why it bothers me, but that last blow toward Charlie makes me want to punch him square in the face.

From the corner of my eye, Jackson moves closer at the same rate Dakota does, much to Katy's dismay. Hey, at least it won't be two on one. Both girls look at the scene with horror, and now we have even more onlookers. Shit, there's no way Joseph won't find out about this now.

Cooper starts to say something else, but a deep voice cuts through the tense air: Chief Sloan. "Alright boys, break it up!" The Bezer chief of police cuts through the crowd at the same time Cooper's handler, Old Man Red, does. "Cooper get the fuck out of here. We don't need any trouble tonight. Go on!"

Cooper is about to argue when his handler gives him the same look he had outside Sullivan's a few days ago, and it shuts Cooper up immediately. With a huff and an eye roll, Cooper stalks off into the crowd, Dakota not far behind.

"You got him?" Sloan asks Red.

"Sure. They won't be causin' any more trouble tonight." Red glances my way, eyes narrowing slightly, before he tips his cowboy hat toward the group of us and disappears in the same direction his boys went. When I met his stare, I got the same feeling I did outside Sullivan's. There's something familiar and dangerous in his eyes. Something that tells me maybe there is more to Cooper, Dakota, and Red than meets the eye.

"Get them home," Sloan says to me, meaning Charlie and Katy.

Charlie tries to argue—she doesn't want to leave yet—but I give her a look to shut up. Katy isn't as upset about the news, clinging to Jackson, who wastes no time leading her through the crowd. I plant a hand on Charlie's lower back and guide her. The night is over, and so is this date.

sixteen

I DRY THE WATER from my head and step out of the shower. When we arrived back at the ranch, I only wanted to crawl into bed, but I needed to wash away the day. The hot water helped loosen my muscles, still tight from the altercation with Cooper and Dakota. The ride back didn't help—Charlie gave me the cold shoulder the whole way back from town. She's mad. Who exactly is she mad at? I don't know. I was getting mixed signals, but her irritation rolled off her in seismic waves, making me more tense. She practically tucked and rolled before I could park the truck outside the house, ignoring my calls from behind to wait up. I wanted to apologize for how the day had turned out, but she wasn't in the mood, letting the door slam behind her.

I tried to give Charlie what she wanted, but it only seemed to make things worse. There are too many unanswered questions—things I don't know or understand. I asked for a sign and got one—the lilies—but what did it mean? And the woman who has haunted me from day one, who is she? Is she my wife? My girlfriend? An ex? The latter seems most likely considering the note in the bouquet. The mix of anger and anxiety I felt reading it had to be some indication she was important to me, but maybe I wasn't as important to her.

However I feel about Charlie (or don't feel about her), I know I haven't been fair to her today. I was distracted and distant the whole time; I didn't give her a real chance like I promised. And for that, I'm sorry—genuinely.

I wrap the towel around my waist and walk out of the bathroom. I don't notice her standing in front of my room until I'm practically on top of her. "Holy shit! Charlie?"

"Oh my gosh!" She takes a step back, backing into the doorframe. "I'm so sorry. I—I didn't know you were—Sorry!"

"What are you doing?" I resecure the towel with my hand, making sure it still covers my lower half. It's not unusual to leave the bathroom in only a towel when my room is right next door. It's never been a problem, until now. I make a mental note to bring clothes with me next time to avoid another run-in like this.

"I just...I came to apologize. I was rude, and—" The whole time she's stumbling through her words, she tries not to stare at my bare chest. And if I'm honest, it's kind of cute. Her eyes roam around the entire hallway—the floor, the ceiling, the wall, the window—anywhere but at me. "So, yeah, I...uh... came to apologize for being bratty and not taking into account how today was probably a lot for you. And for Cooper. Oh my gosh, can you put a shirt on or something? This would be easier if you were...you know, clothed."

"You're kind of blocking my way," I say with a smirk, motioning to the door she still stands in front of.

"Oh! Right. Sorry." Charlie takes one big step to the side and keeps her eyes glued to the floor when I walk by.

Closing the door, I change in record time, pulling a pair of sweatpants up my legs and a T-shirt over my head. After running the towel over my shaved head one final time, I toss it onto the back of the desk chair.

I don't expect her to be so close when I open the door again, and I don't account for her to be on me like a damn fly on honey, either. Her mouth molds against mine, and it stuns me at first, but slowly I ease into her kiss, and she greedily accepts my offer. My hands reach up to cradle her face, and I swallow her moan when I nip at her bottom lip. Everything about her is foreign, the way she feels, the way she moves, the sounds she makes...Despite the differences, I can't deny it feels good to have someone this close. And that's why I don't pull away when I know I should.

Charlie gasps when I set my lips at the juncture of her neck and shoulder, her head falling back as I move up the length of her neck with open-mouthed kisses. I can't help but smile as she arches into me when I find an extra-sensitive spot. "Zay," she whimpers, her voice thick with need.

"Get on the bed," I demand, and she does without question. This might be the most compliant she's ever been.

Charlie sits on her knees on the edge of the bed, her fingers already working the hemline of her cropped T-shirt, letting it fall to the floor and leaving her completely bare from the waist up in front of me. Her breasts are like small mounds, but they fit her body, and I swoop down to take one of her hardened buds in my mouth. She moans at the sensation, fully unprepared for it, but she's not complaining, wrapping one hand around the back of my neck to keep me right where she wants me. I massage the pale skin of her left breast and swirl my tongue around her nipple, letting my teeth scrape against the bud every so often, and the sensation drives her crazy.

Her body vibrates with anticipation, need rising in her veins when my hand skates down her sides, which lacks the curves I'm used to.

Wait, what?

The thought stuns me briefly, but she doesn't seem to

notice, too engrossed in the way my hand feels against her skin. When I reach her pajama pants, Charlie's purrs of satisfaction spur me on, and I dip my hand beneath the waistband. "Did you fucking come in here bare?" I ask, not feeling anything between my fingers and the skin under her pants.

Charlie doesn't answer, only smirks, pulling my mouth back to hers.

I climb above her, and she rakes her nails across the thin hair of my buzz cut. "You should grow this out," she says, fingers ghosting across my neck.

"Why?" I chuckle.

"I want to see what it looks like." Her fingers trail around my neck to my chest and down the front of my T-shirt. She lifts the hem and tugs, pulling it over my head, and her eyes darken. She slides her hands down the bare skin of my chest, fingertips ghosting over my left pectoral before her lips follow.

Drawing in a sharp breath at the sensation, I slide my hand back into the waistband of her pants, between her thighs, and her head falls back against the pillow. She's already soaked, and she bucks against my hand when I slip one finger inside her.

"Zay," she moans when my lips find her collarbone.

I shush her and scrape my teeth against the delicate skin, dipping my tongue into the groove where her neck and collarbone meet. I push another finger inside her and she bites down on the meat of her hand to muffle her moans. She moves her hips greedily, needing more, and rubs her clit against the heel of my palm. She's close. I can feel it when I slip one more finger inside and take her nipple back into my mouth. With each swipe of my tongue across the sensitive bud, she loses more control, and when I bite down, she's a goner. She comes hard, her fingers white where they clench the blue quilt beneath her. Her body milks my fingers, vibrating underneath my touch with each stroke of my fingers, which continues to work her through her orgasm.

Pulling my fingers from her, I step off the bed and grip the back of the desk chair, taking a steadying breath. Things between Charlie and me are already complicated, and I have no doubt this will only make things worse. I wipe my hands on my towel and try to think of a way to end this without causing a scene. I don't want to hurt Charlie—any more than I have already—but I shouldn't have let this happen. I shouldn't have let my desire for the connection I've been missing overtake my common sense. She's going to think this means something. She'll think what happened means more than it does, and I'm dreading what comes next.

"Did you come here knowing something might happen?" I ask, but it's a silly question. Of course, she did. Why else would she come here without any underwear on? Okay, that doesn't mean anything. Plenty of people sleep in the nude...or commando, but still. I don't think she showed up at my door tonight to *talk*. And I have a feeling if I don't get her dressed in the next few seconds, she will try and "talk" some more.

"I had an idea," she answers, and her voice is closer than it should be. Charlie reaches across my chest and tugs, spinning me around to face her. She delicately drapes her arms over my shoulders, and lust-filled eyes look up at me from under her long lashes.

Her lips are on my skin, leaving a trail of wet, open-mouthed kisses down my neck, shoulder, and chest. She goes lower and lower until she's on her knees, fingers in my waistband and tugging my sweats down my thighs.

I need to stop this. Right now. But how do I—*Holy fuck.* A sharp inhale passes my lips as she frees my cock, touching the sensitive skin as she does so. Her tongue pokes out to wet her lips at the sight. I wrap my fist around my cock, stroking it a few times while her palms run the length of my thighs. Charlie watches my movements like she's under a spell before her hand reaches out, thumb swiping over the head.

"Fuck," I breathe, my head falling back. I have to grip the back of the chair to steady myself. I groan when her fingers run over my length. It's been too long since I've been touched by a woman, and come to think of it, I can't remember the last time I took care of myself. A shiver runs down my spine when she wraps her hand around me. Her hand is too small. Her fingers don't connect around my width.

Charlie licks from base to tip, smiling when she takes me fully into her mouth, and I curse under my breath. She takes me as deep as she can, sucking me the whole way back. With a quick sweep of her tongue, she cleans the leaking head of my cock.

"Eyes on me, Charlie," I rasp when her eyes close as her head bobs down my shaft. My hips twitch with restraint, trying not to fuck her mouth, letting her have the control. "That's it. You're so fucking good at this."

The words of praise make her mouth smile around me. I push a strand of hair from her face and push my fingers into the auburn locks, and she moans when I tug. Charlie twists her hand around my base, which doesn't fit in her mouth, but I want her to fit the whole thing.

"You can do it, Charlie," I say, flexing my hips to push more of myself into her mouth. And she takes it, finally relaxing her jaw, as her hand disappears beneath her waistband. "Are you touching yourself?" Her moan is enough of an answer. "There you go. That's good. Make yourself feel good."

She flicks her tongue across the head again and I can't take it anymore. I fuck into her mouth. Hard. Her eyes water, but she lets me do what I need and whimpers when I twist her hair around my fist, keeping her where she is. And with two more pumps, I let go. Hot streams hit the back of her throat, and my head falls back with a deep moan.

Charlie takes every last drop, and when I look down, she

runs her tongue across her lips as I pull my softening cock from her mouth.

Holy shit.

Oh, no.

No, no, no. That wasn't supposed to happen. None of this was supposed to happen, but *that* was especially not supposed to happen.

She stands from the floor and wastes no time closing the space between us. Her hands wind around my neck.

"Charlie, wait." I gently push her away when she tries to pull my mouth back to hers. "Charlie, stop."

Her brow cocks as she looks up at me. The realization slowly hits her. "You're...You want to stop?"

"Charlie, look—"

She jumps away from me, using a blanket on the chair in the corner to cover herself. I do the same with my towel, folding it inside of itself on my waist. "Save it, Xavier," Charlie hisses. "I don't want to hear your fucking excuses."

"Would you listen to me?" I reach for her, but she shrugs out of my grasp.

"I'm good enough to suck your dick, but not enough to fuck?"

"That is not..." I pinch the bridge of my nose and take a deep breath, trying to collect myself. Do not let her get to you. She's upset about everything, not just this.

"You know what, don't answer." Charlie scoffs, collecting her clothes from the floor and slipping it back over her head. When she straightens out her shirt, Charlie crosses her arms tightly over her chest and glares at me. "What did Danny want earlier? And don't even try to say *nothing*, because we both know that's not true. What the fuck did he want?"

My shoulders rise and fall. "Don't worry about it. It's nothing you need to concern yourself with."

"What did he want, Xavier?" She shoves into my bare chest

with her hands.

"It doesn't concern you!"

"Yes, it does!" The nail of her pointer finger sticks into my muscle. "You were supposed to be on a date with me and your mind was everywhere but on *me!*" Charlie scoffs, running a hand through her messy waves. "Look, I get it, this is hard for you. It's been hard for you. But don't drag me into something you're not ready for. I deserve—"

"Drag you into—" I scoff. "Charlie, *you* wanted this! You're the one who wanted to go on a date. You've been—"

"So, what, it was a pity date?" There's a new level of emotion in her eyes. Part of me feels bad, but I can't deny what's right in front of us. It wasn't a complete pity date, but it wasn't wholly something we both wanted, either. "Save your fucking pity. I don't need it."

"I didn't say—"

"You didn't have to! You don't have to." She takes a step back. "I can see it written all over your face. But you know what, Xavier? When you decide to pull your head out of your ass and you want to finally move the fuck on with your life… don't come to me." Charlie shoves past me and leaves my room, and after a moment I hear the door to her room slam.

Am I supposed to go after her? Continue to apologize for something she started? Maybe I should, but I don't. I quietly grab my sweatpants from the floor and go to the bathroom to clean myself up.

seventeen

THE AIR IS THICK and muggy today. It has been since I got out to the fence this morning. While the sky looks like it could unleash its fury at any moment, it has yet to do so. Until it does, I'll continue mending the fence. I need the space to think after last night. Even though I only got a few hours of sleep (if that), I was out of the house well before Joseph and Charlie got up this morning, thankfully. I wasn't ready to face that beast, yet. I was grateful to find Joseph had restocked the coffee. There was no way I would make it through today without it. The thought crossed my mind as I prepped the pot this morning that maybe I should talk to Joseph about moving out.

Joseph tries to hide his concerns, but I think it's obvious things around the ranch are tight—tighter than before. I notice it whenever conversations about money or needing materials get brought up, or when Charlie goes out one too many nights a week. I can't help but wonder if I'm part of the cause, too. I've considered asking Joseph to cut the small stipend he started giving me, but I don't think that talk would go over very well.

If I move out but still work around the ranch, it might

alleviate some of Joseph's concerns. It might diminish some of the tension with Charlie, too. If I stick around, I think it'll only make things worse.

The hairs on the back of my neck stand to attention and goosebumps rise across my skin as I finish securing one of the barbed wire knots. The weight of a heavy presence draws my attention over my shoulder and I sigh. "Fuck." The word slips past my lips when the two figures approach.

They've come to finish the job, and something tells me this will be a fight to the death...literally. What was it Dakota said the other day in town? *You're supposed to be dead.* That means I've already won before, right? Maybe I can do it again...

"If you're looking for Charlie, you've come to the wrong place," I say, standing from my position on the ground.

"You best stay away from my girl."

"Your girl?" I laugh. "That's not what she told me."

"Better be careful. Wouldn't want your *wife* to find out you've been stepping out on her while you've been gone," Dakota says with a wicked grin.

What did he say? *Your wife.* Wife...I have a wife?

I look between them and a smirk tugs on Cooper's face when he realizes my confusion. "She's been raising holy hell to find you, too. I'm surprised the feds haven't stormed the castle by now."

My heart stops at the thought as the image of the woman plaguing me since I arrived in Bezer fills my mind. It has to be her. My wife. And she's looking for me—has been looking for me. *Raising holy hell to find you,* is what Dakota just said. So, why hasn't she found me? Shouldn't the police know where to find me if I'm in the missing person database?

"My wife?" I ask.

Cooper rolls his eyes. "Don't act like you don't remember."

My lack of response is enough to elicit a laugh of disbelief from them. Dakota clamps down on Cooper's shoulder. "Oh, this is rich! You mean you really don't remember? I thought Old Man Red was blowing smoke up my ass."

"Kind of takes the fun out of killing you," Cooper adds.

My hand tightens around the pair of pliers I'm holding—not that they'll do me any good compared to whatever these two have in their arsenal.

"Maybe—" Dakota glances at his counterpart before he smiles my way. "Maybe we oughta pay her a visit, too."

My words come out between gritted teeth. "Touch her and I'll kill you myself."

A chuckle rumbles in Cooper's chest as he reaches into his pocket. He pulls out a black square—a wallet. Flipping it open, Cooper studies something inside the wallet before looking up at me. He nods and tosses it over to Dakota. "What do you say, Koda? That him?"

Dakota does the same, but when he looks up at me, there's a hint of mischief in his eye. "I don't know, hair's a bit different. But I think he could pass."

"I wonder if he still could with his face caved in?" This time when Cooper makes his threat, he takes a step closer, and I see the oversized blade at his side.

Shit.

What good are a pair of pliers going to do against that? That's like bringing a knife to a gunfight.

Wait.

Gun. I have the gun Joseph gave me *just in case,* especially when I'm out in the fields. The last thing you'd want is to be caught out here empty-handed if something snuck up on you. Little did I know it would be two things.

Dakota moves at the same time Cooper does, coming around the side. They're going to try to pin me against the fence. I could run for the truck—for the gun—but Dakota could easily intercept me.

I have to do something. I can't stand here and wait for

them to finish me off. I have to try and fight. I have a *wife* waiting for me. If I walk out of this alive, I'm going straight to Sloan to tell him.

My feet are heavy the first few paces toward the truck. Realistically, it's only about ten feet, but it feels like a damn football field in this moment. Cooper yells something at Dakota and when I reach the truck, one of them grabs hold of my shoulder and throws me back onto the hard dirt. The impact steals the breath from my lungs and sends a jolt through my skull. I cry out when Dakota steps onto my injured hand before he applies all his weight when he sits on top of me. He lands a blow to my left cheek and another to the side of my face. I extend my good arm toward the pliers on the ground barely out of reach. My finger grazes the handle, and I gently ease them between my fingers until I can grasp them and slam them against Dakota's temple. The blow only temporarily stuns him, and the look of fury in his eyes when he composes himself tells me I better do something fast.

I punch him in the ribs three times and slam the pliers against the same temple before finally leveraging him off me. I try to scramble to my feet, but Cooper is already there. He grabs hold of my ankle, slamming my face back into the dirt. He raises the machete in the air and I twist to try and use my other leg to kick his chest, but the blows don't land properly and he twists my ankle into an odd direction—the same ankle that had been sprained a year ago.

Gunshots ring through the air before hoofs against the dirt ride up to meet us. Joseph holds a shotgun toward the sky as he and Lady approach the scene. Getting closer, he lowers the gun, aiming directly at Cooper's head. "One move and I'll drop you both right here."

Cooper chuckles, dropping my ankle and sending me crashing to the earth. "Oh, c'mon, Joe! Don't be like that."

"I don't care if you have Red in your back pocket. This

is *my* property and not only are you trespassing, but you're assaulting one of my employees. I'm within my rights."

"We weren't meanin' no trouble, Joe," Dakota says, rubbing his head.

"You okay, Xavier?" Joe asks without looking.

"Fine," I say, pushing myself up from the ground.

"You hurt?"

"Nothin' I can't handle." I wince applying weight to my ankle—it'll be sore, but I can live with it.

Joseph motions toward the road in the distance, speaking to Cooper and Dakota, "Unless you want Red to find your brains scattered across my field, I suggest you get moving."

Cooper narrows his gaze at me before he turns back to Joseph, the blade still dangling between his fingertips. I don't trust him, and I sure don't trust Dakota. They won't give up this easily, not when I'm within their reach. They've waited long enough. They want to finish the job. Dakota reaches into his waist and I lift the gun from the holster between the seat and center console—another thing Joseph suggested when he realized I'd been keeping it in the glove compartment. "I'd think twice before doing that," I say, aiming the barrel at Dakota.

Dakota looks at me and then at his friend. Lady stamps her feet and huffs in anticipation, but no one moves, locked in a standoff no one seems ready to lose. From here, I can see Joseph apply a little more pressure to the trigger, and finally Cooper relents.

"This isn't over," Cooper says.

"Step foot on my property again Hayes and I'll make sure you never leave." Joseph continues to follow his every move with the barrel as Cooper and Dakota begin their retreat. Only when they turn their backs and get a few more yards away does he finally lower the gun, never taking his eyes off them until they've disappeared down the highway. "Sure you're okay?"

"Fine," I say, rolling my shoulders and touching my cheek. I'm sure it's bruised, I can already feel it swelling beneath the skin. "Maybe it'll knock something loose."

Joseph chuckles. "Wouldn't that be nice?"

"Thank you. If you hadn't shown up—"

"I've been looking for an excuse to do that since the day Charlie brought him home her sophomore year." Joseph stuffs the gun into the holster on his back. "Seems like they've taken a liking to you. You know 'em?"

"I don't, but apparently they know me."

"What'd they say?"

"Not much. Said I was supposed to be dead…and I have a wife."

Joseph leans forward a bit on the saddle horn. "She lookin' for ya?"

"Raising holy hell, too, according to them."

"Where she at then?" Joseph rights himself, tugging on the reins to direct Lady back the way they came. He poses a good question—one that I need to ask Sloan. If he and the sheriff had put my picture out there, why hadn't she shown up yet? "Well, pack up and come on back to the house. I was 'bout to start dinner before Charlie goes to work. Fair warning, she seems to be a bit in a mood."

"Yes, sir."

"And from now on, Xavier"—Joseph looks back over his shoulder—"you don't come out here alone. Got it?"

eighteen

HOT WATER RAINS DOWN my back, relieving some of the soreness in my muscles. It's a nice contrast to the cold compress I've been holding against my face since I got back from the field. A bruise has already started to form along the cheekbone with some of the discoloration bleeding up toward my eye, and right in the middle of it all is a small laceration from where Dakota's knuckles made an impact I hadn't noticed until I saw my reflection in the hallway mirror. Charlie was doing her best to avoid me; however, she couldn't help but stare when she did look at me. I looked like hell, and I knew it. Her unwavering gaze only confirmed it.

"Are you okay?" she asked, and it shocked me. I didn't think she would speak to me for at least two days after last night.

"Yeah, your boyfriend says hi." I tried to give her a tight smile, but the small twitch in my face sent a shockwave of discomfort through my cheek and into my skull.

I didn't wait for her to respond, trudging into the kitchen to find something cold—frozen peas, frozen meat, or a frozen compress, I didn't care—to put against my face. Luckily, Joseph had already pulled the compress out, instructing me to take a load off. And that's what I did.

When Charlie tried to press me for information about what happened, Joseph stepped into the living room, telling her to mind her business and help him with dinner. From my spot on the couch, I could hear bits of their muffled conversation but tried to block them out, piecing together what I wanted to say to Sloan when I visit him tomorrow.

After dinner, I dragged my aching body up the stairs and straight into the bathroom to take a shower, hoping it would bring some more relief, and it did.

Closing my eyes, I let my head fall into the steady stream and my mind wanders to a bedroom somewhere far from here. The windows showcase city lights expanding as far as the eye can see. A reflection stares back at me in a floor-length mirror. It's me, but I look different...My hair is a tad longer, and I'm dressed in a white button-up with black dress pants. A black tie hangs from my hand. From the open door, I hear the sounds of her heeled footsteps before she appears, digging through her purse for something. The light pink shade of her dress brings out the warmth of her skin tone and the way it hugs her every curve is fucking delicious. My fingers clench at my sides at the mere thought of touching her. Long hair falls over her shoulders in delicate chocolate waves, they've been placed perfectly to make sure she looks good from any angle, and damn does she. When she catches me staring, she smiles and raises a brow. "Can I help you?"

Fuck yes, she can.

All I want to do is strip her out of that dress and have my way with her. It seems she has the same idea. She drops the purse on the dresser and closes the space between us, wrapping her arms around my shoulders from behind and kissing my neck. A soft hum rumbles in my throat in response as I lean back into her embrace before she tugs my shoulders turning me around. I plant my hands on either side of her neck, pulling her mouth to mine, and when her fingers brush over my already semi-hard cock, it sends all the blood rushing there.

My need for breath is greater than I'd like it to be. When my lungs force me to take a deep breath, it pulls me from the memory. I brace my palms against the wall.

Without even thinking about it, my fist wraps my cock and the image of her dropping to her knees infiltrates my mind. Her mauve-painted lips form an "O" as she bats her lashes, looking up at me. My fingers tangle in those warm chocolate waves, tugging her hair as her tongue laps the underside of my dick.

Fuck, why can't this be real? There is something different here than last night. Something I've never had with Charlie: a longing to have this woman wrapped around me, to feel her heart beat against mine as she comes undone. I stroke myself, imagining she is here, and my mental image changes. Suddenly she's on her knees on the floor of this very shower.

I groan as she licks the head of my cock, and after a few more, she takes me fully into her mouth, as far back as she can. "Fuck, beautiful. If you're not careful, I'll come in that pretty mouth." My words make her smile, and she simultaneously moves her hand and mouth.

My throat grows tight as my hand tightens around my base, pulling and stroking, eyes screwed shut as the water beats down on my back. I want this to be real so fucking bad. No, I need it to be.

She switches between deep sucks and long strokes of her tongue. When she looks up at me through her thick eyelashes, there's a slight quirk in the corner of her mouth. She feels so good, according to my imagination, and she knows it. That's the sexiest thing of all.

I fist my hand in her hair, pushing my cock deeper down

her throat. There's no hesitation from her. She opens her jaw and takes me deep, and when she moans, I come. A stream of cum hits the tiled wall. My fingernails dig into the tiles above me, using the wall to brace myself as my legs quiver beneath me. This release is hot and all-consuming, completely different from last night.

I continue to stroke myself and let every last drop fall until it's washed away.

"Shit." I sigh, my left palm still braced against the wall.

A daydream isn't going to be enough. I need the real thing. But it's not just my body that longs for this woman...

My heart does, too.

An ache deep inside me has kept itself concealed until today. Hearing someone is out there looking for me—

But not just anyone. My wife...It still didn't feel real to hear the words spoken, but they are real, and she is real. And I will do whatever it takes to find my way back to her...Starting with talking to Sloan to figure out what the fuck is going on.

When the water finally runs cold, I turn the dial until it's at its coldest and let the water rush over me for exactly two Mississippis before turning it off. Rubbing the towel over my head, I wrap it around my waist and meet the reflection in the mirror. I let out a sharp inhale when my fingers graze over the laceration on my cheek, tender to the touch and only going to get worse by tomorrow. At least he didn't give me a black eye.

For the first time since I arrived in Bezer, I allowed myself to stare at my reflection. Almost every time I've come into contact with a mirror over the last year, I avoid lingering in it too long. Why? I can't stand looking at someone I don't recognize. Someone I can't remember.

How do you wake up with no recollection of who you are? Charlie's words from when I first arrived echo through my mind. And isn't that the million-dollar question?

Maybe if I had the answer, I'd be able to find a way home...

to her...my life.

Find a way back to me.

I stare into the eyes of the reflection again, willing it to remember something—anything—that would help me. I begin to take inventory of the rest of the man in the mirror: shaved head; dark brown hair; facial hair that has started to grow from lack of shaving the past week; almond-shaped, hazel eyes with flecks of gold; a longer-shaped face with a broad forehead and pronounced cheekbones that narrow into a defined jawline; freckles dusting my right cheek and extending up toward my forehead with a single one on the left side of my nose; and four tattoos, but not a single one shakes a memory free.

"Who are you?"

The answer sits at the edge of my mind. I can practically hear it screaming from the edge of the abyss, trying to break through the fog, but it can't. It's trapped there, in limbo. I just wish there was an easier way to free it.

nineteen

A LARGE BLACK ESCALADE pulls through the tree line as I leave the barn. From here, I can make out two people in the front seat, and when they get closer, it's easier to recognize the two men Joseph was talking to at the festival.

Because I don't know how much longer I'll be in this town, especially after I tell Sloan about what happened yesterday, I got up early this morning to clean out the stalls and save the horses—and me—from dealing with Charlie's wrath. It had returned full force last night when she returned from work, and while I'm not sure what set her off, I know seeing my face when she came upstairs didn't help. She stomped up the rest of the way and slammed her bedroom door behind her, rattling the frames on the wall. Joseph stood at the bottom of the stairs, shaking his head with a sigh before disappearing down the hall to retire for the evening.

The front door slams, catching my attention as Charlie stomps down the steps toward my truck. She flings open the passenger door, climbs in, and slams it behind her.

Great. This is going to be a fun day.

Maybe I shouldn't go to the station today. I don't think dragging her along on that particular errand is the best idea. I didn't want to bring her with me in the first place, but Joseph insisted she tag along instead of making multiple trips into town. She and I shared a look. It was obvious neither of us wanted to be in such quarters, but we couldn't tell Joseph that. He didn't question when she complained about it—her father was used to Charlie being hot and cold toward me—but if I refused, it would look suspicious and require more explanation than I was willing to give. So, I gave up the fight and told her to be ready by eight o'clock sharp.

"Good luck, Xavier, she's in one of her moods," Joseph calls from the porch when he walks out of the house. Settling a cowboy hat on his head, he glances toward my truck and shakes his head.

"Anything in particular?" I ask.

"Take your pick." Joseph chuckles. "Well, would you look at that? A hummingbird!"

Sure enough, fluttering at the far end of the porch is one of the small birds with rapid-fire wings and a long, slender beak that flows into a fiery red throat. The sun reflects off its iridescent feathers—vibrant shades of green, blue, and purple—hovering near one of the Morello flowers Charlie planted a few days ago.

"First one I've seen this year. She's a pretty thing," Joseph says, walking down the steps.

The distinct thud of a car door pulls my attention away from the bird. The two men have finally exited the oversized SUV, and the shorter one stares straight at me as they walk toward the house.

"Well, I'll see you when you get back. Don't take too long and don't get more than is absolutely necessary for the fence, you hear?" Joseph instructs.

"Sure, Joe," I say, holding the man's gaze. Something about

him feels…familiar, but it's not the same feeling as when I first saw Cooper or Dakota. This is different.

When I get in the driver's seat, I keep the many thoughts running through my mind to myself. Does Charlie know who those men are? What are they doing here and why were they meeting with Joseph alone? Every time a new question forms, I think about asking her, but the irritation rolling off her tells me to leave her alone…for now.

About fifteen minutes into the drive, I called off my trip to the police station. I'll have to make the trip down tomorrow during my lunch break when I can talk to Sloan without Charlie's lingering presence. As I load the supplies from Sullivan's into the back of the truck, she hasn't moved from her spot in the front seat, but I know she's breathing because her arms are no longer crossed, and she sits on her hands. Her eyes are set forward, gaze narrowed as she chews on the corner of her mouth. I'm starting to think her irritation with me is about more than what happened between us…

"You wanna talk about it?" I ask, closing the door after I climb into my seat.

"No."

Any other day, I would let it go, but not today. Charlie seems extremely bothered by whatever is happening and I know what happened between us isn't helping. I hate being part of her problems. So, if she will let me, I'll try to be part of the solution.

"C'mon, you can tell me. What's bothering you?"

Charlie scoffs. "And why would I tell you?"

"Because it's better than holding it in," I say, backing out from the hardware store.

Charlie pulls her hands from under her legs and cracks her knuckles before wringing her hands together. She fidgets the whole way to the post office, the one errand she had to run today. I expect her to jump out of her seat and run inside as soon as I park, but she does the opposite. With a heavy sigh, she rubs her neck and pinches the skin between her thumb and forefinger, clearing her throat.

"He's selling the ranch," she says so quietly I almost don't hear her. Charlie scoffs before she takes a shaky breath. I don't have to see her eyes to know tears have begun to spring in the corners of her eyes. Shaking her head, she leans back against the headrest, and a tear trails down her cheek. "Says it's become too much and he can't keep up with it. Can't afford to keep up with it. He's gonna sell it off to those vultures before the bank can take it."

"Is that who showed up before we left?" I ask, and she nods. "I'm sorry, Charlie. I wish I could do something."

"Yeah, me too." Flinging her door open, she storms out of the truck and into the post office.

My shoulders fall with a sigh, staring at the door she walked through. I can sympathize with her. When things seem to be looking up, everyone—me included—pulls the rug out from under her.

Isn't that how it always works?

Within minutes, Charlie stomps back to the truck, a package in her arms. She tosses it onto the floor beneath her feet without care for whatever is inside and sits back in her seat, folding her arms tightly across her chest and gluing her gaze to the windshield.

"How 'bout we go grab something to eat? Might make you feel better."

"Not in the mood," she says, looking out the window instead.

"My mom used to say there wasn't anything a good meal couldn't fix." We both freeze as soon as the words leave my mouth.

"You just remembered?" Wide green eyes turn to me.

"Y-yeah, I guess so." I don't know where it came from, either. The words popped into my head, and I said them... but when I tried to think of my mom, there was only a vague outline of a woman.

"Better hope it all comes back before you don't have anywhere to stay." And she's back to being a brat.

I roll my eyes and back out, driving to the end of town where my favorite diner awaits us.

Charlie looks around at our surroundings, quickly realizing we are not headed for the ranch. "I said—"

"I know, but I don't care. We're going in here to get something to eat. I know you haven't eaten much since the other night."

"What do you care, Xavier?" She practically spits my name, and I remind myself not to fall into her trap. She's in a bad mood because of everything going on. I shouldn't take it too personally. Maybe a little, though.

Parking at the diner, I say, "Charlie, get out of the truck now." Before she can challenge me, I repeat myself. "Now."

With a loud huff, she does as she's told.

Mom was right. Nothing a good meal can't fix or make a little better. Charlie's mood had improved significantly after getting some food in her stomach. Helen took one look at her and immediately knew what to give her: one of their famous chicken pot pies and a slice of lemon meringue pie. By the third bite, Charlie was a brand-new person.

However, that new person disappears when we drive through the Blackwood Ranch gate. She sees the Escalade still parked in front of the house. It's now joined by another vehicle I don't recognize—a silver Jeep Wrangler. They can't be from around here. Most people in Bezer drive older SUVs, and most aren't Jeeps—surprisingly.

Charlie slams the passenger door, takes off toward the house, and lets the front door slam behind her. The door slams one more time when she comes back outside. "They're not inside. Where in the hell—"

"Charlie! Xavier!" I hear Joseph shout from behind me. He waves, walking down from the barn with the same two men behind him. "There you are. I was starting to wonder if you were ever coming back. I want to introduce you to some people."

"No, thanks," Charlie says, her voice laced with enough venom to poison all four of us were she to strike.

Joseph ignores her, introducing them anyway. "Jace, Ben... I'd like to properly introduce you to my daughter, Charlie, and our house guest, Xavier. He's the one I was telling you about who has been doing all the work around the ranch."

Both men stare straight at me. Neither one tries to hide it, and the shorter one fails to hide the smile tugging at his lips. It's not a normal smile you give to someone you just met. It's the kind of smile when you *know* something everyone else in the room doesn't. He steps forward and extends his hand. "Hi there, I'm Jace. It's nice to meet you...Xavier, was it?"

"That's what they call me," I say, shaking his hand.

"Yeah, because you don't even know your own name," Charlie says with a slight scoff, earning a glare from me and Joseph. Why in the hell would she say that? These guys don't need to know what a nutcase I am.

"You don't know your name?" Jace asks, cocking his head

to the side.

Joseph sighs, glaring at his daughter one more time. "Xavier was in an accident and unfortunately lost his memory. He's been with us since we found him wandering the woods last—Oh, good! She's here."

Joseph beams, staring past Jace and Ben back to the barn. When I follow his gaze, my heart stops.

It's *her.*

I have no doubt it's her—the woman I've been dreaming of.

When our eyes meet, she braces herself against the barn door. Little by little, the fog that has infiltrated my mind for the last twelve months lifts, and I can see everything.

I know who I am.

I know who she is.

The pieces of the puzzle are starting to fit together. We may be almost a football field apart, but I can see the emotions displayed across her face. The tears in her eyes. The flush in her cheeks. The way her chest heaves with each shuttered breath. She wants to, but she doesn't make the first move.

She waits to see what I'm going to do…

I can only imagine what she's been going through the past year, and I hate myself for putting her through it. I'd do anything to take it back, and I will. I'll do whatever it takes to make this right. But right now, all that matters is the woman in front of me—*my wife.*

"Dee."

Part Two

Her

twenty

Now

ONE YEAR.

That's how long it's been since the last time I saw my husband. One year since the last time I heard his voice. One year since he walked out of my office, and got on a plane to his brother's bachelor party without saying goodbye, only to go missing three days later.

Life has been a mess since I got the call he was gone... No, I take that back. Life has been hell. When I got the call from my brother, I thought it was some practical joke—an extremely mean one, but a joke, nonetheless—until I got to Haven, Colorado, and realized it wasn't a joke and Nick was missing. He had been for days.

I've done my best to hold the family together, but it's been hard. A lot harder than when Daddy died almost ten years ago.

Shit...Has it been that long?

This December will mark the tenth anniversary of my father's death and I've been so preoccupied with everything else going on I barely even noticed.

There's tension within the family, more than I can handle

on my own, and instead of dealing with it, everyone acts like it's not there. I think the issue lies with the many unanswered questions about what happened that day and the ones that followed. The only thing we know for certain is Nick left the house on April 8, drove out to Mount Achor for a hike, and never came home.

Since his disappearance, I've stayed at our home in Haven, except when I have to be in New York for work. It's not hard to work from here for either of my companies—my design firm, DV Designs, or the family business, Villa Incorporated. The board of Villa Inc. didn't fuss much about the lack of my presence at first, but I know they're getting antsy. They want my feet on the ground full-time, not once a quarter or whenever I decide to show up. I've spoiled them the past ten years, taking over the company when I was originally only supposed to have a supporting role. My role should have been to attend board meetings and consult with my brother. Daddy left the company to Kai when he died, but my brother wanted to take a step back when he became a father, so I took over. Everyone, especially the chairman of the board, liked it that way. They preferred it when I was in charge. Don't get me wrong, my brother is good at his job—Daddy wouldn't have trusted him with the company if he wasn't—but he's not me, and the chairman has had no issue making it known.

The entire Villa-Davis clan is supposed to be here on Saturday, two days from now—the day before the one-year mark of Nick's disappearance. They wanted to be together, to celebrate him. I would have much rather spent it alone with my daughter, Elena, but Nick's brother, Alex, insisted when he called me two weeks ago. He had already talked to the rest of the family, and they were excited. I was the only one who didn't seem to like the idea. I don't want to celebrate. What is there to celebrate?

Nick is gone.

That's not a cause for celebration. He's still missing…Well, his body is still missing. We haven't found it and after a year I'm starting to think we never will.

"It will be good for everyone to be together," Elizabeth said when she called me a few hours after Alex did. "We haven't *all* been together since Thanksgiving. Besides, I don't want you to be alone."

That was true. It had been a while since everyone could sync their schedules, but that didn't make me want to. It only made me feel like I had to.

Now, I have to host all eighteen of them at my house. Yeah, you heard me: *eighteen.* My brother, Kai, and his wife, Eileen, with their kids, Ophelia, and Fallon (their latest addition, almost two years ago); my sister, Elizabeth, and Nick's cousin, Josh, and their kids, Brie and Nova (who was born last Christmas Eve); Josh's little sister, Michaela, and her husband, Finn, with their daughter, Raegan (born early last December); Nick's little brother, Alex, and his fiancée, Lara; Josh and Michaela's parents, Pat and Jenny; Nick's father, Jimmy, and his girlfriend, Tessa; and Blake Evans, Brie's best friend. All eighteen members of the family, not including Elena and me. But at least I know I won't have to deal with my mother, even if my brother wishes I'd change my mind.

Luckily, I won't have to deal with them long.

"No ifs, ands, or buts," my brother said when he called yesterday to inform me the board wanted me in New York next Wednesday for a meeting. Why it can't wait until the quarterly meeting the following week is beyond me, but I don't have a choice. The board isn't going to let me out of this one.

This is the meeting where they tell me I have to be back in New York full-time, which may not be such a bad thing… As we approach the one-year mark, I've been contemplating whether or not I should sell the house in Haven and move back to New York permanently. It's hard to consider staying here when there's a constant reminder of my husband everywhere I look. Everything about this place screams Nick, from the renovated fireplace he designed to the stairway railing he handcrafted alongside his father to the playhouse for Elena that he designed and built two years ago with his own hands.

Kai and I are slated to leave the evening after the anniversary, much to the family's dismay. They didn't understand why this meeting couldn't wait until the following week when we'd already be in town. I didn't have it in me to go back and forth about it; instead, I reassured them they were welcome to stay at the house through the rest of the week for spring break, and left it at that.

"Momma?" a small voice calls from behind me.

Looking over the back of the couch, I meet the warm, honey eyes of my almost-four-year-old, Elena Joanna Davis. She looks like me when I was her age, but she has her father's eyes. She clutches her pink fleece blanket, rubbing her eyes when she yawns. The sound of her bare feet against the wood floors follows her to the couch. Elena crawls into my lap and snuggles into my neck. Her small fingers toy with the chain around my neck that holds her father's wedding band on it until she frees the ring from underneath the neckline of my sweater.

"What's wrong, Bird?" I kiss her forehead.

"I couldn't sleep."

"No?"

Elena shakes her head and buries herself further into my neck, still clutching the ring. "When is Daddy gonna come home?"

My heart clenches. "Elena, your daddy loved you very much, but remember what I told you before?" I smooth down the hair on the back of her head and lift her away from my shoulder so I can look at her. Clearing my throat, I try to keep my voice from breaking under the weight of the emotion.

"Sometimes daddies have to go away. Sometimes they...have another job and can't be with us anymore."

"But he's coming home, right?"

What am I supposed to say? I've had this conversation with her on more than one occasion and it's getting harder every time...for both of us. Every time I have to remind my daughter her father isn't coming home, it feels like we're starting the grief cycle all over again.

I have to be honest with her. I can't lie and give her the false hope that he'll walk through the door one day. If you ask the authorities, that isn't going to happen. The moment they found the bloody piece from his shirt, it officially turned into a recovery instead of a rescue.

"I don't know," I whisper, kissing her temple. For tonight, though...I'm choosing not to upset her. I pat her leg and give it a gentle squeeze. "C'mon, let's get you back to bed. You have preschool in the morning."

"I don't want to go to school." Elena grumbles the whole way out of the living room, dragging her blanket behind her as she kicks something invisible in front of her feet.

Following my daughter down the hall, I can't help but think of how things could've been different if Nick and I hadn't fought before he left for Alex's bachelor party...If it wasn't for those damn flowers. If I had stopped to say 'I love you.' If I had just made him listen...Maybe things could have been different.

twenty-one

One Year Ago
April 2028

YOU'VE GOT TO BE fucking kidding me. Did this asshole not leave anything untouched? I try to rub out the pounding in my temples, taking one of the longest deep breaths of my life. Then another. It's fine. Everything is fine. We caught this before it became an even bigger problem. That's what matters.

Three nights ago, I got a call from my DV Designs CFO, who was concerned about how far over budget our Dallas office is, considering it's only the beginning of April. How much over? Approximately thirty-thousand dollars. The discrepancy was discovered while she was putting together numbers for the quarterly meeting coming up next week. I told her to send me what she had, and we'd look at it this week. But I never expected this…

We sat on the phone all night until we discovered the problem: one of the project managers was misallocating funds. The discrepancies stretched back to last October when they were first hired. It started with small things, a purchase here or there until it turned into larger things like paying someone an extra thousand dollars here, two there. The whole thing is a shitshow.

I need to finish combing through these transactions tonight because I should be focused on the Villa Inc. networking event tomorrow afternoon before I take the rest of the week off.

Nick comes home from Haven tomorrow. He spent the last week at his little brother's bachelor party—a phone-free event. Alex's friend planned the whole thing, but Alex's one request was no phones. Elizabeth thought it was sweet, but I thought it was annoying. You try telling a two-and-a-half-year-old she can't call her dad for that long. Truthfully, I didn't put up much of a fight. I assumed Nick would find a way to call anyway, but he hasn't called once. The last time we talked was last Wednesday night when he got to Haven. If they are taking the whole "no phone" thing this seriously, my only hope is he comes home a lot more levelheaded than the way he left...

"Knock, knock," a voice calls from my office door. Luke Benson. The fresh-out-of-college, know-it-all business major I've been mentoring for the past two months. His presence is not going to help my headache.

"Can I help you, Luke?" I ask, continuing to look through the papers in front of me.

"You haven't returned my calls." Luke crosses the threshold of my office, his left hand toying with the tie around his neck before he sits in the chair across from me.

He's right. I haven't returned his calls. I know it's wrong, but this man is why I'm on thin ice with my husband, or one of them anyway. I can't give him all the credit. I got myself into this predicament without anyone's help. Luke was simply the cherry on top. And instead of confronting him, I chose to push him off on one of the managers here at the corporate office, who he should've been under from the start. I'd only been mentoring him as a favor for one of Daddy's old acquaintances.

"I'm sorry, I've—"

Luke cuts me off. "Got a lot going on, I know, Nina."

A heavy sigh falls past my lips.

"Don't get me wrong, Andy has been great, but he's not you."

"Luke, I'm sorry, but I don't think it's a good idea for us to work together anymore."

"Did I do something?" Luke seems genuinely confused.

"Luke." I sigh. "We need to talk."

"Uh oh, that doesn't sound good."

"Look, I don't want you to get the wrong impression of what's going on here. I'm only here to help you figure things out, help you get your feet on the ground before—"

"Nina, what are you talking about?"

Is he going to sit there and act like he doesn't know? That's a bold move. "The flowers," I say.

Last week before Nick left for Haven, he stopped by my office while I was going through the documents I had requested from Luke after our discussion two nights before. I didn't get too far into them before my door swung open to reveal my husband, leaning against the frame with a casual smirk.

"Hey there," Nick said with a hint of flirtation. "You got a man?"

"You're looking at him," I said without looking away from my computer.

"Oh, c'mon, Dee, have a little fun." Nick walked to the other side of my desk and sat on the edge.

"*Mi dispiace.*" I apologize, lifting my glasses on my head. I rubbed my eyes and leaned back in my chair to look at him. "I have a lot to get through."

"You will always have more stuff to get through. It will always going to be there," Nick says. I had been putting in extra hours since Kai decided to take another small leave from the company when Eileen gave birth last fall. "Let's go grab lunch. The break will be good for you."

I sigh. "Nick, I can't. I—"

"No, you're right." He sighed, standing up from my desk. "You're busy. I should go…What is that?"

I looked around the room to find the source of his question. What is he talking about? *"Cosa?"*

"That." Nick pointed at the large bouquet of roses and lilies on the conference table.

I shrugged, fiddling with the pen in my hands. "The courier dropped it off earlier." I hadn't given the bouquet much thought since my assistant brought it in this morning.

Nick pushed through the flowers, looking for a card, which I hadn't done yet. "What the fuck?" He held the card up in the air as he walked back to my desk, and I stood to meet him. *"Thanks for an unforgettable night. Can't wait for the next one,"* my husband read the card aloud. "Nina, *che cazzo è questo?"* *What the fuck is this?*

I was as confused as he seemed to be. I grabbed the card from his hands and read the words for myself. *What the fuck?* There wasn't a name, only an "x" where there should be a signature. I turned it over, looking for any indication of who they came from, but there wasn't one.

"The other night when you were 'working' with Luke?"

Did he just…Was he seriously implying I was having an affair with the guy I've been mentoring?

"Nick." I scoffed. "You cannot be serious."

"Well, what am I supposed to think, Nina? You work late every fucking night. You spend more time here or with him than you do at home. I can't remember the last time we had a meal together that wasn't business-related or with someone else there. And now, I walk in here to find this. I can't—*Non posso farlo,* Nina." Nick hung his head, pinching the bridge of his nose. He can't do this?

What does *that* mean?

"Nick, nothing happened. How could you even suggest that?" I took his face in my hands, not missing the way he leaned into my touch. *"Fossette,"* I said, trying to butter him up with the familiar nickname meaning *dimples.* "I know things have been hard with me stepping in for Kai this time. I know that. But you have to believe me. Nick, I would never—"

"You didn't even come home that night!" Nick ripped himself from me, taking two steps back. "I went to bed alone and woke up the same way. And you…You flitted off to fucking Chicago without a fucking care in the world."

There was nothing I could say to make this any better. He was too riled up, and most of his anger was my fault because of my focus on work over our family the past seven months.

Nick scoffed and walked out the door without saying goodbye. I tried to follow him, but my assistant Sydney intercepted me, blocking my path with a desperate plea to call the chairman. He had already called twice, but his impatience would have to wait. Pushing by her, I promised Sydney I would call him as soon as I talked to Nick. By the time I reached the garage, he was already gone.

My attention returns to Luke when he asks, "What flowers?" He seems genuinely confused, but I can't tell if it's an act or not.

I say, "The flowers you sent last week…to me."

"I didn't send you flowers." Luke chuckles. "I sent flowers to my…girlfriend, but I didn't send—Shit." Luke sighs. "Now that I think about it, she did get the wrong ones. They sent her a bouquet with roses and peonies and…"

I stop listening to him ramble because I don't need to hear anything else. It all makes sense now. Roses and peonies are staples in any bouquet Nick sends me. Nick must have sent me flowers on the same day Luke sent his girlfriend flowers, and the courier mixed up the two orders.

"Thank God." One of the weights on my chest dissipates.

"You seem pretty relieved that I didn't send you flowers."

A smile spreads across my lips. "You have no idea."

"Does this mean you can still help me?" Luke looks hopeful and I almost feel bad for what I'm about to do.

"Actually, I think it's best if Andy takes over indefinitely."

Luke groans at the same time my phone begins to ring. Turning it over, I see my brother's name. Weird…They're not supposed to have their phones until tomorrow.

"Kai?" I answer the call. "What are you—"

"Nina." Kai sounds exhausted on the other end. His voice is calm, too calm, and it sends a wave of anxiety rolling through me.

Something's wrong.

"Kai, what's wrong?" I ask.

"Have you…Have you heard from Nick?"

What kind of question is that? He knows I haven't heard from Nick. My face must say everything I'm thinking, because Luke doesn't hesitate to get the hell out of dodge, walking out of my office without me having to ask. When the door clicks behind him, I ask, "Why are you asking if I've heard from my husband? He's with *you*."

"Shit." My brother sighs.

"*Sputalo fuori*," I say between clenched teeth. *Spit it out.* "Enough of the fucking games, Kai. What is going on?"

"Nick is…missing."

My initial reaction is to laugh. This is a terrible joke. It's not even funny, because obviously, he's joking. What does that even mean? *Nick is missing.*

"That's funny, Kai." I chuckle. "Now, let me talk to my husband."

"Nin, I'm serious."

"Kai, this isn't funny anymore. Let me talk to my husband. *Proprio adesso*."

My brother remains silent on the other end.

"Right *now*, Kai. I'm not—"

"Nina, I'm sorry." He sighs. "I'm so sorry. I don't—I don't

know what happened."

"I'm on my way."

twenty-two

April 2028

"KAI JAMES VILLA, WHERE the *fuck* are you?" I walk through the door of our Haven home at seven o'clock on the dot the next morning. I wanted to be here sooner, but I had to pick Elena up and take her to Michaela's condo so her grandfather, Jimmy, could get her this morning. He and Tessa are taking her down to Florida for the week, which gives me time to figure out what's going on before I have to explain anything to her.

I struggled to hide my feelings from my daughter before I dropped her off at Michaela's, but it helped that Elena was exhausted from a long day at the zoo and then the park. I don't think she noticed something was wrong. At least, I hope not. When we walked into Michaela's, she crashed on the couch, but Michaela had just gotten off the phone with Finn and was doing her best not to freak out. The severity of the situation was starting to hit everyone. One of our own was missing and no one knew where he was. Before I left, Michaela told me she had plans to join me in Haven as soon as Jimmy arrived to get Elena.

Walking through the mudroom into the kitchen, I find all

the guys stationed at various places, a mixture of emotions playing across their faces—some pity, some fear, others sadness…and some a mix of all three. They look like hell, like they haven't slept in days.

Good.

"Does anyone want to tell me what is going on?"

"Nina—"

Alex cuts him off. "We don't know."

My glare doesn't waver as it moves from my brother to my brother-in-law. Alex is the reason they're all here in the first place. This week-long trip was for *his* bachelor party.

"You don't know?" Each word is perfectly enunciated.

Josh steps forward, hand extended like he's going to offer a comforting hand, but I shrug him off. I don't want their comfort. I want to know what is going on. I want facts.

"How long has he been gone? Where did he go? Did he leave a note? Someone doesn't just *disappear!*"

Finn takes hold of my hands and bends to be eye level with me. "Nina, we understand, and we've spent the past two days looking for him. But we can't—"

"Due giorni?" I yell. *Two days?* "Two fucking days! So, today makes it what…Three? You *idioti* waited *tre fottuti giorni* to tell me my husband is missing?"

This is unbelievable. Why would they wait three days to say something? What the fuck is wrong with them?

The silence afterward is maddening. The eight of them look at one another before my brother finally speaks up.

"I thought we would find him," Kai says. "I thought…Well, I just…I thought he went for a run or something and would be back. But…"

The weight of his unspoken words begins to settle on my heart. He doesn't have to finish the statement. I already know what comes next.

This isn't some cruel joke. Nick isn't going to pop out and

yell *Gotcha!* at any moment because he is...*missing.*

A heaviness gets lodged in my throat and the pounding of my heart drowns out any other sound. The air feels extremely hot, or maybe it's me? I claw at my burning skin as a weight crushes down on my chest. I have to get out of here. I can't... be here anymore. Turning on my heel, I make a beeline for my bedroom on the other side of the house.

Climbing the stairs of the turret, I ignore Kai's pleas. As soon as the door closes, I'm met with incredible stillness compared to the hurricane inside me. Closing my eyes, I let my head fall back against the door, my hand keeping a death grip on the knob. The coolness of the metal feels good against the burn beneath my skin, but it's not enough.

Moving through the sitting room into the bedroom, I open the balcony door and step outside as a cool breeze blows, and the beginnings of a snow flurry touch my skin. When my hands grasp the metal railing, I force myself to take a few slow, centering breaths. The burn settles into a simmer and the weight on my chest lifts enough that I can take a full breath.

Daylight has begun to rise behind the snow-covered peak in front of me. The house we bought after we sold the old family house in Haven sits further out in the wilderness, offering lush greenery and mountain views from every room. Our bedroom in particular has an unobstructed view of Mount Nebo, one of the trails Nick and I like to hike together. Taking one final deep breath, I glance back at Nebo and walk inside.

Everything inside appears to be in place. The bed is made, including the dark gray blanket draped across the foot of the bed that Nick *always* forgets to replace. Three receipts are stacked on top of each other on the dresser along with a few dollar bills, next to his belt coiled in a tight circle. Nothing stands out in the bathroom as unusual. A towel hangs on the hook next to the glass-walled shower and the vanity is clean and tidy with his everyday items resting in their typical order of usage. His clothes hang in the closet in the exact order they should be—color-coordinated with the shirt front facing to the left. My fingers graze the fabrics as I look around the rest of the closet to see if anything seems out of place. The only thing noticeable is the pair of shoes missing from the far right of the line they are laid out in—the pair he likes to wear when we go hiking.

"This is how we found it," Kai says when I come out of the closet. How long has he been here? I didn't even hear him come in. "Nina, I—"

"Kai, I love you, but right now...you are the last person I want to see."

My brother shoves a hand through his already disheveled hair. I'm so angry with him, but part of me feels bad for being so mad. I can tell he hasn't been getting much sleep or putting much effort into his appearance. Kai has never been one to go a day—even staying at home—without styling his hair and making sure his clothes are pressed.

He sighs. "I know you're mad. You have every right to be, but you have to believe me, Nin. I am so sorry, I—I didn't think he was missing. I never...Nina I—I didn't know what to do."

"You should've called me!" My anger deflates slightly when he looks up with wet eyes. I cross my arms over my chest. Taking a deep breath, I rub my face and try to piece together what led to this. I should ask him for the whole story without the rest of them around. I'll get a better answer without the constant interruptions. "Kai, what happened?"

Kai sits on the edge of the bed, letting his hands fall between his knees. "We were supposed to go out, but Nick...He didn't want to. He said he wasn't feeling up to it. Feeling under the weather. Frankly, he seemed off the whole time we've been here. He tried to hide it, but I could tell. We all could. He was trying to get through this weekend for Alex and—"

"And you didn't think to tell me this before?"

Kai sighs. "I was trying to be respectful of the no-phone thing."

I roll my eyes. Stupid fucking request.

"Anyway, Nick insisted we go without him. Was pretty adamant about it. Said he didn't want to put a damper on things. So, we went without him...Didn't get home until late that night because we went to Petra."

Petra Creek is a ski resort about an hour and a half north with some of the better skiing slopes that would still have snow this time of year.

Kai continues, pushing a hand through his brown hair. "I didn't see him when we got home, and I assumed he was in bed. Then Sunday came and we all slept in. When he wasn't here for breakfast, I assumed he was up and out for a run. But when he wasn't back by lunch, I checked on him, and...he wasn't here." He looks up at me, but I don't flinch, waiting for him to finish. "We started looking for him, everywhere, but no one has seen him. No one. He didn't leave a note, he didn't send a text, he didn't do anything...He was just gone."

My gaze narrows. "Someone doesn't just disappear, Kai."

"I know that."

"Why wouldn't you call me? My husband goes missing and you decide to keep it to yourself for three days? *Questa è una stronzata!*"

"I know it's *bullshit,* Nina. I know. But I thought we would find him. I thought he would show up. I didn't...I didn't think it was going to turn into this. I thought it would be something we'd all get to laugh about and never have to tell you. But yesterday it became pretty damn obvious that wasn't the case."

"Did you even go to the police?" I don't know why I ask, I'm sure I already know the answer. *"La polizia—"*

"We did." A different voice answers. Josh, Alex, and Finn stand at the end of the hallway connecting our bedroom and sitting room. Josh continues, "Alex and I went Monday morning."

"You sent *them?*" I ask my brother, and he shrugs. Am I dealing with idiots? Kai should know better than to let them go alone. "Why in the hell wouldn't you go? Beau would've known—"

"He's my brother, Nina!" Alex pipes up. "I wanted to be there."

"Where are the police now?" I repeat the question when they don't give me an answer.

"The deputy we spoke to said Nick has a right to go off if he wants," Josh says.

"Mi scusi?" I scoff. "I'm sorry. Did you say the police told you my husband can 'go off' if he wants to?"

"He's an adult," Alex says. "He has the right to disappear without telling anyone."

"Ha il diritto di scomparire?" I repeat my brother-in-law's words. "He has the right to leave his wife and his child?"

"There weren't any signs of foul play, Nina," Kai says. "Nothing indicates that something happened or went wrong. The only thing missing is Dad's old Jeep, the one Nick fixed up."

The 1985 Jeep C-7 Laredo Wrangler. Cream-colored with a dark brown fabric top. It was my dad's favorite car, but my mother was adamant he needed something more professional and reliable. Daddy tucked it away in the garage at the Haven house after that. Eventually, it broke down, but he couldn't bear the thought of parting with it, so the old car sat in the garage for years until Nick got his hands on it. It's been running like a champ ever since. Daddy would be happy to know someone is getting some use out of it.

"I cannot believe this," I huff, pulling my bottom lip between my teeth, and look up at the ceiling. How could they let it get this far? How could they go so long without telling me? Had they come to me earlier, we probably could've found him by now. The weight begins to build in my chest again, mounting with an ever-increasing pressure that feels like it's going to implode at any moment. "He didn't...He wouldn't. I can't—"

"Nina, breathe." My brother reaches for me, but I push him away.

"Don't. Don't fucking touch me."

With a shaky breath, I order them all out of the room. They try to argue, but I don't have time for arguments. When they're gone, I barricade myself in the bathroom, falling back against the door and finally letting the tears fall.

Nick is gone.

I'm in Haven because my husband is missing. He's been missing for at least three days, maybe four. No one seems to know for sure.

The only thing that keeps coming to mind is how we left things the last time we saw each other. We were too busy fighting and now I can't remember if we told each other we loved each other.

Did we? I don't know.

The whole fight was stupid, a simple misunderstanding that I now have answers to. The problem wasn't just the flowers though, it was a culmination of all the other small things that led up to him finding the card and the flowers. The pot had finally boiled over and now I may never get the chance to make it up to him...

"Nina, what a surprise!" As I walk into the sheriff's station, the older woman at the front desk lights up. On a normal day, I would stand and chat with Flo for a few minutes, but not today. I can't even bring myself to give her much of a smile as I walk up to the desk.

"Where is Beau?"

"Well, he's in a…meetin' right now. But I'm sure he'll—"

I don't wait for her to finish, marching past the front desk straight to the office door labeled *Sheriff Beau Turner.* Whatever *meeting* he's in is going to have to wait. Flo calls after me, but I don't hesitate to open the door without knocking. A shriek sounds from behind the desk, and a pair of wide green eyes look around the bare-backed blonde to meet my gaze.

"I am so glad this is what my tax dollars go to."

"Nina! What the hell?" Beau scrambles to cover himself and the girl does the same, jumping away from him. She collects her belongings, tripping over her feet and running out of the office. This isn't the first time I've caught him in a compromising position, but it will be the last if he doesn't get his ass in gear and do something to find my husband. "You can't just—"

"Honestly, Beau, now is not the time for your shit."

Beau Turner is the current sheriff of Spruce County, headquartered right here in our town of Haven, Colorado. He is the youngest sheriff elected to office in the jurisdiction's history. While Beau has proved himself to be a great leader in the community, he wouldn't have been elected three years ago without our support—something he, luckily, hasn't forgotten. It's nothing I like to hold over his head, but in this instance, I'm going to do just that.

Beau shuts the door and finishes buttoning his shirt, straightening it out, and rolling up the sleeves. He adjusts the belt buckle and briefly stretches his knees before falling into his chair behind the desk. He motions for me to do the same, but I continue to stand in the middle of the room.

"Are you ready or do you need a few more minutes?" I ask, brow raised.

"What can I do for you, Mrs. Villa?"

"Cut the shit, Beau. You have a missing person's case you're four days behind on."

"Excuse me?" It's his turn to raise a brow. "And tell me, *who* is missing?"

"My husband."

I can visibly see his heart stop and start back up again. The color drains from his face and his green eyes look like they might bulge from his head. His mouth opens and closes.

"Two days ago, my brother-in-law and his cousin came in to file a missing person report. However, it would seem one of your deputies told them the person probably needed some time...some space. Not to worry too much, because they'd come back when they're ready."

Beau scrubs his hands down his face with a heavy sigh. "Nick is—"

"Missing. Has been since either Saturday or Sunday, the guys aren't completely sure."

"Nina—"

"While you've been too busy screwing little whores in the office, he has been god knows where for *days.*"

Beau straightens in his chair. "And why are *you* telling me this now?"

"Because I had no idea! Because not a single one of them picked up the damn phone until last night to tell me. They've been off on their own trying to find him without any help from you guys—the ones who can do something about it."

Beau curses under his breath.

"You want my advice?" I ask, waiting until I have his full attention again. "Find my husband or find a new job, Sheriff."

twenty-three

April 2028

I CLOSE MY EYES for a brief moment, pulling myself up on one of the kitchen island barstools. It has been a long two and a half days of sunup-to-well-past-sundown searches resulting in *nothing*. Even after the search parameters were extended, there have been no signs of Nick. This morning is the first time since Wednesday night we haven't gathered to continue the search. Beau told everyone to stay home, we'd regroup tomorrow after some time to rest and recoup.

Our house has been filled with people—family, friends, police, searchers—but I still feel alone. There's a gaping hole where Nick should be, and it's only getting worse as more time ticks by. I'm doing my best not to think the worst. Not to let the nightmares win. But every day, that little voice in the back of my mind gets a little louder.

It's been a week since Nick went missing, and three days since the police finally started their search. Our house has become the official headquarters of the search party. Beau wanted to start within our immediate radius because no one had any other ideas of where to start. Even when I pointed out Nick's hiking shoes were missing, Beau was skeptical of changing the course. We don't know which trail he went to—there are at least seven within a twenty-mile radius of us—and if he is trying to find his way back home from one of the trails nearby, at least rescuers would find him.

Every morning before we leave the house to pick up where we ended the day before, Beau begs me to stay behind. On the off chance Nick shows up, I should be home. I should be waiting for him. Every day, I say no. I refuse to sit around doing nothing while my husband is missing. And every day, Beau meets my *no* with a resounding sigh before he rolls his eyes and opens the passenger door of his SUV, grumbling on his way to the other side. Sheriff Beau Turner is stuck with me whether he likes it or not.

Sitting at the kitchen island, the coffee mug is hot in my hands when I lift the rim to my lips and take a long sip of the burning liquid. The heat trails its way down my system, warming parts of me still cold from being out in the elements the past few days. Setting it back down on the marbled counter, I open my eyes to find my adopted sister, Elizabeth, standing on the other side of the island. Her brown eyes are full of pity.

"Stop looking at me like that," I say.

"Like what?" Elizabeth asks.

"*That.*"

The same way everyone looks at me lately and I hate it. The only person who hasn't been treating me like I might break any second is Beau, but I think he's scared to. I don't want anyone's pity. I want my husband. I want my best friend back.

"Everyone looks at me like that. I don't need you doing it, too."

"Nin, I know you want to find Nick—we all do—but you can't find him if you're not taking care of yourself. You should rest."

"Rest?" I scoff. "Elizabeth, how can I rest? My husband is

out there! Who knows where he is or if he's hurt or lost or..."

"Or what, Nina?"

I refuse to say it. I refuse to believe Nick is dead. He can't be. We haven't been able to fix things...I haven't been able to fix things.

"We're going to find him, okay?" Elizabeth reaches her hand out toward mine, but I pull away. "But please...You're not going to be any help to Nick or Beau if you don't take care of yourself."

Tears begin to blur my vision. "This is all my fault."

"Your fault? Nina, why would you say that? This is not your fault."

"We had a fight right before he left." I sigh. "I can't help but think that maybe if he wouldn't have gone off alone if we didn't—"

"Nina." Elizabeth cuts me off. "A fight doesn't make this your fault."

It only makes it partly my fault.

I take a final drink of my coffee before pushing the mug toward her. "I have to go. I'm meeting Beau."

"Nina—"

"I heard you, Elizabeth," I say without looking back. "I heard you."

Because it's a Sunday morning, Beau and I will be the only ones in the station other than the one deputy who is officially on duty. Pulling into the parking lot, Beau climbs out of his SUV wearing civilian clothes—jeans and a maroon button-up—but his badge still clings to his hip. I can see it from here. I park next to him and before I can even turn off my car, he opens the door, like he has every time we've been together lately. I can't remember the last time someone opened the door for me who wasn't hired to do so.

"Thank you," I say, taking his hand and stepping down from the driver's seat. He closes the door and motions for me to lead the way inside.

"Get any sleep?" Beau asks, opening the station door.

"Did you?"

We both know the answer.

"Hi, guys!" Deputy Johnson calls from his desk in the corner of the bullpen.

I stifle a yawn and wave toward him, walking straight to Beau's office.

"You want a coffee?" Beau asks, earning an enthusiastic nod from both me *and* Johnson. "I wasn't asking you, Johnson. I was asking her."

"Well, I thought if you were offering…"

Beau rolls his eyes, and I can't help but chuckle, leaning against the wall outside the locked office. The sheriff grumbles to himself, pouring three cups of coffee and walking one over to Johnson. "Not one word," he mumbles when he greets me with my cup.

"I wasn't gonna say a thing." I bite down on my lips, trying to hide a smirk. I've enjoyed my time with the sheriff and his deputies, despite the reason *why* we're together. They are like a breath of fresh air compared to the stifling fog inside my house.

"The chopper is out," Beau says from behind me when we walk into the office.

That's news to me. I thought everyone was taking the day off.

Beau closes the door and comes to sit at his desk. "The guys wanted something to do, so they went ahead of us to see what they could find."

"Find anything?"

"Nothing unusual."

Of course not.

Beau keeps talking, but I don't hear him. I'm too busy racking my brain for any information over the past ten years that could help us find Nick. When we sold the old Haven house four years ago and moved, it put us further off the grid, which we love, but also means there are any number of places he could've gone, and we've combed through almost all of them.

"Nina." Beau sighs, catching my attention again. "We need to talk about something."

"Isn't that what we've been doing?"

Beau tries not to roll his eyes, sipping his coffee before he cracks his knuckles and plants folded hands on the desk. "It's been a week, Nina..."

"I'm aware."

"...and it's still pretty cold at night and conditions on some of these mountains are less than optimal. We have to be realistic about what we're going to find." Beau clears his throat when I don't say anything. "We may be walking into a recovery, not a rescue."

Despite knowing this was coming, hearing the words doesn't hurt any less. I don't want to hear that they think Nick is gone—not just gone missing but *gone.* They haven't found anything pointing to that and I know he's not gone...He can't be.

"Beau, he's not dead."

"Nina, we need to be realistic—"

"You *just* started looking for him! You are not giving up on him. Not yet. You need more money? More resources? Fine. Tell me what you need, and I'll make it fucking happen. But I don't want to hear any more excuses. You have a lot of time to make up and a lot of ground to fucking cover. We are not giving up on him."

Beau doesn't say anything, only takes a deep breath, maintaining his composure.

"Start by calling your guys in first thing tomorrow. Gonna be overtime? Fine. I'll pay the difference. Need to feed them? Great, I'll do that too." I stand from the chair and plant my hands on his desk, leaning over him. "In case you've forgotten, Sheriff Turner, I'm the reason your ass is even in this chair. If it wasn't for me and my family, Nick included, you'd still be a beat cop. Or have you already forgotten?"

"I am well aware of—"

"I don't care what it takes, Beau. You bring him home. Do you understand me?"

Beau nods.

"Good, then I'll see you bright and early, sunshine. And you better bring your A-game."

twenty-four

April 2028

THE TRAIL UP TO the peak of Mount Achor is my favorite when I need a little space—a little me time—but moving added about forty-five minutes to the already hour-and-a-half drive. Still, after the week I've had, some alone time on the trail seems the perfect way to clear my head. Approaching the trailhead, I notice the only other vehicle in the lot on the dead-end road and my heart stops. There's no way. I pull up behind the old Wrangler parked at the far end—cream body, brown top. My body buzzes as I slowly step out of my Wrangler. Despite my mind yelling at my hand to let go of the door so I can walk forward, it doesn't, maintaining a death grip on the silver-colored body. I'm scared to approach it. Afraid of what I might find.

"What are you doing out here?" I whisper.

Why hasn't anyone reported this being out here? They put a BOLO out on it. Surely someone had seen it and thought it was suspicious a car had been sitting there for days. Then again...not many people hike Achor, especially right now, when it could still have snow in some places. It's one of the harder trails and not most people's first pick. Maybe no one has come out here recently.

I dial the number of the first person who comes to mind. The call rings and rings until finally, "Nina?"

Walking up to the old Wrangler, I finally look inside the window, at least if there's something in there, I won't be alone (per se).

Nothing appears out of place—it's clean as a whistle, the way Nick always keeps it. His Boston University sweater is tossed on the passenger seat, which seems weird. He definitely would've folded it first.

"Beau, I found something," I say.

"Where are you?" I can hear him sit up in his chair on the other end of the line as I tug on the handle and freeze when it opens. *Did Nick leave it unlocked?* As if he's standing right next to me, Beau says, "Don't touch anything."

He's right. If there is something in here, I don't want to compromise it.

"Where are you?"

"Achor."

"Achor? Shit!" He sighs. "That's out of my jurisdiction. Just...Nina, give me a few minutes, I have to call Puck County. Do you see any sign of him?"

"Only a sweater."

"Don't touch anything, Nina. Wait for one of us to get there."

I almost snap back at him "I'm aware of how this works," but don't because I almost *did* touch something. Without acknowledging him, I start to end the call, but he calls out to me. I sigh. "What, Beau?"

"This is good." I can almost picture him nodding as he gathers his stuff to run out the door. "It's a sign. It gives us something to go off now. It narrows down the location."

I hang up without saying anything. This might give us an

idea of where Nick went, but that doesn't make it a good sign. It's been over a week, and who knows what the weather has been like out here compared to back home, where it's been on the mild side. Climbing back into my Jeep, I stare at the old car, almost willing Nick to pop out with a laugh and a *Gotcha!*

But he doesn't.

No matter how hard I wish for it…it never happens.

Why would he come here? He's only been to Achor once (maybe twice) with me, usually preferring to stick to the trails closer to home. He could have gone anywhere but chose the trail he knew the least—one of the hardest ones. Why?

There hasn't been any sign of life in the last thirty minutes. How much longer until someone gets here? I pick up my phone to call Beau when I see a black F-150 creeping down the highway before it pulls into the lot. *Puck County Sheriff* is printed on the side.

An older man climbs out of the front seat and settles a cream-colored cowboy hat on his white hair as his feet hit the ground. Wide, black aviator glasses hide his eyes, resting on his nose above a white mustache. "Mrs. Villa?" he asks when he approaches me, and I nod. "Sheriff Rhett Wilson, it's nice to meet you, ma'am."

"You can call me Nina."

"Turner over in Spruce told me a bit about what's going on, said we have your missing husband's vehicle here."

"Yes, sir."

Sheriff Wilson points toward the old Jeep and I nod. "That's an '87, isn't it? Real good condition."

Is he really commenting on the car right now?

Why am I surprised? Everyone does when they see it. Daddy always loved it and was so excited when Nick fixed it up during our first summer together in Haven. It gave him one final opportunity to drive it before…Well, you know.

I frown. There's something about this man I don't like, but I can't quite put my finger on it. Or maybe I'm just annoyed he's too busy being enamored with the vintage car instead of worrying about the case.

"'85, actually."

"Oh, right. Said that in the BOLO." Wilson nods, walking back to his truck and digging through until he finds a pair of gloves. He continues searching before he looks over his shoulder. "You have a spare set of keys?"

"It's open. I accidentally pulled the handle when I saw it."

He pulls the gloves over his hands and says, "Well, let's take a look, shall we?"

Before he starts to search the vehicle, another car pulls into the lot, and the sight brings a wave of relief crashing over me. *Spruce County Sheriff* it reads on the side of the SUV and Beau doesn't waste time. He jumps out, still dressed in civilian clothes from earlier at the station. Rhett says something like "Nice of you to join us," but Beau ignores him, beelining for me. "You okay?"

I nod, I'm just grateful he's here. I don't think I could handle this alone with Sheriff Wilson.

"Anything, Rhett?" Beau calls when we approach the vehicle.

"Clean as a whistle!" Sheriff Wilson yells from inside the cab.

The way Nick liked it.

Beau pulls the Jeep's BOLO up on his phone. "The license plate matches, so we know it's theirs."

"But we don't have anything connecting it to him."

I roll my eyes. "Who else would have driven it out here?"

"There were a handful of other guys with him last weekend, huh?"

"You cannot be serious." I huff, earning a warning look from Beau. "Yes, eight or nine of them, including Nick."

"Well, which is it? Eight or nine?"

I look at Beau, who pleads with his eyes. "Nine."

"So, any of them could've—"

"No, any of them could *not* have brought this out here! The others are all accounted for, the only one not is my fucking husband, Sheriff Wilson. And the sweatshirt sitting on the passenger seat is one of *his.* That leads me to believe *he* was the one driving the vehicle."

Sheriff Wilson shares a look with Beau, who offers him a small shrug, but I see the smirk tugging at the corner of his mouth. For someone who's just as much at fault for this, he's enjoying the show a little too much.

"If you check the glove compartment, you might find his wallet. He used to leave it there when on the trail." Even though I always told him not to.

Wilson walks around to the passenger side, opens the compartment, shoves his hand as far as it will go, and comes out...empty. A second later, his eyes narrow toward the center of the cab. "Wait a minute. I might've found something." Sheriff Wilson's words sink like a rock in my stomach. That can't be good...Can it? I look at Beau, but he hasn't taken his eyes off Wilson's back since he dove back into the car. The older man comes out and drops something into the palm of his hand, examining it before he encloses the object in a tight fist. "Can you describe your husband's wedding ring, Mrs. Villa?"

When I look at Beau for confirmation, he nods, urging me to answer the question. "It's a silver band, with a stripe of black titanium. The titanium would be scratched to hell because—"

"Can you think of any reason your husband would leave his ring in the car?" Wilson lifts the object he'd been toying with moments before, holding the circle between his thumb and index finger. "Seems a little suspicious, don't you think, Turner?"

Beau stands with his hands on his hips, chewing on the thought. His gaze moves from me to the ring and back. "Does Nick normally take his ring off to go hiking?"

"After I got mad when he scratched it up, he started swapping it out with a silicone band," I say.

"Sounds more like a classic getaway, if you ask me." Wilson chuckles.

"Well nobody asked you." My words are laced with enough venom to drop an elephant if I choose to strike, but Beau steps in front of me, shielding the other sheriff.

"Nina," he warns, pushing me back a few paces. "Keep your thoughts to yourself, huh? This isn't just you and me talking. This is a different ballgame now." I refuse to answer, but I know he's right. I can't lose my cool. If I want to find Nick, I need to keep it together, but as soon as we do, all bets are off. "So, no wallet, right?" Beau asks, turning back to Wilson who shakes his head. "Thank God," Beau says, earning a confused look from me. What does that mean? "Look, if Nick has his wallet and ends up in a hospital or something, they can identify him."

The older sheriff looks out over the tree line across the road. "Or if someone finds him on the—"

His words falter when Beau shoots him a glare that says *Shut up.* Like I don't already know what Sheriff Wilson is thinking. It's been a week, and assuming the weather hasn't been the best, someone is more likely to find Nick's *remains* on the trail. And if he happens to have his wallet on him, we won't have to rely on physical appearance, or what's left of it, to identify him.

"How soon can we organize a search of the area?" Beau asks.

"I'll make a few calls," Sheriff Wilson says, returning to

his truck. "I can probably get everyone out here first thing in the morning. Gonna have to call State now that it's crossing county lines."

"I called them already, got ahold of Warren."

"Just what we want. State breathing down our necks."

Beau shares a knowing chuckle with his counterpart before he looks at me. "Stay put, I'm gonna make a few calls, too."

A bird calls from somewhere up the mountain, catching my attention. Another squawks in reply before a black cloud swarms the sky as the flock takes flight from the trees. I watch them until a small movement below catches in my peripheral. My gaze sweeps across the tree line, following the dirt path through the overgrown field and a small opening in the tree line, but I don't see anything. There's absolutely no movement, everything is deadly still, which seems…odd. Come to think of it, there hasn't been much movement or even the normal sounds of nature the entire time I've been here. Those birds are the first sign of life I've noticed all day. The wilderness calls to me like a siren song, but something tells me not to go. And this time, I heed the warning.

A touch on my shoulder sends me five feet in the air, my fist poised and ready, but I stop when I realize who it is.

"Whoa, there!" Beau puts his hands up. "I didn't mean to scare you."

"Sorry! Sorry, I was just—Sorry."

Sheriff Wilson rejoins us. "Alright, folks, we're all set to start first thing in the morning. Turner, I assumed you'd want to be here, too, so I told the guys we'd have some extra hands in the field."

"You'll have me and as many deputies as I can spare," Beau confirms.

"And me," I say.

Wilson looks between me and Beau before a smile creeps up on his face. He rubs at his stubbled jaw. "I appreciate your enthusiasm, Mrs. Villa, but we don't need you out there getting hurt and causin' any—"

"I said, I'll be here. I've been on every one of the searches up until now and that's not going to change because we're in *Puck* County."

"That's right, you are in Puck County, and I don't know what kind of show y'all run over in Spruce, but we don't let civilians run the roost around here."

"Alright," Beau says, stepping between us. "You both can put the rulers away. Rhett, if Nina wants to come along on the search, she can stick with me. That's worked out fine the past few days anyway. And Nin"—Beau turns to me with a tight-lipped smile—"just try to behave, okay? We're making progress. It may not seem like it, but this is good. We're one step closer to finding him."

This may be one step closer to finding him, but in what capacity?

twenty-five

April 2028

"IS THIS PUNISHMENT FOR working too much? For going *back* to work?" I look up at the bathroom ceiling, clutching the edges of the bathtub. It has been four days since the discovery of the Jeep at Mount Achor trailhead and we've had three full days of search activity on the mountain. But tonight, a combined decision was made between Sheriff Wilson and Sergeant James Warren, the leading State detective, to end all search efforts. Beau tried to convince them to give it one more day, but they couldn't be swayed. Even if they were giving up…I wasn't.

I've already decided to ask Beau for his help tomorrow. First, we both need a shower and some sleep—two things we haven't gotten much of in the last few days.

Stepping into the house earlier, I dragged my tired and sore body to my bedroom without a word to the others. I stripped out of the clothes caked in sweat, blood, and dirt from hours on the mountain and climbed into the bathtub. The hot water felt amazing against my muscles, and I wondered why I hadn't done this sooner.

Most of the guys from Alex's bachelor party have left already. Cole, Jeremy, and Elijah left yesterday morning. Dean left last night when we returned from Achor, apologizing profusely the whole way out the door I pushed him out of. I appreciated their help but having that many people under one roof was enough to drive me insane. The family alone was enough to send me into a spiral half the time. Nick would have loved it. He always loved having everyone together. His dad says Nick is like his mom in that way. Don't get me wrong, I love our family, but sometimes they can be…a lot.

"He isn't gone," I say to the empty room, but I'm not sure who I'm trying to convince with my words—me or the big guy upstairs. "So, why can't I find him?"

The room remains silent and still. Despite my desperate pleas for answers and help—not just tonight but this entire time—they go unanswered, leaving me feeling helpless and hopeless. A heaviness settles in my chest as a sob builds. The warmth in my eyes begins to blur my vision. Thickness coats my throat.

My phone buzzes against the vanity.

Who the fuck? It can't be Elena. She's still in Florida, it's too late for her to be awake, and I already talked to her earlier. She will be arriving in Haven with her grandfather in two days, and I'm no closer to finding answers about her dad today than last week. The thought of my impending conversation with her makes me sick to my stomach.

The call ends but picks back up immediately.

Climbing out of the tub, I pull my robe over my shoulders and pick up the phone.

Beau Turner.

"This better be important, Beau."

"Nina…went back…I…trail." His voice cuts out every few words and it makes my heart race. Is he still out on the trail? It's well past ten o'clock, he shouldn't be out there. He was supposed to be right behind me when I left earlier.

"Beau, you're cutting out. What's wrong?"

The call goes dead and when I try to call him back, it only rings until it reaches his voicemail. I curse under my breath. How am I supposed to make out what he was saying or know where to find him? My phone vibrates again, but this time it's a text message.

Beau Turner

We found something.

My heart drops.

They found something? What does he mean they found something? I thought the search was off.

Shedding my robe, I run to the closet to pull on jeans and Nick's sweater from the Jeep. We got the car back this morning after the State police finished running tests. They said they would have the results by the end of the week, but it was only slightly comforting to know they hadn't found any initial traces of blood or a struggle inside the vehicle. Straightening out my bun, I pull on boots as another text comes through.

Beau Turner

Lake.

That single word stops me in my tracks.
The lake.
They found something…in the lake?

The parking lot where the search camp had been set up is clear, minus a few remaining vehicles. Two have searchlights on, lighting up the dark lot, and I can see four figures huddled over the hood of another.

Beau glances over his shoulder when I call his name, motioning for me to join them.

I recognize Sheriff Wilson, Sergeant Warren, and Deputy Max Johnson, one of Beau's deputies, as the other men with him, and they all take turns looking my way. Their expressions are unreadable, unlike Beau's—or maybe I've gotten better at reading him.

A paper map is spread out over the hood of the police truck with a large red X drawn near the lake, but not the one I thought Beau was talking about.

"Nayda?" I ask. Lake Nayda is a smaller lake at least half a mile east of the trailhead, past the dead end of the highway.

"Recognize these?" Beau doesn't waste time, pointing to the evidence bags on the hood. Each one contains a separate item: a phone, a shoe, and a torn piece of fabric. Even from this distance and the shadows cast by the lights, I recognize the shoe as one-half of the missing pair from our closet. And if I tapped on the screen—if the phone works—I'm sure there will be a photo of me and Elena staring back.

I nod.

"You the know the code for the phone?"

"It works?"

Beau lifts the phone and taps the screen through the translucent bag. Sure enough, it lights up with the photo of Elena and me from last June, bright smiles on our faces. However, a large crack down the center stems from an impact point near the top right corner.

"I thought you said it was in the lake."

"Beau and I found it a couple hundred yards south of Nayda," Max says, motioning down the road.

"It was the only place I hadn't personally looked," Beau adds. "The only place *we* didn't look. I didn't realize it until

Max and I were about to pull out and I just had this feeling… We went to do one final sweep. It reflected off our flashlight near the first bend."

"1-0-3-0," I say, still staring at the screen that has since darkened.

My birthday.

Beau types in the number and the screen opens.

"Well, that confirms it's his," Sheriff Wilson says, rubbing his chin.

"Because the photo didn't?" I ask, earning a sigh from Beau and a glare from Wilson.

Sergeant Warren rolls his eyes but continues the conversation, trying to ignore the tension between me and Sheriff Wilson. "Why was it over at Nayda? Does he usually go out that way?"

"This is only the second time he's been out here. He doesn't usually hike here," I say.

Max curses under his breath and gives Beau a worried glance, but Beau's focus remains on the phone. His finger skims across the screen as he searches through it. "The last message to go out is…a failed message to Nina." His eyes meet mine before he extends the bag toward me and I only look at it, glancing between the phone and him. I'm scared to know what the message says, but Beau nods, pushing the bag into my hands.

I look down at the green bubble with a bright red exclamation point beside it indicating it was undelivered.

Dee, I'm at Achor.

I'm sorry. I overreacted about those damn flowers. I've overreacted about a lot of things lately. This isn't us.

I know I'm not supposed to have my phone, but I don't care. I miss you. I need to hear your voice. I'll call you tonight when I get back.

I love you.

Not Delivered

I smoother the sob that escapes my lips, trying not to break here and now, and look up to meet Beau's sympathetic eyes. My bottom lip trembles and I pull it between my teeth to settle it, but it doesn't work as tears build in the corners of my eyes.

"Let's give her a minute," Beau suggests, beginning to usher the others away from me.

"N-no." I clear my throat and dab my eyes. Pinching the bridge of my nose, I take a settling breath. I will not break right here in front of them. I can't. "No. What else did you find?"

"Nina—"

My voice raises when I have to repeat my question. I won't like whatever it is, but it doesn't matter. Now is not the time to tiptoe around my feelings. "What else did you find?"

The sergeant picks up the third bag with the piece of fabric and hands it over to me. "You recognize this?"

"I mean, it could be from one of his shirts. He has a few long sleeves this color, but I don't know for sure." Lifting the bag into the light, there's a splotch of something darker on the fabric. "What is this?"

"We need to test it, but it looks like blood." Beau doesn't sugarcoat it this time.

"This was with the phone?"

"Not far from it."

Gone are the tears and hurt, replaced by pure anger. "We have been *here* for days and you've only now found this shit? You were about to call this off! No, you *did* call it off. You gave up before you'd searched everything!" Beau tries to interrupt me, but I hold my finger up. "Shut up, Beau. Not one more word from you or I'll have your job before the sun rises in the fucking east."

His mouth clamps shut.

I toss the evidence bag back on the hood and meet each one of their stares. "My advice? Figure out what is going on. I am done with the fucking games. I want to know what happened to my husband and where he went. And if you can't do that, then you all better start looking for a new career path."

It's barely past five in the morning when I walk back into the house. The officers plan to do a final extensive search of the area later today, but they need to get back to their respective offices and make a few calls first. Beau had released Max from duty but told him to be on standby. They'd probably need him, considering the amount of ground that would need to be covered before the end of the day. Sheriff Wilson tried to argue everyone needed to get some rest before the search—no one would be any good if they were exhausted. Sergeant Warren smirked and shook his head before he patted Beau on the back and climbed into his SUV. Wilson tried to reason with Beau, with me, but the plans were clear, and they weren't changing. Before I left, I told the sheriff of Puck County that if he didn't want to do his job, I would find someone who wanted to. I was done playing by his rules, it was time we played by mine.

"You're up early," Kai says, entering the kitchen. I can hear his muscles pop and stretch, a few cracks here and there, as he stretches out and rubs his eyes.

"Just got home." I fill a mug with fresh coffee and lean back against the counter, inhaling the scent.

"You just…You just got home?" My brother's mouth hangs open. "Nina, please tell me they didn't—"

"It wasn't him." I take a deep breath, another inhale of the rich, warm aroma emanating from the mug in my hands. "It was his stuff, and his shirt had blood on it."

Looking up to the ceiling, I chew on the inside of my cheek, willing the tears to *go away*, but this time they refuse to retreat. "What am I supposed to do, Kai? He's my best friend. My other half. I don't…I can't do this without him."

"You won't have to," Kai reassures me, but he hasn't seen what I've seen. "We'll find him, Nin. We will."

I swallow back the thickness coating my throat and finally look at him. "I hate you."

"I know. I hate me, too."

"This is all your fault." A sniffle. "If you had just—You should've called me."

"I know that, Nina. I never thought…Had I thought it would turn out like this, had I thought he was *actually* missing, I would have called. The second I realized it. But none of us thought that's what was happening."

In my heart, I know Kai didn't mean any malicious intent by what's happened. He would never do anything that he thought might potentially harm Nick or me or our family, but it doesn't make the sting hurt any less. It doesn't bring Nick back. Finding out the truth sooner may not have changed anything, but the thought still plagues my mind.

TRANSCRIPT OF RECORDED INTERVIEW
WITH DAVINA VILLA

Unnecessary sounds, such as "um" and "uh," have been omitted from the following statement for the purpose of making the statement easier to read.

Between Sergeant James WARREN (State), Sheriff Beau TURNER (Spruce County), and Davina VILLA

On June 9, 2028, 08:05
Location: Spruce County Sheriff's Office

WARREN: Just for the record, Mrs. Villa, you are aware this conversation is being recorded?

VILLA: Yes.

WARREN: Great, thank you for meeting me this morning.

VILLA: Mhmm.

WARREN: And thank you, Sheriff Turner, for allowing me to occupy your space for the past few weeks.

TURNER: Of course.

WARREN: Look, I'm going to cut to the chase…I think we all know this case has come pretty much to a halt. We haven't found anything that could be considered "evidence" since the items Sheriff Turner located at Lake Nayda, and there are no leads.

VILLA: So, we're giving up?

WARREN: We're not giving up…We're just in limbo.

VILLA: a.k.a., giving up. Just call it what it is, James.

TURNER: Nina.

WARREN: No, it's okay. (sighs) I understand this isn't what you want to hear, Mrs. Villa, but unfortunately, not even you can play God in these circumstances.

VILLA: (scoffs)

TURNER: Nina.

WARREN: I just mean not everything has a price to be paid. Sometimes things are completely out of control and no amount of money or prayer will make it right.

TURNER: (sighs) You're not helping your cause, Sarge.

WARREN: (to Turner) I'm not, am I? (to Villa) I am truly sorry. I know this isn't what you wanted to hear, but without sufficient evidence, I cannot, in good conscience, keep pursuing this case. We have to redirect resources toward higher-priority cases.

(Background noise)

TURNER: Nina—

VILLA: What should I tell my daughter, Sergeant Warren? When she asks me where her father is and why the police aren't looking for him…what would you like me to tell her?

(Background noise)

WARREN: (clears throat) I—I…

TURNER: The truth. You tell Elena the truth.

VILLA: Do you have children, Mr. Warren?

WARREN: No.

VILLA: I suspected as much. Do you have siblings? How about your parents? Are they still alive?

WARREN: They are.

VILLA: And siblings?

WARREN: A brother.

VILLA: Great. So, you understand my dilemma here? I have an almost three-year-old waiting for her daddy to come home, and an entire *family* waiting for his return. What, Mr. Warren, would you like me to tell them is the reason he is, in fact, not coming home?

WARREN: (sighs) I truly am sorry. I hoped we wouldn't have to have this conversation, but my hands are tied. I hoped when

Sheriff Turner found those articles belonging to your husband, it would help lead us to the truth about what happened. Unfortunately, all it gave us was more questions.

VILLA: The case has gone cold?

WARREN: No. It is now being considered a "Missing Person Presumed Dead" case.

VILLA: Spell it out for me like I'm a toddler, Sergeant. What exactly does that mean?

WARREN: It means we're in limbo. The case isn't cold, but it's not closed, either. If something we deem to be reliable comes in, we will look into it, but until that happens, we won't be pursuing it any further.

VILLA: Right…And you'd be willing to explain this to the family?

WARREN: Yes.

VILLA: Great. I'll get them on the phone.

WARREN: Now?

VILLA: You want to do this again?

TURNER: (sighs) Fucking hell.

WARREN: No.

VILLA: Great, I'll be back in a few minutes.

(Door opens)

(Door closes)

WARREN: (to Turner) I don't know how you do it, Beau.

TURNER: What?

WARREN: Deal with her on a daily basis.

TURNER: (laughs) You think that was bad? You should've seen her the first day she walked in here.

WARREN: You're gonna keep an eye on her, right?

TURNER: Of course.

WARREN: I'm worried about her.

TURNER: You and me both, Sarge. (sighs)

WARREN: I can't quite put my finger on it, but there's more going on here, Beau.

TURNER: What do you mean?

WARREN: Haven't you noticed that whenever we get one step closer to figuring it out, we get set three steps back?

TURNER: You think we have a mole?

WARREN: (shuffles) Something's going on.

TURNER: (sighs) Fuck.

WARREN: Don't tell her. Not until we know more. If she finds out someone in the department might be involved…she'll have *all* our heads.

TURNER: I can't lie to her, James.

WARREN: Don't let your personal feelings get in the way of doing your job, Beau.

TURNER: What are you talking about?

WARREN: (background noise) You really want this part recorded?

END OF TRANSCRIPT.

twenty-six

October 2028

"**WHERE ARE YOU COMING** from?" Elizabeth asks when I walk through the door. My sister flew into Colorado this morning with her adopted daughter, Brie; Brie's friend, Blake; and Nick's cousin, Michaela. They are in town to celebrate our birthdays—mine is tomorrow, Elizabeth's is two days after—and Halloween. They even talked my brother's wife, Eileen, into making it a girls' trip. And while they did so under the guise of wanting to celebrate, I know part of the reason is to check on me after what should have been the fourth wedding anniversary of our vow renewal two years after getting married at a courthouse in New York. Thursday was a hard day, but it was nothing like what I felt on May 18, on what should have been our sixth wedding anniversary.

Eileen arrives tomorrow with my nieces Ophelia and Fallon, just in time for my birthday dinner and Halloween the next day. Ophelia was ecstatic her mother was letting her miss three whole days of school and had called me every day since they made the plans, updating me on her costume, which Eileen was making.

Did I want to spend the next five days entertaining people? No, but I knew it would be good for Elena. They finally sold me on the idea by saying the kids could go trick-or-treating with Brie and Blake in town while the adults went to dinner at the club where Eileen and I could enjoy some kid-free time.

I don't think Elena likes being in Colorado as much without Nick. I think she feels alone, even with me here and the few friends she has made in preschool. It's not the same as having her dad here to play with her or her cousins down the street. We're halfway across the country from the rest of the family, and seeing how it affects her breaks my heart. I don't want to move back to New York or Winchester—especially Winchester—but if it means doing the best thing for her…I'd do it.

"Oh, I had to run by the station. Talk to Beau," I say, pulling a water bottle from the fridge.

"You do that a lot?" she asks with a raised brow.

"I check in with him a few times a week." I shrug. What's the big deal? Beau has been helping me continue the search for Nick.

Elizabeth sighs, eyes narrowed in thought. She returns to the meal she's been preparing. *Thank God.* I was not in the mood to explain my meetings with Beau to her. Or anyone, for that matter.

"Momma!" Elena races into the kitchen and I sweep her into my arms. "Did Uncle Beau send me a present?"

I laugh, ignoring the look Elizabeth gives over her shoulder. "Of course, and he says to tell his Shortie hello."

Elena squeals with delight as I adjust her to rest on my hip and reach into my purse. I pull out the sucker the sheriff had swiped from the jar on his desk which he kept stocked with blue raspberry suckers specifically for her.

"I will let you hold onto it," I say, holding it out to her, but not letting go. "But you can't eat it until after dinner."

"But, Momma…" Elena groans.

"No, ma'am. You're not going to spoil your dinner."

Elizabeth shakes her head, siding with me when Elena tries to persuade her next. "Sorry, Lena. Your momma is right. Besides, I made skillet mac, your favorite."

"But did you put 'matoes in it?" Elena scrunches her nose in disgust.

"No, I put the *tomatoes* on the side," Elizabeth says, shaking her head as she turns off the burner. "Lena, go tell the Bs dinner is done."

My daughter squirms from my arms and runs in the direction she had come from to gather everyone for dinner.

"So, I have to ask." Elizabeth leans back against the counter, resting her hands on her swollen belly. Seven months pregnant. She and Michaela are both due in December, meaning this is their last trip away from home for a while, another reason I couldn't say no to their impromptu trip out west. "What's going on with you and Beau?"

"What do you mean?"

"Well, they closed the case, didn't they?"

"In a manner of speaking." The case was *presumed closed.* It wasn't *officially* closed, they hadn't found a body, but it wasn't being actively worked on, either.

"So, why are you still running by the station to talk to Beau?" There's a slight twinkle in her brown eyes when Elizabeth asks the question.

"Am I not allowed to go talk to the sheriff?"

"I didn't say that," she says, a slight tug in the corner of her mouth. "You can talk to the *sheriff,* but you didn't call him the sheriff. You called him Beau. Not to mention, Elena seems quite fond of him."

"Elizabeth." I sigh, pinching the bridge of my nose.

"Look, I don't care what you do. I'm just saying you might want to consider how it will look to other people."

"We're not *doing* anything," I snap, and Elizabeth reels back slightly at the bite in my tone. Closing my eyes, I take a deep breath and brace myself against the counter. "Beau has continued looking for Nick when everyone else gave up. I'm alone out here, Elizabeth, and he has been there whenever I need something."

"You have people out here who would help you."

"Not anyone who wants to help." Sympathy seeps from her eyes when I meet her gaze again. "It's been six months, Elizabeth. Six. Half a year since the last time I saw my husband or heard his voice and it's fucking killing me. The worst part? I may never know...I may never get the answers about what happened to him. And the only person who hasn't given up helping me *try* and figure it out is Beau. Please, do not sit there and tell me to consider how it looks to other people when I honestly don't give a fuck."

My sister doesn't get the chance to respond before my daughter gallops back in with Michaela, Brie, and Blake hot on her trail, all eager to stuff their faces.

Beau Turner

Happy birthday, Sweetheart.

I have read his text about thirty times throughout the day. I don't know why, either. It isn't anything special—a simple message with no hidden meaning—but it keeps coming to mind. It's the only one I opened all day, but I haven't responded. I have left it sitting there until I can decide if I'm going to respond or not. The conversation with Elizabeth last night has been running through my mind nonstop, making my mind spiral. Am I doing something wrong letting Beau help me? Am I supposed to accept that the other officials have given up, and we may never know what happened to Nick? Am I supposed to care what it looks like that Beau and I are still in contact? Or that I called him *Beau* instead of Sheriff Turner?

After breakfast in bed—a bowl of Lucky Charms, Elena and Nick's favorite cereal, with a steaming cup of coffee, courtesy of my daughter—I spent the early part of my day in my office, putting out a fire Kai couldn't seem to control. I offered to help Elena bake a cake before her nap, but she shooed me away because it was supposed to be a surprise. Instead, I went for a hike before coming home to get ready for dinner at my favorite restaurant: Little Bird, located inside the Grand Oak Resort in downtown Haven.

Elena's cake was my favorite part of the day by far. The cake was vanilla and coated in a heavy amount of pink frosting and a mountain of rainbow sprinkles. *Happy Birthday, Momma* was written across the top, almost unreadable in her messy handwriting (the use of frosting hadn't helped her cause). It was a beautiful disaster, and I loved every bit of it. After cake and ice cream, we cuddled in her bed, watching a movie before she passed out.

And now, after slipping out of her room, I plan to hide and try to relax for the remaining three hours of my birthday, joined only by a glass of red wine and a hot bubble bath.

"There's someone here to see you," Elizabeth says, opening my bedroom door without knocking.

"Who is it?" I ask, pulling my sweater back over my head.

"Come and find out." The corner of her mouth ticks upward, and it makes me suspicious. Who in the hell would be showing up at nine o'clock at night? Elizabeth motions for me to follow and starts the trek down the hallway. I roll my eyes but follow her retreating figure to the foyer.

When I turn the corner, my steps falter. "What are you doing here?"

"I meant to stop by earlier, but I got a little tied up at the station," Beau says, standing inside the door. I glance at Elizabeth, who stands to the side with a knowing smirk. "When Shortie told me *she* was baking your cake, I figured you might want something with a little less...everything."

I laugh, taking the personal-sized cake he holds out. "Is this..."

"Red velvet."

My smile drops, but I quickly replace it, hoping he doesn't notice.

"You don't like red velvet?" His warm voice is heavy with concern, worried he messed up, but that's not it. "Elena said you and Nick—"

"It is...was Nick's favorite," I say, swallowing the boulder growing in my throat. When I look back to where Elizabeth should be standing, she's gone. Of course, when I want her here, she's gone.

"Oh, Sweetheart." Beau steps forward. "I'm sorry. I didn't—I shouldn't have assumed. I just thought, when she told me—"

"Beau, it's okay." I place my hand on his chest to stop his rambling. I feel his heart racing beneath my touch. "I appreciate it more than you know."

His hand swallows mine, holding it steady against his heart. "I'm sorry he couldn't be here."

Beau's words strike a chord deep inside me. Without warning, my eyes begin to swell. As hard as I try to conceal the tears, I can't, and they fall down my cheeks. His green eyes widen, and he removes the cake from my hands. He pulls me into his arms. Beau's embrace is warm and comforting. One hand grasps the back of my neck, his thumb makes small circles on the skin; the other on my lower back holds me close as I cry into his chest. My fingers clutch the fabric of his tan button-up when a hard sob racks through me. He holds me tighter with each one.

"Let it out, Sweetheart," he whispers against my temple. "I got you. You're okay."

"I can't do this, Beau," I cry into his shoulder. "I can't...How am I supposed to—"

"You can do this, Nina." Beau pulls back slightly to look me in the eye, maintaining his hold on my neck. His thumb continues to trace warming circles on my skin. "You are Davina Villa, and you are the strongest person I've ever fucking met." There's a soft smile on his lips when he pushes my hair from my face, cradling my cheek. "You can and will get through this."

There's a deep ache in my chest, a longing for something I will never know again, something that can never be replaced. All day, I've done my best to ignore it, but I can't anymore. This is the first time I have spent my birthday without him in ten years.

Since our first trip to Haven—when he was pretending to be my boyfriend (but we won't get into that)—Nick has never missed one of my birthdays. Not even when we agreed to separate for the two years he went back to college. The first year we sat on the phone for hours and talked about everything and nothing. We didn't get off the phone until well after three in the morning. Before we hung up, he said, "I love you, Dee." And the second year, I spent my birthday in Boston... with him. No one knows about it except his brother, and I'm surprised Alex has managed to keep it a secret. I was in town for a lecture and couldn't resist the opportunity to see him. I showed up outside his apartment. I tried to talk myself out of it even though I desperately wanted to see him, and almost did until he found me standing outside...Then it was game over.

A fresh round of tears fills my eyes and my chest tightens.

"I don't want to do this without him, Beau."

"I know, Sweetheart." Beau sighs, brushing through my hair and pressing his lips to my forehead. "But you're not alone. Okay? I'll be here every step of the way...And your family, they'll—"

"The family," I scoff. "I'm the only one still holding on to some kind of hope that we'll get real closure."

"I doubt that." He wipes away another tear before it falls down my cheek, and I lean into his touch. Everything about him is comforting and familiar. It's the only thing that has brought me any sense of security since I got the phone call from Kai six months ago. "Nina, we are all here for you. You just have to let us in."

twenty-seven

January 2029

"CAN'T BELIEVE I GAVE him the week off," I mumble, shoving my laptop in my purse. There is about a foot of fresh, powdered snow on the ground, and I can already feel the chill blowing in through the open door at the front of the plane. There's at least a twenty-degree difference between here and New York. I finally landed in Colorado after spending the last month and a half on the east coast. Elena and I bounced between New York and Winchester, spending our weekdays in the city and weekends in the Lowcountry. And because I didn't originally plan to return until next weekend, I gave everyone here this week off. I got lucky when I called Steve, he was free to fly me back on such short notice. I couldn't spend another day in the city (or around my family). I needed space, and the only place I wanted to be was Haven.

The end of the year is a busy time for our family. Between September and December, there are a million things to do and celebrate. With the multitude of birthdays, wedding anniversaries, holidays, death anniversaries, and company events, it is truly the busiest time of the year. By the time my birthday rolls around at the end of each October, I'm ready for it to be January when work is the only thing I have to worry about.

And this past holiday season was no exception.

The holidays were…interesting. The gaping hole Nick left at the dinner table was joined by the absence of Michaela, Elizabeth, and their husbands. Granted, Mic and Elizabeth had a good excuse: they both gave birth in December and weren't ready to be around outsiders. Alex and Lara played host for both Thanksgiving and Christmas at their new home in Charlotte, and while I was glad not to worry about hosting everyone, it only added to the awkwardness.

Alex and I have grown distant in recent months. Why? I'm not sure…Part of me wonders if Alex thinks I blame him for what happened. Part of me worries he blames me for not finding his brother. I'm Nina Villa. I'm supposed to be able to do anything…At least that's what my brother-in-law has always believed. Our relationship has shifted as more time has worn on in the search for Nick, especially after Sergeant Warren explained the case is (essentially) closed from the State's perspective.

"You need me to give you a ride home, Nina?" Steve asks from the cockpit door.

"No, I'll be fine. Please enjoy the rest of your time off, Steve. I'm so sorry I bothered you."

"Not a bother." He waves me off. "Kai requested the plane on Tuesday anyway." At least I know Kai will be bringing Elena back on the plane. She begged me to stay a little longer with her cousins and her uncle couldn't say no. "You call me if you need anything. I'm gonna stick around until Sunday."

I press a chaste kiss to Steve's stubbled cheek on my way out of the plane, freezing at the top of the stairs, and not because of the drastic drop in temperature.

What is he doing here?

He's not supposed to be here…yet here he is. I haven't seen him in almost two months, but we've been in contact almost every day while I was gone. He keeps me informed if there are any new updates (there haven't been) and I bother him to see if there are any (even though there aren't). They aren't long conversations, but he'd check in, ask me how I was doing, and if I needed anything. Then he'd ask about Elena (Shortie, sorry), and then, he'd check in on the rest of the family. Once a week, he'd say he ran over to the house to check on it since it had been so cold. The conversation was easy and flowed naturally—no pressure, no expectations. Being gone made me miss him, and I didn't even realize it until now.

He leans against the Spruce County Sheriff's SUV, legs crossed at the ankles and arms folded over his broad chest. A smile spreads across his face when our eyes meet.

"What are you doing here?" I ask, stepping down from the jet steps.

"Figured you might need a ride," Beau says, wrapping his hand around the handle of my suitcase.

"But I didn't—"

"Your brother told me."

"Kai told you I was coming home?"

Beau nods. "Asked me to keep an eye on you." He pushes a strand of hair that has fallen out of my braid behind my ear, gently caressing my jaw, and the motion sends a shiver down my spine. "C'mon, Sweetheart, let's get you home."

"Thanks for bringing me," I say, pulling a water bottle from the fridge. I'm surprised to find the house awaiting my arrival: the fridge is restocked, the heat is turned up to a comfortable temperature, and firewood has been brought in from outside and neatly stacked in the holder. "You did all of this?" I ask, turning back to Beau.

"Figured it would help you unwind a little more if you didn't have to worry about it."

"Beau—"

"You don't have to say anything, Sweetheart." He lifts his hand from the white marbled countertop and chews his bottom lip. "I wanted to make sure you had what you needed. I know dealing with the family and going back and forth has been hard on you. Just wanted to lighten the load a little."

I don't know what I would've done without this man for the last nine months. He has been my rock and my shelter in the hurricane. He has made sure I'm taken care of when I don't remember to take care of myself. When I'm too busy worrying about what comes next in the list of things to handle, what someone in the family needs, what I can do to continue the search for Nick…Beau worries about me.

Our fingertips graze on the island and the feeling draws my gaze up to his when a charge spreads across my skin. The feeling is something I haven't felt since…Nick. And from the look on Beau's face, I know he feels it, too.

"I should…I should go." Beau rips his gaze from mine, pulling his hand away to rub the back of his neck. "If you need anything, you know how to get ahold of me." Without giving me a chance to respond, he bolts out of the kitchen and straight out the front door.

When the door closes, I finally allow myself to breathe.

I pour scalding water from the kettle into a mug filled with lemon juice and honey. Pouring the rest of the water down the drain, I bring the mug to my lips and inhale, letting the aroma fill my senses. The sweetness of the honey mixed with the acid from the lemon juice creates a warm, harmonious scent. Before I take a sip, there's a knock at the front door.

When I open the door, my heart stalls. Beau stands in the doorway. His hands have a death grip on the frame and his gaze raises to meet mine. There's something in his green eyes I've never seen before, or maybe I've never noticed: want, need, desperation…A mix of all three? Whatever you want to call it, the heat in his gaze makes my skin flush.

"Hi." My word comes out more like a question. What is he doing here?

"Nina." It comes out strangled. His hands flex on the frame.

"Beau." Before I can fully get his name past my lips, he steps inside and his mouth is on mine. I don't know what I was expecting, but I don't think it was this…Or maybe it was. I don't know. All I know is his kiss ignites a fire inside me that was dampened a long time ago.

His tongue strokes mine as he reaches out to close the door with one hand, the other hugging my waist to keep me as close as possible. He bends slightly, sliding his hands under my ass and lifting me off my feet. My legs wrap around his waist, and he carries me through the house in a frenzy.

Beau sets me on the island, and I gasp when his mouth trails down my jaw, nipping at the sensitive skin behind my ear.

"Fuck." Beau rips himself away from me and takes two large steps back. "Fuck, Nina. I—I'm so sorry. I don't know what came over me. I—" His green eyes meet mine before he scrubs a hand down his face.

"Don't apologize," I say, stepping down from the counter. Two of his steps equal three of mine as I cross the room. He tries to take another step back, but I reach out for him, pulling him back to me. "Beau," I whisper, hands gripping the front of his sherpa-lined jacket.

Warm hands cradle the sides of my neck, his face so close to mine I can smell the mint on his breath, mingling with his cologne, and it's intoxicating. His eyes remain closed as his tongue darts out to wet his plump lips, biting down on the bottom one.

"Nina." He groans. "You gotta tell me you don't want this."

"I can't."

His forehead rubs against mine as his face contorts almost in agony. He says my name again. Green eyes open to meet mine, thumbs grazing across the skin of my cheeks before his right traces my lips. Eyes heavy with want, he groans when I tug him another step forward, his hips pressing against mine.

Fuck.

We are toeing a dangerous line, and if we cross…He has to know I can't offer myself to him. Not wholly. Not now, and maybe not ever. But for tonight…

"I can't promise you anything, Beau," I whisper. "I can't promise you tomorrow or the next day, but I can promise you tonight."

"Say it," he demands, his lips ghosting over mine. "Tell me what you want, Davina."

"I want you."

His mouth covers mine in a bruising kiss, all teeth and tongue, as his fingers grip my jaw. His kiss is different than what I'm used to, what I know, and it offers a different spark than the ones I shared with my late husband. The guilt begins to settle in already and we haven't done anything.

Why do I feel guilty? Nick is gone. He's not coming back. This isn't supposed to be a long-term thing, one night to get it out of our systems…So, why do I feel like I'm doing something wrong?

"We can stop," Beau says, parting from me again. He tucks

a strand of hair behind my ear, letting his fingers trace down the side of my face and jaw, lifting my chin to meet his gaze. "No hard feelings."

I bite my bottom lip, never breaking our stare, and shake my head, pulling his mouth back to mine.

In one quick motion, my feet leave the floor when he lifts me onto the island again. His tongue sweeps across mine and they dance together in a fight for dominance—one I'm happy to let him win.

I push the jacket from his shoulders and he shrugs out of it, letting it fall as my fingers make quick work of untucking the plaid button-down from his waistband. A soft whimper passes through my lips when Beau parts from me. I already miss his touch, watching as he kneels before me.

He lifts my left leg, kissing the inside of my thigh as his fingers lightly trace down the length of my leg to my boots. He undoes the lace, slipping the first boot from my foot before repeating the process on the other side. His green eyes burn when he stands, looking down at me as he drags my ass to the edge of the counter.

"Up," he commands, lifting my hips.

I leverage my feet on the handles, and he shimmies my leggings off my hips and over my ass, removing them one leg at a time.

Beau kisses me again. "Stand for me, Sweetheart," he commands. His eyes never leave mine as I slip from the counter, sliding down his body the entire way. I hold my breath, waiting to see what he does next. The air surrounding us grows thicker with each passing second.

Beau doesn't waste time, hands flying to my hips and spinning me around. The edge of the counter digs into my stomach with his body flush against mine. His breath is hot against my ear when he moans softly at the connection.

"Beau." I gasp when large fingers splay across the bare skin of my stomach beneath my sweater, igniting a fire across my whole body. His right hand comes to my neck, holding me steady as he grinds against my ass. I can already feel how hard he is through the denim. I can't stop myself from thrusting my hips backward to meet his. His lips and teeth meet the left side of my throat, no doubt he's left his mark on the skin. I don't care because it feels too fucking good. Beau Turner knows exactly how to please a woman.

His fingers tighten around my neck with the slightest pressure, and his mouth trails from my neck to my bare shoulder where the sleeve of my oversized ribbed sweater is halfway down my arm. Warm lips ghost over my shoulder, scruff bringing every nerve to attention, and the sensation elicits the slightest whimper from my lips. I feel him smile against my skin.

"You're not wearing a bra," he rasps against my ear. His hand releases my neck, trailing down my chest. He cups one of my breasts through the fabric before he reaches under my sweater, palms rough against the sensitive skin. His fingers tease my hardened nipple and it sends a shockwave through me.

He pinches my nipple again before trailing further down my body until he reaches the waistband of my underwear. His hand slips beneath the fabric until it finds what he's looking for and my legs practically fall out from under me at his touch.

"You're a needy thing, aren't you?" I can hear the smirk in his voice and, normally, I'd roll my eyes at his sense of pride, but right now all I can think about is how his hands feel against me. And what I wouldn't give to feel all of him against me. Beau dips one finger between my folds and I claw at the countertop. "Fuck, Nin, you're drenched," he moans and pushes another one inside me.

"Beau," I whine.

"Stay put, baby." Beau kisses the back of my neck. "You got

that?"

I nod in response, sucking in my bottom lip.

One of his feet comes between mine, widening my stance, before he pulls my hips out from the counter.

"Holy fuck, just look at you," he moans, grinding against my ass once more before the weight of his body disappears.

"What are you—" I gasp when I see him back on his knees, and the ache between my legs grows.

Beau shrugs out of his flannel, leaving him in a T-shirt, and he gently nudges my legs a little farther apart, pulling my underwear down. "Put your hands on the edge of the counter and lean forward. I want to watch as you come undone on my tongue."

Holy fuck.

My body craves his touch. I don't have time to think about how this would look if someone were to walk in because I'm so desperate for him. His mouth moves to where I need him most and I have to grasp the counter to keep from falling, eyes screwed shut, as I call his name.

"Eyes on me, Davina," Beau commands, and when I meet his hooded gaze, I practically come right then and there. His tongue moves in languid circles against me, drawing out deep cries of pleasure. I haven't felt like this in so long, I'm not going to last. One hand threads through his hair, tugging, when his lips suckle on my clit. He does it over and over, building the weight of ecstasy in my veins. I feel like I'm going to combust. When my legs begin to buckle, he tightens his already firm grip on my ass. No room for escape from his assault. Licking. Biting. Sucking. Nipping. It's all too much.

"Beau." I whimper, my orgasm building stronger, and he slips two fingers inside me. "Holy fuck," I cry out, unable to contain myself at the feeling. I feel so full and all I can think about is how good it will feel when his fingers are replaced by his cock. He crooks his fingers inside me, and it sends me spiraling, chasing my orgasm.

"You wanna come?" he asks against me, and I nod my head frantically. Beau spreads me wide again with one long lick from top to bottom before his mouth finds my clit.

I'm so close. The pressure in my belly tells me I'm right on the cusp, and when his teeth graze the sensitive bud at the same time his fingers thrust inside me, I step right over. I can't contain the scream that rips through my throat as shockwaves of pleasure course through me. His moans spur me on, and I grind against his tongue as he continues to work me through my high.

My breaths come out in heavy pants when his assault finally relents. He stands from his knees, but I still lean over the counter, trying to catch my breath.

Beau pushes the hair from my shoulder, pressing a soft kiss to my skin, and I smile lazily at him.

"You look pretty on your knees, Beau Turner." My statement makes him laugh—a hearty, full belly laugh—and the sound makes me smile. Finally catching my breath, I stand to meet him, draping my arms over his broad shoulders. His hands rest on my hips.

"You sure you wanna do this, Nin?" he asks, gaze never leaving mine.

"A little late for that, isn't it?"

Beau shakes his head. "Not if you want to stop. I'll walk away...No hard feelings and no questions asked."

I trace the side of his face before pushing my fingers through his hair, tugging at the ends, earning a grunt in response. I don't deserve the man in front of me. The same way I didn't deserve Nick. Both men too good for the world we live in. The world I live in. "Beau, I can't give myself to you. Not in the way you deserve...I just...I'm not there yet."

"I know, Nina." He pushes the dark waves behind my shoulder, cupping my face. "I'd never push you."

"I meant what I said earlier...I can promise you tonight, but that's all I can offer."

"Then let's stop wasting it."

Beau pulls me in for a kiss that will forever be burned in the back of my mind. He kisses me the way every woman wants to be kissed—soft, yet rough all the same. He devours me. He isn't trying to win a battle, seeking only the closeness of another person who yearns for the same thing he does. Two people sharing the same breath...the same sensation...the same moment.

Fisting the cloth of his T-shirt, I pull him closer, and I can feel the heat rising in my cheeks as his tongue dances with mine, tasting me as if he's been deprived—quick and delicious, then firmer and more determined. There's a yearning deep inside me to make him feel as good as he's making me...made me. Something tells me Beau hasn't often been awarded the same opportunities he has given others, and I can't wait to show him what it's like...

The morning light shines through the windows of the guest room as I watch Beau sleep. Last night, I couldn't bring myself to enter the same room I had with my husband so many times, instead opting for one of the many guest rooms. My eyes trace the dips and curves of Beau's strong body, committing every inch to memory as his chest rises and falls with each slumbering breath. The scents of blue cypress and vetiver, with a hint of the coast, cling to him, and when he shifts beside me, the sunlight catches the curve of his jaw as his dark hair falls across his forehead.

I woke up about an hour ago but haven't been able to

force myself to climb out of bed yet. Because once I do…this all ends. And when it ends…I go back to being Davina Villa: widow, mother, and CEO; but when I'm with Beau, I get to be just…Nina.

Last night was the first time I felt like I could breathe again. Like I wasn't barely keeping my head above water, at risk of drowning in depths of uncertainty. No one in the family understands the massive weight crushing down my chest every time I think of my husband. The guilt knowing that had we not fought before Nick left, maybe, just maybe, he wouldn't have gone hiking by himself. I knew the only reason we had been fighting so much was because I chose my career over my family, and it killed me to know Nick left thinking he and Elena weren't enough for me. They were all I ever truly needed. I'd give it all up for them.

I close my eyes, willing away the monster of grief trying to deepen the grasp it has on my mind, but my attempts are useless. The past nine months have been anything but easy. They've been the biggest fucking rollercoaster of emotion and grief and hopelessness I've ever experienced, a pain far worse than the one I felt when my dad died almost ten years ago.

And now…if anyone finds out what I've done—what *we've* done—they'd never forgive me. They'd never forgive Beau. My family would never look at either one of us the same.

I can't let Beau know. I refuse to let him think I regret what happened between us. Because…I don't. I don't regret what we did. I only regret not waiting until I could fully offer myself to him. Beau Turner is a good man—too good—and he deserves better than this. Deserves better than me. Better than the fucked world my life is rooted so deeply in.

Tears cloud behind my lids, refusing to be willed away, and a few slide down my cheeks. I've made a complete mess of things and have no idea how to clean it up.

Beau shifts beside me and a warm hand drags up my back,

along my spine, until it settles on the nape of my neck. He pulls me toward him, pressing a kiss against my forehead. "Mornin', Sweetheart," he murmurs.

I wipe my cheeks, hoping he hasn't seen the tears already. His eyes are still heavy with sleep, but he smiles at me, and it pulls one of my own out from the depths of my core.

"Did you sleep at all?" he asks, and I lean into his touch when he traces the side of my face.

"A little. I don't sleep much anymore."

Beau hums in response, pulling me back into his chest. "I have to go soon," he whispers against my hair. "I gotta meet Max at the station."

"Okay," I say, because what else is there to say?

"Okay," he agrees, and the weight of the word chips away at the small piece he had mended back together.

<h1 style="text-align:center">twenty-eight</h1>

February 2029

MY ASSISTANT SYDNEY COMES running into my office with wide eyes. She braces on the door, catching her breath, to say, "Nina, there's someone here to see you. I tried to tell her you were busy, but she said she didn't care. She says she's—"

"Your mother." Brina stands behind Sydney with an unimpressed expression. Her thin brows are peaked and her lips are drawn into a tight line. *What is she doing here?* I haven't seen this woman in over nine years and there hasn't been a single day in all those years that I've found myself missing her. "Hello, Davina," she says, and a sickening smile spreads across her red-painted lips. She pushes Sydney out of the way to finally walk through the door.

"*Stai scherzando. Cazzo.*" I sigh. *You've got to be fucking kidding me.*

"Nina?" Sydney asks, an unsure look in her eye.

"It's fine, Syd," I say, waving her off. "She won't be any trouble, will you, *Brina?*"

"Cross my heart," Brina says, one of her bony fingers making an X over her heart. She falls into the chair from across my desk, resting her oversized red YSL bag on her knees. It's from the new collection later this year. How did she get one of those? She can't afford one—she doesn't get that much money from the estate. I would know, I'm in charge of the damn thing. Maybe she's dating someone. In that case... good for her. I might still have my investigator Ed look into it, because if it's one of her former boyfriends from when Daddy was still alive—

"So, Davina...How are you?"

I roll my eyes. "Cut the act. What are you doing here?"

"Act?" She places a perfectly manicured hand over her heart. "Davina, I don't know what you mean. I've only come here out of concern for my *daughter.*"

"Okay, I'll bite," I say, lifting my glasses from my nose and folding my hands over the papers on my desk. "Why are you so concerned?"

"Why, Nicholas, of course." Brina's face pulls into a solemn expression, and my heart drops at the mention of my husband's name. She sighs. "It's so terrible. I can't believe he'd just up and leave."

"He didn't up and leave, Brina. *Chi te l'ha detto?*" I ask.

She stares at me blankly. Oh, that's right. I almost forgot she likes to pretend she can't understand Italian.

Rolling my eyes, I repeat the question. "Who told you about Nick?" It's probably those gossipmongers at the private club she frequents. *"Questo non ti riguarda."* This doesn't concern her. Nothing about our lives should concern her.

Brina reaches across the desk to cover my hands. "Oh, you know, I heard through the grapevine he left you and Elena. That is my granddaughter's name, isn't it?"

How does she know so much about me and my family? Kai wouldn't tell her, and as far as I know, he hasn't spoken to her since Daddy's death, either. When the truth came out about our mother and my ex-boyfriend sleeping together—

yeah, you heard me, my mother was having an affair with my *ex-boyfriend*—it was the final straw for my brother. Not to mention the way she conducted herself during the reading of our father's will, plus finding out she had been having multiple affairs for practically their entire marriage.

Was I surprised? No, not really, but it was a tough pill for my brother to swallow.

Kai was our mother's pride and joy. Brina loved him in a way I had never known. We never got along, I was the child she never wanted but got anyway, and she always reminded me. Daddy used to say the reason she and I butted heads was because we were so much alike, but I resented that. I still do. I don't want anything to do with her and she doesn't want anything to do with me—we like it that way. Since the truth about her and Lee came out after our summer trip to Haven ten years ago, I haven't seen or spoken to my mother, even concerning matters of the estate and her monthly stipend. The family attorney plays middleman so I don't have to deal with her.

"My daughter is none of your concern," I snap, ripping my hands away from her.

"You cannot keep my grandchild away from me, Davina."

Her statement is almost laughable. "I can't keep her from you? I am her mother—"

"And I'm *your* mother!"

This time, I do laugh. She cannot be serious. Is she trying to guilt me by pulling the "I'm your mother" card?

"I think you're confusing me with your other children, Kai and Elizabeth."

"Elizabeth is not my child."

"Well, you sure treated her more like a daughter than you ever did me." I rub the crease between my brows. "Now, if you don't mind, I have far more important things to worry about than whatever *this* is. If you thought using my husband was your chance to weasel your way back into my life or the life of my daughter, you are sadly mistaken."

"And what will you tell her when she asks why she doesn't have grandparents, hmm? That day will come, especially when she realizes all her friends have something she doesn't. Something you can't buy her. This isn't some family vacation where you pay someone to pretend to be your boyfriend. Are you sure your dear Nicholas wasn't still pretending all this time? Maybe that's why he left you."

My jaw tightens, and without a second thought, I reach across my desk and smack her.

Her blue eyes burn when she looks back at me, fingers grazing across the reddened skin.

Shaking my head, the words come out in a low hiss. *"Come osi?"* How dare she come into my office and speak so terribly of my husband?

"Speak English, Davina. You know I cannot—"

"Stop pretending like you don't understand me!" I slam my hand down on the desk. "I know damn well you can. You understood Daddy perfectly for however many fucking years you held him hostage."

Brina's face pulls into a straight line.

Rising from my chair, I brace myself against the desk and tower over her. "How *dare* you speak ill of my husband? You walk in here pretending like you care about him. About me and Elena. You don't care about anyone but yourself and whoever your latest fuck is. Why are you here, Brina? Run out of money for the month, or are you so bored you have to show up here and fuck with my life some more?"

Brina rubs her cheek gently before she scoffs, looking around my office before her gaze lands back on me. "Your father would be disappointed to see how this place has turned out. To see *you* at the helm. This was never meant to be *yours,* Davina."

She stands from the chair, looping her arm through her bag strap, letting it hang from the crook of her elbow. Rolling her shoulders, she lifts her chin and purses her lips, looking me up and down with disdain.

"Alaric Villa is rolling over in his grave at what you've done to this company—to his empire. How you have taken what he worked so hard to build and destroyed it piece by piece."

Every word she utters hits me harder than the last, but I swallow the emotions threatening to spill over my already overflowing cup. I cannot let her know how much her words affect me. She can't know she can still rip me to shreds with a single look. This woman…this monster who has done nothing but pick me apart and try to ruin any ounce of confidence I've had my entire life.

"I will not stand by and watch you continue to ruin Alaric Villa's legacy."

"*È una minaccia o una promessa?*" I narrow my gaze. *Is that a threat or a promise?* "Because if you're going to make threats, you better come prepared to back them up. And if it's a promise—"

"*Ti prometto che acquisirò la proprietà di questa azienda prima che tutto sia finito,*" she says.

I promise you I will have control of this company before everything is said and done.

Her words draw the corners of my mouth up. I knew she faked not understanding for all those years. There was no way she was married to Daddy for so long and not picked up something.

"I'd like to see you try, *puttana,*" I say, leaning further over my desk.

The fire in her gaze burns hotter than before, and she swings her palm toward my cheek, but I catch it. "You dare call me a *whore?* You watch your mouth, you little bitch!"

"*Vattene via dal mio ufficio, cazzo.*" The words come out in a low hiss as I shove her hand from me. "Get out before I call security."

"What the fuck is going on in here?" My brother's voice echoes around us. He storms into my office, not even bothering to close the door behind him. "Mother, what are you doing here?"

"Oh, Kai, darling! I was coming to—"

"To start shit with me," I finish for her. "We haven't spoken in almost ten years, but she shows up now, pretending to care that my husband is gone."

Kai glares at her. "You're about ten months too late."

"Ten months?" Brina's head whips around to me, this time a look of what I think might be genuine concern in her eyes. That's a first. "He's been gone ten months? But I thought—"

"Get the fuck out," I say, and when she doesn't move an inch, I repeat the sentiment in a less-than-friendly way.

"Tell Ophelia I look forward to seeing her," Brina says when she passes by my brother, whose gaze narrows even further.

Kai slams the office door behind her but stands with his back to me for a moment longer than I feel he should. What did she mean by she looked forward to seeing Ophelia? Had he been in contact with her? After everything she has done… he wouldn't crawl back to her, would he?

"Nina—"

"*Stai parlando con lei?*" I cut him off before he can begin peddling whatever lie he's about to spew. I watch his throat bob with a hard swallow and it's all the confirmation I need, but I want to hear him say it. To admit he's going to let that bitch back into his life, and ultimately into mine. I repeat myself, "Are you speaking to her?"

"Nin, I…I wanted to tell you, but I didn't know how. She… she came by not long ago and asked to talk. She apologized for everything."

"Oh, I'm sure she did. You know what, Kai? *Vaffanculo.*

Fuck you. I have worked my ass off for this company. And for you. So you can come and go as you please, playing pretend CEO when you *feel* like it. I'm the one who made this company into what it is, *non tu.*" I roll my shoulders and straighten my back. "Not you, Kai. Me. I'm the one who sacrificed *my* family so you could have yours! You, this company—you're the fucking reason my husband went missing. *Tu sei la ragione per cui se n'è andato!* You and this company are the reason he's gone. And I will not let his death be in fucking vain. I will not stand by and watch as that gold-digging *puttana* weasels her way back into our lives and this company because that is all she wants."

"She wants to know her grandchildren, Nina."

"If you believe that…you're dumber than I thought." I scoff. "Now, get the fuck out of my office."

"But Nina—"

"Esci!" I slam the palm of my hand on my desk, breathing out an exasperated huff.

Kai stands there a moment longer with a pleading look in his eye, one I've seen many times over our lives. The same one that used to appear when Brina and I would get into one of our arguments and he'd stand there, idly, trying to decide what to do. And ultimately, he always chose to side with her, because it was easier than ending up on her shit list, where I held permanent residence.

twenty-nine

March 2029

"PLEASE TELL ME YOU'RE coming to your niece's birthday." Eileen doesn't waste time getting straight to the point when I answer the FaceTime call. I can't remember the last time she called me out of the blue like this.

I was disappointed I didn't hear from her when everything went down with Brina last month, but I wasn't completely shocked, either. We're both busy. Not long after Nick went missing, Eileen opened a salon on the Upper East Side, and when she's not with her girls, she's behind the chair or handling the business. On the screen, the streets of Manhattan pass behind her, either on her way to the salon or to pick up Ophelia from school. Judging from the lack of Fallon on her hip, I'd guess it's the salon.

"Hello to you too, Lina," I say, sitting back in my chair at the DV Designs Denver office. I have two hours before I need to leave so I'm back in Haven to pick Elena up from school. Beau offered, knowing I had a lot to do today, and while I appreciated the offer, she and I were going to have some uninterrupted mommy-daughter time this weekend. That included a movie marathon tonight, a trip to the neighbors' for horseback riding lessons tomorrow, and a spa day on Sunday.

"Nina, I'm serious." Eileen pauses at a crosswalk, glancing both ways before she jaywalks. "Ophelia wants you and Elena here next weekend. And, personally, I don't want to be the one to tell her you're not coming because you and Kai aren't getting along."

"You and I aren't exactly on the best terms, either." I stare her straight in the eye. She blinks away, closing her eyes with a deep sigh. "Why didn't you tell me, Lina?"

"It wasn't my place, Nin. Your mother is a…touchy subject. For both of you."

That's an understatement.

"I can't say I was happy about his decision to let her meet the girls, but—"

"But you let it happen."

Eileen sighs. "Despite everything, she is your mother, and if Kai wants to have a relationship with her—"

"He can," I say, and it seems to surprise her. Her brows raise and her steps halt in the middle of the sidewalk. "If Kai wants to have a relationship with her—and only God knows why—he can. That doesn't mean I must subject myself to the same fate."

"What does that mean, exactly?"

"It means that as long as I know she's going to be somewhere, I'm not coming, and neither is my daughter."

Eileen is still skeptical. "You're being surprisingly…calm about this."

"Lina, I know Brina Villa won't be able to keep the ruse up for the rest of her life. The mask will come off eventually and she'll remind my brother why he stopped talking to her in the first place."

"I don't like it when you say things like that," she says with a deep sigh. With her eyes still closed, she circles back to the reason for her call. "Can we expect you next Saturday or not?"

"Will Brina be there?"

"I don't...I don't know. Maybe?"

"Well, then you have your answer."

"Nina, please don't separate the girls! They're going to be heartbroken if we—"

"I've made up my mind, Eileen. As long as Brina is there, we won't be." There's a knock on the open office door, and I'm surprised to see my brother standing there. "What are you doing here?"

"I forgot to tell you," his wife says over the phone. "Your brother is in town."

I hang up the phone without saying goodbye as he walks inside, closing the door. Kai and I haven't talked outside of an occasional text or email, keeping it strictly business after our argument last month. I think this is the longest Kai and I have gone without talking since Daddy died. As much as it hurts to think we've taken five hundred steps back from where we've come, erasing all the work put into our relationship, I don't know any other way to get my point across.

"Can we talk?" Kai asks. Hands shoved deep into the pockets of his dress pants, my brother stands in the middle of the room, looking like a scolded toddler.

"I guess that depends on you."

"I'm not sorry for talking to her, Nina, but I am sorry for hurting you and lying about it. I should've told you."

"And you think it would've made it any better?"

"No, but maybe you wouldn't have been so angry."

I laugh in disbelief, letting my tongue run across the back of my teeth. He thinks I wouldn't have been so angry. No matter when he told me, my reaction would have remained the same.

"She wants to know her grandchildren, Nina. That's it."

"I said before and I'll say it again, if you truly believe that, you're dumber than I thought. Kai, she wants the company.

She wants—"

"She has no right to the company!"

"You think that will stop her? This is *Brina Villa* we're talking about. She will find a way, she always does."

He finally crosses the room to sit down and is anything but his normal poised and composed self. His weighed-down posture exposes the truth about how my brother has been faring, and I wonder if there's more going on than he's telling me. "Nina, I don't want this to come between us again."

"Kai, if you feel this strongly about wanting to have a relationship with her, go for it. I won't stop you, and when she proves to be the same person she has always been…I'll be here to pick up the pieces. But if Brina is going to be somewhere, I won't be, and neither will my daughter."

"Nin—"

"Did you tell her about Nick?"

"Why would I tell her about Nick?"

"I don't know, but someone did. Why else would she show up?"

Kai scrubs his hands down his face and sighs, but it's one of those soul-crushing sighs that only confirms what I thought earlier. There's something else going on.

"What aren't you telling me?"

My brother stares at the ground. He gnaws on the inside of his cheek and fiddles with his hands. Finally, his gaze raises to meet mine, and for a moment I swear I'm looking at Daddy. He takes a deep breath, and says, "She's dying, Nin."

The pen in my hands clatters down to the desk. What does he mean she's dying?

"She…She begged me to meet her, and after putting it off for practically a month, I finally sat down with her at the end of January. She has cancer, Nina. Pancreatic. They're only giving her a year. Max."

"You're going to bring her into Ophelia and Fallon's life

only to rip her away from them in a year? If she even makes it that long. Do you know how fucked up that is?"

"She deserves to know her grandchildren, Nina."

"And do the girls deserve to have their grandmother ripped away from them as soon as she comes into their lives? I can't believe you would subject your children to something like this. This is unbelievably selfish, Kai."

"She is our mom, Davina!" He practically jumps out of the chair, slamming his hand on my desk. "And we have spent the last ten years pretending she didn't even exist because—"

"For good reason."

My brother's eyes are red with unshed tears and his hand grips the edge of my desk like it's his only lifeline. "Our *mom* is dying, Nina."

And if Daddy was still alive, I know he would try to convince me to let her back into my life, too, regardless of what happened between them. He was always the peacemaker between me and Mother. He was the only one who could quell an argument before it started or end one with a single look. But Daddy isn't alive, and even if he was, I wouldn't subject Elena to more pain and loss than she has already had to deal with. She still hasn't fully accepted Nick being gone. There are nights she calls out for him. Nights she comes to our room looking for him. Days she still asks me when he's coming home. And I'm left to pick up the pieces of a three-year-old's heart when she remembers Daddy is not coming home. Why would I want to subject her to even more of the same pain?

"Do you really hate her *so* much you don't even care she's going to die?"

I don't know how I feel about her impending demise. I'm not sad, but it doesn't make me want to jump for joy. Regardless, I've made up my mind: Brina will not be meeting Elena.

I push up from my chair and come around my desk to sit

beside him. Giving his hand a gentle squeeze, I say, "Kai, I'm sorry. I am. And I get it—why you want to have her around. You and Brina were always close. You had a relationship with her, I never did, so while I may not like that she's around, I understand."

His head hangs low, and he bites down on his bottom lip to keep it from quivering.

"It's not right to involve your children, Kai. You *know* how this ends...and it's going to end sooner than later. This doesn't change my mind about being around her. I won't subject Elena to more loss any sooner than I have to."

"I'm sorry, Nina." Kai pushes his fingers into his eyes, hoping to prevent the tears from falling. "I'm so sorry. I should've...If I had just—"

"Kai, stop." I put my hand on his knee. "I don't blame you for what happened to Nick. My husband made his choice. He chose to go out for a hike alone without telling anyone. Nick did that, not you." Now giving his knee a comforting squeeze, I say, "I'm sorry. Truly, I am so sorry you're going through this."

My brother nods, his head still hung low. I reach over and pull him into a hug, wrapping my arms around his frame. My brother clings to me as the tears begin to flow, soaking the fabric of my cardigan, and tears prick the corners of my own eyes. I hate seeing him in so much pain. I hate there's nothing I can do to make it go away.

I wish I could say I'm upset our mother is dying—that I'm going to miss her—but the truth is...I grieved the death of Brina Villa a long time ago.

thirty

Now

THE FAMILY ARRIVED IN Haven for the anniversary and spring break this morning, and it has been utter chaos since they walked in the door. I keep getting pulled in five different directions at once, trying to manage everyone's needs and wants. You would think they've never been to my house before. I'm starting to regret giving Elena's nanny the weekend off. She would have been a great buffer to some of the chaos, but I didn't want to subject her to the craziness, even if she was used to it. I had to practically shove her out the door last night because she knew what was coming. We both did. But it's fine...I only need to get through the next two and a half days and then I'll be a comfortable distance away with my feet back on the ground in New York.

Until then, I will take every opportunity to sneak away, like now...For the past two hours, I've been hiding in the office. I snuck down after putting Elena down for her nap—which she fought me on, saying she was "too excited to take a nap" and there "was so much to do!" She loves having the family together because she has her cousins to play with and her grandparents to spoil her. But when she crashed ten minutes later, she crashed hard.

I didn't plan on being down here as long as I have been, but I needed a few minutes alone and something to distract me. If I couldn't escape long enough for a hike work was the second-best choice. Then a few minutes turned into almost two hours of researching the house's resale value based on all the work we had done to it.

When Nick and I bought the house a few years ago, we gutted it down to the studs and redesigned the entire thing, together. Bringing our combined visions to life was the most fun I'd had on a project in years, but now…it made my heart yearn for those moments again. I couldn't go anywhere in this house without thinking of him.

"You have a minute?" Someone knocks and I'm surprised to see Nick's little brother, Alex, standing in the doorway.

"Sure," I say, motioning to the chair on the other side of my desk. "Everything okay?"

"Yeah, I just wanted to talk."

Alex and I haven't talked much since everything happened. Truthfully, I can't remember the last time we had a conversation outside of a family function, and even then…it was mostly small talk. It wasn't the normal banter I'd become accustomed to over the last decade.

He fidgets with his hands, seemingly unable to get comfortable.

"What's up?" I ask, leaning back in my chair, a little fidgety myself. I grab a pen from my desk to keep my hands busy.

Alex tries to get the words out about five times, but he can't seem to find what he's trying to say. He sighs. "What am I supposed to do, Nina?"

"I'm not sure what you mean."

"I'm getting married next month."

"I'm aware." I stare at him blankly, not seeing his point yet.

What does this have to do with me?

I swear it takes a full minute for him to say, "He's not here, Nina. My brother…He's not *here*. Still. How am I supposed to get married without him?"

It's my turn to sigh, pushing my thumb and forefinger into my eyes to pinch the bridge of my nose.

"I can't push it again. That wouldn't be fair to Lara. We've already pushed it twice. I can't—I can't ask that of her."

"No, you can't," I say.

When it became obvious Nick wouldn't be home in time for Alex's wedding last June, he and Lara decided to push the date back six months. Five months later, they postponed to May this year. Alex didn't want to get married without his best friend. I didn't blame him. Had the roles been reversed, Nick wouldn't have wanted to walk down the aisle without his little brother, but at some point, Alex needs to be realistic and accept that Nick isn't coming home. At least not how we want him to. He'll have to do the unthinkable: get married *without* his older brother.

Alex sighs. "I can't get married without him."

"So, you're not going to get married?"

"Of course, I am!"

"Then I guess I'm a little confused. What is it you're trying to get at here, Alex?"

He shakes his head and tears his gaze away from me to look out the window taking up almost the entire exterior wall. Alex pushes his hand through his hair, cut shorter than it was at Christmas. The curls he shares with his brother when it's long are now gone.

"I have done everything I can to try and bring him home," I say, trying to regain his attention. "To find him. It's not—"

"That's why you spend almost every night with the sheriff?"

My heart stops. Full on stops for at least a second. What did he just say?

His blue-eyed stare is lethal when he turns back to me. "What? Did you think we didn't know? You don't hide it as well as you think, Nina. Hell, you didn't even wait a fucking month before he went missing to jump into—"

"I'm going to stop you right now. Before you say something you're going to fucking regret."

Alex doesn't back down, though.

"I'm going to let that one slide because I know you're upset about your brother and your wedding and whatever else you have going on. But so help me God, Alex, if you *ever* say something like that to me again—"

"What?" He scoffs. "What are you going to do, Nina? Nothing. You're not going to do a damn thing, because—"

"Alex. Shut the actual fuck up."

It's silent for a moment, the only sounds from someone walking above us and the patter of raindrops that have started to hit the window.

"Do you even care that he's gone?"

"How dare you?" I practically spit the words at him. "I have worked my ass off to try and bring Nick home. I have exhausted every resource, every favor, every debt owed to me to find something—anything—that will lead me to him. And do you want to know what I've found? *Niente.* I have found nothing, Alex. It's like he disappeared off the face of the fucking planet."

Alex swallows whatever bullshit he thought of spewing a moment ago.

"You think I don't care? You think I'm not upset?" I scoff and toss the pen I've been holding on my desk, pushing up from my chair. "I don't have the same luxury of being able to break down and worry like the rest of you. Someone has to keep shit going around here. Someone has to hold shit together and it isn't going to be any of you."

"That doesn't mean—"

"Make no fucking mistake, Alexander Davis; I break, too.

And I am completely fucking broken. I could lose everything, every single fucking thing in this world, and as long as I had your brother...I would have been okay. But now, I have no choice. I have to be okay because someone else depends on me. That little girl upstairs misses her daddy, and she spends most days wondering when he's coming home. I have no choice but to continue to be strong for her."

"None of this justifies spending your nights with the sheriff."

A dry, humorless chuckle emanates from my lips. "Alex, I am warning you—"

"You don't deny it!"

"Nothing is going on between me and Beau Turner!"

The sounds from upstairs have quieted down now. Whoever is up there is trying to listen, to hear what's going on.

"Beau feels guilty because *his* deputy refused to take the police report. He feels guilty because he wonders what might have happened if *you* had tried harder to talk to him instead. If *you* had pushed a little harder to make someone believe you!"

"This isn't my fault."

"Need I remind you why your brother was out here, to begin with?"

Too far, Nina.

"You're a bitch," Alex says without remorse.

"Maybe." I shrug. "But at least I know I've done everything to find him. Have you?"

thirty-one

"HEY, KIDDO," JIMMY SAYS when he enters the kitchen. We had gathered about twenty minutes ago to watch a movie at the request of Elena and Ophelia. When Elena cuddled up in Brie's lap instead of mine, I took the opportunity to get a few more minutes of alone time. Jimmy peers over his shoulder into the living room to make sure all eyes are still on the movie before he joins me at the other end of the island. "Doin' okay?"

"I'm fine." A weak smile tugs on my lips. "How are you? We haven't talked in a while."

"Yeah, unless you're pawning that beautiful grandbaby off on me." Jimmy chuckles, and when I apologize, he adds, "I'm kidding. You know I don't mind one bit. Anything you need, Nina."

"Well, she loves it. She misses you when you're gone."

"Of course, she does! She gets spoiled rotten. And not even by me. Tessa beats me by a long shot."

"I believe it." Tessa used to spoil me whenever I'd go to her diner in Winchester. She has always been a kind soul, acting like more of a mother to me than my own. Every time Daddy and I would go into Honeybee's Cafe, she'd be waiting with a stack of Funfetti pancakes for me and a newspaper and a black coffee for Daddy. Tessa would slide into the booth next to him with a toothy grin and little to no space between them. Over the years, I had watched their relationship blossom, but nothing ever came out of it, only a little flirting here and there. Despite my mother's actions over the years, my dad would never step out on her. I had hope for him and Tessa when he finally decided to divorce Brina...until he passed. Tessa was heartbroken when Daddy died, like most people who knew him, and I thought introducing her to Jimmy would give them both a friend with something in common. I never thought they'd be anything more than friends, but I couldn't have been happier when they decided to start dating.

"So," Jimmy says, pulling a water bottle from the fridge. "You wanna talk about it?"

"Which *it?*"

"Any of 'em."

I swirl the red liquid against the sides of my glass, letting it rise and fall with each flick of my wrist. It almost crests the rim but falls back down before it can.

"How 'bout we start with something easy?" I doubt whatever he's about to suggest will be an easy topic of conversation. "Something happen with Alex earlier?"

After our conversation in my office, Alex stormed up the stairs and out of the house. The whole thing left the others stunned and confused, and even from downstairs, I could hear the murmurs trying to figure out what happened. When I came upstairs about thirty minutes later, I didn't say anything about it, and neither did anyone else. Alex returned about an hour ago and we've kept our distance since.

My tongue swipes my bottom lip before I pull it between my teeth. "It's nothing. We had a...disagreement."

"Pretty heated disagreement from the sound of it." Jimmy

reaches over to cover my hand with his own, squeezing my hand. "Nina, you can talk to me."

"Jimmy—"

"Did he say something out of line?"

I could tell Jimmy what happened, but it won't change anything. It won't change how Alex feels about this situation or how he feels about me. Getting Jimmy involved won't fix things. I think it'll make things worse. "He's worried about the wedding coming up next month."

"Worried because Nick won't be here?" Jimmy asks, almost a little incredulously, and sighs when I nod. "Well, my dear, as much as it pains any of us to consider, it's something we have to accept. Think about why we're here! It's not for spring break, as much as I would like it to be."

I fight the tears collecting in my eyes and look away from him to dab them away with the sleeve of my sweater.

"Nina." His tone is fatherly, and he waits until I finally relent and look at him, giving me a teary smile. "You have done so much for this family—for *my* family—and I will never forget that. You have worked endlessly to bring Nick home. And when the time is right, all your hard work will pay off. I'm sure of it." Jimmy pulls me into a tight embrace, eliciting a sob from deep within me.

It's in moments like this when I miss my father most. Daddy would've known what to do. I have no doubt that had he been here, Kai wouldn't have hidden the truth from me and Nick would've been found within hours of going missing. Nick probably wouldn't have gone missing because my brother would've never taken a leave of absence from the company if Daddy was still alive. I wouldn't have taken over and Nick and I wouldn't have been on thin ice. The whole fight leading up to his disappearance wouldn't have happened in the first place...

But my father isn't here, so a hug from Jimmy is the closest thing I can get, and I cling to him.

Jimmy kisses the top of my head before pulling back to look at me. "You're an amazing woman, mother, wife, and business owner. I'm proud of you, Nina." A tear slips down my cheek, but he wipes it away. "It's okay to let your guard down sometimes. You don't have to be strong all the time."

The same advice Daddy used to give me.

Jimmy wipes another tear from my face, but I can see tears building in his blue eyes. The color of his eyes is a softer blue than the ones that sat across from me earlier. "I love you, Nina. And I know that wherever my son is…was…he'd do everything he can to get back to you because he loves you, too."

With a final squeeze, Jimmy returns to the living room, and I retreat to the safety of my bedroom. My feet move so fast that it feels like walking on air as I climb the stairs of the turret.

Walking into my bathroom, I grip the edge of the white marble vanity, trying to push down all the emotion clawing its way to the surface. I take a deep breath and flick on the hot faucet, letting the water run until steam rises. Filling my hands, I splash my face, looking in the mirror. The woman who stares back is not the same woman who stood here last year or the year before. The weight of the past three hundred and sixty-four days shows itself in my features. Despite years of diligent skin care and hydration, the signs of age are still there. I'm only thirty-four, but the formation of wrinkles in the corner of my eyes has started. Gray hairs have begun to pop up here and there. Constant dark circles rim my eyes under layers of concealer and foundation, something I've never had to do before. Makeup was always a choice, never a necessity. I feel like I developed more curves after having Elena, no matter what I do, they stay in place.

Nick never seemed to mind, though. He seemed to crave my body even more after I became a mother, worshipping it in a way only he knew how. And when I'd feel down about myself, my husband always made me feel better—even if only a little bit.

I hang my head and slam the faucet closed. I wish we could skip tomorrow and jump straight into Monday. Straight to getting on the plane that will take me to the other side of the country and far away from here. How can it already be a year since he left? It feels like it was just yesterday, but also a lifetime ago, all at the same time.

"I miss you," I whisper to the air around me. Closing my eyes, I take a deep breath and feel the burn behind my eyes. "I needed you—*we* needed you—and you…left." I try to withhold a sob. "How could you just leave me?"

I don't get an answer.

I never get an answer.

I should've fought harder for that final conversation…I should've told him I loved him. When I walked in the door the night after our final confrontation about the flowers, I fully expected Nick to be there, cooled down and ready to talk. Instead, I was met with a silent condo filled with inky black shadows. I had checked my watch to verify the time. It was too early for him to be in bed, but not late enough for Elena. I shouldered off my black overcoat, hanging it in the entry closet, and stepped out of my boots, leaving them under the table. Walking farther inside, I heard the faint sounds of giggles and the bath faucet being turned off—the sounds of Elena's bedtime routine.

My relief evaporated when I turned the corner to find Elena and her nanny, Alyssa, in the bathroom. Why was Alyssa still here?

"Momma!" Elena garbled the word around her toothbrush.

"Oh, Nina!" Alyssa held her hand to her chest. "I didn't hear you come in."

"Where's Nick?" I asked.

Alyssa reminded Elena to rinse her mouth after she spat,

and with a dramatic eye roll, my daughter did as she was told. "He asked me if I'd stay until you got home, something about needing to get out to Colorado early."

My stomach dropped.

Nick left. Without saying goodbye. Was he really *that* mad? I never thought he'd leave for the bachelor party without saying goodbye. We'd had our fair share of arguments—what couple doesn't?—but things had never seemed this bad before.

"I was supposed to call him in a few so Elena could say goodnight, but since you're home..."

"I'll do it." I nod. "You're free to head home. And Alyssa, you can take tomorrow off. I'm going to work from home."

Alyssa's brows raised, curious, but she didn't question it. She hung Elena's towel on the bar and said her goodbyes.

"I missed you, Momma," Elena said, snuggling into my side when I kneeled to her level.

"I've missed you, too, my girl." I gathered her in my arms and squeezed her tight, kissing her hair.

"Can we call Daddy?"

"Of course. Go get into bed and I'll call him, okay?" I gave Elena a small push and she took off to her room. I sighed when she was out of earshot, pulling my phone out of my pocket, praying he would answer.

I stared at my reflection on the phone screen for what felt like ten minutes as the phone rang. A second before it ended, the screen opened to his side. The camera stared up at the ceiling, a distant conversation in the background before he picked it up and we were face-to-face, but not how I had hoped when I left work earlier that night. Neither of us said anything until I finally broke the silence. "You left."

Nick blinked away from the phone briefly and then back. The warmth of his whiskey-golden eyes was missing.

"This isn't us, Nick."

He sighed. "Nina—"

"This isn't how we handle things. Not anymore." In the background, I can hear Josh calling for him. "You're obviously busy. Tell Elena goodnight, then you can go."

I don't wait for his response, walking into Elena's room. I handed her the phone, took two steps back to stand at the foot of her bed, and listened as Elena recounted her entire day, which I was sure she had done before he left. But Nick listened like it was the very first time.

"G'night, Daddy." Elena blew a kiss to the phone.

"Good night, Little Bird. I love you. Be good for your momma, okay?"

"Mhmm! When you come home?"

"Just a few nights. I'll be home when you get back from Florida with Grandpa."

Elena held out her pinky finger to the screen. "You double-dog promise?"

"Promise," Nick said, and I knew he was doing the same thing. It was something Elena had picked up on after watching us do it over the years—except she added the "double-dog promise," mixing up "double-dog dare" and "promise," but we went with it anyway.

"You wanna talk to Momma?" Elena asked.

"Tell your momma I have to help Uncle Josh, but I love her."

"Daddy says he loves you!" Elena shouted toward me over the screen, and I could only offer her a small smile before I heard the sound of his disconnection. "Sam I Am?"

"Of course, Bird," I said, fingering the thin orange book from the shelf and settling into bed next to her. I recited the book almost from memory as my mind wandered to the man on the other side of the screen more than two thousand miles away.

And now, standing in front of my vanity, what I wouldn't give to go back to that moment and tell Nick I loved him, too, or beg him to tell Josh to hold on for five more minutes so we could talk. What if I had pushed harder? Would he still have gone out for the hike? Would he still be here?

I open the third drawer of Nick's dresser and pull out the old Boston University sweater faded from years of wear—between the two of us, I think it's seen more action than most things in either of our wardrobes. It still faintly smells like him when I pull it over my head and bring the collar to my nose, even though I'm sure it's only my imagination. There's no way it could *still* smell like him. Nonetheless, the notion is comforting as the earthy scents of cedar and cardamom fill my senses.

On my way to rejoin the family, a photo in our sitting room catches my attention. *What is that doing there?* This is the first time I've noticed it since my return to Haven last year, but I haven't spent much time here recently. This room was our safe haven, away from the chaos that filled our home more often than not. It was one reason I fell in love with this house. During the remodel, Nick even added built-in shelves on either side of the fireplace, and a wet bar, usually stocked with water or juice instead of beer or wine.

I stand on my tiptoes to remove the frame from the top shelf of the built-ins. The image grips tight on my heart and squeezes, digging in so deep I feel the pain in every nerve ending.

A prickle in the air caught my attention well before I felt the weight of his hand on my shoulder. His fingers applied a small amount of pressure on the space between my neck and shoulder and I covered his hand with mine, giving it a gentle squeeze. "I can't wait to get you back to the room," Nick whispered in my ear before he pressed a lingering kiss against my hair.

"Okay, time for you two to start talking," Elizabeth said when he sat beside me.

Nick's hand splayed across my thigh under the table. I

tried not to squirm when his fingers inched closer to where I wanted him most. It had been months since I'd been this close to him and as much as I loved my friends and my sister, I was ready to get back to my hotel and consummate this love affair. When he showed up in the park earlier, I never imagined the day would turn out this way, but now I can't imagine a more perfect ending.

"What do you want to know?" Nick asked.

"How about we start with that ring sitting on Nina's finger," Josh said from behind his whiskey glass. The suggestion from his cousin earned a glare from Nick, but a chorus of agreement from the others at the table.

"You guys have been apart for years! Now you're…married?" Elizabeth's apprehension confused me. Wasn't she the one telling me Nick and I should set aside our differences and make it work the past two years?

The weight on my left ring finger felt foreign. My thumb was constantly fiddling with the new addition to my jewelry collection—a blue-green emerald-cut stone with a diamond halo and diamond-studded platinum band.

"Well, I think it's romantic," my friend and college roommate Lydia swoons, and Michaela agrees.

"It is romantic, just a little unexpected, I guess." Elizabeth shrugged.

"I love her," Nick said, his gaze focused on his hand resting on my thigh. Squeezing my thigh, he looked up and met my stare. "Yeah, there are some things we still need to figure out, but I didn't need time to decide if I wanted to be with her or not…I've known for a long time. I'm just lucky she felt the same way."

After that, the conversation shifted to Michaela's new job promotion, but I knew the interrogation was far from over. Elizabeth and Michaela would question me…later when we weren't sitting at dinner meant to be celebrating Michaela.

"I love you." I looked at my husband. That sounded weird to say...husband. Every time I thought it or said it, a quick wave of adrenaline shot through my veins.

"Ti amo da morire."

I love you to death. The words held such a weight, but I knew he meant them.

"To death, huh?" I asked.

Nick gripped the bottom of my chair and dragged it closer to his. He wrapped his arm around my waist and leaned in. "Till death do us part, Princess," he whispered. The nickname was one of the many he'd used over the years, but I'd come to prefer Dee or Princess over all of them. I giggled when his mouth hovered over mine, bringing my left hand to caress his stubbled cheek.

"And after," I answered.

"And after," he agreed.

The flash caught me off guard. When we parted, Michaela had her phone pointed in our direction. "You guys were so cute, I couldn't resist," she said before returning her attention to the table conversation.

"Nin?" Michaela's voice pulls me from the memory. She stands in the open door of my bedroom with wide blue eyes. "Is everything okay? You never came back, so I wanted to check on you. I knocked, but you didn't answer. Then I saw you crying and—"

"It's fine, Mic. I'm fine," I say, wiping under my eyes, and return the frame to its place on the shelf. "I'm just...thinking about things."

Michaela glances at the frame, a sad smile on her lips when she sees the photo from almost seven years ago. Next month should be our seventh wedding anniversary. "That's still my favorite."

"Yeah, me too." The corners of my lips lift briefly when I gaze at the photo one last time. With a sigh, I usher Michaela out the door. "Well, c'mon, before we miss the end of the movie. Elena would never forgive me."

The stars twinkle in the sky above the mountaintop through the window wall in the great room. When Michaela and I rejoin the family, my daughter climbs over Brie and into my lap, gripping the fabric of Nick's sweater between her tiny hands. Kissing the top of Elena's head, I think back to the photo in my bedroom. I think about that lovesick couple, how unfair life can be, and how blissfully unaware they were of what the future had in store for them.

thirty-two

THE STATION IS QUIET this morning as I follow Elena inside. She skips through the lobby and past Flo's desk without a care in the world. I half expect to see Deputy Johnson sitting at his desk in the corner, but it's empty. The whole place is empty—which isn't unusual for a Sunday—but I know at least one person is here, I saw his SUV parked outside.

Elena woke up early this morning, begging me for a hot chocolate from Vintage House in downtown Haven. And who was I to deny her a warm, chocolatey beverage and some breakfast from her favorite restaurant? It was the same place Daddy and I used to go when we were in town for some father-daughter time and I loved sharing the same tradition with my daughter. Besides, it would be nice to get some time for ourselves before the rest of the day started. Today would be filled with family activities, including a lantern ceremony before dinner.

While sitting at breakfast, Elena suggested we get some breakfast for Uncle Beau because he was probably hungry, too. Little did she know it was already on my agenda to order at least a coffee to-go for our favorite sheriff. I wanted to stop by on our way home and see how he was faring this morning.

Elena likes Beau. I'm not surprised. I suppose her fondness for him is par for the course considering how often he's been around the past year.

I like Beau too, but…it's a little more complicated.

Elena continues to skip through the bullpen until she comes to Beau's office and bolts through the door without knocking. A squeal of delight echoes from inside, which means Beau already has her in his grasp.

I lean against the frame, and a real smile tugs at my lips. Beau kneels in front of my daughter, talking in hushed tones as he offers her a blue raspberry-flavored sucker.

Elena nods her head and greedily takes it, rushing over to me. "Momma! Look what Uncle Beau gave me!"

"I see. Did you say thank you?"

She turns over her shoulder. "Thank you, Uncle Beau!"

"You're welcome, Shortie." Beau chuckles, pulling himself up from the ground, and wipes his palms on the thighs of his jeans.

"Momma, can I get some juice and watch cartoons?" She turns back to me and gives me her best doe-eyed expression, lip pout included. Beau keeps a secret stash of juice for her in the fridge—and everyone knows it—in case I have to bring her along when we meet at the station. He even taught her how to work the tiny television on the counter to keep herself entertained after she called our conversations boring once.

"Sure, Shortie. You know where it is." Beau answers for me, and Elena doesn't wait for my confirmation, dashing out of his office. "Don't look at me like that," he says when I give him a questioning glance.

"What if I was going to say no?"

"You weren't." He sits on the edge of his desk, arms crossed over his broad chest, which strains against the fabric of his khaki-colored button-up. I quickly avert my gaze from his arms. "I was wondering if I'd see you today."

I shrug, lifting the paper bag and tray with two coffees in the air. "I wanted a coffee, and Shortie wanted a hot chocolate, so we went to Vintage House for breakfast. Picked you up something." Walking around the back of his desk, I drop the items on top of the paperwork and fall back into his chair. "I needed a break from the chaos inside my house."

"You have everyone there?" he asks without turning around completely, and I nod while allowing myself a moment to take in his side profile.

A small dip in his forehead from the crease in his brow that I know too well. An almost perfect, Grecian nose. Full lips. A strong, defined jawline that could cut fucking glass. His warm, beige skin was peppered with dark stubble from a few days without shaving. I prefer it that way.

He sucks in a breath, turning away from me. "Damn, that's a lot of people."

"You're telling me." My head falls back against the headrest of the leather chair with my feet planted on the floor, twisting from left to right. I keep my gaze locked on the ceiling tiles above, but I can feel the heat of his stare, sending a wave of fire across my skin. He's moved to the back side of his desk now and if he came even an inch closer, our legs would touch. Actually, with each twist, my jeans swipe against his.

"How's it going?" Beau asks and I shrug, still staring up at the ceiling. "That good, huh?"

"You know how it's going," I say, finally looking at him. "Everyone walks on eggshells. No one quite knows how to be. I mean, how could they? And then—" I scoff. "Then Alex and I got into a fight yesterday."

"About?"

"It doesn't matter."

"Sure, it does, Sweetheart."

I sigh. "He said some shit and...I let it get to me."

"Like?"

"None of your business." My tone earns an eye roll from Beau before he stares down at me from his desk, patiently waiting for me to continue. "He thinks I don't care that Nick is gone." With every word, I can see his jaw clench a little tighter. "And then he brought *you* up."

"Me?"

I nod, biting down on my bottom lip. "Yeah, he thinks we're sleeping together. Thinks we've *been* sleeping together."

"And why would he think that?" Beau tries to hide his shock at the accusation. "Do they know about—"

"No," I say quickly. "I didn't tell them, but I've never hidden that you've been helping me, even after the case went cold. They all know, but now...I can't help but wonder if they all think it."

"That's something I can't answer for ya, Nin. You gotta talk to them, and I would...Talk to them, I mean. If you're that worried about them thinking you and I are together—"

"Don't," I cut him off. "Don't do that."

"What?" His lips have been pulled into a thin line, and I can see the walls coming up between us.

"It's not like that, Beau. You know it's not."

A burst of giggles comes from the kitchen, catching our attention. Elena races back to the office, her sucker now in her mouth, as she tries to retell the joke she just heard on the television. Without waiting for our response, she runs back to the kitchen, giggling. When I'm sure she's gone, I stand to meet Beau at his desk.

"Beau—"

"Nina, don't." He withdraws slightly from my touch.

"I'm sorry," I whisper, pulling him back. "It has nothing to do with *you*. And I am so sorry, but I...I'm not ready. I don't know when I'll be ready. Not just because of me, but because

I have a little girl to think about. How do I explain something like this to her?"

I cradle his cheek and lift his chin to bring his gaze back to mine. A wild mix of emotions swims in his green eyes before his lids flutter closed and he leans into my touch. His hands come to rest on my hips, pulling me to stand between his legs. A small gasp escapes me at the connection. My body is already reacting to being so close to him.

"I am so appreciative of you and everything you've done for us...for me. I wouldn't have made it this past year without you." My fingers play with the hair at the base of his skull, and a small hum of approval sounds in his throat.

"I think you've been doing alright." When his eyes reopen, they glance down at my lips and back, and he swallows the thickness growing in his throat.

"I don't."

There's a gentle tug between us and we don't deny it this time. Like magnets drawn together, unable to resist the pull. His nose brushes against mine. I feel the ghost of his lips and I'm almost certain he can hear my heart pounding. We pause there, neither of us taking the final step forward.

"Nina." A hint of icy mint ghosts across my skin. I can practically taste it on my tongue.

"Beau." His name is strangled on my lips, and I want nothing more than to push forward and claim him as my own. Everything in me screams to close the gap between us. My body remembers the way his felt against mine. Remembers how good it felt to be close to someone, and not just someone... him.

But as much as I want to—and I really, *really* want to—I know we can't.

"Beau, Elena is here."

Those words break the trance once and for all.

Beau clears his throat and slips away from me, scrubbing a

hand down his face. "Shit, Nina. I'm—"

"Don't." My tongue swipes across my lips, still tasting a hint of mint. "Do not apologize. There is nothing to apologize for. This...us...God, Beau. I wish I could give this to you. You have no fucking idea how badly I want to, but—"

He kisses me quickly, stopping my rambling. "It's okay, Sweetheart."

Fuck is the only thing crossing my mind. The only thing I want to do is finish what he started. Holding his gaze a moment longer, I clear my throat and do what *has* to be done. Taking a step back, I say, "We should probably get back before they send a search party."

Beau doesn't offer a verbal response, only nods, and I grab my coffee from the tray before slipping past him.

"Thank you, Beau," I say from the door. "For everything."

"Anything for you, Sweetheart."

I smile, standing there for a brief moment longer before I force my feet to move forward.

thirty-three

OUR FAMILY IS GATHERED for a lantern ceremony in an open field outside downtown Haven. We extended an invitation to anyone in town who wanted to join. I swear the whole town showed, including Beau, other members of the sheriff's office, Sergeant James Warren from State, and Sheriff Rhett Wilson from Puck County. I wasn't surprised to see Beau or the other officers. Hell, I wasn't even surprised to see Sergeant Warren. There was only one person I was surprised to see: Sheriff Wilson. Why was he here?

I had developed a rapport with the others, but not him. He was the only person who avoided me unless he *had* to speak with me. Not that it bothered me much. Something about him makes me feel uneasy…It's hard to explain.

"Uncle Beau!" Elena waves wildly when she sees him. Before I can tell her to wait, she sprints in his direction. Beau doesn't hesitate, lifting her off her feet and swinging her through the air; a chorus of giggles follows. He sits Elena on his hip. Her arms wrap around his neck tightly, and she presses her head against his cheek.

"I think I found something that belongs to you," he says, finding me in the crowd.

"Momma, can I stay with Uncle Beau?" Elena asks, electing him as her official handler for the ceremony. She tightens her grip around his neck, giving me her biggest and brightest *please, please, please* eyes.

"If he's okay with it, I'm okay with it," I say, unable to deny her request. I wasn't going to deny her any source of comfort today, even if it was bound to piss off her Uncle Alex.

Beau readjusts Elena to sit on his shoulders and her hands grip the top of his head, patting his skin affectionately. Her eyes scan the crowd, an advantage from her new height, and she waves at someone in the distance. When Beau is comfortable with her position, he raises his eyes to meet mine again. "Hi," he says with a small smile.

"Hey." Some of the anxiety I have been feeling disappears when I hug him and he returns the gesture. We stand in the embrace for a moment longer than we probably should, but I don't care. "Thank you for being here," I say when we part.

"Whatever you need, Sweetheart." He wraps his hands around Elena's calves and motions me forward to where the rest of the family waits.

"You guys know Sheriff Turner," I say, approaching them.

"Beau." Jimmy is the first to step forward, extending his hand, which Beau takes without question. "Good to see you."

"Wish it was under better circumstances," Beau says.

"Don't we all?"

One by one, everyone welcomes Beau without a second glance, except Alex, who keeps his distance. Every so often I notice the sideways glances he shoots at Beau or me, but at least he keeps his mouth shut. After our conversation yesterday, I wouldn't be surprised if Lara warned him against causing a scene today. I make a mental note to thank her when we get home.

The ceremony happens in the blink of an eye, and before I know it, Jimmy invites Beau to join us for dinner. I thought about it but didn't want to push the boundaries, especially not today. But if Jimmy is okay with it, who am I to say no? Beau looks at me for confirmation and I don't hesitate to nod.

When we get to the table, I smile when Beau sits on the other side of Elena without hesitation. Halfway through dinner, I feel his touch on my shoulder, sending a wave of fire across my skin. It makes me crave his touch everywhere else. Makes me yearn for him in a way I know I shouldn't. And it makes me want to finish what we started this morning in his office...and the only thought I have is, *I am so fucked.*

"That was Mom," Kai says, walking into the kitchen. I stand with my hands under the faucet, filling them with cold water before bringing them to my face, trying everything I can to erase the thoughts of Beau from my head, at least for now. It doesn't feel right to have these kinds of thoughts on today of all days.

Fucked.

I am so fucked.

"You good, Nin?" Kai asks when I come up for air. His brow is cocked so high it's practically in his hair.

"Fine." I sigh, wiping my face with a clean towel. "What did Brina have to say?" At the mention of her name, his eyes drop to the marbled counter, his fingers picking at an invisible speck. Placing my hand on top of his, I squeeze his fingers. "Kai, what's going on?"

"She's in the hospital."

Shit. I sigh. Already? It's barely been three months.

"Nin, it's not..." He presses the heels of his palms into his eyes, taking a deep breath to wrangle in his emotions. "I had to talk to the nurse because Mom was irritated and distracted. She couldn't understand why I wasn't there. Why we *both* aren't there. She even asked about Dad."

"She doesn't remember?"

"The nurse said pancreatic cancer can affect the memory, especially with the chemo."

"How long?" I ask.

Kai shrugs. "Honestly, the nurse said to be prepared."

I sigh, pulling my brother into a tight embrace and rubbing my hand down his back. "I'm sorry, Kai."

We stand there for a few quiet moments before he finally pulls away and wipes under his eyes.

"We'll be in the city tomorrow. You should go see her."

"Do you...Do you want to come with me?" His voice is small, asking the question he already knows the answer to.

No, I don't want to go with him. But without Eileen there, who else is going to do it? And it's not like Elizabeth will go. She wants nothing to do with her, either.

"I know you said—"

"Sure," I say, a bottomless pit forming in my stomach. The thought of going to visit Brina in the hospital makes me sick, but I know it's the right thing to do. "Yeah, Kai. I'll go with you."

Maybe it sounds terrible, but at least talking about my dying mother helps take my mind off a certain sheriff.

"It was nice to see Beau tonight," he says.

There goes that sentiment.

I avoid making eye contact with my brother, and now it's my turn to pick at an invisible speck on the counter.

"I guess I didn't realize how close he and Elena were."

I shrug. "He's been nice to her through this whole thing."

"I think it's a little more than that."

"Kai—"

"Nina, if he makes you happy, why not—"

"Because I'm not ready," I snap, finally looking up at him. "I'm not…" I sigh. "I'm not looking for anything right now. I'm still trying to navigate this new life without Nick and it's not… It hasn't been easy, but having Beau's help has made it a little easier."

"You like him?" My brother asks.

"Non posso."

"How do you not know?" Kai lifts my chin so I'm forced to look at him. "Nina, it's okay to admit you like him. It doesn't mean you love Nick any less."

Tears flood my eyes, and when I try to pull away from him, he doesn't let me.

"I'm selling the house," I say without thinking. "I'm—I'm moving back to New York."

"Oh." Kai drops his hold on my face and chews on the inside of his cheek. "Yeah, I guess that does change things. Does Beau know?"

I shake my head. "Not yet. I just…I just decided a few days ago. I'm supposed to meet with a realtor next week."

"And what if you tell him and he says he wants you to stay?"

"Non lo farà." I scoff. *He won't.*

"Sure he would, if he thought it would change your mind." Kai shrugs. "What if he asks to come with you to New York?"

This time, I laugh. What is he smoking? My brother is delusional if he thinks Beau Turner would ever pack up and leave Haven for New York. This is his home, this is where his life is. He's the sheriff for godsakes. *"Ora stai delirando."*

"I am not. From what I saw tonight…I think anything is possible."

"Stai zitto, Kai. Just shut up."

My brother raises his hands in surrender. "All I'm saying is he's not a bad option."

"I'm not looking for an *option* right now, Kai."

"What are we talking about?" Elizabeth asks, joining us from the hallway after putting her daughter, Nova, to bed.

"Nina and Beau," Kai says, taking an apple from the fruit bowl on the counter.

"Oh my...*Stai zitto!*" I hiss at my brother, swiping at him across the island. Kai dodges the swings, laughing the whole time.

He needs to shut up, right now.

"Why? He's not wrong," Elizabeth says with a smile. "You guys are cute together. Besides, he loves Elena."

I wonder if they know how impossible they are making it to take my mind off Beau and the way my entire being has yearned for him since I was in his office this morning.

"*Lascia perdere! Entrambi.*" I plead for them to drop it before someone else overhears the conversation. My siblings share a glance and laugh as I roll my eyes, stalking out of the kitchen to my room. "You're both insufferable."

thirty-four

DO YOU EVEN CARE *that he's gone?*

Alex's words echo through my mind as my feet pound against the dirt trail. They haven't left me alone since he said them, not even after I talked to Beau about them yesterday. I know it's Alex's grief talking, but it doesn't make his words hurt any less. I want to talk to Alex, to try and fix the damage done by our argument, but every time I try, something pulls me back. I think it's my fear of escalating the situation further. Beau's presence last night only pissed Alex off further, but the rest of the family didn't seem to mind, and it made Elena happy. Her happiness was all I cared about.

My pace slows as I round the bend leading to the Marah Lakes, a group of three large bodies of water off the trail. The largest one is a bit farther off the path but has the best views. Slowing even further, I take the path veering to the left of the main trail. After another ten minutes, I finally step through the tree line where a gorgeous (and worth the new bruise on my shin) view awaits me. A rocky beach leads to crystal waters where the mountain peak rises high into the sky, and the day's last sunlight reflects off the remaining pure white snow yet to melt away. I don't have long before it's dark on the trail, and I don't want to be out here without any light.

Not alone, anyway.

Sitting on one of the bigger rocks on the shore, I take a deep breath and hold it before exhaling.

Do you even care that he's gone?

Those words hit me like a freight train, and every time I hear them, it makes me think of the fight Nick and I had the September before he disappeared. The fight we had before we returned to New York...I can still remember it like it was yesterday.

"What did Kai want?" Nick's voice caught me off guard. *When did he get there?* Turning away from the window, my husband stood in the doorway of my home office. His arms were folded, his gaze slightly narrowed.

I sighed.

I wanted to digest this before telling him. Hoped I could find the right time, but I knew that wasn't possible, considering the time constraint. From the look on his face, I was ninety-nine percent sure he already knew what my brother wanted, and I hadn't even said anything yet. It wasn't hard to guess what it meant when I said Kai wanted to talk business.

"Oh, hi, *Fossette*," I said, offering a smile, the familiar nickname rolling off my tongue.

His brow raised, unimpressed with my attempt to deflect. "Dee, what did your brother want?"

I bit down on my bottom lip, setting my phone back on my desk. Nick was going to be mad, there was no doubt about it, but I didn't have a choice...

"Eileen is about to pop any day now and he wants to be able to be there for her." I shrugged. "He asked me if I'd consider stepping in for a bit."

"He's not giving you much time to think about it. Eileen is

due in two weeks."

"I know…I said yes."

"You said…" Nick scoffed, shaking his head in utter disbelief. "Nina, we didn't even talk about this! Don't I get a say in this, too?"

"I can't let the company fall into anyone's hands."

"What about us?" The word *us* had a particular bite to it. "What about our break? We're supposed to pack up and move back to New York because Kai doesn't want to do his job anymore?" He gripped the other side of my desk, staring me dead in the eye as my face fell. "I don't want to go back to New York, Nina. And neither does our daughter. She likes it here. I like it here, and I thought you did, too."

"I do! It's just—"

"It's not enough for you."

"Nick, that is not what I said."

"You've been going nonstop your *entire* life, Dee. You have always been there to step in for Kai when he didn't want to do his job, but who steps in for you? Even now, you're still helping out with DV Designs. You're still on the board of Villa Inc. You haven't fully stepped away."

"I can't—"

"You could, but you don't."

"Non capisci," I pleaded with him.

"But I do understand, Dee. Probably better than anyone." Nick's hand reached for mine, his thumb grazing the back of my hand, and his touch spread fire across my skin. "You think you owe it to your dad to make sure things run a certain way, to live up to the expectations people have set for you because of him—"

"Non farlo." Don't do that. I pulled my hand from under his. "Don't you dare bring my dad into this."

"I don't want Elena to grow up with parents like yours, Nina," Nick said. "And I know you don't, either. Your dad left the company to Kai, Nina, not you. *Non tu.* He didn't want this for you. And yet, you've been running things since Ric died, and Kai is only there when he wants to be." He reached for me again, but I stepped back from the desk, staring at the ground. He sighed and walked around the corner of my desk, lifting my gaze back to him. "You finally get a chance to have a break, to enjoy life, and now you're letting them suck you back in. *Non è giusto.*"

"*Giusto?*" I scoffed. What did he know about *fair?* "I have to do this, Nick. I have to—"

"Davina." His tone silenced me. "Your brother has had his time. He had his chance to play house and not worry about a damn thing while still getting the title and all the credit. When do you get yours?"

"Now, that's not fair. Kai is—"

"There's no getting through to you." He sighed. "You know…I guess I hoped this would be enough for you…That we'd be enough for you, but I knew better."

We'd be enough for you.

Those words cut me to my core. What did he mean? Of course, he and Elena were enough for me. I'd give up everything for them if I had to. But there wasn't any reason I couldn't go and fill in for my brother for a few months while he helped Eileen adjust to having two kids. We could return to our sabbatical once they were more adjusted and settled in their new life as a family of four.

"Nick—"

He cut me off, his tone void of the same sense of reassurance from before. "When are you leaving?"

"I, um…"

When am I leaving? That's an odd thing to say. We're all going…Aren't we? I didn't plan on leaving them in Haven.

"There's a board meeting in two days. Kai wants to tell them I'll be taking over then." I reached for Nick's hand when he turned away and for a moment, I thought he would keep walking. When he stilled, his back remained facing me. "Nick, I'm sorry."

A dry chuckle escaped his lips, and he looked up to the ceiling, shaking his head. "No, you're not, Davina." He pulled his hand from my grasp and left me standing there.

It's hard being back in my home office after that argument, but it's also one of the only places I can find solitude when the house is full. And when I can't find it there, I come here, despite Beau's continued warnings against it.

I don't care if this is the trail where Nick went missing. It's where I find the most peace. Sometimes it makes me feel close to him—even if it's all in my head.

Things had been going well those ten months we lived exclusively in Haven, starting in late December three years ago. Nick and I had taken a step back from work, occasionally helping out when someone needed some support or when I had to be in the city for a board meeting…but it was the first time we had truly taken a break.

"Six months tops," Kai said on the phone that day. I thought about saying no…Highly considered it, but I knew that I had to go. I couldn't sit by and watch someone else run the company I had worked so hard to grow since Daddy died. And there was no way the board could find someone else in such a short amount of time. From my conversations with other board members, they'd been waiting for the day I decided to leave behind the quiet, mountain life and return to the city.

Nick and Elena did come with me to New York the next day, but neither of them was happy about it. Scratch that, Elena was, at first, because going to the city meant getting to see her aunts and uncles, but her excitement seemed to dwindle when she realized we weren't returning to Haven anytime soon. Nick didn't have to say the words *I told you so,* they were written all over his face from across the plane.

The tension between us seemed only to grow when the plane landed on the tarmac in New York. He carried a sleeping Elena off the jet into the back of the SUV, and we rode in silence the whole way to our Upper East Side condo.

It wasn't until he climbed into bed, pulling me flush against him and kissing the back of my neck, that I felt some of the walls come down.

"I'm not happy about this, Dee." Nick sighed. "But I don't want to fight. I support you. I would've supported whatever decision you made if you would've talked to me first." His warm, whiskey-golden eyes met mine when I turned in his arms. "We're in this together, Davina. I just ask that you try to remember that."

"I love you, *Fossette*," I whispered and kissed him.

A few months in New York turned into six sooner than expected and by the time Alex's bachelor party rolled around in the seventh month, there were no signs of Kai returning anytime soon. Nick had decided to pick up a few projects here and there—nothing daunting, but it still meant he needed help with Elena. I had to hire a nanny, which was something I never wanted to do, but it was necessary. Not only was I working on current projects, but I had a backlog of projects to catch up on that my brother had failed to mention. There was a lot of work to be done. More than I anticipated, and that was saying something...I was spending less and less time at home. Nick and I started getting into more fights—most of them small, but the divide was noticeable to both of us.

It was becoming too much, and a few days before our last fight, I had a difficult conversation with myself. Maybe this life wasn't what I wanted anymore. I loved my work. I loved my companies—both DV Designs and Villa Incorporated—but it wasn't worth the cost of my marriage or family.

Now, the only things I have left are Elena and my work.

And Beau.

But do I have Beau?

He isn't mine. I've made it clear that I'm not ready for anything resembling a relationship, but it seems like the harder I fight it, the harder it pushes back. It isn't even Beau's fault. He respects the boundaries, and he respects me, but neither one of us can deny there is *something* there. Something that continues to draw us together. There is also the guilt I feel, it keeps me from even dipping my toe in. Whenever I think about what I could have with Beau, the guilt creeps up from its hiding place and reminds me why something with Beau wouldn't even be possible.

The more I think about it, the more I can't wait to return to New York. Going back will be good for both of us—Elena and me. She'll be happy to be closer to her cousins again and it will give me the fresh start I've been looking for. Maybe it will allow me to start healing once and for all.

Now, I have to tell Beau…

thirty-five

KAI WILL KILL ME if we miss our flight, but there's no way we'll make it now. I have been out here far longer than I should have, but it was hard to leave the lake. It's always hard to walk away from this place…Being here makes me feel close to Nick. Is that morbid? Maybe a little, but sometimes I hope some answer will magically appear if I keep coming out here. A sign to let me know what happened because, despite what the police speculate (a wild animal is their best guess) I still don't know for sure, and that haunts me.

My pace slows at the base of the mountain. I try to catch my breath, approaching the mouth of the trailhead. When I step through the tree line, a cool wind blows through the field and the tall grass bends to its will. It wraps around me, cooling the exposed skin on my legs and face, warm from my final push the last half mile. A chill runs through my veins, a hyper-awareness of my surroundings as goosebumps rise across my skin. When the wind recedes, the air feels still and suffocating. The birds no longer share their song with me. Everything around me ceases and it feels like the world stands still.

Something isn't right.

A prickle on the back of my neck forces me to look in every direction for the source, but I find nothing. Something is out here with me. Or is it someone?

I stuff my hand into the front pocket of my hoodie, gripping my keys and stuffing one of them between my forefinger and middle finger.

The feeling of being watched is overwhelming, but I don't see anything out of place. Any predator would know how to hide—know how to conceal itself long enough to strike at the right moment. I press the auto-start button on my keys, but nothing happens. Of course, this is the one time it wants to follow the rules about range. My feet automatically pick up the pace, but not enough to trouble whatever is watching me.

My gaze sweeps across the fields on either side of the parking lot. There's nothing out of the ordinary. Like earlier, my silver Wrangler is the only car in the lot, making me feel paranoid. Am I being paranoid? No? Maybe?

Two steps from the highway, I click the button again. This time, the engine turns over, taking the edge off my anxiety.

Snap!

"Don't do it, Nina. Keep moving," I demand, but I don't listen. Turning over my heel, I find the source...

A man towers over the opening of the mountain. He doesn't move, only stares.

I'm scared to move, but I can't stay here. I'm closer to the car than he is to me, but what if...I whip around to look back at the lot and make sure there isn't someone else lurking there. No sign of anyone, but that doesn't mean they aren't hiding nearby. I didn't see this guy until he made his presence known, so who knows how many others there could be? Looking back, I half expect him to be closer, but he stands in the same spot.

I step back, finally on the road, keeping my eyes on his as I edge toward the lot. When I finally reach the other side, stepping onto the gravel driveway of the lot, the man takes one step forward. And then another. And another. Until he's halfway across the field. I run the final distance to the car, expecting to see someone else waiting for me, but there's no one.

I slam my hand into the ignition button and lock the doors. When I reach the exit, the man stands at the edge of the highway, and we're locked in another standoff.

Without taking my eyes off the man, I dial the all-too-familiar number.

"Nina?"

"Beau." His name comes out slowly, concentrated, as I try to remain calm. This is not the time to freak out.

"What's wrong?"

I smile at how well he's come to know me. "There is someone out here."

"Out where?" Sounds of him gathering his stuff can be heard in the background. A door closes and keys jingle. "Nina, where are you? I'm on my way."

"Achor."

"What the fuck are you doing out at *Achor?*"

"I needed some air," I say, watching the man stand there. *What is he doing?* I'd swear he was a statue if I hadn't seen him walk a few moments ago.

"You needed air?" Beau tries to keep his voice down. He hates that I come out here, especially alone. He's pleaded with me multiple times to at the very least give him a heads up or let him come with me. I tell him he's being paranoid. That I'll be fine...even if there was always a voice in the back of my mind telling me he might be right. This was where Nick went missing, after all. "Nina, if you need air, go to one of the one-fucking-million trails we have around *here.* You don't have to drive to fucking Achor where I can't—"

"You are not helping!"

There are no signs of anyone joining us on this dead-end highway. If I try to pull out, will he bumrush the car? The doors are locked, he can't get in, but what if he has a weapon? He could blow out a tire. Then I'm really screwed. I could try to outrun him, but...

Holy shit.

Is that what happened to Nick?

My mind flashes back to the thought of the bloody shirt and the broken phone. Was this man the reason my husband went missing? So many scenarios run through my head of what could've happened...Each ends in my husband running for his life as this man chases him through unfamiliar territory. Each ends with my husband left bruised and bloodied—or worse—in the wilderness, left for nature to take its course.

The man heaves something out of his pocket and tosses it in the middle of the road, his eyes never leaving mine. When I realize what it is, tears prick the corners of my eyes and nausea rises in my throat.

Nick's wallet.

The black Louis Vuitton wallet I gifted my husband for Christmas four years ago. He rolled his eyes playfully when he opened it, saying he didn't need something so expensive to carry around his credit cards and ID. Despite his protests, he kissed me and began transferring his stuff over. My husband would have no problem buying me something so expensive— he liked spoiling me—but he'd never do it for himself, so I did it for him. I didn't look at the wallet as a symbol of status. It was a gift, something he *needed,* not just something he wanted.

When my eyes rise from the road, the mystery man smiles victoriously.

"Nina!" Beau's voice rips through my head.

"W-what?"

"For fuck's sake, I've been saying your name for a straight minute." His voice sounds a little more distant and I can hear the wind in the background. He's driving. But he's almost two hours away, he'd never make it in time if this man decided to do something.

"He has it." My eyes lower to the wallet again.

"What?"

"Nick's wallet."

"You can't possibly know it's—"

"I know what it is, Beau! I bought the damn thing. I'm telling you—"

"Listen to me right now." Beau's voice is deadly on the other end of the line. "Do not get out of that car. Rhett is on his way. You need to leave."

"But B—"

He cuts me off before I can even say his full name. "Davina, I do not care if it's Nick himself out there, do *not* get out of that car. You leave right fucking now. Do you hear me?" He stops me when I try to protest again. "Let Rhett handle it. I'm on my way and if you're there when I get there, I'm going to arrest you."

"Good thing you have no jurisdiction here, then."

Beau doesn't laugh at my attempt at a joke.

I scan over the man on the other side of the road again. He is so still. He stands as tall and stagnant as the mountain above us. I'm not sure he's even blinked in the last three minutes. Has it really only been three minutes? It feels like we've been locked in this stalemate for hours.

"Nina," Beau pleads. "Let us handle this. Please. Let *me* handle this."

"Because that's gone so well for me up until this point?"

Beau sucks in a breath. "I will have Rhett arrest you for interfering with an investigation."

He wouldn't dare.

"Do not get out of the car."

"What if he's gone?" I ask, starting to let my foot off the

break.

"We'll find him."

How? I barely saw him to begin with. Not until he wanted me to. Who knows how long he's been hanging around? Watching. Did he watch us search last year? Was he a volunteer? Has he been here the whole time, hiding in plain sight?

"Nina, we will find him. I promise. Please, you have to leave. Elena can't lose both of her parents." Beau's words lift my foot the rest of the way.

To my surprise, the man doesn't move when I pull out of the lot. Glancing in the rearview mirror, I watch him. He turns his head, watching me leave, and my heart stops when I see the other person standing in the lot, directly behind where my car had been sitting seconds ago.

When I pull into the garage almost two hours later, I kill the engine but don't get out. I rest my head against the top of the steering wheel and take slow, deep breaths. What is going on? This cannot be real life. This kind of stuff doesn't happen in real life. This is the kind of thing you see in movies. The ride home was silent, minus the phone call I got from Beau ten minutes ago.

"Did you find them?" I didn't waste time on the niceties when I answered the phone. I had been impatiently awaiting his call since I received his text when he arrived at Achor forty minutes prior, managing to cut at least twenty minutes off the typical drive time. I wondered if cops were subject to speeding laws like the rest of us, or if this constituted a necessary reason to break the law.

"There's no one here, Nina." Beau sighed on the other end. I could picture him in my mind, jaw set, pinching the bridge of his nose, eyes screwed shut, as he stood in the middle of the parking lot.

"They were there, Beau! There was someone there, I...I saw them. I'm not crazy."

"I'm not saying that!" The bite in his words startled me. That was the first time he had spoken to me like that. Ever. "Fuck. Nina, I'm sorry. I didn't—I didn't mean to snap on you. It's just..." I could hear someone in the background—Sheriff Wilson, or maybe Max—but I couldn't understand what they were saying. "Let me call you back."

The line went dead.

He called back a few minutes later and this time the sounds of a moving car were in the background.

"Everything okay?" I asked when he didn't say anything.

"Fine." Beau sounded like he was wound as tight as a pissed-off rattlesnake.

"What's wrong?"

"Nothing is wrong." I could practically hear the grind of his teeth.

"That was convincing," I said, navigating the road toward the house, hoping he would finally open up and tell me before I arrived. "Beau, please don't lie to me. What is going on?"

A heavy sigh on the other end mixed with the sound of the road and the wind pouring in from an open window. "I'm sorry, Sweetheart. I shouldn't have snapped at you, I'm...I'm trying to make sense of all this, but I can't. Nothing about this makes any fucking sense. We know it's his wallet—you ID'ed it and his license is inside, but it doesn't tell us anything."

The confirmation hits me like a freight train. I don't know why the confirmation of what I already knew sends an unexpected wave of emotions flooding my system. I clear my throat, trying to hide the thickness of my voice. "Are they gonna reopen it?"

"Rhett said he'd get in touch with James."

"And you believe him?"

"You don't?" Beau asked, a hint of something in his tone. Was he fishing?

"I think things have been wonky ever since Rhett got involved," I said, gripping the top of the steering wheel. It was the first time I had admitted it out loud, but the thought had crossed my mind more than a handful of times.

"I agree," Beau said before he sighed. I didn't know whether to be relieved or concerned that we shared the same thought. "Will you be home when I get back to town?"

"I shouldn't be, but probably. I don't feel like sitting on a plane with my brother for five hours after the day I've had. You try being stalked by some weirdo on the trail and then see if you want to be stuck in such tight quarters with Kai James Villa."

Beau laughed, and the sound made me smile.

"You'll let me know when you hear something?" Parking outside the garage, my knuckles turned white against the wheel, and I rolled my lips between my teeth.

"The minute I know something, you'll know something, Sweetheart. And Nina, I really am sorry for snapping at you." The sincerity in his voice took me by surprise. I can't remember the last time someone apologized to me and seemed so sincere about it.

Now, the longer I sit here pondering what's going on, the more I'm starting to believe Sheriff Rhett Wilson is somehow involved in Nick's disappearance. It's the only thing that makes sense…And if he is involved—

Knock! Knock!

"Whoa!" A voice shouts outside the car window when I practically jump out of my skin. Turning to see who it is, I'm face-to-face with Elizabeth. She tugs on the handle, opens the door, and leans in. "You alright?"

"Fine," I say, rubbing my eyes.

"I believe that like I believe Brie when she says she didn't take the last piece of cheesecake from the fridge. You about jumped to the moon and back when I knocked on the window. What's going on?"

"I'm fine, Elizabeth. Just…tired."

"I'll pretend I believe you for the sake of not wanting to make whatever this is"—she waves her hand in an all-encompassing circle before me—"worse. But don't think we're not talking about this later."

I wouldn't expect anything less. "Where is Kai?" I ask, walking into the house.

"Out back, he was getting antsy when you didn't show up on time. Please tell me you're packed and ready to go because—Wait, where are you going?"

"I need to talk to him. We're not leaving tonight." I don't wait for more questions I'm sure she has, like *why* we aren't leaving tonight.

No one needs to know why I want to postpone the flight. When Kai asks why, I'll go with whatever excuse comes to mind, even if it's as simple as not wanting to be in such close quarters with him right now. It's better than the truth. If I tell them the truth—if I tell them I was face-to-face with the person (people?) who I think did something to Nick—they'll have a million other questions to replace the handful they're going to have about a postponed flight. This is a case of picking your battles, and I'm choosing the easier one.

thirty-six

MAGNOLIA CAFÉ IS A small coffee shop in the heart of downtown Haven. It's the perfect place to grab a coffee before I'm stuck on a plane with Kai for five hours. He wasn't happy I wanted to push back our flight, mostly because he wanted to go to the hospital to see Brina, which I wasn't in any rush to do. I reminded him we didn't *have* to be in the city until Wednesday morning. Anything else was extra time to get ahead (or to let me see what he had fallen behind on). When he started to argue, I told him to drive down to Denver and catch a commercial flight if he wanted to leave so badly, but our flight was leaving this morning at eight-thirty sharp.

The morning air is warm, and the sunshine already beats down from the clear sky above me as I stand outside Magnolia's to-go window. Normally, I'd be comfortable in my current outfit—jeans, white camisole, and a flowy caramel-colored button-down left open—on an early spring day, but it might be too much today.

"I thought you'd be on a plane by now." The gruff voice brings a smile to my lips.

Beau stands behind me with his hands on his hips. He is dressed in black trousers and a tan-colored button-up, with the top two buttons undone and the sleeves rolled up below his elbows. The material hugs his arms in a way that almost makes me jealous. His badge sits on his left hip, opposite of his holstered weapon. The layers of his short brown hair are styled this morning, but left tousled, giving it volume most women would kill for.

"I should be."

One of the baristas calls my name, setting my coffee on the windowsill. Not a moment later, she calls out the window again, "Here you go, Sheriff."

He didn't even order yet, how did they—Shit. How could I forget? Beau gets his second cup from Magnolia's every morning before he heads into the station.

Beau plucks our coffees from the window, dropping a five-dollar bill in the tip jar. "You have a minute?"

"Not really, but we're already here. It won't kill my brother to wait a few more."

"Sure about that?" He chuckles, leading me down the steps of the patio to where his SUV awaits.

"What's wrong?" I ask, ignoring the joke.

Beau sets both coffees on the hood and uses my hands to tug me two steps closer. "I'm sorry, Nina, for snapping at you yesterday. I—"

I cut him off. "Beau, you already apologized."

"I need to say it again because I was wrong. Going off on you wasn't acceptable...or professional. So, I'm sorry."

"Are you saying this as Sheriff Beau or just...Beau?" My fingers tug on the front of his button-down, just enough to earn a small grunt in response when our bodies collide.

"Nina." It's a warning.

We're not even one hundred feet from the coffee shop, barely shielded by his SUV, and technically he's in uniform...

This is not the place.

I take a step back and take a deep breath, rolling my shoulders to stand straighter. "Beau, I need to tell you something." I chew on the corner of my mouth and my stomach sinks meeting his gaze. This is going to hurt. "I'm going back to New York."

"Yeah, I know."

"No, I'm going back...for good. Elena and I are moving back."

Beau's green eyes narrow at the unexpected announcement. "What do you mean you're moving back...to New York?"

"I—I think it's time. It's been over a year, and I can't stay in the house when...he's *everywhere*. Everything about it reminds me of him. I can't keep living like this, Beau. I can't. I can't keep sitting here hoping he's going to walk in the damn door one day, because he's not. Nick is gone and he's not coming back. What happened yesterday only proves it."

Every time I close my eyes, all I can see are the eyes of the strange man staring back at me. They were so cold, so distant...like he was there, but he wasn't at the same time.

"Will that make you happy?" Beau asks. The question is so simple, but so heavy all at the same time. Will it make me happy? I don't know, but it's the only way I know how to start over.

"I don't know," I say.

"Nina—"

"Beau, don't. Please." I shake my head and pull my lips between my teeth. "Please don't make this decision harder than it already is."

Beau sighs and nods once. He crosses his arms over his chest and blinks away from my gaze. He scrubs his face with a hard sigh and changes the subject. "You know what I still don't understand. How did they know you were there? And why show up now?"

Those were the questions I'd been trying to figure out.

Nothing about any of this made sense. Why would the man risk showing himself now? Why did he let me go? I had seen his face, clear as day, but he still let me go. I think it's pretty obvious he is the one who attacked Nick, but why? Was it a case of wrong place, wrong time? Did he know Nick? Or was someone trying to get to me? All questions no one seems to have the answers to.

And what about the other man? The one I had seen in the rearview mirror. He couldn't have been more than two feet from the back of my car. What if I hadn't left?

"Have you heard anything from James?" I ask, but Beau shakes his head. "You don't think Sheriff Wilson—"

"I don't know, Nina," Beau says, pushing his hands through his hair, the sun warming his natural dark brown color. "Honestly, I don't know what to think anymore. Something in me says there's more going on here. Someone knows something. Whether that's Rhett or—"

"Oh, you've got to be fucking kidding me," a different voice says, and my stomach lurches at the sound. A humorless chuckle follows the statement.

No, you've got to be kidding *me.*

"You know, for someone who says nothing is going on, you're not doing a good job of being convincing."

"What are you doing here, Alex?" I ask. I don't have the energy to fight with him right now.

"Well, I came to grab a coffee while Lara's in yoga class. The barista said you were around here somewhere, so I thought I'd come to talk to you. Try to apologize for how I handled things the other day, but..." Alex shakes his head, the hurt palpable behind his eyes. "I see you're doing just fine."

"Alex—"

"No, Nina. I don't want to hear it." My brother-in-law takes a deep breath. "Did you even wait for him to get cold? Or were you so happy to be rid of him it didn't matter?"

"Enough, Alex," Beau says. He wraps his arm around me and pushes me behind him.

Each word Alex said is like a stab to the heart. This time I can't fight off the tears as they prick the corners of my eyes. Can't stop a few of them from slipping down my cheeks. Can't stop the nausea as it rises in my throat, nor the crushing weight building in my chest.

His murderous gaze falls on Beau. "And you—"

"Shut the fuck up, kid. Someone needs to knock you off your high horse before you forget who you're talking to. You don't speak to her that way. Do you have no respect?"

"Where's the respect for my dead brother?"

Beau shakes his head and scoffs. He looks up to the sky, begging for patience to deal with this situation. If he wasn't in uniform, I doubt Alex would still be vertical.

"The rest of the family might be okay ignoring it, but I'm not."

"There's nothing to ignore or not ignore, Alex," I say. "We aren't together!"

"I can't believe you still deny it when I just caught you! You're not even trying to hide it anymore. You're messing around in plain sight—"

"In plain sight?" I scoff. "Alex, you didn't walk in on us fucking around. We're standing here, as you said, in *plain sight*, fully clothed and talking about Nick…Your *dead brother*, as you so eloquently named him."

"Now, I'm no lawyer, just a lowly sheriff." Beau scratches at the scruff on his chin, staring down at Alex. "But isn't there something called innocent until proven guilty? Or does that not apply in your little witch hunt?" He looks over his shoulder and meets my gaze with a brief smile. It chips away at my already fragmented heart. "Nina has done nothing wrong, and neither have I. The only thing we're guilty of is trying to find the answers to what happened to your brother. When the rest of you packed and left, she stayed here and worked tirelessly trying to get those answers." Beau looks at me again. "You tell him about last night?"

"Beau, don't," I whisper.

"What about last night?" Alex looks between the two of us, but I avoid his stare.

Beau shakes his head, offering me an apologetic smile. "Nina was followed off the trail by two men, one of them in possession of your brother's wallet."

Alex's eyes are wide. "Nina, why—You could've been hurt! Why wouldn't you tell us?"

I scoff again. Is he serious? "Why would I tell you?"

"Why wouldn't you tell me?"

"You and I aren't exactly on the best terms right now, Alex. Or have you forgotten you accused me of being *happy* about this? Happy that I was robbed of my happy ending with the man I love."

Alex gnaws on the inside of his cheek, considering my words, and from my peripheral I see Beau brace himself to prepare for whatever else my brother-in-law may throw my way. Clearing his throat, Alex looks at the sheriff. "Are you going to reopen the case?"

Beau shrugs. "It's not my call, but it might be enough for Warren to consider it."

My phone rings in my pocket and I pull it out, rolling my eyes when I see the name.

Jace Powers.

Jace Powers is a former developer at the Villa Architecture Firm. He worked with Nick for a year or so before leaving the company to start his own firm, centralized in Denver. From what I can tell, he has done well for himself over the years, focusing more on developing some of the smaller towns to bring tourist activity to them. When he left Villa Inc., I jokingly warned him to stay away from Haven. We were fine. I didn't want him picking apart my city. If anyone should be in charge of the further development of Haven, it was me.

When I was leaving this house this morning, I noticed a missed call from him. I assumed he called because he needed help, but I didn't have time to clean up whatever mess he'd made. I had enough going on today, so I left his voicemail unheard and put him on my list of things to do on Thursday morning.

It seems strange for him to call again. Normally, he'd wait for me to return the call. Maybe it wasn't about a project...

"I have to take this. Don't leave, it'll be two minutes tops," I say to Beau, glaring at Alex over my shoulder.

Beau nods without looking away from Alex. I hear the sheriff say something to my brother-in-law, but his voice is too low to know what it is.

"What do you want, Jace?" I answer the phone when I'm far enough away from the duo.

"Where are you?" Jace asks, his voice quieter than I've ever heard it before.

That's an odd question. "I'm about to leave for the airport. Why?"

"Which airport?"

"Jace, why are you asking—"

"Nina, what fucking state are you in *right now?*" The tone of voice shocks me.

"Colorado...What does any of this matter? Jace, what's going on?"

"We found him."

thirty-seven

BLACKWOOD RANCH IS BREATHTAKING. Black wrought iron letters spread across the top of the gate spell out the family name as I pass through. The bed and breakfast becomes visible in the distance with the rest of the farm. Based on looks, I'd say this place was built in the late 1800s, and normally that thought alone would excite me. I'd salivate at the chance to learn its history and hear all the stories from its lifetime, but not today. Today my focus remains on the words Jace Powers said. *We found him.* Those three words led me to walk away from Beau and Alex without any explanation other than: "I have to go."

Since I left them on the side of Main Street, Beau has called my phone repeatedly, and so have Alex and Kai—almost like the three of them are sitting together, calling in rotation to see who I would answer first. After the fifth rotation, I turned my phone off. If they wouldn't take the hint, I'd make them.

My hand grips the gear shift long after I park the car in front of the beautiful two-story farmhouse.

My heart feels like it's going to beat out of my chest. Is this really happening? Am I moments from seeing my husband for the first time in over a year? It feels like a dream I'll wake from at any moment.

There's another car parked next to me, a black Escalade, and I can only assume it belongs to Jace. The others under the carport don't have the same look as the sleek black SUV. They're more suitable for life on a farm. Before I kill the engine, the Escalade's driver's side door opens and Jace jumps out. He shakes out his leg and wipes some invisible dust off his jeans before his attention turns to me. He waves me forward.

No going back now...

My finger presses the ignition button and Jace rips open my door, pulling me out of the seat. "Nina, you made it!" He pulls me in for a hug and whispers in my ear, "Play along."

"What are you talking about, Jace? Where is—"

"Play along." He drags me toward the Escalade where his partner, Ben, and an older gentleman now stand. Jace says, "Mr. Blackwood, I want to introduce you to someone. This is Nina. She's one of the best designers in the country and I thought she could lend a hand with some ideas for the ranch."

What in the hell is going on? I'm not here to help them develop this fucking ranch, I'm here to find my husband. Jace didn't say anything about this on the phone. He didn't say anything other than he and Ben had seen Nick—*alive*—at a ranch in Bezer.

"It's nice to meet you, Nina," Mr. Blackwood says, extending his hand toward me. *Who is this man?*

Jace gives me a look that says, *Play. Along.*

"You as well, Mr. Blackwood," I say, still trying to gather my thoughts.

"Joseph, please."

It's hard not to offer the older man a genuine smile before my gaze sweeps over the house. It's a beautiful home. Well-maintained, with a lot of charm. Black shutters shoulder each window. A wide porch extends the front of the house and wraps around the right side, with six steps up to it. Mountain-blend stones layer the foundation, climbing up the chimney on the far-left side, a warm contrast to the pure white siding. It could use a new roof, but it doesn't look to be in terrible shape. Rolling hills of the mountain extend past us on all sides, and I can imagine the sunsets here are otherworldly. I can't imagine why he'd want to sell to Jace. Knowing Ben, Jace's partner, the whole thing will be torn down and they'll slap a resort on it.

"Have we done a tour yet?" I ask.

"You want to see the house?" Joseph's shock tells me he figured the same thing.

I meet Jace's annoyed glance and smirk. If he wants me to play along, that's exactly what I'll do. Turning back to Joseph, I say, "Jace told me a little, but I'd love to see for myself. Being here…I have some ideas of how we can maintain it."

Joseph raises a brow to Jace and Ben, extending his arm to me. "Right this way."

The inside is even more charming than the outside. Original hardwood floors flow throughout each room, intricate wallpaper designs line the walls in some rooms while a mix of white and colored paints decorate the others, cozy furniture dots the living room and bedrooms, and knickknacks from years of travel and gifts from returning visitors rest in various places throughout the house. This is not the same kind of farmhouse aesthetic you see nowadays—it's the real deal, and I'm in love with it. A warmth radiates from the inside out, making you feel like part of the family, and I can tell Joseph is a big part of it. The second we walk inside, he offers each of us a cup of coffee—which I happily accept, but Jace and Ben decline.

The kitchen, painted a bright yellow like sunshine on a warm, summer day, houses a four-seater handcrafted wood table in front of the window overlooking the side yard. White cabinets, tan countertops, and white appliances fill the space. Square, white tile backsplash lines the walls behind the stove, and utensils and small pans hang from black hooks on two rails on either side. It's exactly what you'd imagine walking into a farmhouse untouched by modern society and its call to rid homes of what makes them unique.

Joseph hands me the coffee in a ceramic blue mug with a hummingbird, and I try to hide my surprise. Surely, he didn't see my tattoo—it's hidden beneath my shirt sleeve. "I love hummingbirds. How'd you know?"

"I saw your necklace." He smiles, and my left hand instinctively reaches for the small bird resting on my collarbone. The hummingbird hangs a few inches above the second chain holding Nick's wedding ring above my heart.

A gift from Nick for Christmas years ago—the second Christmas we spent apart when he was in Boston—the hummingbird necklace arrived with a handwritten note. The note reminded me of what Nick and I had talked about two months prior when we'd secretly seen each other in Boston. We didn't speak for five months after that. Not until another note arrived with a bouquet after one of my speeches. A few days later, he found me in Central Park and asked me to marry him...We got married at the courthouse the same day.

"You got lucky. Normally, it's in the sink. Our guest who's been with us uses it every morning before work. Guess he didn't have any coffee this morning."

"He had a to-go mug when I saw him leave with your daughter," Ben says from the hallway.

"Oh, right, they had to run into town and grab some things. They should be back at some point, hopefully before you leave. I'd love to introduce you."

Jace stares straight at me and offers a subtle nod, confirming the "guest" is Nick. I do my best not to react when my heart does a flip, trying to escape the confines of my ribcage.

"Well, c'mon, let's see the rest of the house," Joseph says, offering me his arm again.

The house has just as much history as I imagined, probably more than Joseph could know. His family restored it to its former glory when he was a child. While he's done his best to maintain the property, it has become hard to manage with his declining health. As we walk through the house, Joseph tells me stories from his childhood and of his daughter, and I fall more in love with it. I can't fathom the thought of tearing it down. A lot of love and hard work has gone into this house over the years, and the idea of losing such craftsmanship seems unthinkable.

My fingers graze over the wall of the upstairs hallway. It's stark white with a smooth and even texture that only comes from a fresh paint job, confirming what I already knew from the smell in the air. "Did you recently have some work done?"

"How can you tell?" Joseph smiles.

I point to my nose. "I can smell the fresh paint on the walls."

"That guest I told you about, he's been lending a hand around the ranch."

"You put all your guests to work, Joe?" Jace laughs.

"Poor kid came wandering into town 'bout a year ago without a dime to his name—or a name, for that matter. Needed a place to stay. I've been letting him stay here and help me get some work done around the property."

Or a name, for that matter. What does he mean?

"Awful kind of you, sir," Jace says, meeting my gaze briefly.

"Hard worker, too. Been a real help around here since Doctor Sanders said to lighten the load after my health scare."

"Well, let's look at the barn," Ben suggests. "You said you had some work done in there recently."

"Oh yes!" Joseph's face splits with a bright smile. He begins ushering us toward the stairs at the other end of the hallway. "Xavier has done some great work in there."

Xavier? Who the hell is Xavier?

I hang back a few steps. "Do you mind if I use the restroom? I'll be right out."

"Course, darlin'. Right through that door." Joseph points at the door over my shoulder at the furthest end of the hallway.

I smile in thanks and walk to the bathroom, but don't go in, gripping the handle until their voices disappear and I hear the front door close. When I see them through the window overlooking the front of the house, I go to the bedroom door directly to the left of the bathroom. When I turn the handle, I'm happy to find it unlocked. Joseph wouldn't let us in this room earlier, saying he wanted to respect the privacy of his guest, and I knew I had to get in there. It may be my only chance to figure out what in the hell has been going on.

The door swings open, smooth as butter, and I smile, because I know it's something Nick is a stickler for. If there is so much as a creak in a hinge, it will be gone the same day. While I never thought it was a big deal, it came in handy with a sleeping toddler.

The room looks like the other three guest rooms—nothing special, nothing out of place. Only two things in the room indicate someone has been staying here: the folded pajamas hidden behind the pillow—something Nick always did—and the desk full of sketches, notebooks, and a file. A medical file. The name on the tag reads *John Doe* in scribbled penmanship. I flip it open to find a medical chart and a police report, neither filled with much information. I scan the file and find a scribbled note on the last page of the medical chart:

No memory of the incident or how he arrived in Bezer.

Patient found by Bill Wyatt and Joseph Blackwood on April 10, 2028. Patient has amnesia. Definite cause is unknown, appears to be some kind of trauma to the head with a deep laceration, along with bruised ribs and a sprained ankle.

"Oh my God," I whisper.

Amnesia.

Nick has amnesia. He doesn't remember me or our life together. He doesn't remember our daughter, our home…He doesn't remember anything.

There's a Post-it Note inside the file with five facts in my husband's handwriting. The fifth one makes my heart ache: *No one has come looking.*

Closing the file shuffles a few drawings, and one catches my eye. I gasp, dropping it as soon as I free the drawing from underneath the others. Tears prick my eyes when I see the sketch of our home in Winchester—the house I built long before Nick and I were together. The house I had worked hard to pay for because I wanted something of my own without feeling like it had been handed to me because of my name. The one Nick moved into after we got married in New York and turned it from mine to ours, making it feel less like a house and more like a home. A tear drops down my cheek, falling onto the paper, and I smile.

Maybe he didn't remember everything, but he remembered something…

And I could work with that.

When I find the others in the barn, they're gathered in the stable area behind doors that look like they've been recently redone. "I'm sorry, I got caught up looking at the paintings in the hallway," I say.

Not a total lie, I *had* been admiring them earlier when we passed by them.

"Nice, aren't they?" Joseph asks, a sense of pride in his words.

"Did you do them?"

"Oh no!" He chuckles. "No, I'm no artist. My mother painted those. She had dementia, but painting gave her a way to express herself even when she couldn't *express* herself."

"I'm so sorry to hear that."

"Oh, don't be, sweetie. Mother lived a good life. Happy till the day she went to be with the good Lord."

"Shall we?" Jace extends his hand farther into the barn. He and Ben are getting antsy, but Nick isn't back from town yet... What's the rush?

"Oh, yes, of course. Let's start with the arena," Joseph says, leading us down the main stretch. He begins in the tack room, recently renovated by *Xavier.* After bragging about the new indoor shower, Joseph pulls open a rolling door at the end of the long hall, revealing a riding arena where three barrels sit in the open space.

"You been barrel racing, Joe?" Ben chuckles.

"Charlie," Joseph corrects him. "Finally got her back on the horse last year after her accident, thanks to Xavier. Remember, she competed at the Blossom Festival this past weekend and won. I'm not surprised, she just needed a little shove in the right direction."

"She and Xavier close?" Jace asks the question I want to know.

"It's a bit complicated." Joseph laughs, scratching his beard. "I wouldn't say they're close, but definitely something goin' on there."

Not exactly the answer I wanted to hear. If he's built a life here, how am I supposed to convince him to come home?

What if he doesn't want to come home?

"But enough about all that," Joseph says as we walk out of the arena and back down the hallway. Two horses stand at the gates of their stalls, heads protruding through the open spaces. One of them is a chestnut brown with a white star extending down the bridge of its nose. The other reminds me of the horse Elena fell in love with on the property next to us. Not long after we moved to Haven for those ten months, our neighbors (if you can call them that when they live over a mile down the road) invited us for dinner. Their horses were out in the fenced portion of a pasture near the house and Elena was enthralled when she saw them. This one is a little darker than the one next door, its coat as dark as the shadows that move in the night, the kind of black that protrudes through darkness with each movement. The nameplate under him reads *Shadow.*

Fitting, I think, and our steps halt in front of the horses.

"Time to get down to business, don't you think?" Joseph says.

"Actually," I say, interrupting Ben before he can do what he came here to do. I have so many questions, some about the future of Blackwood Ranch, but most are about *Xavier.* For now, I'll keep those to myself. "Joseph, can I ask you something a little personal?"

"You can ask me anything, darlin.'"

"You love it here. You have so much history here. Your family practically built this place…Why are you selling?"

Joseph's lips curve into a sad smile beneath his white mustache. "How'd I know you were gonna ask me that?" He chuckles, leaning against the door of an empty stall. "We've had a bit of a rough patch the last few years. From bad crops to disease spreading in the cattle…Then that big resort opened a few towns over. It took a good chunk of the B&B customers. Unfortunately, I had to let all my guys go, so it's just been

Charlie and me, now Xavier. Don't get me wrong, he's been a big help, but I'm not getting any younger, and I don't imagine he wants to make less than minimum wage the rest of his life."

If only Joseph knew who he was talking about. My husband might have grown accustomed to the lifestyle of a Villa, but Nick had continued to be the humble man who grew up in the small town of Bridgeport, South Carolina, working in his family car shop, making just enough to make ends meet.

"With the bank breathing down my neck to pay the loan I borrowed a few years ago, I can't afford to keep going. I'd rather sell it to someone like Jace, who might keep it somewhat intact instead of someone who wants to build a skyscraper in its place."

Shadow, the black horse, whinnies, catching my attention, before it nickers at me. When it catches my eye, it moves its head in a combination of up-and-down and side-to-side movements, and I close the gap between us. Reaching my hand out, Shadow nuzzles his muzzle into my palm, nibbling my hand affectionately.

"You shooed us off the first time," Ben says.

"Damn straight." Joseph laughs, his gaze falling on me briefly before he turns back to the boys. "You wanted a number right then and there, but I hadn't accepted the truth yet. I wasn't ready to admit defeat."

"It's not defeat, Joe," Jace says.

"This place has been in my family for a long time, boy. I planned on spending the rest of my life here. It's a little defeating to know I couldn't keep it goin' the way my parents hoped, but I think it's time to let it go."

I sigh, petting the bridge of Shadow's nose. "This place is special. I hate to see what these two might do to it."

"Which is why you're here, Nin," Jace says.

I hum in response, smiling at Shadow, who seems content with the affection received before I catch Joseph's eye.

"Y'know, that horse doesn't usually let many people near it," he says with a twinkle in his eye. "The only one he's taken a liking to besides you is Xavier."

My heart constricts at his confession, but I try not to react, locking my jaw and returning my gaze to Shadow.

"Speak of the devil." Joseph's voice has a new level of excitement when a car door slams outside. "Sounds like they're back. Come on, I'll introduce you!"

I hold my gaze on Shadow, my fingers trailing down his nose. I could be mere seconds from seeing my husband, but I can't make myself move. I'm scared—No, I'm terrified.

What if he doesn't remember me? What if he never remembers me? Do I say something, or do I walk away? He's made a life for himself here, but it's a life that will soon be ripped out from under him. Where will he go when Joseph sells this place? And then there's Charlie. Joseph said it was complicated. Are they together? Has he moved on without even knowing it?

"You coming?" Jace asks from the door.

Without looking, I ask the question that's been on my mind since I got out of the car. "Why did you bring me here, Jace?"

"What do you—"

"You never said anything about all of *this* on the phone. You only said you found him. You forgot to mention the part about him having amnesia or that he had built a life here."

"I didn't know, Nina. When I called you...Joseph hadn't told us anything until after we spoke. I figured it was better to ease you into it than to let you come in guns blazing. This is still a matter of business for us, Nin."

"You sure about that?" I ask, looking over my shoulder. The second he asked me to play along, he brought me into this deal, and I'm not sure I want to see what he has in store for Blackwood Ranch. Jace stands there a moment longer before he sighs and leaves the barn.

Then it's just Shadow and me. The horse offers a small huff in my direction. I rest my forehead against his nose, take a deep breath, and try to swallow back the tears that have started to build in my eyes. When I step back, I whisper, "You know, don't you?"

Picking up one of the apples nearby, I offer it to him, letting him eat it from the palm of my hand before petting him a final time.

"Now or never, huh?"

thirty-eight

MY MIND COMMANDS MY feet to move forward, but they don't obey. I'm stuck in the same loop of what-ifs…each one terrifies me more than the last. I can't do this. I can't walk out that door if he isn't going to remember me. That's a fate worse than I've been living the past year.

Shadow huffs and stomps his foot behind me.

"Yeah, yeah, I'm going," I say, taking a deep breath. I lift feet that feel like they're trudging through wet cement.

When I reach the door, my eyes are drawn to the man who has joined Joseph, Jace, and Ben near the truck parked in front of the house. My breath catches in my throat, and my right hand maintains a death grip on the wood frame as I try to contain the sob building in my chest.

It's him.

It's really him.

"Nick." The name comes out in a broken whisper.

As if he can hear me, warm, whiskey-golden eyes look my way. Even from this distance, I can see the wheels of recognition turning. Slowly, moving forward from their stationary position, kicking the dust off, until finally, it all clicks in place. He takes one step forward, then two, then three, until he's sprinting up the hill.

"Dee," Nick says. He sweeps me off my feet and into his arms in a soul-crushing hug, so tight it's sure to leave an imprint on me. I hang on for dear life, never wanting to let go. He pulls away enough to meet my gaze before his mouth covers mine in a bruising kiss. The kiss is all-consuming. I have no choice but to get lost in it.

Lost in him.

Our bodies...Our souls are not strangers. They are familiar in a way I can't explain, but being in his arms feels right. Feels whole. The yearning I've buried deep inside me is now satisfied when every one of my senses is full of him. I will never let this man go again. My heart has craved the beat of his against mine. My body has craved his touch on my skin and the comforting smell of him when he's near. Everything about this kiss feels like coming home.

He's finally home.

"You remember me?" I ask when we part, breathless, his forehead against mine.

His eyes meet mine and he smiles, calming the storm behind them. "I could never forget you, Dee." Nick kisses me again.

"I thought you were gone. I thought I'd never see you again," I whisper. "I didn't—"

"You found me, baby." Nick brings the back of my hand to his lips, then holds my hand to his chest. I can feel the beat of his heart underneath my fingertips. The sensation fills my eyes with fresh tears. He's here. He's really in front of me. My fears have been put to rest because he's standing here, and he *remembers*. "Elena?" he asks, a bit desperately.

"She's okay." I smile at the thought of finally bringing him home to our daughter. "She misses you, but she's good." I notice the white bandage on his left hand and a deep purple bruise on the left side of his face fades into the skin beneath his eye. "What happened to your face? And your hand?"

"It's nothing, Dee. I'm okay," he says, trying to reassure me. "I promise. I'm better than okay."

"I guess it's time to come clean," I hear Ben say when the others make their way up the hill. His tone holds a hint of humor like he's about to let the others in on a private joke.

I refuse to take my eyes off Nick, scared if I look away, he might disappear and I'll wake up to find the whole thing to be a dream.

Jace chuckles. "I have to apologize, Joe. You see, when we arrived this morning, it *was* to discuss the sale of your property. However, our true intentions shifted when we saw him leaving with your daughter."

"You know him?" Joseph asks.

"Sir, I'd like to introduce you to Nick Davis."

Nick smiles at the sound of *his* name. I do the same when he tugs me into his side, turning to face the others, but still holds my hand to his chest.

There's a woman with them now, or maybe she was there all along. I didn't see anything besides him. Her narrowed gaze sweeps across the different members of the group before landing on Nick, but he doesn't even seem to notice, re-introducing himself to Joseph. Her pale green eyes move to me, and she looks me up and down before her gaze narrows even further.

"And this is my wife, Davina Villa," Nick says, drawing my attention away from her.

"It's nice to properly meet you, *Nick* and Nina," Joseph says with a smile.

"I have to apologize, Joseph; I came here under false pretenses. You see, I've spent the past year thinking my husband was dead. When Jace called me this morning to tell me he'd seen him, I dropped everything and ran." I smile up at Nick briefly. "But after seeing this place, I've fallen in love with it."

"What a load of bullshit." The woman scoffs, shaking her head. "Villa? You're married to a *Villa?* You're exactly who I thought you were."

A slight fall in Nick's features catches my eye. "Charlie—"

"I can't believe I fell for it." Her burning gaze turns on Joseph when he tries to calm her. "No, Dad! How can you sit back and let them pull this—"

"Charlie, that's enough," Joseph says.

"Seeing her won't magically bring back his memory."

"Actually, it can; especially if he's been recalling things that have to do with her. These things aren't certain. You remember how it was with Grandma. And Doctor Sanders said—"

"This is insanity. They've done this whole elaborate scheme to get you to sell the ranch!" Charlie backs away a few steps before turning on her heel and running inside.

That was...dramatic.

Her father's body rolls with a heavy sigh when the front door slams.

"Joe, I'm sorry," Nick says. "It wasn't like that. I swear. I—"

"You have nothing to be sorry for. That's how these things work. All it takes is one trigger to set the whole thing in motion." Joseph shrugs, adjusting the hat on his head.

Nick turns to me, cradling my face in his hands. "I should go talk to her. It'll just take a few minutes. Okay?"

I don't want to let him go. Don't want to let him out of my sight, but he reassures me it will be okay. He kisses me one more time when I nod before he follows the same path Charlie took moments ago. When the door closes behind him, I turn back to Joseph. "Can I get a minute?"

"She means you two," he says to Jace and Ben, who finally take the hint and head toward the house.

"I cannot thank you enough. Truly, you have no idea how much the generosity you've shown him means to me. The past year has been...the most difficult year of my life. We looked everywhere. We thought he was dead. And now, to find him alive and well, knowing he was taken care of—"

"Don't think I didn't put him to work."

"I have no doubt. He probably loved every second of it. I know he missed working with his hands while doing more of the corporate side before all of...this. He's not much of a suits guy."

The thought of being a few hundred feet from Nick still doesn't seem real after this past year. I've discreetly pinched myself a few times to make sure I won't wake up from this dream, but I'm still waiting for it to happen. The moment I wake up, alone, and look at his side of the bed, finding it empty.

"He's a good one," Joseph says, stopping my thoughts in their tracks, and I smile. "You are too, Nina. You're a bit harder to read, a lot more diplomatic than he is, but you have a big heart."

"I get it honestly."

"Do you mind if I ask *you* something?" Joseph pushes his hands in the front pocket of his jeans as we begin a slow walk down the hill. "Charlie seemed awful upset when she learned your name, but to be frank, I wouldn't know the difference between a Villa and the man on the moon."

His words make me laugh. It's refreshing to be around someone who doesn't know who or what a Villa is. "Let's just say, my family is kind of known around the world for being good with money."

"So, you're not a designer?" Joseph lifts a brow.

"Oh no, I am. I have my own design company and help run my family company. When Daddy died ten years ago, he left it to us. Well, he left it to my brother, but I've been the one running it for the most part."

Joseph hums in response with a single nod, his gaze on the gravel path.

"Joseph, I'd like to help. I hate to see you walk away from this place. It's been in your family for generations and I hate to see it change. You've done something for me that I can never repay, but I want to try."

"Change is part of life, Nina. The only repayment I need is knowing you'll be in charge of the design for whatever happens after the sale."

"Joseph—"

"Nina." There's no room for argument in his voice. "I can't keep up with this place, and it's too much for Charlie to do alone."

"What if you could afford to hire at least one ranch hand?"

Joseph rolls his eyes, shaking his head. "You don't give up, do you?"

"No, I don't." I smile. "I want you to think about it, please. And if you decide you still want to go through with the sale, I'll make this my last one."

"Your last?"

"I've been a bit of a workaholic the past...well, my whole life. And this whole thing has been a wake-up call. I don't want to blink, and it's been forty years, and I haven't been able to enjoy my life. My family. I don't want to end up like my dad." My arms fold over my chest as I rock back on my heels, staring down at my feet.

The thought breaks my heart. Daddy never got to experience a life without work. Even on vacation, he would still be handling business affairs—I can't remember a single time he didn't. And when he finally started to consider retirement—and divorcing Brina, but that was a whole other problem—he died a few months later. It didn't seem fair that when he was about to start enjoying life, it was ripped away from him. I don't want the same thing for me.

"It's time to loosen up the reins a little. Let other people do their jobs and handle it for me. That way, I can finally enjoy time with my husband and our daughter."

"A daughter?"

I smile and pull my phone out of my back pocket, opening it to show him a photo. "Elena. She'll be four in August."

Joseph places his hand on my shoulder, giving it a comforting squeeze. "I can attest that the work will always be there and there will *always* be more after it, but the memories with your family are what stick with you. Don't waste this time you have with your daughter. You won't be able to get it back."

"Thank you." I step forward into his embrace and he squeezes me again before we part. "I should help him get his stuff together so we can go home. We have a bit of a drive ahead of us and a family wondering where I am."

Part Three

Them

thirty-nine

Nick

CHARLIE GLARES UP AT me from the door of her bedroom. It had taken five minutes just trying to convince her to open the damn thing. She's hurt. I think she's more upset about this than what transpired the other night.

And me? I don't know how I'm supposed to feel.

The biggest part of me was fucking elated to see my wife standing there. After all this time, to finally remember something...someone. Her name was the first thing on my mind and then my own. No one and nothing else mattered when I saw her. But then, the smallest bits of concern and regret pushed their way through the elation. What changed back home in the year I've been gone? Did Nina move on? Does Elena even remember me? Did Alex get married? What about Joseph and the ranch? What about Charlie? Will Nina be mad when I tell her about Charlie? Does it matter what happened with Charlie?

"I'm sorry you feel like I was leading you on, that was never my intention, Charlie." I sigh, leaning back against the banister. "I told you I wasn't ready for something like this. I didn't even know who I was. I didn't—"

"Whatever you say, *Nick.*" Charlie practically spits my name, and I won't lie, it hurts a little. "Why don't you run back to your perfect life with your perfect wife? I'm sure you even have a kid waiting for you in your mansion back home."

"Enough, Charlie." She can say what she wants about me, but I won't let her bring Elena or Nina into this. This is not their fault. "I can't help it if you choose not to listen to me. I made it very clear I wasn't looking for anything."

"Didn't seem that way the other night."

My gaze narrows.

Charlie smirks. She knows she has me backed into a corner. "That was nothing, too?"

I pinch the bridge of my nose and pray Nina doesn't walk inside. The thought of her hearing any part of this right now…I don't want her to find out like this. I need to break it to her at the right time. I don't know how she'll feel about what happened here.

"You can't tell me it meant—"

"Charlie, it didn't mean anything," I say and meet her eyes again. "I'm sorry if I gave you the wrong idea, but—"

"You didn't even think they were looking for you!"

There's a creak at the bottom of the stairs and I don't have to look to know who it is. Charlie doesn't, either. Her heated gaze doesn't flinch, remaining on me. "*She* wasn't looking for you," Charlie says, loud enough for Nina to hear.

She's angry, and I suppose part of her anger is valid, and if she could, I'm sure she'd set me ablaze right here and now. It would be easier than facing the heartbreak she brought upon herself. I can't give her what she wants. I can't. I don't love her. I care for her, but the woman standing at the bottom of the stairs will always be the one who owns my heart.

"You're right, Charlie, I didn't think anyone was looking for me. But obviously, I was wrong." I motion toward the window at the end of the hallway overlooking the front of the house. "She's here. And she is the *one* thing I had to hold on to this entire time. Almost every memory I've had since I woke up in the hospital, she was there...I may not have known who she was, but I knew she was the answer to finding myself again."

I can see the tears blurring her vision, and when I step toward her, Charlie takes two steps back.

"I wish I could be who you want me to be, but...I'm not."

"You could."

"No, I can't, because my heart belongs to someone else."

"You don't belong there, Nick," Charlie pleads. "You aren't like *them.* They're what's wrong with everything in the world, the kind of people who step on people like me and my dad to get what they want. They don't care—"

"Stop talking," I hiss, taking another step closer to her. "You will not speak about my *wife* or my family that way. You don't know them. You don't know what they've been through."

Her tongue pokes out to wet her dry lips before her throat bobs with a deep swallow.

"You don't know *me,* Charlie. You only know the shell of a man who didn't know where he belonged."

Her eyes leave me, glaring to my right, where I know Nina stands at the top of the stairs. My wife looks between us, only allowing her gaze to remain on Charlie for less than half a second. Then she walks between us toward my room without a word. Charlie scoffs. "Well, then, you better go. Wouldn't want to keep the princess waiting."

There is so much more I want to say, but I know nothing will change her mind or the way she feels about what has happened. I have to be okay walking away from the ranch knowing it means leaving Charlie heartbroken. It's not my job to fix her. It never was.

"Nina," I say when I walk into my bedroom, but she's busy pulling together the contents of my desk, shuffling them into a neat pile one thing at a time. Taking her left hand in mine, I stop her movements and tug her to me. My thumb swipes across the stone on her ring finger before I bring the back of her hand to my lips. "Dee, it's not what you think."

"I don't care, Nick." She shrugs and tries to move past me to finish collecting my things, but I stop her.

"I know you, Davina. I know what's going through your head right now, and what happened here is not what you're thinking."

"Even if it did, it's not my business."

"It is your business, and I was going to tell you later, not right now. Not when I just got you back. Charlie, she...she's not you, Nina." I tuck a strand of hair behind her ear and lift her chin to bring her mouth to mine. Being with her, feeling her body against mine, her heartbeat against mine...is the best feeling in the entire fucking universe. "I've missed that," I whisper when we part, finally earning a smile from her.

Nina buries her face in the crook of my neck, and I wrap my arms firmly around her. Taking a deep breath, I inhale the familiar scents of magnolia and sandalwood, mixed with her vanilla-coconut shampoo.

"Let's go home," I say, and kiss the top of her head.

My arm extends over the center console, hand resting on her right thigh as Nina drives home. She asked me if I wanted to drive, but I said no, I'd ride passenger this time. Besides, did she really trust me to remember the way home? It was meant to be a joke, but I don't think she found it as humorous as I did. Not right now, anyway. Maybe in a few days once the dust settles. While the joke may have had some truth, I didn't want to drive because I wanted to take the opportunity to be present. I wanted to take my time, re-memorizing her features and learning the new ones she's acquired. I wanted to listen without distraction as she told me everything that happened the last year. To soak in every moment of the little alone time we had remaining. Nina warned me everyone was at the house...literally *everyone*. And I'm not sure whether the thought should excite or scare me.

"I was supposed to be on a plane right now," Nina says, glancing over at me. "The board wanted to talk to me tomorrow. I haven't been very...present lately."

"You're still running things?"

She shrugs. "Yes and no. I've been working, but mostly from here. They want me back in New York, and before today, I'd been considering it."

That's...disappointing to hear, though not surprising. My wife is nothing if not a workaholic and a bit of a control freak. She gets it honestly. Her dad, Ric, was the same way. Her constant need to go behind her brother and fix things is one of the reasons we ended up in this situation.

"I thought about selling the house and moving to New York. Elena has enjoyed it when we're there off and on, and work would have given me something to take my mind off things."

"Nina—"

"Nick, I don't want to fight about this. Not right now. Please."

I squeeze her thigh before moving my hand to caress the side of her cheek. "I'm not fighting, Dee. I just want to know what's going on in your life."

Her phone buzzes in the cup holder between us like it has been every few minutes since she turned it on about twenty minutes ago, but she left it disconnected from the car so it wouldn't continue interrupting us. Nina ignores it, but it's getting harder for me to do so. Who in the hell is blowing up her phone? Didn't she tell the others where she was going?

"You want to get that?" I ask, looking down at it.

Nina sighs. She doesn't look, but finally answers the call, reconnecting the phone to the car. "Yes?"

"Where are you?"

I do a double-take when I see the name on the screen.

"I'm"—she glances over at me and chews on her bottom lip, her gaze returning to the road—"driving home."

Holy shit. She didn't tell them. They have no idea she left to find me.

"How far out are you?"

"About an hour away." Her answers remain short and sweet, to the point. She's trying not to give anything away to either one of us—me or him.

"Anything I need to know?"

"Nope. I'll fill you in when I get there."

He sighs. "Okay. Be careful, Sweetheart."

She hums in response, hanging up the call.

I count to five, waiting for her to say something, anything, but she doesn't. Her eyes are glued to the road ahead. Her thumb fiddles with her wedding ring, her left hand resting in her lap. When I get to five, I take a deep breath and ask, "Why the fuck is Beau Turner calling you *Sweetheart?*"

forty

Nina

FUCK.

I wasn't ready for this conversation yet. What am I supposed to say? I'm not going to lie. I planned on telling Nick about Beau and everything that happened, but I didn't plan on doing it right now.

Thanks, Beau.

No, this isn't his fault. I should've told him Nick was sitting next to me, but then he'd follow that up with a million other questions. The first one being: Why didn't I let him go with me? The answer was simple. I needed to do this alone, but what if Nick hadn't remembered me? Having Beau there would've been a smart idea.

My fingers white knuckle the steering wheel for a count of three before they relax, straightening out.

"Nina," Nick says, removing his hand from my leg. "Why is Beau—"

"It's a nickname, Nick. That's it."

"Not when it comes to *my* wife, it's not. What is going on?"

I sigh, closing my eyes for less than a second. When I

reopen them, I stare at the road ahead. "Nick, I'm not going to lie to you."

He interrupts me. "Did you fuck him?"

When I glance at him, there's a hint of betrayal in his eyes. It hurts to see it there, but I can't lie to him. I sigh, pushing a hand through my hair. "Yes, Beau and I slept together about three months ago. It only happened once, but—"

"Wow." Nick breathes, scratching the stubble on his cheek. "You and Beau."

"It's not like that, Nick. I promise it's not. We're not together. It's complicated."

"Seems pretty straightforward to me. You didn't wait long, did you, Nin?"

He's digging in deep using that nickname. My husband doesn't call me Nin. He calls me a variety of things, but never *Nin.* He has only called me that once before, and just like then, he's using it to get under my skin.

"You cannot be serious." I scoff.

"I mean, first it was Luke, and now—"

"Stop," I say, cutting him off. We are not about to compare Luke Benson and Beau Turner. "This is not the same. Nothing happened with Luke. Nothing. Those flowers…They weren't meant for me. Luke sent his girlfriend flowers and they got mixed up with the ones you sent."

"That's not the point, Nina."

"Then what is the point?"

This is unbelievable. How can he sit there and act like he didn't have his fair share of extramarital activities while he was gone? At least I have a good excuse, I thought he was dead. He'd been gone for nine months and there were no signs of him returning from the grave any time soon. I can't help but wonder if it wasn't for Jace and Ben, would I have ever found him?

"You and Charlie—"

"Didn't sleep together!" Nick's voice explodes around us and my shoulders fall when I huff. "I didn't sleep with her. I couldn't. Why? Because *you* were the one thing on my mind. I'm glad to know I was, too."

"That's not fair," I say, tears building in my eyes. "I thought you were dead."

"And yet, here I am."

"I don't want to fight with you, Nick," I say, taking a deep breath and trying to keep the tears from spilling. "Not about work and not about this. I just got you back. Please, don't do this."

He doesn't say anything in return. His gaze remains on the passing landscape that goes by in a blur. We're less than an hour from home now and I don't want to show up during an argument. Especially not this argument.

"Nick—"

"I need a minute, Davina."

From my peripheral, I see his shoulders rise and fall with a deep sigh, the window fogging from the warmth of his breath against the cool glass.

We're two minutes from our driveway and we still haven't talked. The rest of the drive has been in complete silence, and I almost wish he'd yell at me—get it over with so I'm not walking on eggshells. Instead, he gives me the cold shoulder and sits there letting it stew and brew. I understand he's hurt, but I don't understand being angry at me when he and Charlie spent their own time together. And how she reacted tells me there was more to it than a simple kiss to test the waters…She was too upset, too hurt for that to have been the case.

The house comes into view a few minutes after we've twisted around the curves leading up to the door. Light floods from the windows, creating a warm glow as the sun sets behind the trees.

"I'm sorry," he whispers, eyes set on his lap when I pull to a stop in front of the garage. I haven't opened the garage, yet, hoping to give us a few more minutes before the others discover I'm back. "Nina, I'm sorry. I shouldn't...I shouldn't have yelled at you. You're right, it wasn't fair for me to react that way. I can't be mad at you or him; and honestly, I don't think I am. Mad, I mean. I'm upset, and I'm allowed to be upset." When his eyes meet mine, they hold a level of grief I know all too well. "I just need time to...adjust."

"We both do, Nick."

Nick reaches across the console and his fingers caress the side of my cheek before turning my face toward his. "I love you, Davina Bay. *Ti amo da morire.*"

I love you to death. We've expressed those words a few times over the years, but they hold a greater weight now than before.

A smile tugs at the corner of my lips when he speaks Italian. I whisper, *"Ti amo da morire."*

"Good, because that's what it'll take to fucking get rid of me." He kisses me. "Just please don't give up on me...on us."

"None of it matters if it's not with you, Nick."

He kisses me again. "Please be patient with me. I promise I'll get there. I'll be normal again."

I don't think we'll ever be *normal* again. Normal went out the window when he walked out the door last year.

Nick sighs, glancing at the house. "I need a minute before I...go in there. Before the chaos starts."

"Come in when you're ready." I squeeze Nick's hand and climb out of the car, but I barely make it up the front steps before being swept into a pair of strong arms. Beau frets over me, touching my hair, my cheeks, my neck, my shoulders, my hands, and finally my cheeks again, cupping them in his warm hands. Instinctively, my fingers grip the front of his shirt, pulling him close. When his green eyes meet mine, I can see the worry being replaced by relief.

"Don't do that again." Beau finally takes a breath. "Do you understand me? I was worried fucking sick about you. What in the hell was so important—" His words falter and his gaze travels over my shoulder. "Is that…?"

I nod.

"Holy fuck."

My hands fall from his shirt at the same time his hands fall from my face. Nick walks up the sidewalk and Beau's head swivels between us, trying to determine if this is real. Before either of us can say anything, before I know what's happening, Nick's arm pulls back, and his fist extends straight into Beau's face. Beau stumbles back two paces, and I start to reach for him, to check on him, but stop myself.

"Sheriff!" Beau's deputy, Max, comes down the stairs. "You just assaulted—"

"No!" Beau extends his arm, catching the deputy as he rushes down the sidewalk toward us. "No, it's fine." After a deep breath, Beau glances my way. "I deserve that."

"What is going on out here?" I hear Kai call before he and Elizabeth appear. "Holy shit." My brother runs down the steps, past me, past all of us, and pulls Nick into a full embrace. I swear the impact knocks Nick back a step, but he returns the gesture. When Kai pulls back, he grips Nick's shoulders, before one of his hands cradles Nick's cheek. If I didn't know better I'd think they were the long-lost couple.

"Get a room!" A voice calls from behind us.

"Shut up, Sheffield!" Kai yells back at Finn before he clamps down on Nick's shoulder one more time. "Fuck, it's good to see you."

One by one, everyone comes out of the house and greets my husband. Each time, there's a look of disbelief before they rush down the steps and sweep him into a hug, not waiting for the person before them to finish. It's a wild rush of emotions watching the scene unfold. I stand to the side, next to Beau, letting everyone have their moment. The same way I had to when I first saw him at Blackwood Ranch.

"What's all the commotion out here?" I hear Jimmy ask and he finally emerges from the house, Alex not far behind him. His blue eyes sweep across every face until they land on Nick, and I can see the tears begin to well. Jimmy slowly makes his way down to his oldest son before he pulls him into the tightest embrace of anyone here. "Where have you been?"

"It's a long story, Pop." Nick smiles, tears brimming in his eyes.

"And I want to hear every bit of it," Jimmy says, stepping to the side so Alex can have his turn. Jimmy's eyes find mine and he smiles. For the first time since the others joined us, it feels like I'm not an outsider watching a family reunion.

"We'll tell you guys everything, but first, I need to see my daughter," Nick says when Alex tries to push for answers.

"She's inside with Brie," Jimmy says, motioning toward the house.

My husband glances my way as if asking for permission, and I nod, motioning for him to lead the way. "Don't leave," I whisper to Beau, only loud enough for him to hear, and he responds with one curt nod.

Elena hasn't left her father's side since I stepped aside to reveal him standing there twenty minutes ago. Tears fell down her cheeks as she clutched his neck, and every few seconds, she would pull away and look him dead in the eye to make sure it was really him. Another piece of my world slid back into place watching them cling to one another. When Nick's gaze met mine, I half expected him to reach out for me to join them like he always did, but his arms remained wrapped securely around our daughter. He offered me a half smile before returning his attention to Elena, who finally pulled away to chastise him in half English, half Italian for being gone for so long.

Even now, Nick sits in the middle of her room, listening intently as she moves in every direction to show him every little thing she owns, even the things he's seen before.

"You have a minute?" Beau whispers, joining me in the doorway. His eyes land on Elena as she hands her dad the Barbie horse Beau had gifted her for her birthday last year. She explains what each button and tassel does—one makes it bow, another makes it dance—four in total and I still forget what each one is meant to do.

"Yeah, I don't exist to them right now, anyway," I say with a small laugh, and follow him down the hallway.

Beau waits until we get out the front door and to the driveway before he asks, "You want to tell me what in the hell that's all about?" His hands rest on his hips and his stance tells me he's not leaving until he gets an answer.

"What?"

"That." Beau motions toward the house. "That... awkwardness between you and Nick. Nina, you just spent the last year looking for him, hoping he'd walk through the damn door, and if I'm being honest, you don't exactly seem—"

"He knows." My gaze falls to the ground before I look up to meet his gaze.

"Yeah, I got that." Beau points to his face, where discoloration has already started to set in on his cheekbone.

"I am so sorry, Beau." I touch his cheek, and my thumb

gently skates over the bruise. "He's not exactly happy with me. Actually, he's pretty mad about the whole thing."

"Mad at you?" Beau scoffs when I nod. "How can he be mad at you? If he should be mad at anyone, it should be me. I'm the—"

"Absolutely not." I shake my head. "You did nothing wrong. This is all on me." I step back from him, rubbing my eyes with the heels of my palms. "Do you know what it was like to get that phone call? After all this time, to hear that he might still be alive?"

"You should've told me, Nina. I would've gone with you."

"I needed to do it alone."

"Alone? Sweetheart, I didn't even know where you were! What if something had happened? What if it turned out *not* to be him?"

"But it was."

"But what if it wasn't?"

Truthfully, I hadn't thought about that possibility. When I heard Jace say they had found Nick, my sole focus was getting there as soon as possible. I didn't stop to think about the other outcomes.

"I don't know, Beau." I look to the sky, closing my eyes with a deep breath. "He had amnesia. That's why he never came home…Whatever happened on the trail—"

"Did you ask him what happened?"

"No, not yet. We were too busy trying not to argue over the fact that I was about to move back to New York and that you and I slept together."

"I'm sorry, Nina. I—I should've stopped, I shouldn't have—"

"Don't. Don't do that," I say. "I don't regret it, Beau. And I don't want you to, either."

Beau stares for a moment before his gaze falls to the ground. He folds his arms and sighs. "He seems to remember everything just fine now."

"I wouldn't call it perfect, but it helped jog his memory when he saw me. He'd been…having small memories, but nothing clicked." I sigh. "Do you know what it was like to see him today? I didn't know what to expect or if he'd even remember me. But then I saw him…I touched him for the first time in over a year, and it was like my whole world came back into view. But I still have this ache inside of me because I don't know what's going to happen, Beau. We aren't the same people. I'm not the same."

Tears begin to fall down my cheeks. I should pull away when Beau reaches out to wipe them away, but I don't.

"How do I know he still loves me? That he won't want to return to the life he was living back there? How do I know we're going to make it?"

"You don't, Nina."

"And then there's you. For the past year, I have carried this…pain, this agony thinking my husband was gone. Not just gone…*Dead.* And the whole time, you were this shining light in the dark. You pulled me out of the dark and helped me keep going even when I didn't want to. You were here for me. You made sure I was okay when no one else did…I care about you so fucking much and the thought of losing you makes my head spin. I won't let him be mad at you. This isn't your fault."

"Oh, Sweetheart." Beau exhales.

"What am I supposed to do, Beau?"

Beau cradles the sides of my neck. "You walk back in that house and tell your husband everything you just told me. Because I know you, Nina, and I know that despite whatever feelings you have toward me, whatever feelings I have for you…I'm not the one for you. He is."

When I try to look away, he doesn't let me.

"You have spent the past year looking for him, never giving up. Don't give up now. Nick is hurt. But he's only hurt because he loves you."

"Beau—"

"I'll be okay, Nina." He smiles and I tighten my grip on his arms when he kisses my forehead. We stand there for a moment longer before he finally takes a step back and readjusts his posture to stand straighter, arms folded over his chest. "Where was he?"

And just like that…Beau Turner has transformed into Sheriff Turner right before my eyes.

"Bezer."

His gaze narrows. "Where is that?"

"Some small town about an hour and a half from the trailhead. It's barely a blimp on the map. Blink and you'd miss it as you drive through."

"Still in Puck County?" Beau asks, and I shrug. "How many miles would you say it is from Achor?"

"Maybe forty miles from where you found his stuff, but driving it's longer because of getting through the mountains."

Beau disappears into his thoughts, and I watch an idea form behind his eyes. "Where exactly is Bezer?"

"You take 133 to one of the county roads south of Achor. I don't remember which one."

"That has to be Puck." Beau shakes his head. "He was right under our nose the whole time."

"Nina." We both turn to see Nick standing only a few feet away. His eyes roam every inch of the scene before him, scrutinizing every detail—how close Beau and I stand apart, the flush in my cheeks, the fresh tear tracks on my face—as he walks closer. "Everything okay, Sheriff?"

"Yeah," Beau says, keeping his gaze locked on Nick, a quirk in the corner of his mouth. "Just trying to get some details from your wife. Help fill in some blanks."

"You don't want to talk to me?"

"I do, but—"

"I told him it could wait until tomorrow," I say, interrupting them. Nick glances at me, then back at Beau; whether he means to or not, his eyes narrow slightly. "Tonight is about family. They can interrogate us tomorrow."

"First thing in the morning," Beau says, looking at me. "Be at the station at nine."

"We'll be there," Nick says before I can.

forty-one

Nina

I LEAN AGAINST THE frame of Elena's room and watch Nick read *Green Eggs and Ham* as she begins to fade, and for a brief moment, all feels right in the world. Life feels normal. The way it did before everything happened…Before I took back over at the company.

Kai left about an hour ago to catch our flight to New York. He said he would handle the board for now. I'd have to go back sooner rather than later and face them, but he'd find a way to hold off their demand for my presence a little longer. There was no way I could fly to New York right now, and if that meant the board decided to remove me permanently, then so be it. Do I think they would? No, but they're not going to be happy.

Nick closes the book as he finishes the last line and smiles down at Elena, who has finally succumbed to sleep. He slips out of the bed with the utmost care, gently resting her head on the pillow he'd been leaning on. Tucking her in, he flips the switch on her night light, casting an array of stars on her ceiling. He turns off the lamp on her nightstand, kissing her forehead. He tiptoes out of the room and meets me in the hallway, closing the door behind him. "Should we head to bed?"

I nod, and he tugs me back by my hand when I start to walk down the hall, sweeping me off my feet. "Nick!" I giggle but cover my mouth to stay quiet and not disturb Elena or the others who have already gone to bed. "What are you doing?"

"Just wanted you close," he says, kissing my temple, and finds his way through the house to our bedroom. I nuzzle into his neck and kiss the exposed skin above the neckline of his shirt. Despite the tension that has wormed its way between us, the thought of him being home feels surreal.

When Nick sets me on my feet behind the privacy of our bedroom door, he pulls me into a tight embrace. His arms wind tightly around me, and he inhales deeply. A contented sigh follows before I feel something wet on my skin. Another inhale confirms my suspicions, and I look up, meeting his teary gaze.

"Oh, *Fossette.*" I sigh, wiping a few tears from his cheeks.

He smiles at the word. "Say it again."

"Fossette."

"I missed that," he says, eyes closed.

"I missed *you.*"

Whiskey-golden orbs meet mine and a fresh round of tears makes them glassy. The sight makes my own blurry. "I missed you so much," I say, wiping another tear from the corner of his eye. "Nick, I'm sorry. I—"

"Stop," he interrupts me. Gathering both of my hands in his, Nick kisses them before holding them against his chest. "Nina, I don't want to do this right now. I don't want to spend my first night home talking about Beau Turner or Charlie Blackwood or Luke Benson or whoever or whatever else there is standing between us. Tonight, I just want to be with my wife. I want to enjoy the feeling of you in my arms and hear you say you love me as much as I love you. As for the rest…We can deal with it tomorrow."

"Tomorrow," I agree.

Nick pushes my hair behind my ear and his fingers trace my jawline before he pulls my mouth to his. I missed this. Missed him. I moan against his lips, and he swallows the sound, cupping the back of my neck. He pulls away briefly to let his eyes roam across my face, memorizing every feature, and his thumb traces across my bottom lip. He smiles when I gently nip at his finger. *"Ti amo,"* he says softly, his hand still splayed across my neck, a slight pressure in his grasp.

"I know," I say. "I love you too, *Fossette.*"

He hums in approval, his eyes practically rolling in the back of his head. "Fuck, I love when you say that."

Without warning, Nick swoops down to catch my lips in another kiss. He traces the line of my bottom lip with his tongue before biting down on the flesh and swallows my gasp as he devours my mouth. Our tongues locked in a desperate embrace, I didn't even notice he was leading me farther into our room until the back of my thighs hit the bed.

His warm mouth caresses every inch of my skin down my neckline. The urgent need to have him as close as possible ignites inside me when I plunder my fingers through the short hair across his scalp, missing the length he used to keep and how it used to end in soft curls. His fingers drift along my curves, tugging my white satin camisole free from my jeans. He leaves gentle love bites against my collarbone when he pushes the caramel-colored button-up from my shoulders, and it lands in a heap on the floor.

Lifting my shirt over my head, I'm met with a soft smile before his eyes roam across the exposed skin of my chest. His fingers make note of every new mark I've earned in the last twelve months: the small scar on my shoulder, the result of a scratch from a branch full of thorns on the trail; three new freckles on my chest; and a new tattoo embedded in the skin where my right shoulder and collarbone meet, a simple *N* with a delicate heart. Fingers trace the letter before his eyes meet mine again, and I nod, the right corner of my lips tugging upward. Nick leans his forehead against my shoulder, taking a deep breath, before his breath ghosts over the tattoo, followed by his lips, and the sensation sends a shiver up my spine.

His fingers dig into my flesh as he reaches around, unhooking the clasp of my bra, and takes one of my nipples into his mouth.

"Nick," I whimper, wrapping my fingers around the back of his neck.

His teeth graze the peak, sucking greedily. It's a mix of teeth and tongue against the sensitive bud and it fills my veins with pure ecstasy. His fingers tremble slightly as he works the buckle of my belt. I take his hands in mine, gently removing them to undo the buckle and then the button of my jeans. He slowly peels the denim from my waist, shoving it down my thighs, and I shimmy out of it.

Before I know it, I'm standing bare, and he hasn't shed a single piece of clothing.

"No," he says when my fingers play with the end of his shirt. His hand caresses the side of my face. "No, Davina. Tonight is about you. Only you."

Nick lifts me off my feet, setting me on the edge of the bed, but his fingers aren't gone long before they brush against my core. One finger slips between my folds, dipping inside me, and my body reacts immediately to his touch.

"God, I missed this," he whispers against my neck. "You are so fucking wet already and I've barely even touched you, Davina."

I gasp when he slips another finger inside me, and I clutch his shoulders in desperation.

"That's my favorite sound." He hums before his tongue trails up the column of my neck to my ear, all while slipping a third finger inside me and curling them. His name falls from my lips like a prayer. "I take it back. *That's* my favorite sound."

I whimper when he pulls his fingers from me, but anticipation floods my entire being when he climbs onto the bed and sits behind me. His legs plant on either side of me before he caresses down the length of my left leg and bends it upward, planting my foot on the bed. His mouth attaches to my right shoulder, his tongue following the love bites on my skin.

"Keep your leg up, Davina. Understand?"

I nod, unable to get the words out. Normally, I know it wouldn't be enough for him—he likes a verbal response—but he seems too invested in the moment to care. His lips trail up my neck and down my other shoulder. His right arm hooks around my middle while the left reaches around, under my leg, until his fingers brush against my wet folds.

"Good, baby," he whispers when my hips buck against the sensation. He slips two fingers inside me and his thumb begins a relentless assault on my clit. Nick kisses my temple when my head falls back against his shoulder. His right hand slides up my chest, stopping for a soft squeeze of my breast before slipping around my neck, applying soft pressure to the sides. There's a deep inhale below my ear and I whimper when his teeth graze the skin. "Just look at you, Dee. Fuck, I love watching you like this."

My hips move against his hand, craving more friction, and before I know it, he slips another finger inside me. The heel of his palm plants firmly against my clit and it lights every one of my nerves on fire. The pressure around my neck tightens and he pulls my mouth to his in a forceful kiss. The new angle makes his fingers reach deeper inside me before he curls them, scratching an itch that hasn't been satisfied since he left.

Pressure in my belly builds and I know it won't be long if he keeps going at this pace. I want to make this last. I don't want it to end. But my husband has other plans, deepening each circle of his palm against my clit and elongating his fingers inside me before curling them forward in such a painfully slow manner it makes my body ache with the need for release.

"You want to come?" Nick breathes into my ear, nibbling on the lobe. My head nods and he applies the same pressure to my neck. "Come when you want, but I want you to look forward."

"W-what?"

Nick motions ahead of us and forces my gaze to follow his, keeping his hand on my neck, and suddenly I'm staring straight into the floor-length mirror across from the bed. The sight is otherworldly—him wrapped securely around me as I sit between his legs spread out on the bed, one hand gripping the column of my throat, the other positioned between my legs in a deliciously possessive way. I meet his eyes in the mirror and a devilish smile forms on his lips.

"Keep your eyes on the mirror, Davina," he commands, and I cry out when his fingers begin to move in and out of me at a brutal pace. Sounds of wet skin fill the room and he peppers my skin with warm, wet kisses, but his gaze stays on the mirror.

My body clings to his fingers, begging for release, and when he commands me to reach between my legs and rub the sensitive bud, I don't hesitate. My fingers work the bundle of nerves, bringing me closer and closer to the edge, but it's the sound of his moans and watching us in the mirror that pushes me over.

"Watch," he commands when my head starts to fall back against his shoulder. He forces my gaze back to the mirror. My body trembles under his touch, fingers still slipping in and out of me as my pussy clutches onto them with each thrust, and when I can't force my fingers to move against my clit any longer, his replace mine.

Tears sting my eyes at the pressure rebuilding in my core when he continues the brutal assault, and when Nick bites down on my shoulder, I come again.

"That's my girl," Nick whispers against my skin, his fingers slowing down until he finally pulls them away from me, bringing them to his mouth and slipping them between his lips. He moans at the taste, and I swear I could come from the sound alone. "Fuck, Dee."

His hand grips my chin and he kisses me, his tongue delving into my mouth, swiping against mine so I taste myself on him.

"I love you," he whispers, brushing his nose against mine, still holding my face between his fingers.

"Lo so." I know.

forty-two

Nina

NICK AND I SIT in the same chairs I have spent many days in over the past year. Poring over the different reports, photos, and maps of Mount Achor and its surrounding areas, Beau and I searched for answers and clues about where my husband could have been. Little did we know, he was right under our noses the whole time. The bigger question remains *why* did his presence go undetected for so long? The police in Bezer would have (or should have) reported his appearance in town to the State authorities, or at least the sheriff, and that would've closed the case almost immediately. So, why didn't that happen?

Nick's knee bounces with anticipation. He's ready to get this over with. And after what I witnessed last night I can't say I feel much different.

I woke up in the middle of the night feeling the weight next to me continuously shifting—not shifting, thrashing. Nick's body practically vibrated as he lay in bed, his head moving from side to side, arms flailing as beads of sweat lined his face. He'd mumble, so low I couldn't understand him, but then he screamed. A terrified scream that rattled me to my core, and if I wasn't awake yet, I was after that.

Nick refused to wake up when I tried rousing him. He began repeating a mix of *no* and my name before he jolted awake. He bolted straight up, and his fingers held my wrist in a vice grip. His eyes were blown wide with fear and confusion as his chest rose and fell violently.

"Hey, it's me. You're home. You're safe," I said, touching his face, but he ripped away from me, still looking around the room. His breaths became panicked, his chest rising and falling violently. "Nick, look at me." I gripped his chin and forced his eyes on me. "It's me," I said, annunciating each syllable.

He blinked a few times, glancing on either side of my face before locking eyes with me again. Finally, the recognition set in. "Dee?"

"Yeah, baby. It's me. You're home." My fingers glided through the short hairs, nails grazing his scalp, before he leaned forward and buried his face into my neck. "You're okay, *Fossette*. I got you," I whispered and kissed his temple, tightening my hold on him.

The whole ordeal scared the shit out of me. We sat there for at least fifteen minutes. It took another twenty for him to fall back to sleep, and me another twenty. When we woke up this morning, he pulled me into another hug, breathing out a quick "thank you" before we got ready to leave for the station. Maybe I should've pressed the topic further—asked him more about it—but I got the feeling he didn't want to discuss it...

The door of Beau's office swings open, Beau leads Sergeant James Warren from the State inside before sitting at his desk. Warren introduces himself to Nick, offering me a nod, and finds his place leaning against the filing cabinet to the right of the desk. A moment later, Sheriff Rhett Wilson from Puck County walks in the door.

Nick's grip on my hand tightens and his leg movements

halt. His eyes remain fixed on the newcomer, narrowed slightly, following his every move.

"What's wrong?" I ask, but he doesn't move or respond.

"Nick, this is Rhett Wilson, sheriff out there in Puck County," Beau says. Looking up from the paper in his hands, he notices Nick's death grip on my hand. I watch Beau's eyes trail from Nick's hand to his face and finally to mine.

"Nick," Sheriff Wilson chuckles. "Glad you finally decided to join us."

My husband doesn't respond, instead looking back at me. Something isn't right. When I look at Beau, he continues to look between Nick and Wilson, putting the pieces together. The tension in the room finally catches the Sergeant's attention. He gives Beau a knowing glance, subtly lifting his brow, and nods.

Do they know something?

The other sheriff seems oblivious to it all, staring out the window of Beau's office. "Ms. Villa," Wilson says, turning back to us. "I'm sure Beau told you, but we looked all 'round that trail, and didn't see any signs of your mystery man."

"Men," I correct him. "There were two of them."

His face twitches near the corner of his left eye, but you probably wouldn't notice if you weren't looking.

"Hey, Rhett, can you grab Max from outside?" Beau asks, and the older man raises his white brow. "I want him to be here for this since he's been part of the investigation. He can take notes for me."

Sheriff Wilson rolls his eyes, grumbling, but does as he's asked.

When the door closes behind him, Beau looks directly at Nick. "Okay, what the fuck is going on?"

Nick doesn't seem to notice. His attention is now directed to a spot on the floor and his fingers absentmindedly pick at the fabric of his jeans.

"Nick." I gently touch his cheek, causing him to jump in place. When his eyes meet mine, I stroke his cheek with my thumb. "You gotta tell us what's going on. Do you know him, the sheriff?"

Nick looks around the room at each of us, ending on Beau. "He knows the guys that attacked me." The sentence hangs in the air for a moment. You've got to be fucking kidding me… Did Nick just confirm what Beau and I had been suspecting this whole time? "I saw him…in Bezer, with them. I—I didn't know he was the sheriff. No one ever said…He goes by Red there."

"I'm sorry." Beau pinches the bridge of his nose, eyes screwed shut, working through this new information. "Did you just say Sheriff Wilson is *working* with the men who attacked you? And they may be the men your wife saw at Mount Achor a few days ago?"

"They're definitely friendly."

Beau scrubs a hand down his face, cursing under his breath.

"Do you have any proof?" Sergeant Warren asks.

"I didn't exactly have a phone to be able to capture a fucking picture," Nick snaps, and I squeeze his hand, a gentle reminder these aren't the two we're supposed to be fighting. "But I'm telling you I saw him with my own two eyes. He's part of whatever is going on out there."

"And you're sure it was him?"

"Pretty damn sure."

"That's not solid enough," the sergeant says a millisecond before the door reopens. He pulls his phone out from his front pocket and begins typing. He looks up at Rhett, then returns to his message moments later.

Something is going on here, I know it, but what? I can't tell if Warren believes Nick, but when I meet Beau's stare, he nods discreetly. Despite whatever Sergeant Warren may think,

Beau believes him. His confidence is enough for me—as long as one of them does.

"Great, now that we're all here, can we get started?" Sheriff Wilson asks, looking around the room. His baritone voice displays a deep annoyance at the situation, and if I wasn't suspicious of him already, I would be by his eagerness to get this over and done.

Beau pulls a voice recorder from the top drawer and sets it near the front of the desk, pressing record...

TRANSCRIPT OF RECORDED STATEMENT
BY NICHOLAS DAVIS

Unnecessary sounds, such as "um" and "uh," have been omitted from the following statement for the purpose of making the statement easier to read.

Between Nicholas DAVIS, Sheriff Beau TURNER (Spruce County), Sheriff Rhett WILSON (Puck County), Sergeant James WARREN (State), Deputy Max JOHNSON (Spruce County), and Davina VILLA

On April 11, 2029, 09:10
Location: Spruce County Sheriff's Office

TURNER: Whenever you're ready, Nick.

DAVIS: (clears throat) Where should I start?

TURNER: Let's start with something simple. What day did you go missing?

DAVIS: April 8, 2028.

TURNER: And what were you doing on April 8, 2028?

DAVIS: I was in Haven for my brother's bachelor party.

TURNER: How did you end up at Achor Hiking Trail?

DAVIS: I didn't feel like going out with everyone, so I stayed home while the others went out. I had a lot going on and needed some space. A hike seemed like a good way to clear my head.

WILSON: So, you went to Achor—two hours away?

DAVIS: Yes.

WILSON: Even though there are a million other trails around *here?*

DAVIS: Yes.

WILSON: (scoffs)

WARREN: What made you decide to go to Achor that day, Mr. Davis?

DAVIS: It's my wife's favorite trail. I thought it might make me feel closer to her. We'd gotten into a fight before I left home and there was this stupid no-phones rule for the party—

WILSON: Which you broke because we found your phone with a text to your wife on the trail.

DAVIS: I wasn't going out there blind.

WILSON: Your wife said you didn't normally hike that trail. Said it would be unfamiliar to you. Why would you go to an unfamiliar trail alone?

TURNER: I think we already covered that.

(Background noise)

TURNER: Go ahead, Nick…So, you went out to Achor to clear your head. You get out there and then what happens?

DAVIS: Everything was normal. I hiked out with no issues. I don't remember seeing anyone else on the trail. Seemed unusually quiet…I didn't think anything of it because Nina has always said she liked how it wasn't a very populated trail. On my way back, I got just past the lakes area, around the bend, and heard a commotion.

WARREN: What kind of commotion?

DAVIS: Three guys were talking on the edge of the trail.

TURNER: What did these guys look like?

DAVIS: One was a smaller guy, a bit scrawny, but I don't remember much else about him, to be honest. The other two were bigger guys, one a bit heftier than the other. They give off "thug" vibes.

WARREN: What does that mean?

DAVIS: They just looked like trouble. The bigger one was leading the small guy off the trail, it looked like a shakedown.

TURNER: Okay, so you come across this "shakedown." Then what happens?

DAVIS: It was too late to try and get away. They saw me the second I rounded the bend. Without a second thought, the smaller of the two pulled a gun and shot the smaller guy point blank.

VILLA: (gasps)

TURNER: You okay, Nina?

VILLA: Sorry.

WARREN: (to Wilson) You guys find a body out there?

WILSON: (clears throat) Nope.

WARREN: Huh.

WILSON: What?

WARREN: Seems odd someone wouldn't report finding that.

WILSON: Unless it wasn't there.

VILLA: If he says it happened, it happened.

TURNER: Nin.

VILLA: (clears throat)

WARREN: We're not discounting that it happened, just trying to put the pieces together.

TURNER: (sighs) Okay, then what happens?

DAVIS: I ran. Figured it was better than standing around and waiting for the same thing to happen to me.

TURNER: Did they follow?

DAVIS: Yeah, and they seemed to know those woods like the back of their hands. No matter where I went, they were always right there. The bigger one got to me first, though. He had something on him, used it to hit me on the head.

WARREN: You didn't see what it was?

DAVIS: If I did, I don't remember. There are still some fuzzy bits.

WILSON: How can we rely on any of this, then?

TURNER: Okay, so the bigger one hits you on the head. Then what happens?

DAVIS: (background noise, sighs) I tried to get away, I don't remember a lot after that. Just trying to get away, until everything went black.

WILSON: You're not giving us much to go on, Mr. Davis.

DAVIS: I saw them again in Bezer. The men.

TURNER: Okay, let's hold on a second. Back up. So, everything goes black, what is the next thing you remember?

WILSON: (mumbled) This is useless.

DAVIS: Waking up in a hospital room.

WARREN: Do you remember what day that was?

DAVIS: April 10, 2028.

WARREN: And when you woke up—

DAVIS: I had no idea who I was. I couldn't remember *anything.* After a few days in the hospital, Joseph Blackwood— one of the men who found me—offered to let me stay and work at his ranch while I tried to figure out my next steps.

TURNER: When you said you saw these two men in the town of Bezer, did you recall *knowing* who they were at the time?

DAVIS: I didn't *know,* they just looked familiar.

TURNER: Where did you see them?

DAVIS: The first time was at a bar for Charlie's birthday.

TURNER: Who is Charlie?

DAVIS: (shuffles) Joseph Blackwood's daughter.

TURNER: The ranch owner?

DAVIS: Yes.

TURNER: And you went out to celebrate her birthday? Were you friends?

DAVIS: We had gotten close over the time I spent there.

TURNER: And they were at her birthday celebration?

DAVIS: Charlie used to date one of them. He was trying to convince her to date him again, but she wasn't interested.

TURNER: Because of you?

VILLA: Beau.

TURNER: (clears throat) Right. Okay, you see them at this bar, then what happens?

DAVIS: They seemed to recognize me, but it wasn't until a few days later when I was in town at the hardware store that it became obvious to me they knew who I was.

WARREN: Why do you say that?

DAVIS: They said, "You're supposed to be dead." Before anything else could be said, Chief Sloan showed up.

WILSON: (clears throat)

WARREN: Who is Sloan?

DAVIS: Chief of Police in Bezer.

WARREN: And Sloan made them leave?

DAVIS: Him and their father, or whoever he is.

TURNER: Their father?

(background noise)

WARREN: Mr. Davis?

(background noise)

WILSON: Cat got your tongue, boy?

TURNER: Rhett. Nick, we can't help you if you don't—

DAVIS: (clears throat) His name was Red.

TURNER: Okay, can you tell me what this 'Red' looked like?

(background noise)

VILLA: Nick.

DAVIS: I don't—Y-Yeah…White hair, mustache, kinda tall and slender.

TURNER: That all you got?

DAVIS: …Wears a white cowboy hat.

WILSON: (chuckles) If I didn't know any better, I'd say you were talkin' about me.

(Background noise)

WARREN: (clears throat) So, Mr. Davis, you said you saw them outside the shop…Sullivan's? Is that the only time you saw them?

DAVIS: No, they showed up at the Blossom Festival a week later, and then they cornered me on the ranch the next day.

WARREN: They cornered you?

DAVIS: I was working on a fence that needed repaired, and they showed up. They started talking about my wife and a bunch of other things, and pulled out a wallet that looked like my old one…Then they attacked me. Honestly, came pretty close to finishing the job, but Joseph showed up. Got rid of 'em.

TURNER: Did you see them again after that?

DAVIS: No. And two days later, my wife showed up.

WILSON: This still doesn't tell us anything we don't already know.

TURNER: Could you pick those men out of a lineup?

DAVIS: Yes.

WILSON: Why didn't you go to the authorities when you saw them? When they attacked you?

DAVIS: What was I supposed to say? I didn't even know my name let alone what happened between us. And Joseph ran them off. Everyone seemed pretty used to them around there, even Sloan.

WARREN: The police chief?

DAVIS: Yes.

WARREN: So, Joseph knew these men, as well?

DAVIS: Yes. Everyone did.

WARREN: What about the man you said was with them? Their father (?).

(background noise)

TURNER: Nick?

DAVIS: (clears throat) Yeah, they knew him. No one talks about him much around there.

TURNER: And could you point him out? (slight pause) In a lineup, I mean.

DAVIS: Yes.

WILSON: This still isn't much to go on. It's about as useful as your wife's disappearing mystery men.

WARREN: (sighs) It's not much but it's a start.

TURNER: It's more than we've had.

WARREN: I want to get ahold of Mr. Blackwood. Find out what he knows.

WILSON: You? This is *my* jurisdiction!

WARREN: And you haven't been able to keep up with things happening in *your* jurisdiction.

WILSON: James—

WARREN: You want to help, Rhett? Stay out of the way. (To Davis) Thank you for your time, Mr. Davis. I'll be in touch very soon. (To Turner) Beau, you can end the recording.

END OF TRANSCRIPT.

forty-three

Nina

"YOU CAN'T TAKE ME off this case!" Sheriff Wilson yells. I'm almost certain he's been holding that in since the interview began. Through most of the interrogation, Wilson kept his eyes glued to the floor, arms crossed tightly over his chest, listening to Nick. He analyzed every word Nick said, looking for anything he could use against him, instead of anything that might help the case.

I stared past my husband directly at the sheriff, watching for any confirmation of what Nick said earlier. I wondered if he really could be involved. Beau had questioned things about him before, but how do you accuse a fellow officer when you have no concrete evidence? All we had was a gut feeling, which now seemed spot on.

The final time Wilson looked up was when Nick mentioned the name "Red." He glared at the back of Nick's head before his eyes met mine. There was so much anger and fear in those cold blue eyes. It was at that moment, I knew he was involved. How involved? I don't know, but he knows something. I'm sure of it.

"I'm the one who brought you in. I'm—"

"Actually," Sergeant Warren interrupts him. "Beau brought me in. While you were pussyfootin' around, he was the one who recognized this was going to take more manpower than you could offer."

Sheriff Wilson's next argument falls short. When he looks around the room, he meets the gaze of everyone except my husband. Nick doesn't look up from his hands. Wilson scoffs. "This is ridiculous."

"You know this Joseph Blackwood?" Warren asks him. "You don't live far from Bezer, right? That's a pretty small community. You've probably run into him up there."

"Just because I live around there doesn't mean—"

"Yes or no, Rhett?" the sergeant demands, but Wilson doesn't reply. "You can either answer me right here or from the other side of an interrogation table. Your choice, Wilson."

"Excuse me?" Sheriff Wilson hisses.

"You heard me."

I look between the two men, then at Beau, whose eyes are locked on Wilson. I still feel like I've missed something. There has been a silent conversation between Beau and Warren this entire interrogation, one that I wish I had been included in.

Wilson chuckles humorlessly. "You've got to be kidding me, Sarge. What has your panties in a wad, huh?"

Nick tenses when Wilson steps off the wall, closer to him. I reach over, taking his hand, but he doesn't notice. His fist is clenched so tight that I'm sure his nails will leave indents in his skin. Slowly, I work his fingers away from the meat of his palm and lace mine through his, breaking whatever spell he's under. Nick looks at our hands, and I offer him a brief smile when he looks at me.

Warren looks up from his phone with a smile in the corner of his mouth and nods to Max. When Max opens the door, two men stand on the other side with badges draped around their necks. They look a lot like other detectives I've seen around the sergeant. The taller of the two says, "Rhett Wilson, you're under arrest."

Nick squeezes my hand.

"Under arrest?" Wilson's voice booms through the office. "I'm the Sheriff of Puck—"

"Save it for the jury," the shorter one says.

"Get the hell off me," Wilson says when they reach for him. "What are the charges? You can't—"

"You wanna go there, Rhett?" The same one says with a cocked brow.

"Yes! You have no right to come in and—"

The taller one begins rattling off a list of offenses and looks bored as he does so. "Conspiracy to kidnap, kidnapping, possession and trafficking of drugs, conspiracy to commit murder, obstruction of justice, extortion, bribery, and tampering with evidence."

Wilson struggles against the two men when they turn him around and push him against the wall. One finally pulls the sheriff's hands behind his back, and the other reads his rights as they drag him out the door.

"That went better than expected," Beau says, shaking hands with Warren.

"You knew what was happening?" I turn around so fast that I think I give myself whiplash.

Beau lifts his phone. "We've been in contact with a few guys on the outside."

"I already had two guys on their way out to Bezer this morning," Sergeant Warren says. "I wanted them to sit down with Joseph and Sloan and find out what they knew. They were right outside of town when Nick said he recognized Rhett, so I put a word out to them to get their asses in gear. They said Sloan was tough to crack, but Joseph provided the names of the men who attacked Nick and confirmed Rhett knows 'em. He confirmed a lot of what Nick just said in his statement.

Commissioner gave the green light to take Rhett into custody and the signed warrant came right on time." He lifts his phone. "We've put a BOLO out for the other two."

"Cooper Hayes and Dakota," Nick says.

"Dakota Thompson, yes." Sergeant Warren stands from his seat on the cabinet and cracks his neck. "Thank you for your help, Mr. Davis. I don't know who you've got lookin' out for you, but you got lucky. We've been after those boys for a while, but couldn't get anything to stick. Now, I think we know why." He reaches over me to shake Nick's hand before squeezing my shoulder. "Beau, I'll be in touch," Warren says, waving over his shoulder. He lifts his phone to his ear as he leaves.

"I don't know about the rest of you, but that's enough excitement for the next ten years," Beau says when Sergeant Warren is gone. He scrubs a hand down his face and lifts his feet onto the corner of his desk.

I squeeze Nick's thigh. "Are you ready to go home?"

"Please." Nick sighs, wiping his palms on his thighs before standing.

"I'll be out in a minute, okay? I need to talk to Beau."

Nick looks between us before he holds his gaze on Beau. Admittedly, I'm a little scared of whatever he might say. "Thank you...For not giving up and keeping her out of trouble."

"It wasn't easy," Beau says, his feet falling from his desk.

"No, I'd expect not." After a small laugh, Nick gnaws on his bottom lip and looks back to me. "Had something happened to her—"

"We're just glad you're home."

My husband looks at the sheriff, who offers him a genuine smile. Nick nods once before he kisses me and follows Max out of the office.

When I turn back to Beau, he's already on the other side of his desk. With his hands on his hips, he stands barely a foot from me but doesn't come any closer. "Does this mean I get to keep my job?"

"I suppose it does." I laugh and take a small step forward, happy when he doesn't move away. "Thank you, Beau. For everything."

"Happy to be of service."

A silence falls between us because neither of us knows what to say. There is so much left unsaid, but now that Nick is back...None of it matters, not anymore.

"Nina—"

"I should go," I say, because I have to. There is no more space for conversation outside of Beau Turner, Sheriff of Spruce County, and Davina Villa, resident of his jurisdiction.

"Right." Beau nods, taking a step back. "Yeah, you're right."

I close the gap between us, pulling him into a tight embrace, and his arms wind around me. He squeezes me and inhales before I feel his lips on my forehead.

"Take care of yourself, Sweetheart."

When we part, I walk to the door, pausing at the threshold. "Beau?" He looks up. "I couldn't have done it without you."

Green eyes soften when Beau smiles. "I'll see you around, Nin."

forty-four

Nick

"MIND IF I JOIN you?" I hear from a few feet behind me, and I wave Pop over without looking. I knew one of them would find me eventually, I just wasn't sure who would be first…him or Nina.

Leaning over the fence, I hold the neck of the beer bottle loosely between two of my fingers and stare out at the black void before me. The sun set about two hours ago, leaving the mountain shrouded in darkness and the starry sky glittering above its peak.

"How are ya feeling?" Pop asks.

I sigh, letting my head drop.

"That good, huh?"

"Honestly, Pop…This is all kind of a lot."

"What did you expect?" He chuckles. "You've been gone a long while, Nick. There's going to be an adjustment period. You can't expect to come home and have everything go back to normal. *That* normal went out the window when you stepped out of this house last April, along with the people you once knew. While you were gone, the rest of us spent the past year

364

adjusting to a different normal—without you in it. Now we have to pivot to *this* normal—the one where you're back."

Is he right? Is that what I was expecting? To walk in and everything returns to the way it was before? To the way Nina and I were before? That's been the hardest thing to accept since I got home…The way my wife and I seem to be strangers.

When I learned about her and Beau, I think it's fair to say I subconsciously put up a barrier between us. When I saw them together…how close they were…how comfortable they were…it only reinforced the space between us. Just like today when she asked me to leave so they could talk. The request made my stomach drop and my heart ache. A few minutes later, when she left his office, she seemed sad but did her best to hide it. It made me wonder if we'd ever be able to move on…If I could move on.

"Everyone is different to some degree, including you. You're not the same person you were before, either. Are you?"

I shrug, but he knows the answer: No, I'm not.

"No, you're not. And that's okay. Neither is your wife."

At the mention of Nina, I look up at him.

Pop sighs, planting his hands on the top board of the fence. He looks out into the wilderness. "I have never seen a woman—or anyone for that matter—hold themselves together the way your wife does. It should be studied."

I can't contain my laugh, because Pop isn't wrong. His words take me back to when Ric died and Nina was the only one holding things together. Kai broke. Her mom was playing the role of a grieving widow. Eileen was too busy taking care of Kai. Elizabeth was dealing with her own grief, losing yet another parent. But Nina…She held it all together when no one else could. It didn't help that Ric put Nina in charge of *everything*—his estate, his personal effects, and his funeral. It shouldn't have come as a surprise to me that she did the same this time around with my supposed "death."

"While the rest of us were too busy thinking about ourselves—about you—she was worried about all of us. Taking care of everyone while still going out and searching every square inch of these mountains. I doubt she slept more than an hour each night. She is the only reason we're still here. I don't think we would've made it this far without her."

"I don't doubt it," I whisper, swinging the bottle between my fingers. "You know when I saw her standing there"—I close my eyes and smile, thinking back to seeing her the first time at Blackwood Ranch—"I felt everything click into place. My world came back into view. I have been stuck in this fog for the past year, scratching and clawing, trying to remember something...anything...about myself. But I could never get more than a vague memory, a vague image. It was like I was trapped in this cloud of thick smoke behind a foot of glass and there was nothing I could do to reach them. I was at the mercy of this monster who enjoyed torturing me, giving me small crumbs here and there, but never enough to get the full picture."

Looking up at the stars in the sky, I fight back the burning growing behind my eyes. "But when I saw her...it all just clicked. I don't even know how to—There's no way to explain it."

"Then why are you avoiding her? Oh, don't give me that look, you think I haven't noticed?" Pop shakes his head. "Nick, I'm your father, and you may have been gone a while, but I can still tell when something is bothering you."

Tugging at my beer, I avoid his stare. Changing the subject, I ask, "What's going on with her and Alex?"

I would have never expected tension between Alex and Nina, but it was palpable from the moment I saw them together yesterday. They avoided each other, avoided being alone together, and kept their distance whenever being around each other couldn't be avoided.

Pop sighs. "I think you'd be better asking them."

"Something happened?"

It's his turn to avoid my stare. He braces the fence and bites down on the inside of his cheek.

"Pop. What is going on?"

"Nick, this whole ordeal has been hard on the whole family, but especially your brother. He took your absence extremely hard, and it's led to some tension between him and Nina."

"Obviously. They've been trying to hide it but they're not very good at it."

"Well, they got into a pretty big fight not long ago."

Alex and Nina got into a fight? That seems out of character for both of them.

Pop shrugs. "You'd have to ask one of them about it, but I don't think either of 'em will tell you the truth. Neither one has said anything since it happened a few days ago. But if I had to guess, it probably has something to do with the sheriff. Alex struggled with how much time Nina spent with Sheriff Turner during all of this. He's convinced she slept with him."

"She did."

Pop's brow raises at my confession.

Shit, I don't know why I told him that.

"She did?" he asks.

With a soft *mhmm* in response, I stare down at my feet. "A few months ago."

"And how do you feel about that?"

"I was mad. No, I was angry. At her. At him. At the situation."

"You still angry?"

"No." I shrug. "I don't know, maybe. Or maybe I'm upset and hurt. But how can I be, when I did the same thing?"

"You did?" Pop seems even more surprised than he did about Nina and Beau.

"Joseph's daughter, Charlie…We weren't close, but we were

friendly. She liked me, and I guess, I became more open to the idea as more time passed." I shake my head, looking back up at the sky. "I should've never let it happen, I knew better, but she kissed me one night and I let it go further than I should've."

"You sleep with her?" Pop asks, but I shake my head. "Nick, I say this with all the love in my heart, but you're being a fucking hypocrite."

"I know." A bitter laugh I can taste on my tongue rises out of my chest. "I fucking know, Pop. And for some reason, I still can't get past it. The thought of him touching her, knowing her the way I do...it makes me sick."

"Nick, listen to me." Pop grips my shoulders and turns me to face him. "Nina thought you were gone. No, she thought you were *dead.* Even when they told her there was no use looking...She did it anyway. And do you know who was by her side the entire time?"

Beau.

"Beau Turner. He didn't leave her side or let her go out there alone because he wouldn't let whatever happened to you, happen to her. When she refused to sit on the sidelines, he made sure she came home every night, he made sure she ate when she forgot, and he made sure she had what she needed to keep going. While the rest of us were too busy worrying about ourselves, he was worried about her. You should be thankful for Beau Turner. Without him, I don't know if Nina would even be remotely as close to normal as she is today."

His words sink like a boulder in my stomach.

"You want to be upset? Fine. Give yourself five minutes and then get over it. Do you honestly believe that your wife— that Davina Villa—would have done *anything* like that had she thought you were still alive? Had she known you were out there somewhere in need of rescue?"

"No," I whisper.

"No," Pop confirms. "She would have burned the whole

world down until she brought you home. And that's what she did until she couldn't anymore."

His words are only confirmation of what I already know.

"You were dead. Did you expect her to stay miserable and alone for the rest of her life?"

"No," I say again. I would never want that for her. I'd want her to find happiness again. I'd want her to find someone who could take care of her and Elena and would love them both.

"It's not like they were dating, Nick. So, what if they—"

"I think she's in love with him," I say.

Pop laughs a full, hearty sound. "Oh, you've got to be joking."

"You haven't seen them together, Pop." He didn't see them yesterday. The way she looked at him. The way she clung to him. The way she instinctively went to check on him after I punched him was like it was second nature. And anyone who saw how he looked at her would notice it immediately.

There was no denying it.

"I have seen them together and I can tell you she doesn't love him. Maybe she has some feelings for him, but I'm gonna tell you something, Nicholas. That woman only loves one man and it's *you*."

Tears prick the corners of my eyes.

"She never stopped loving you, regardless of what has happened. Regardless of how stubborn and bullheaded you've been over the years, or how much you have harassed her about her job and all that comes with it, or you lying to her about her mother...Nina Villa has always loved *you*. She never stopped looking for *you*. She dropped everything and ran to *you* when she heard you were alive. Where is she right now? It's not with Beau. It's right here...with *you*. You're too wrapped up in your feelings to see the truth."

"What if she doesn't want me when she realizes I'm not the same man she fell in love with?" I bite down on the inside corner of my mouth, swallowing the thickness growing in my throat.

"Are you still Nick Davis?"

"Yeah, I guess...But—"

"That's all that matters. You're still you, Nick. You're just a little different, or maybe a lot different. We all are. You and Nina, you two will figure this out, but you gotta give yourselves the grace to do it."

My wife kisses our daughter on the forehead, pulls the blanket up to her shoulders, and turns off the light. There's a level of surprise in her eyes when she looks up and meets my gaze, but we don't speak as she closes Elena's door and I follow her to the kitchen. Thankfully, everyone else has already gone to bed, so there isn't anyone left to distract us from finally having the long overdue conversation.

Nina begins to pull dishes from the dishwasher and put them away, but I stop her. Taking her hand in mine, I remove the plate from her grasp and set it on the counter. "What are you—"

Her words are lost when I kiss her, and she melts into my embrace. Her hands grip my shirt, and she tugs me forward as I explore her mouth, eliciting a moan from her.

"What was that for?" she asks when we part, her eyes still closed.

"I missed you."

Dark emerald orbs blink open, meeting mine, but she doesn't say anything. She doesn't have to. I can see every emotion running through her mind behind her eyes.

"Can we talk?" I ask, tucking a strand of hair behind her

ear and running my fingers through her hair. "Please."

Nina sighs and closes the dishwasher in silent agreement.

When we get to the bedroom she closes the door and leans back against it. After a few heartbeats, she creeps farther inside, arms folded over her chest, waiting for whatever is about to come. We've never been like this. Even when we've had disagreements in the past, there has never been this air of uncertainty between us, and I hate it.

I hate that it feels like we're dancing around each other, avoiding the well-placed landmines waiting for an unsuspecting victim. We haven't done this dance since I was hiding the shit about her mom and ex-boyfriend, trying not to slip up and tell her when hiding it felt like the only way to protect her and my family.

I take a deep breath and say, "I'm going to ask you something and I want you to say the first thing that pops into your head, okay?"

Her brow raises at my question. "Interesting way to start this off, but okay."

I swallow the lump of nerves building in my throat, pushing it back down into my stomach. I don't know what will happen next, but I know I have to ask. I need to hear the answer straight from her lips. "Do you love him?"

Nina freezes. "W-what?"

"Do you love him?"

Her gaze narrows. "Do I love who?"

"Beau! Nina. Do you love Beau?" I pinch the bridge of my nose. The longer we play this game, the more it makes me sick.

The next moments feel like a lifetime, waiting for her to answer.

Nina sighs, falling onto the edge of the bed. "Not like I love you."

"That's not good enough, Nina."

"Not good enough?" She jumps up from her seat. "No!

Nick, no. I don't…I do not *love* him. But I won't lie to you. There are feelings there for him, but they're not…" Nina takes a step toward me but stops herself. "I love you! It's always going to be you, Nick."

"Even if he loves you?"

"Even if he loves me. I will always choose you. I am yours." Nina takes the final step, taking my face between her hands. Her palms are warm against my cheeks. "My heart and soul belong to you. I only ask you to give me the grace to figure this out. The same grace I've extended to you about Charlie."

"Nina, we—"

"I don't want to know, Nick." She shakes her head, dropping her hands and taking a step back. "I don't need to know. Whatever happened…or didn't happen, you weren't yourself." Biting down on her lip, she blinks away from our shared gaze.

"*Ti amo*, Davina," I say. It's the first thing to cross my mind. I gently grip her chin and pull her mouth to mine in a quick kiss. "The only things that matter to me in this world are you and that little girl down the hall. I could lose everything, but as long as I have you…I know I'm gonna be okay."

"You have me. You'll always have me."

I stick out my right pinky and tears form in her eyes when she looks at it. With a soft laugh, she sticks out her own, wrapping it around mine tightly.

forty-five

Nina

OUR FINGERS STILL INTERTWINED, Nick uses them to tug me forward, into his embrace. His left hand grips my neck and brings my mouth to his. It's soft and leisurely like we have all the time in the world, and I suppose we do.

I untwist my fingers from his and trail my hands up his chest, gliding around the sides of his neck. The slow, languid strokes of his tongue become more desperate as he urges me backward until the backs of my thighs press against the bed. He reaches down, cupping my ass, and lifts me off my feet. My back hits the mattress and Nick wastes no time crawling up, covering my body with his. His lips dot along my jaw and neck, fingers skating across my stomach when he lifts my sweater. The familiar roughness of his touch warms my skin.

Nick tugs the fabric over my head and leans down to press a lingering kiss on the initial branded into my shoulder. He traces the letter with his pointer finger before he looks up, tears coating his whiskey-golden orbs.

Wrapping my hand around his neck, I bring his lips to mine, and the soft kiss quickly turns hungry. His tongue sweeps across my lips, and I open to him, letting our tongues tangle in a desperate embrace. A hand tangles in my hair, tugging my head back to give him full, unadulterated access. Wet, open-mouthed kisses trail down my jaw and throat to my chest. Unclasping my bra, he kisses between the valley of my breasts.

"Where did *he* touch you, Davina?" His mouth is hot on my skin. "I want to know every place that his mouth"—a gentle bite on the swell of my breast—"and his hands"—he caresses down my stomach—"and his dick"—he cups me through my leggings—"touched you because I'm going to remind every inch who you belong to."

The simple words ignite a fire under my skin, and I can already feel the pulse intensify between my legs. My husband has always been a possessive lover, a dominating force when it comes to lovemaking, and it's one of the things I love most about him. This is the one place he doesn't hold back no matter the circumstances. It's the one place where I'm not forced to be in control, to clean up after everyone else, or to worry about the repercussions. Because when we are behind this door, we are not Nicholas Davis and Davina Villa—entrepreneurs, business owners, investors, and every other title associated with our names—we are just Nick and Nina, an ordinary couple trying to show their love for one another.

"Do you know who you belong to, Davina?" My husband whispers against my stomach. His lips brush against the skin above the waistband of my leggings.

"You." I gasp as his tongue licks a stripe up to my navel, dipping inside. That's new, and not something I'd expect, but fuck...it felt interestingly good. He tugs my leggings and underwear down my hips, and I kick them off before his fingers find my center. "Nick." I moan when he touches my swollen folds and pulls back, satisfied.

"I've barely touched you and you're fucking soaked,

Davina."

"*È la tua bocca.*" A breathy laugh passes my lips after I say, *It's your mouth.*

"This mouth?" Nick asks. He spreads my legs and blows against my entrance, and I breathe out a soft, "Yes."

One finger swipes up my center, followed by his tongue, and the sensation bows my back off the duvet. Nick chuckles against me, wrapping his hands around my thighs and dragging me to the edge of our bed. He winds my legs around his waist and lifts me into the air, carrying me to the chair next to the fireplace. My ass hangs halfway off the edge, but his grip on my thighs is firm and supportive, pushing my legs apart as far as they'll go.

"Dee," he groans, staring up from under his lashes. He licks a single stripe up my center, letting his nose brush against my clit, and it sends a shiver up my spine. "Fuck, I've missed tasting you." He smiles before his mouth returns to where I need him most.

"Yes." I sigh, digging my nails through his short hair. Each swipe of his tongue that follows brings me higher than the last. "Oh my god." I gasp when he flattens his tongue against my clit, dragging it across the sensitive bud, and pushes two fingers inside me at the same time. But it's not only the feeling of his tongue or his fingers that drives me higher, it's the look on his face when I stare down at him. Pure euphoria is the only way I know how to explain it—like he's enjoying this as much as me. His eyes meet mine again and with a final brush of his tongue, it sends me soaring.

His hands brace against my legs, keeping them spread when I try to squeeze them closed, and he laps up my release with a heavy moan. My perfectly manicured nails dig into the arms of the chair as I let my head fall behind me, unable to control the strain of expletives falling from my lips.

My body arches forward without warning when he does

a final suckle on my clit before sitting back on his heels. He wipes the corner of his mouth with a smirk. My nails still dig into the wooden arms, but I nod in response when he offers his words of praise.

Nick stands before me and bends down to swipe his thumb over my cheek before covering my mouth with his. "You were such a good girl."

When I open my eyes, he's already pushing his jeans down his thighs, leaving them in a puddle at his feet. His cock strains against the fabric of his underwear.

"As much as I want to fuck your mouth, I don't want to wait any longer to be inside you," Nick says, pushing the cotton down his legs and fisting his cock.

He's fucking beautiful. And he's all mine.

Planting my feet on the floor, I wrap my hand around his cock alongside his and the sound it pulls from him is heavenly. Stroking him, I feel the anticipation vibrate through his entire being and glide my other hand under his T-shirt to the planes of his chest. He removes the shirt in one swift motion, and I attach my lips to his chest. Tears cloud my vision when I see the tattoo on his left pectoral. I thought I'd never see it again. The black ink engrains the image of the Tree of Life in his tanned skin, the leaves designed to be birds flying from its branches.

Nick lifts my chin to meet his gaze and kisses me softly. With his hands on my hips, he guides me back to the bed, lifting me with ease onto the plush mattress. I laugh when he crawls on top of me, this time peppering my neck with kisses, his stubble tickling the skin.

"I lied. *That's* my favorite sound." His words refer to last night when he said everything was his favorite sound, but I think he means it this time. Pushing the hair from my face, he leans down to kiss me again.

We kiss for what feels like hours. No pressure, no need to

rush things, just enjoying being wrapped in each other.

Nick pushes inside me without warning and my body arches off the bed, flush against him as I adjust to the fullness of him. The sensation is so familiar, yet foreign at the same time. He takes his time, pushing further until he's seated fully inside me, filling me completely. He moves slowly at first, pulling out and pushing back in at a steady pace, each thrust bringing me closer and closer to the edge already. This might be a new record for how fast he's made me come, but between the anticipation and coming on his tongue, I know it won't take long until I'm cresting over the edge of ecstasy again.

My nails rake down his forearms and his back, they dig into the flesh of his shoulders as I grasp for anything I can hold on to as he rolls into me repeatedly at a deliciously, torturously slow pace. He's taking his time, devouring every moment we are connected as one.

"Do you know how many nights I dreamed about this while I was gone?" Nick thrusts into me, filling me to the hilt, hips pressed firmly against mine. He maneuvers them in a deep circle that draws a low groan from me. "Of the woman who plagued my mind from the moment I opened my eyes until I saw you standing there. Dreamed of what it would feel like to be this close to you again. To feel you wrapped around my cock." His breath pushes through gritted teeth when he pulls out—almost completely—and pushes back in. A guttural moan rumbles in his chest, and he presses his forehead against mine, his fingers digging into the comforter beside my head. "To remember how fucking good it felt to love you."

When Nick opens his eyes, there's a hint of fear inside them. It's a look I haven't seen before, but one that I recognize immediately. It's the same feeling I get, the fear of waking up and he will be gone again.

"Come back to me, *Fossette*," I whisper, tracing my finger down his face. A tear slips down his cheek, landing on my chest, and I wipe another that follows. "Right here, Nick. It's you and me. I'm not going anywhere, and neither are you."

Nick nods, his forehead still against mine, and his eyes screw shut to fight back the tears in his eyes. Our bodies continue the familiar dance, expressing the love we have shared for almost a decade that only we know, but there is something different this time. Each movement is more sensual, more spiritual, than ever before.

"I love you, Nick Davis," I say, and kiss him. "I love you so much it fucking hurts, and it makes my heart ache because the thought of losing you is too much. If I ever lose you again, I won't survive."

"Nina," he whimpers, letting his forehead fall to my shoulder.

"Let go, baby," I whisper against his temple, my fingers splayed out across the back of his head. "*Va tutto bene. Basta lasciar andare.*" *It's okay. Just let go,* I whisper and gasp when he pulls all the way out and pushes back in. He does it one more time, and moans when he comes, continuing to fuck me through his orgasm. I slide my right hand between our connected bodies and rub the bundle of nerves already on fire. It won't require much to follow him, and when he rocks his body against mine, applying even more delicious pressure against me, I come.

"*Brava ragazza,* Davina."

Good girl.

The words draw a whimper from my lips, and he kisses me, swallowing the moans of my release. He pushes up on his palms to stare down at me, to watch as I come undone beneath him, and I feel his dick grow hard again still inside me.

"You feel that, Dee?" He moans. "That's all for you."

I clutch at him, interlocking my fingers behind his nape, and hold on as he rocks his hips into me, fucking me again. With only a few pumps, he comes again, and this time the sensation is almost too much to my already sensitive body, but he holds my hips steady so I can't writhe away from him as he finishes.

"Fuck, Dee." He sighs, rolling to my side, his hand resting on my hip where it traces invisible circles. I hum in response, eyes closed as I let my body fall from the high it's still riding. Opening my eyes, I turn my head to the side and find him staring at me. He cradles the side of my face and kisses me. It's soft and slow, his tongue moving in languid strides against mine. *"Sei mio,"* he whispers when we part.

You're mine.

"Tuo," I say in agreement and it makes him smile. Taking his hand, I hold it against my heart and repeat, "Yours. This belongs to you, always."

Nick wraps his hand around the chain holding his wedding ring and slips it over my head. He unclasps the chain and drops the ring into his palm. He stares at it, and I wait for him to put it on, but he only stares. I caress the side of his face. Taking the ring from his hand, I slip it on his ring finger.

Nick

HER BACK RISES AND FALLS with each slumbered breath and I trace every inch of her skin, the same way I've done every morning since waking up next to her again. It's been five days since my wife showed up at the ranch, and every day when I wake up, I'm still scared to open my eyes and find I'm back in my room at Blackwood Ranch with no recollection of who I am or where I've come from.

So far, so good…I wake up every morning next to my wife with most of my memory. Some things are still foggy, but the neurologist Nina got me into two days ago said everything should become clearer with time. The nightmares come and go, but at least they aren't as consistent as they once were.

Her dark hair falls down her bare shoulders, her skin still exposed from our time together under the sheets last night. We made love twice—first when I walked in to find her fresh out of the bath, and again in the middle of the night when she returned to bed from tucking Elena back in. I feel like a high schooler, unable to get enough of her, but every time the opportunity arises, it's hard to fight the urge. We have a lot of time to make up for, and I don't plan on wasting it. I'll take any opportunity to relearn her body and discover new things about her.

Nina shifts beside me, looking up at me through one eye, the other still hidden in the white pillow. "Why are you awake?"

"I like watching you."

"You're creepy."

"And you love it," I whisper, slinking back under the covers. My hands find her sides and without warning, my fingers dance across her skin. She laughs, trying to get away from the tickle assault, but her attempts only push her body against mine and it does nothing to help soothe my already hard erection. Without warning, I wrap my arm around her waist and pull her body over mine.

Nina gasps when my cock rubs against her entrance. "Shit. That all for me?"

"You, and it's the morning, but mostly you."

She hums in approval, grinding her hips against me, and if it's even possible, my cock hardens further.

Fuck.

Nina braces her palms on my chest and sits upright, giving me a full view of her body, and it's a fucking sight. How did I get so lucky? I swear she's gotten more beautiful in the last twelve months…or maybe it's because I haven't seen her, but I'm more inclined to believe it's just her. She has always been beautiful, but the new curves she developed since having our daughter drove me wild. I think about when she was pregnant and I couldn't keep my hands off her. There was something deep inside me—a primal instinct—that loved seeing her pregnant, knowing I had left a permanent impression on her. A feat that no one else would ever be able to accomplish.

"Dee," I moan, my fingers digging into her hips as she rubs against my length.

She bends down to kiss me. Our tongues tangle in a

desperate embrace. Her left hand digs into the sheet beside my head, but her right wraps around the base of my skull, her nails scraping against my scalp. She's craving the length I used to have. She hasn't said anything since I got home, but I remember she was upset when I shaved my head last January. She liked it when it was long enough to curl on the ends, the same length it had been when we got married the first time.

My hands roam across her body before I reach down to cup her ass and she gasps when my length teases her entrance. I pull her bottom lip between my teeth and nibble on the pink flesh. "You want my cock, baby?" She whimpers in response. "Words, Davina."

"Yes." She gasps when I roll my hips into her, and she sits upright. Nina lifts on her knees, fully expecting me to guide myself into her, but I'm not going to give her what she wants yet.

I smirk. "Yes, *what?*"

Her green eyes darken when she looks down at me.

"Yes, what?" I ask. The anticipation of being inside of her is fucking brutal when the tip of my cock rubs against her again, teasing her. She whimpers, desperate and needy, but I wait for her to say the words.

"Yes, *sir.*"

Her words send a jolt straight to my dick and I push into her with a shared gasp. She lowers herself until she is fully seated and stretched around me. No matter how many times I've had this woman around my cock, every time feels better than the last.

"Fuck, Dee," I moan when she begins to slowly rock her hips. One of her hands reaches behind her to grasp my knee and her tits bounce with her. This image is one of my favorites.

I reach up to cup her right breast, kneading the doughy flesh. Her head falls back when I pinch her nipple and the ends of her hair feather across my legs, raising goosebumps across my skin.

"Nick," she breathes, her hands fisting in her hair, tugging slightly.

"You look so fucking beautiful, Dee. I love when you ride me. Fuck, just like that."

She whimpers in response, her pace slowing down, and I can feel her pussy tighten around me. She's close. All it would take is a few strokes of her clit and she'd be a goner.

I reach up to grip her throat, applying a faint amount of pressure on the sides, and pull her mouth down to mine. In one quick motion, I wrap my arm around her waist and roll so I'm on top of her. "You feel so good wrapped around my cock, baby," I say, pulling out a bit and thrusting back in until my hips meet hers.

Nina's back arches off the bed and her fingers grasp for purchase on the headboard. I leave open-mouthed kisses on her neck before tracing back up the column of her throat with my tongue.

She gasps when I lift her right leg and thrust deeper inside of her. *"Sì, amore mio." Yes, my love.*

Fuck. I grit my teeth. She knows what her Italian does to me when we're like this. I'm not going to last if she keeps it up.

"Ci sono vicino," she breathes in my ear. She's close. I know the words are true when I feel her pussy tighten around my cock.

"Dee," I groan. "You gotta stop doing that, baby."

"Lo so." The words and her smirk tell me she knows exactly what she's doing. She reaches between us, fingering her clit, and the response from her body is enough to throw me over the edge.

My fingers dig into the flesh of her hip as I drive into her through my orgasm. I kiss her neck, swirling my tongue along her skin in slow, languid strokes as her walls clench around me and her body trembles reaching the peak of her orgasm. Pure, unadulterated ecstasy runs through my veins, and I push into her one final time.

"*Buongiorno, amore mio,*" Nina whispers when we've both come down from the high, and her fingers lightly trace my face.

"Good morning, *vita mia.*"

She kisses me and I roll next to her. Parting, she runs her nails along my jaw through my stubble. "Elena will be up soon." She yawns and snuggles into my chest despite what she just said.

"Should probably get moving, then." I kiss her forehead and with one final kiss on her lips, I peel myself away from her and force myself out of bed.

A few minutes later, she follows me into the bathroom. We get ready for the morning in a dance that feels so familiar it makes my heart soar. The tension—the awkwardness—that had been there the first two days of my return is gone. Our bodies move in tandem with one another.

"Your life, huh?" Nina asks when she finishes brushing her teeth. Hip leaning against the bathroom counter, she waits for me to pull the sweater over my head.

"What?"

"That's what you said...*Good morning, vita mia.*"

A blush creeps up my neck into my cheeks when she repeats the words I said not ten minutes ago.

She drapes her arms over my shoulders and stands on her tiptoes to kiss me. "You're adorable, *Fossette.*"

When I walk into the kitchen later, the wall of silence practically smacks me in the face. I can almost feel the chill radiating off my brother as he moves from the fridge to the sink and finally the breakfast nook with a bottle of water and a yogurt. Nina watches him from the corner of her eye but focuses on the pizzas she's making for lunch at Elena's request. Are these two ever going to talk about what happened between them, or are we going to continue to act like nothing happened? It's been this way all week with no signs of it getting any better. No matter how much I ask Pop what happened, he still won't tell me. He says I have to ask them, but I don't think they will tell me.

"Oh, don't leave on my account," I say when my brother gets up after finishing his yogurt. "Seems like you two are having a good ol' time in here."

"What are you talking about?" Alex rolls his eyes.

I cross my arms, blocking the doorway. It's time to have this conversation. "I'm talking about whatever is going on between you two."

"There's nothing—"

"Cut the crap, Alex. I may still be trying to remember some things and some stuff may be a little hazy, but I can tell you whatever is happening here wasn't before." I raise a brow and look between them, but Nina still hasn't looked up from making pizza. "Nina?"

She sighs, but still doesn't look up when she asks, "What?"

"You want to tell me what's going on?"

"Nothing!" Alex throws his hands up in the air.

"Nick." Nina sighs. She drops the pepperoni she's been spreading across the dough, and when she looks up, the fight behind her green eyes is obvious. She's protecting him. Whatever it is, she doesn't want me to know. "It's nothing."

"See," Alex says. "I told you. It's nothing." My brother shoves into my shoulder when he pushes by me to leave the kitchen, like a little kid throwing a tantrum.

I join my wife at the island. "Dee, what is going on?"

"Nick—"

"Davina Bay, don't you dare say *nothing* again." I grip her chin and force her to look at me. "Nina, please tell me what's going on. Tell me whatever stupid thing he said so we can move past this. I hate seeing you two avoid each other like this."

Nina bites down on her bottom lip and steps back, rubbing her eyes. "Nick, please don't get mad. I'll tell you if you promise not to get mad. Not to…start something."

Well, that depends on what he said.

"Nick, promise me."

"I can't do that, Nina."

My wife stares at me for a moment longer before she lets out a defeated sigh. "He was just…concerned."

"About?"

"Nick, please. Please let this go. Don't make me do this."

I have no intention of letting it go, especially not when I know how much it's affecting her.

Slowly, her resolve breaks, and she takes a deep breath. "He felt like I didn't do enough to bring you home. He thought I was…happy you were gone. He had his opinions on me and B—"

Without hearing the rest, I leave to find my brother. Nina calls after me, following me through the house and pleading with me to let it go. I won't let this go. I can't. Not when he's treated her with utter disrespect.

It doesn't take long to find him. He's playing in the treehouse in the backyard with Lara, Brie, Ophelia, and Elena.

"Brie, take the girls inside," I demand before adding a quick "please." Without question, Josh's oldest daughter does as she's told, only looking over her shoulder once before they disappear into the house.

"I'm not doing this, Nick," Alex says, trying to follow, but I grip his shoulder and push him back a step.

"Did you tell Nina she wasn't doing enough to find me?" I ask, starting small, but he doesn't say anything. My brother shoves his hands into the crooks of his elbows, eyes downcast on the ground beneath his feet. "I'll take that as a yes. Did you also say she was *happy* I was gone?"

He looks up at me before his glare turns to Nina, now next to me. "Of course, you told him. I will say, I'm surprised you lasted this long."

"Don't blame her. She is still trying to protect you, but I'm over this avoidance game between you. We're adults, Alex, take ownership of your part of the problem."

"My part of the problem? She's the one who was fucking the sheriff! Instead of looking for you, she was too busy spending her nights in bed with him and—"

"So what if she fucked Beau?"

"So, it *is* true," he hisses toward Nina, and I step in front of her. "And you're okay with it? She cheated on—"

"She thought I was dead, Alex. She slept with him one fucking time. And I'm not blameless, either. I messed around with the daughter of the guy who took me in."

"You didn't know who you were! You have an excuse."

"And she doesn't?" I scoff. "What is she supposed to do? Spend the rest of her life alone because I'm gone?"

"She stopped looking, Nick! She didn't even try—"

"How would you know? Were you here with her every day for the past year?" My hand reaches out to my wife behind me. At first, she ignores the gesture, but then she interlocks her fingers with mine. I give her hand a gentle squeeze. "No, you weren't."

"You weren't even that far away. She should've been able to find you! She didn't look hard enough."

"There is more to this situation than you realize, Alex. You need to take a step back, take a deep breath, and get a fucking grip. Nina *and* Beau are the only reasons I'm home. Neither of them stopped looking for answers. She never stopped trying to find out what happened. Did you know she was almost attacked by the same people who attacked me?"

Alex's wide eyes meet hers. "Nina?" he asks, but she looks away from him. "Is that what Beau meant outside of Magnolia's?"

"Alex, it's time to let this go," Lara says from behind him. "Nina has been nothing but gracious to all of us, including you, and you've been nothing but an asshole to her lately."

My brother looks between his fiancée and Nina, and I don't think Lara knew what happened either. I'm not surprised, Alex knows Lara wouldn't stand for him acting this way.

"I didn't mean to call her a bitch," Alex says and the fire that had started to dampen reignites. "It just came out!"

He called her a bitch?

"Alex." Nina sighs from behind me.

I take a step forward. "Did you just say you called my wife a *bitch?*"

"Oh, you tell him everything else, but not that?" Alex asks her around me, but I step back into his view, blocking her.

"You *dare* speak to my wife that way? To the woman who has given you everything on a silver fucking platter for the last decade. No matter the cost, she always made sure you got whatever you needed...whatever you wanted. And you would dare walk into my house and not only accuse her of being happy that I'm gone but call her a bitch?"

Alex might be slightly taller than me, but I tower over him right now. There is no way I'll allow him to disrespect Nina when she has been nothing but good to him. To all of us.

"Nick," Nina says, taking hold of my arm and trying to pull me back. "Nick, it's okay. It's not a big deal, let it go."

"He doesn't get to talk to you like that, Davina."

"But she can tell me it's my fault you went missing?" Alex scoffs. "Glad to know she gets away with everything, per usual."

"Alex," I warn with a dry chuckle.

"Alex," Lara says with a warning glare. "That's enough."

My brother looks between the three of us in disbelief before finally landing on me. "This is unbelievable. Nick, I—"

"Unless your next words are an apology to my wife, get the fuck out of my house, Alex."

He looks at Nina, then back at me. He won't apologize. My little brother is just as hardheaded as me and as stubborn as Pop. He doesn't want to be wrong, and he doesn't want to admit defeat. Alex knows he's wrong—he's known, and that's why he's been sulking around the house and avoiding her—but he doesn't want to admit it.

And Nina being Nina...She knows he feels bad. That's why she hasn't said anything to me. Despite the hurt from his words, she accepted his nonexistent apology before I ever walked through the door. But it's not good enough for me. If he wants to be around us, around me, he will apologize to her.

"And you know what? You don't have to worry about me not being at your wedding because I'm missing. I just won't be there."

Nina gasps. "Nick, you don't mean that!"

"Until he decides to get off his fucking high horse and say the words 'I'm sorry' for the way he's treated you, I refuse to be around him," I say, walking away from them without looking back.

forty-seven

Nina
One Week Later

A SENSE OF DÉJÀ vu ripples through me when I park in front of the white farmhouse. Before I have the chance to get out of the driver's seat, the front door squeaks open and Charlie walks out onto the porch. This should be fun...

"What are *you* doing here?" Her voice is laced with venom, and if it were a bite I'm sure it would sting like a bitch.

"Your dad home?" I ask, ignoring her tone.

"Nope."

"I have something for him. Can I trust that you'll give to him?" I can't stand the thought of leaving this with her, but I have no choice. I have to get back to catch our flight to New York. Steve said we have to leave on time. A storm is coming and he wants to get ahead of it.

"Depends," Charlie says, placing her hands on her hips. "What is it?"

"None of your concern. I'd wait for him, but I have a flight to catch. Can you please make sure he gets it?"

Charlie takes the envelope when I offer it to her but doesn't agree or disagree with my request. "What is it? Hush money?"

For the love of God. I sigh.

"Should it be?" I ask with a cocked brow.

"You tell me."

"Just make sure he gets it," I say, turning my back to get into the car. Time to leave before I say something I shouldn't. I know better than to let her get to me, but to put it simply, I cannot stand this girl. How in the hell did Nick put up with her for a year? I've only been around her for a few minutes and it's been more than enough for me.

"We don't need your handouts!"

I roll my eyes, hand gripping the door handle.

"He was falling for me!" Her words make my blood run cold.

Get in the car, Nina, I say to myself. *Get in the car right now and go home to your husband.*

My fingers flex on the handle, preparing to tug it open, but Charlie opens her mouth again and I've had enough. "Do you honestly believe that?"

Charlie doesn't waver—she stands tall on the porch, looking down at me.

"You know what." I scoff. "I'll give you the benefit of the doubt. Maybe *Xavier* was starting to feel something for you, but the problem is there would have always been a piece of him missing. You'd never have the whole thing. You couldn't. And you want to know why?" My hand rests on the hood of the Wrangler, waiting for her to answer, but she doesn't. The only response is the scowl forming on her face. "That's not who he is. That man is not Xavier. He is Nick Davis. Not only that…He's a Villa, and it would serve you well to remember that the name Villa means something."

"He isn't a Villa." She practically spits out our last name as if it's bitter on her tongue.

"Oh, make no mistake, Charlotte. Nick *is* a Villa. You only got to see a glimpse of who he is. You don't know the real him."

Charlie scoffs, shaking her head. "He didn't even miss you."

Does this girl never learn?

"Maybe Xavier learned not to miss something he never knew, but what was your plan when he finally woke up one day and remembered who he was?" I ask, but she doesn't have one of her snarky answers this time. "Let's say things had turned out differently. God forbid, I never found him. Even if you had won Xavier's heart, there would always be a piece of him you'd never win—a piece of him missing. Because no matter what happens, Nick Davis will always be *mine*."

Charlie's face falls, but is quick to recover, returning to a scowl.

My phone rings from inside the car and I know I'm cutting it close. I didn't tell him where I was going. I only said I had to run an errand—an errand three hours away. Satisfied with the end of our conversation, I turn on my heel to get back into the car before he starts freaking out because I haven't answered the phone.

"Where are you?" Nick's voice fills the cab, and I recognize the hint of panic. I wonder how long it will take before we don't have the small amount of fear that settles in our stomach when the other doesn't answer their phone. I almost had a small panic attack two days ago. He went into town and didn't answer when I called to ask him to make one more stop. The only thing that kept me grounded was Elena in the next room. Two minutes later, his name flashed across my screen and the panic finally subsided.

My hand rests on the gear shift, but I don't put it into reverse yet. I watch Charlie rip open the envelope, scanning over the documents in her hands—the deed to the property and a paid-in-full bill of sale. Her eyes lift to meet mine through the windshield with a look of disbelief. When I called Joseph two days ago, I made him an offer he couldn't refuse. I wanted to pay the remainder of the loan he'd taken out on the property and pay a year's salary for two ranch hands. He had done something for me I could never repay, but I thought giving him his home back and a few helping hands was a good start. And I may have added a small request: keep Shadow for a little longer until we can bring the horse home with us.

I smirk, finally putting the car into reverse. "On my way home."

forty-eight

Nick

I KNOCK ON THE office door before opening it without waiting for her answer. She's hunched over the desk, tracing over the lines of a document with her finger before glancing up at the screen and back down. This will be the first time she has faced the board since they learned of my return—alive and well, back from the dead. No matter how much I ask what she thinks will happen, she says she doesn't know. I know her better than that. She has a plan. She always has a plan. Nina Villa never walks into a board meeting without some idea of the outcome. Whatever the outcome is this time…she doesn't want me to know.

Things between me and Alex haven't smoothed over since our fight last week. He left Colorado the same day—or, he left the house, I should say. According to Pop, my brother and his fiancée drove to Denver to catch a flight the next morning, and Alex spent the whole drive sulking. Pop wasn't exactly happy with me kicking him out, but he understood why I did it.

Should I reach out to Alex? Maybe, but I'm sticking to my guns about this. I don't care if he's my brother, he's not allowed to disrespect my wife and get away with it. And until he apologizes to her, there won't be a conversation between us.

"Hey, you," I say.

Nina looks over the rim of her glasses on the edge of her nose. The line of her lips finally curves upward.

"Want to grab lunch after your meeting?"

"That would be great."

"You think it'll be a long one?" I ask, coming to the back side of her desk and sitting on the edge next to her, our faces inches apart.

"I don't know, maybe." Nina stretches. She's been here since at least seven this morning after coming in for a few hours last night after we landed. "They'll have a lot of questions."

"What could they have questions about?" I chuckle. "It's not like they need to know—"

"I'm stepping down."

It takes a second for me to register the words, and at first, I think she's kidding, but nothing about her expression says this is a joke.

"W-what? Nina, you can't. You—"

"I think it's time."

"Nina, if this is about—"

"No, it's okay. With everything that's happened, I think it's best."

With her hands in mine, I pull her to stand before me. Tucking a strand of hair behind her ear, I kiss her. "Nina, I don't want you to walk away from this if it's not what you want. This company, the work being done here…it's all you. You've taken what your dad started and grown it into something greater. I can't…No, I won't ask you to walk away from it."

"But you and Elena—"

"Will always be here." I wrap my hand around the side of her neck and my thumb grazes her cheek. "We're not going anywhere. What I said before…it wasn't fair. I'm sorry. You have always made us a priority. Always. I shouldn't have ever suggested otherwise." She melts into my embrace when I kiss her again, hands gripping the front of my polo. "I only want you to step down if that's what *you* want. If that's what will make you happy."

Tears brim in her green eyes, and she rolls her lips between her teeth, looking away. I know she doesn't want to walk away, not yet. Maybe in a few years, but she's not ready.

"Nina, the board is—Oh!" The door flies open when her assistant, Sydney, walks in. "I'm sorry, I didn't see you come in, Nick. Still gonna have to get used to seeing you again."

I chuckle. "Good to see you too, Syd."

Nina wipes under her eyes and takes a step back. "I'm on my way, Syd. *Due minuti.*"

Sydney nods, agreeing to the two-minute request, and closes the door behind her.

When Nina looks back at me, she smiles. Before she can say anything, I close the gap between us. She gasps when I deepen the kiss, her fingers raking over my shoulders. A satisfied hum fills the air when we part.

"I have to go," she whispers, wiping the corner of her lips.

I wipe my lips, pulling away to find some of her red lipstick on my hand.

"Red looks good on you, *Fossette.*" She giggles.

"Go to your meeting," I say, ushering her out of the room with a smack on her ass.

When Nina reaches the door, she looks back and holds her hand to me. I take it, walking her down the hallway to the conference room. Standing outside the door, I see the way her shoulders begin to tense.

"Hey," I say, turning her to face me. "Relax, you have nothing to worry about. Whatever you decide, I'm right here. My life is wherever you are. Whether that's here in New York or Haven or Winchester."

Her shoulders loosen and she smiles when I repeat the same words I said seven years ago when I found her in Central Park and asked her to marry me. I meant them then, just as I mean them now. No matter where life takes her, next to her is where I want to be. As long as I'm by her side, that's enough for me.

"*Ti amo, Fossette.*"

"*Ti amo*, Dee," I whisper, kissing her again.

"Oh, before I forget." Nina pauses mid-step. "There's something I need your help with. I left it in that conference room," she says, pointing to the door two down from the one she's about to walk into. "Can you work on putting it back together for me?"

"What is it?"

"You'll see," she says with a soft smile, kissing my cheek. Nina takes a deep breath before walking through the door Sydney holds open. Before it closes, I hear her begin, "Good afternoon, everyone. There are a few things I'd like to discuss before we get to the quarterly numbers..."

Twisting the knob of the conference room door, I'm shocked to see the *thing* I'm supposed to help my wife put back together. "What are you doing here?"

My little brother looks up from his folded hands where he sits at the other end of the table. He looks disheveled like he hasn't been sleeping much. His normally clean-shaven face bears a few days' worth of scruff.

I grip the back of the chair at the head of the table and stare down at him, still waiting for some answer to my question. "Well?"

Alex looks back down at his folded hands. "Nina called."

Why am I not surprised? Of course, she would try and fix this. Still, I ask, "Why would she call you?"

"Because she wants us to fix this."

The air between us is thick, awkward, and weird. It's never been this way between my brother and me, ever. We've been by each other's side for over three decades, but there has never been this much tension. Not even the one time I punched him because he was *right* about the reason Nina was upset with me—you know, the whole Brina and Nina's ex-boyfriend thing—but I didn't want to hear it. Not even then was there this suffocating awkwardness.

"There's only one way to fix this, Alex, and until you apolo—"

"I apologized."

"But did you mean it?"

"Of course, I meant it, Nick! I never...I would never call her a *bitch* and mean it. I was hurt. I was upset. I was..." Alex scoffs. "You have to understand, I was facing a reality where you were gone. I was supposed to get married twice already and kept pushing it back because I thought you'd come home, but you didn't. Nina...she—she's supposed to be able to *do* anything, *be* anything. She's a Villa for godsake." He shakes his head and blinks away the wetness in his eyes.

"So, your first instinct is to attack her for getting help from Beau?"

"Is that what you call it?"

I sigh, white-knuckling the chair. "Alex, you have got to let this go."

"Have you?"

"Yes! I'm not going to hold it over her head when she thought I was dead. How can I?"

Alex locks his jaw. "Have you forgiven Beau, too?"

"Beau is the reason my wife is still here!" I slam my palm down on the table. "He's why my wife and daughter were taken care of the last year. There is nothing to forgive."

"I'll take that as a no." He shakes his head.

Breathing through gritted teeth, I rub the crease building

between my brows. The truth is, yes, I have forgiven Beau, but it's hard to forget. Especially when I'm not whole. I'm not who I once was, and I don't know if that's good enough anymore.

"Alex, I don't need you to go to battle for me about this. This isn't your fight. The only thing you need to do is let this go and apologize—" I stop him from trying to argue. *"Apologize. A real, sincere apology to my wife. She is the only person in this world who never gave up on me and I will not let you take that away from her, Beau Turner be damned."*

Nina looks exhausted when she walks into the conference room two hours later. While waiting for her to finish the board meeting, I allowed Alex to ask me anything and everything he wanted, and vice versa. Things between us aren't perfect, but I think they'll get better with time. My wife smiles when she sees us having a conversation instead of my brother dead on the floor, but it doesn't quite reach her eyes. As much as I want to ask her what happened, and what she decided to do, it can wait.

"How'd it go?" Alex asks, not willing to do the same.

"Fine."

That doesn't sound good.

She looks between us, placing a hand on my shoulder. "Things seem to be okay between the two of you. I half expected to walk in and find one of you dead and the other bleeding."

I bring her hand to my lips before she caresses my cheek. "We're getting there."

"Yeah, we'll get there," my brother agrees. His eyes meet mine briefly before he looks up at her, rubbing the back of his neck with a sheepish grin. "Hey, Nin, I—I just want to say, I'm sorry. I've been a real dick to you lately and…you didn't deserve it. I should've never said those things I said to you. I was upset and grieving. I know it's not a good enough reason to take it out on you."

Nina squeezes my shoulder and I return the gesture, giving her hand the same amount of pressure. I'm with her. No matter what she decides, whether she accepts the apology or not, I'm with her. "Thank you, Alex."

"Does this mean you guys will come to the wedding?" Alex looks between us, eyes full of hope, and they only brighten when I nod. He jumps up from his chair and pulls my wife into a bone-crushing hug; one she's not expecting, based on her expression. But slowly, her hands relax on his back, and return the hug. When they part, he outstretches his hand to me. I take it, shaking his hand. "I have to go call Lara and tell her. She's going to be so happy."

The door practically slams behind him, a product of his happy mood, and I laugh when Nina flinches. That isn't exactly how things go at the corporate office, especially this one, where the suits are stuck-up and boring compared to the laid-back atmosphere you'd find at any of the DV Designs offices.

"Are you still going to the hospital later?" I stand from my chair and follow her out the same door my brother just ran out of. Our hands intertwine as we walk down the hallway to her office.

"Unfortunately." Nina had agreed to go with Kai to the hospital to visit Brina. She regretted extending the offer she'd made well before we returned to the city, but she didn't want her brother to be alone, either. Eileen can't go with him. Correction: Eileen won't go with him. His wife uses Ophelia and Fallon as her excuse. She could ask the nanny to help, but she doesn't want to. Like the rest of us, she isn't Brina's biggest fan.

As someone who lost their mother, I empathize with my wife because despite what she says, I know Nina is upset about her mother's diagnosis. Upset by the reality that she will never know the same person her brother did at one time, nor get the closure she deserves about everything that has happened between them over the years. She grieved this loss a long time ago, but having to face this prognosis head-on is like reopening the wound.

"Want me to come with you guys?"

"You don't like hospitals, and you're supposed to watch Elena," she says, walking into her office. "Nick, I'll be fine. Spend some time with our daughter and when I get home, you can help take my mind off things."

My brows wiggle in a suggestive wave and she laughs, slapping her hand on my chest. I take hold of her hand, not letting her slip away from me, and pepper her neck with kisses. Giggles fill the air as my beard and lips tickle her skin. "I love that sound."

"And I love you," she says, swiping her finger across the tip of my nose.

"What happened in your meeting?" I ask, looping my fingers in the belt loops of her pleated black dress pants, pulling her waist to mine.

Nina sighs and stares down at her feet. "You promise you won't be mad?"

"You didn't resign. Did you?"

Nina shakes her head and looks back up. There's a small amount of fear in her eyes and I hate that my past actions are the reason for it.

"Good," I say, cupping the side of her face. "I want you to do this, Dee. I want you to take this opportunity and run with it for as long as you can...as long as you want to. We have been given a second chance at life. A chance to right the wrongs we made the first time and one of those wrongs was me trying to make you choose between me and your job." Her eyes shine with tears beneath my grasp. I press a light kiss to her lips. "I want this. I want you. I want us. None of this matters if it's not with you."

She fingers the placket of my navy blue polo.

"I didn't realize it was a problem until now. I assumed you knew I would be by your side no matter what. It wasn't until you told me you were thinking about stepping down that I understood you were doing it because of me...because of what I said before." I bring her gaze back to mine. "Nina, I don't care where we are. I don't care if you're working here or if we're taking time off in Haven. As long as I'm with you, I don't care. Because my life will always be with you. Wherever you go, I go. That's how this works, Princess. And it's time for us to begin again."

"What would you say if I told you I had an idea?" There's a mischievous gleam in her eyes.

"I'd say okay, as long as it's not another wedding."

Nina's laugh is like music to my ears, bringing a smile to my lips, and I kiss her. "It's not another wedding."

"You promise?" I stick my left hand out between us, pinky finger hanging in the air.

My wife rolls her eyes but wraps her finger around mine anyway. *"Prometto."*

Two Years Later

Nina

"GOOD MORNING, PRINCESS." HIS breath is warm against the shell of my ear before his lips find my temple. I groan in protest and turn to bury my face in his chest. The action prompts a rumble in his chest as he wraps his arms securely around my waist, and I half expect him to continue to try and draw me from bed, but he doesn't. He buries his face into my hair and inhales, settling further into bed. We lay there a few heartbeats longer before he sighs, kissing the top of my head. "You have to get over to the office before graduation."

I groan at that.

Today is the day the board will vote on a handful of different things, including where we will open the new Villa Incorporated corporate office. When I proposed moving the main corporate office to Colorado two years ago, the answer had been a resounding no. However, they've finally come around to discussing it further. And while I'm happy they're open to change, I'm not sure the board will be too happy when I suggest a different location: Winchester. Or, should I say, I plan to suggest a move *back* to Winchester, instead. Recently

I've begun to wonder if a permanent move to Colorado is a good idea after everything that has happened…Ultimately, it's a decision Nick and I have to make together.

I have to get up and moving if I'm going to make the meeting and be back in time for Elena's kindergarten graduation.

"Is there coffee?"

"Made it after getting Elena ready," he says, planting another kiss in my hair.

"You're a saint." I glide my hands underneath his T-shirt, across the planes of his chest, and kiss my way up his neck. His dick comes to attention through the fabric of his sweatpants.

"Dee," he warns, and I hum against his warm skin. "You cannot be late."

"I won't be if you stop talking."

Nick rolls us so he's on top of me and kisses me. He pushes my underwear to the side, slipping his fingers inside me, and I moan against his mouth. I rake my fingers through the hair at the base of his skull. He finally grew it out last year and I begged him never to shave it again. I missed running my fingers through the tapered dark brown curls too much.

He pumps his fingers in and out of me, using his thumb to circle my clit, and it's pure bliss, this feeling of waking up next to him after going to sleep each night in his arms, knowing when I open my eyes he will be there…It's everything. Sometimes I forget there's an entire year he was missing from our lives, but then I notice little things about him or me or us, and it reminds me. Reminds me we aren't—

My thoughts are interrupted when Nick brings my nipple to his mouth, biting down gently through the fabric of his gray T-shirt I wore to bed. I start to grind myself against his hand, but as soon as I feel that pressure building in my abdomen, he pulls his fingers from me.

He pulls my underwear down my legs and shoves down his sweatpants. Nick positions himself at my entrance, stroking his cock two times before thrusting inside me. And if there's one thing I'm sure of, I will never get tired of this.

Nick makes breakfast while I take the fastest shower I've ever taken in my life. Just before I walk out of the bathroom, I notice two marks he left on my neck, and if looks could kill... Well, you get the idea.

When I walk into the kitchen, I'm ready to give him a verbal lashing but my words falter. Nick crouches in front of Tobias—our six-month-old son—who squeals with delight from his highchair. He just tossed a fistful of mashed avocado onto the floor, much to my husband's dismay. I giggle and kiss the top of our son's head.

"You're going to be late," Nick says, standing up from the floor. Passing me an egg and avocado sandwich and coffee to go, he plants a hard kiss on my lips and smacks my ass, urging me toward the door.

"I'm going, I'm going," I say before wishing them good luck and leaving.

Nick isn't a full-time stay-at-home dad but spends most of his days with the kids. They love it, and so does he. When I decided not to step down two years ago, we had a long discussion about what our life would look like while I was still heavily involved in Villa Inc. But the clock was ticking on my time at the company. I prefaced my decision to remain at the helm with the notion that by the end of the year of my brother's fortieth birthday—which is now less than a year away—I would be taking a step back. My brother had less than eighteen months before I'd officially resign from my position as CEO and he'd have to step in. I'd remain on the board of both

Villa Incorporated and DV Designs, remain a shareholder, and be involved in some projects, but it was my turn to enjoy the life my husband and I wanted five years ago. For now, though, we're making the most of being in the city until we can return to our quiet life.

Occasionally, Nick works on a small project or offers expertise where needed, but mostly with DV Designs and less with Villa Inc. He and Michaela's husband, Finn, get together once a week to "shoot the shit" and have time away from their wives and kids. Michaela gave birth two months after Tobias was born to Emerson Rose, so our husbands are in the trenches together and we know they need a break sometimes, too. The boys love it when Josh and Elizabeth come to town because it's like a Three Musketeers reunion.

Nick stood up at his brother's wedding, and while things aren't perfect between the Davis brothers, they're better. While he's been patching things with his brother, I've been helping mine deal with the deal of our mother almost two years ago.

The board meeting runs over exactly thirty minutes and, naturally, they save the new location discussion for the end, which leaves me in an impossible situation. I told myself if the meeting went over more than thirty minutes, I would get up and leave regardless, and I did. Thankfully, it was already over.

Now I have exactly five minutes to get inside and find my seat before the ceremony begins. Nick is already inside, reserving two extra seats next to him and Jimmy; they left Tobias at home with Tessa. Luckily, Elena has no idea I'm late, and I'm hoping I'll make it to my seat before she notices.

"I thought that was you," a voice calls from my right. When I turn to see who is about to make me even later, a wide smile spreads across my lips.

Before I know what my feet are doing, they bring me to him instead of running up the steps. I don't hesitate to return his tight embrace, which lifts me off my feet. "I thought you'd be inside already!"

"Got a little held up at the airport," he says, setting me back on my feet.

I cradle his face between my hands. "It's good to see you under better circumstances, Beau Turner." We had seen Beau last month when Nick had to testify at the trial of the former Sheriff of Puck County. Rhett "Red" Wilson was finally being tried for his involvement in my husband's disappearance, along with at least twenty others, maybe more. Nick was only a small piece in the puzzle, but his testimony was integral to the State's case against Wilson. Cooper Hayes and Dakota Johnson had taken plea deals, agreeing to tell the police everything in exchange for fifty years each, instead of life behind bars. After an investigation into Chief Sloan, it was discovered he knew about Nick's true identity but didn't report it because Sheriff Wilson had threatened him. Sloan was forced politely asked to retire. He had no other choice; his options were either to step down or face charges of obstruction of justice and bribery. However, Wilson refused to consider a deal. He was willing to take his chances in the courtroom. Two weeks ago, he was found guilty. We'll be back in Colorado next week for his sentencing, but I'm not sure it's a good idea considering how the trial affected Nick. His nightmares returned first, and then he began to recede into himself, barely speaking to anyone, including me. It took at least a week after our return to New York before he seemed more like…him.

"You too, Sweetheart." Beau covers one of my hands with his, giving it a gentle pat, before he motions toward the stairs. "We should probably get in there."

"Nick and Jimmy are inside already."

"How's he doing?" Beau asks.

"Better every day."

When we get into the school, I follow Beau through the crowd to our seats, and I'm surprised Nick left the two empty ones next to each other. Beau lets me go in first and we climb over the three people at the end of the row before I fall into the seat next to my husband.

"Was starting to think you were never going to make it," Nick says, sweeping his gaze to the side without letting it fall on Beau.

"Hello to you, too," I say, ignoring his tone, and kiss him as the lights go down to signal the start of the ceremony.

While he doesn't like to talk about it, I know Nick is still getting used to having Beau around for some occasions. I wasn't sure how to explain to my daughter Beau wouldn't be around anymore. It felt like starting from scratch, similar to when I had to tell her about Nick's disappearance, except this time there was a real possibility she *would* see him again. He wasn't *gone,* he was just...gone. And how was I supposed to explain that? The topic had come up a few times as we settled into our new life with Nick back home, but the first time it became an issue was Elena's fourth birthday when she wanted to invite Beau to her party. And even though we had moved back to New York, she didn't care—she wanted Uncle Beau there.

I could see the sting flash across Nick's features when she made that request. It wasn't until she had gone to bed that night that he finally let it show. He sat on the tub ledge, head hung low, and asked me, "Why is our daughter asking for Beau to be at her party?"

"Because she likes him."

"Nina—"

"Nick, if you feel this strongly about Beau not coming, you can have that conversation with our daughter. I don't see why he can't come." I sat up further in the water and stared at him, waiting for a response, but got none. His eyes remained downcast, staring at his folded hands. I gently placed my hand on his knee. "Are you worried something will happen between me and Beau?"

He sighed. "I didn't say that."

"I don't think you had to."

Finally, his eyes met mine. The uncertainty in them broke my heart. I thought we had gotten past this, and had come to terms with everything that happened the year he was gone.

"I won't sit here and beg you to let Beau come." I bit down on my bottom lip. "But I wasn't the only one he looked after while you were gone, Nick. And our daughter loves him. Beau became part of her life. If you have a problem and don't want him around for things…then you have that conversation with Elena."

He never had the conversation. Instead, he walked into the closet as I got dressed the next morning and told me to invite Beau.

When I see how tense Nick gets when Beau walks into a room, I wonder if I made the wrong choice; maybe I should've pushed him harder to talk to Elena.

Not to mention, my husband wasn't the only one who felt uncomfortable with the idea. Initially, Beau wasn't sure he should come, regardless of how much he loved Elena. While Nick had been gracious the morning of the initial interrogation, and during any follow-up interviews, that was business. This was personal.

It took a little convincing from yours truly to get the sheriff to agree to show up, and even then, I wasn't sure he was going to show. When he did, Elena was over the moon. Her Uncle Beau had shown up to her party and thus began the newest family tradition of Beau joining us for (most) Elena-related events.

The graduation ceremony goes about as well as one would expect. Elena beams from the stage, and for a moment the image of her all grown-up, receiving her high school diploma flashes before my eyes. Before I can wipe the tears in my eyes, my husband wraps his arm around my shoulders with a gentle squeeze and kisses my temple.

"I love you," he whispers against my hair.

"I love you more," I say, turning to meet his own teary gaze.

Nick isn't rude after the ceremony but isn't particularly nice either. He and Beau shake hands, but my husband keeps his distance to maintain a level of cordiality. Jimmy, on the other hand, hugs Beau the moment we stand up. When Elena is released from the line, she runs straight to her father but wiggles out of his arms the second she sees Beau. I make a mental note of who she ran to first like I always do, in case I need to remind my husband who she loves most.

Nick

"So, I have a question," my wife says, walking into the kitchen after she puts Tobias to bed. Our son is vastly different from his sister at this age—he's wild and manic and adventurous—but the one thing that remains the same is his sleep schedule. Even at six months, he sleeps almost through the night.

Elena crashed about thirty minutes ago. She didn't even fight it like normal, asking me to put her to bed when she couldn't keep her eyes open a second longer. Normally, she would still be up for another hour, but after the day she had, I can't say I'm surprised.

I'm running on fumes myself.

After graduation, we had dinner with the whole family, including Beau, at Elena's request. She pleaded with him to join us as he looked up from her to meet my stare. I wanted to say no, but I nodded, and he finally agreed.

Beau's eyes widened when he walked through the door of our new Upper East Side penthouse, and Elena reminded him it wasn't polite to stare. The last time he was in town, we still lived at the Plaza, but we had outgrown that condo. Now that we lived in the city full time and had another body in the house, we needed more space, much to Michaela's dismay. We gained one hundred additional square feet compared to the condo she and Finn owned on Park Row. It had become the running joke that their condo was the one thing my cousin had that my wife didn't (i.e. a bigger condo). Nina rolled her eyes and laughed every time it got brought up, but Michaela fiercely defended herself. Do with that information what you will.

"What's that?" I ask without looking up from the design I've been working on at the breakfast nook. Everyone left about an hour ago, including Beau, who was set to fly back to Colorado tonight.

"Is the reason for these two marks on my neck because you knew Beau was coming today?" Her accusation catches my attention, and I look up to meet emerald eyes sparkling with a hint of mischief. "I'm only asking because it took me an extra five minutes this morning trying to cover them up."

"I'm not dignifying that question with an answer."

She sighs. "I'll take that as a yes."

"I don't know what you're talking about."

"Yes, you do." Nina slides into the booth next to me, placing her hand on mine when I try to return to work. "Nick, I love you, but these feelings you have about Beau being around—"

"Dee, it's not…" It's my turn to sigh, lifting my hand from her grasp before I scrub it down my face. "I don't hate him. I don't particularly like that he's around for some of these big events, but I see how it makes Elena light up and I could never take that from her."

"Then why—"

"Because of the way he looks at *you*, Nina." I cover my face with both hands and rub my eyes with the heel of my palms.

I know I shouldn't hold on to the fear that one day she will wake up and leave me for him, but I can't help it. I'm not whole. I'm not completely myself. Some memories are still foggy, and others I've only remembered over time. I've seen her eyes narrow when she says things and I don't get them right away or remember at all. I worry that one day she'll grow tired of dealing with someone who can't always remember everything anymore. Someone who isn't all there.

"Nina, I—I..."

She looks at me expectantly.

Do I tell her the truth? Do I tell her how unworthy I feel to be here? She deserves someone who can be wholly who she needs them to be. She deserves better. Our children deserve better.

"Dee, I'm sorry." Taking both of her hands in mine, I turn my body toward her and look up to find confusion in her eyes. "I love you so fucking much, Davina Bay. And I am trying my damnedest to be everything you need me to be. That our kids need me to be. But I'm not...There are days I wake up and I'm worried it'll be the day you decide it's not enough...That I'm not enough."

"What are you talking about? Nick, you—"

"I am not whole, Dee. I still forget things. I'm still dealing with my own issues from my time away, from what happened on the trail. I—I'm still catching up to you." Tucking a strand of hair behind her ear, I caress her cheek. "And Beau...Beau doesn't have to do that. He is whole and he can give you things I can't. Not anymore. When I see how he looks at you and Elena—hell, even Tobias—I know he loves you."

"*Così anche tu*, Nick," Nina says with a light scoff. *So do you.*

She catches me off guard after that, speaking so fast

in Italian that I can barely keep up. I miss a few words here and there. Her words are a ramble of emotions, and not understanding why I can't accept her choices. Desperate to know why I continue to try to push her away...

"Is it enough for you?" I ask. My voice is a low whisper, but it breaks her spell. I'm afraid her answer will be *no*. I'm even more afraid her answer will be *yes* and she'll only say it because she feels obligated to. The inner workings of my mind are a deep, dark place sometimes, telling me the only reason Nina took me back is because she *had* to. That she doesn't want me...Doesn't love me. "Is it enough that even though I love you more than life itself, I'm not—" I take a deep breath, swallowing the tears. "I may stumble and fall. I am not the same person I used to be. And I don't know I'll ever be *him* again."

"Yes." Nina takes my face between her hands, her thumbs grazing my cheeks. "Nick, you don't have to be the same person. I just need you to be *you*—whatever that means. And remember when you fall, I'll be there to catch you."

"Dee, I—" I don't get to finish because Nina kisses me.

"Nick, I love you," she says when we part, our foreheads pressed together. "I love you, Nicholas Davis, and nothing will ever change that."

"Momma?" A small voice calls out and we both turn to see Elena. She rubs her tired eyes with her right fist, clutching a blanket in her left. Nina doesn't waste a second, scooping our daughter into her arms and bringing her to sit on the bench with us.

"What's wrong, Lena?" my wife asks, pushing the hair from the little girl's forehead to kiss her.

"I had a bad dream."

"Wanna tell me about it?" Nina asks, stroking her hair. Elena shakes her head, burying her face into Nina's neck. "Alright, let's get you back to bed. Tell Daddy g'night."

My daughter reaches over and wraps her arms securely around my neck.

"Good night, Little Bird," I say, kissing her forehead. Nina offers me a small smile before gathering Elena back in her arms and carrying her down the hall to bed. I stare after them for a few heartbeats before packing up my work, ready to call it a night. I was already having a hard enough time focusing, and there's no way I'll be able to get anything done now.

Walking into our closet, the sight of my reflection in the floor-to-ceiling mirror catches me off guard. The man in the mirror looks vastly different than the one I met two years ago when I finally forced myself to face the stranger who stared back at me. This man doesn't wear the same weight on his shoulders, nor the dark circles under his eyes. Despite the worries in the depths of his mind, he looks happy and content. That's because he is…

The day my wife showed up at Blackwood Ranch, I got a second chance. When I was forced to confront my demons at the trial last month, it drudged up so much of what I had worked to bury. And instead of soaking up every moment of this new opportunity I've been given, I know I've been wasting it. I spent my time worrying about losing it all over again, afraid that I'm not enough, and I've been letting it slip by me.

"*Fossette.*" Her voice breaks through my thoughts. I meet the reflection of her gaze over my shoulder. "*Stai bene?*"

"Yeah, I'm okay, Dee." My feet carry me to her and I close the gap between us.

She moans softly when I pull her mouth to mine, tugging her bottom lip between my teeth. After a round of quick kisses, I stare into her eyes.

"*Ti amo,* Davina Villa. So fucking much. I'm so sorry I've been too wrapped up in my own head to love you properly for the last two years. I guess…No, I know, confronting what happened at the trial put me back in a bad headspace. It made it hard to see what was right in front of me, but I'll do better, be better…I'm going to fix this…Right here, right now. Because if there's one thing I know…it's that I love you."

Nina smiles, sticking out her pinky finger. "Promise?"

"*Prometto.*"

Thank you!

Did you enjoy *Begin Again*? Please consider leaving a review on Amazon, Goodreads, etc!

Interested in more from Jensen Parker? Scan the code below to sign up for the newsletter

WHAT'S NEXT?

This book concludes the *Strangers* Series
(at least for now, you never know what might come up)

You can check out my other books on jensenparker.com!

<u>*Strangers* Series</u>
Until Now
Strictly Business
Terms & Conditions
Begin Again

acknowledgments

I've been dreaming about this concept for over three years. Begin Again sat as a note on my phone for so long with small bits of information added over the years until the time came to put it on paper. The idea came from one of those late-night brainstorming sessions that included a Google search of romance tropes and a little too much Apothic red wine. The moment my brain heard the word "amnesia," the plot of this book was born. I knew which couple it would be and who was losing their memory immediately. Keeping their identity hidden was an essential piece to the puzzle and while I went back and forth on the decision to maintain their anonymity, I'm glad I did. It was a lot of fun trying something different and stepping out of my comfort zone, throwing in easter eggs for seasoned Jensen Parker readers to catch. The reactions to the identity reveal have been priceless because none of my early-stage readers guessed correctly, did you?

Begin Again is the final chapter in the Strangers series, the story that made me a published author. Nick and Nina are my first book babies, and returning to their love story was one of my favorite parts of writing this book. Their relationship is one I admire because while they are equally strong as individuals, they understand they are stronger together than alone. They allow themselves to lean on one another (most of the time) and fulfill what they lack individually. I've loved watching them grow throughout this series and I hope you have, too. Nick, Nina, and the rest of the Strangers family will always hold a special place in my heart. It's bittersweet, but this isn't goodbye…it's just see you later. This universe will be back in some capacity (one day). There are other stories to tell here, but it's time to move for now…

This book is about love and loss and grief and trying to keep it together when your world is falling apart. Most times we extend grace to others but not ourselves. We're much harder on ourselves than other people. We don't allow ourselves to feel what we need to feel or to go through the motions. We force ourselves to pick back up and keep going. I'm guilty of doing it and I know many others who are too. This is your reminder to give yourself some grace. It's okay to lean on those around you and ask for help. Life can be tough, but you're tougher.

First, I need to thank the good Lord. Each time I sit down to start a new book I worry about finding the words to tell the story. How am I supposed to come up with over 80,000 words? This time I strung together 26 letters to produce almost 120k words…That seems insane, but we here are! I couldn't do it without the gift of words

Second, my husband. Without your support and love, I couldn't do this. You believe in me even when I don't believe in myself. You give me a kick in the ass when I need it and never let me give up on my dream. And you're the best damn assistant at a book convention anyone could ask for. I love you to the moon and back.

Third, my mom. Your help with CJ doesn't go unappreciated, even with all FaceTime calls when I'm working. It wouldn't be a work day outside the house without them. And let's not forget, if not for your suggestions my signing table wouldn't have looked half as good as it did.

To my editor, Sophie. Let me start by apologizing (again) for this one. This book went through many different versions, but I think where we've ended up is the best one. You let me vent and bounce ideas off you throughout the whole process (even let me spoil it for you because I needed feedback on things). And even let me change the entire layout in the middle of editing…Phew, that was crazy. Your attention to detail is one of the best aspects of working with you. I remember coming to you with this idea and asking if I was crazy for keeping the main characters' identity hidden…The answer was yes but do it anyway. You handle every story you work on with the utmost care and respect, offering sound advice and suggestions while maintaining my vision. I couldn't ask for a better partner in bringing these stories to life. Can you believe we just pumped out two books and a short story in less than six months? We need a vacation.

My incredible alpha readers, Ashley, Samantha, and Miriam… Your feedback made me realize that I could do this and that I wasn't crazy for keeping the identity of my main characters a secret for almost half the book.

Holly Whitworth. Your friendship and support mean the world to me. You have no problem giving me a good kick in the butt when I need it and provide me a place to vent with someone who gets it. Thank you for letting me spoil parts of this book for you so I could get an honest opinion. Author friends are hard to come by (for some reason), but you're one of the good ones and now you're stuck with me (and Kristin!) LOL

Nick and Nina…thank you for being my guinea pigs. Your story has been my favorite one to tell. From the moment I met you, I knew you guys were the ones I'd been waiting for. Thank you for making my dream of being a published author come true.

And finally, to the person who was there when this story first became an idea…Thanks. Things look a little different now, and that's okay, but I'll never forget the moment the idea for this story came to be.

So many people have supported me in my writing journey, I can't even begin to name all of you, but I appreciate and love you all.

I told myself I was going to take a break after this, but my brain has other plans and has already started working on what's next… I'm excited to share more details about what I have in store and open you up to a whole new world.

Until then…

Jensen Parker is a wife, mother, and contemporary romance author. Her hobbies include coffee, wine, travel, and books. A former retail store manager and real estate professional, but her heart has always belonged to writing. She recently moved back to her home state of Indiana with her husband, daughter, and their zoo. When she isn't writing, you'll find her reading, playing with her daughter, cooking new recipes from scratch, or planning a vacation.

For sneak peeks, giveaways, and more... Sign up for Jensen's newsletter! https://www.jensenparker.com/subscribe

Follow her on social media!

Instagram : instagram.com/jensenparkerauthor

Facebook : facebook.com/jparkerauthor

Threads : threads.net/@jensenparkerauthor

Twitter : twitter.com/jensenpauthor

Goodreads : goodreads.com/jensenparkerauthor

Amazon : amazon.com/author/jensenparkerauthor

TikTok : tiktok.com/@jensenparkerauthor

"I urge you to live a life worthy of the calling you have received. Be completely humble and gentle; be patient, bearing with one another in love."

- Ephesians 4:1-2

#MadeforMore

9 798987 986882